Originally from Houston, Texas, GWENDOLYN WOMACK studied theater at the University of Alaska, Fairbanks. She holds an MFA in Directing Theatre, Video, and Cinema from California Institute of the Arts. Her debut novel, *The Memory Painter,* was an RWA PRISM Award winner in the Time Travel/Steampunk category and a finalist for Best First Novel; her second novel, *The Fortune Teller,* was a bestseller. She now resides in Los Angeles with her husband and her son.

gwendolynwomack.com

ALSO BY GWENDOLYN WOMACK

The Memory Painter
The Fortune Teller

THE TIME COLLECTOR

GWENDOLYN WOMACK

PICADOR NEW YORK

THE TIME COLLECTOR. Copyright © 2019 by Gwendolyn Womack. All rights reserved. Printed in the United States of America. For information, address Picador, 175 Fifth Avenue, New York, N.Y. 10010.

picadorusa.com • instagram.com/picador
twitter.com/picadorusa • facebook.com/picadorusa

Picador® is a U.S. registered trademark and is used by Macmillan Publishing Group, LLC, under license from Pan Books Limited.

For book club information, please visit facebook.com/picadorbookclub or email marketing@picadorusa.com.

Designed by Jonathan Bennett

The Library of Congress Cataloging-in-Publication Data is available upon request.

ISBN 978-1-250-16923-5 (trade paperback)
ISBN 978-1-250-16924-2 (ebook)

Our books may be purchased in bulk for promotional, educational, or business use. Please contact your local bookseller or the Macmillan Corporate and Premium Sales Department at 1-800-221-7945, extension 5442, or by email at MacmillanSpecialMarkets@macmillan.com.

First Edition: April 2019

10 9 8 7 6 5 4 3 2 1

To Kenzo,
My hand is in yours.

*Though with my hand I grasp only a small part of the universe,
with my spirit I see the whole.*

—HELEN KELLER

1. THE MUSIC BOX

EL PASO, TEXAS

ROAN TOOK OFF HIS GLOVES like a man about to duel.

He slid the supple black leather away one finger at a time. He had not been planning to touch anything today, but the enameled singing bird box set with pearls was proving too irresistible—he wanted to make sure the music box was what he suspected it to be.

Earlier in the day, he'd flown to El Paso and rented a car to drive to Hueco Tanks, the low-lying mountains in El Paso County. On the way, a strip mall antique store off the highway caught his eye and he pulled over. Stuart wouldn't be at their meeting point for another two hours and Roan had time. As a general rule, he never missed an opportunity to visit an antique store, the more out-of-the-way the better. Some of his most exciting finds had been in unassuming places such as this.

The elderly shopkeeper glanced up from behind the counter when Roan entered and after a minute offered a greeting.

Roan hid a smile at the man's appraisal. He was used to getting that look, being well over six feet, with dark hair that cut a dramatic swath to his shoulders. He always wore black, a severe choice, but he found it also helped detract from the fact that he always wore gloves.

Before Roan walked in, the man behind the counter had been

squinting hard at an account ledger, tallying numbers while he ate an egg salad sandwich, but his attention was divided now that Roan was in the room. The only sound breaking the silence was the relentless ticking from a wall of cuckoo clocks and the drone from the rusted fan on the counter.

The shop owner finally got up the nerve to ask him, "Just passing through?"

Roan gave a distracted nod, his eyes surveying the showroom. Most pieces appeared to be from the late nineteenth and early twentieth century, the majority Texan and old Americana from Mexico all the way south to Panama. Not an inch of wall or table space was wasted. A dozen well-oiled saddles were on display next to rows of vintage typewriters, assorted crystal, and ceramics riddled with chips and hairline cracks. Old bar globe oil lamps stood clustered in the corner and antique country quilts hung on the wall like tapestries. Behind the register a cabinet with glass doors showcased guns from the Old West.

No other customer was in the store, and Roan doubted anyone else had been in that day. The entire space felt stale and forgotten, like a shoebox full of relics no one wanted. The old man looked to be in his early seventies and ready to retire—perhaps he would have years ago if he could afford it.

Roan's eyes took in every bauble, knowing each one held a story. They were all doorways to the past, to histories tucked away. No item was immune, no matter how small. Even the copper spoon collection for ten dollars contained the moments of every hand that had ever held them.

The vintage costume jewelry glittering in the glass display under the register caught his eye. On top of the counter a delicate gold box, no bigger than a woman's hand, sat like a crown on a piece of velvet.

Roan approached the box in amazement. He had no idea how it had made its way to Texas—or to the United States for that matter. The music box had to be the oldest antique in the store.

He tried to contain his excitement, already deciding he had to touch it.

"That's French I believe, and real pearls," the old man said, clearing his throat.

Roan studied the box, knowing it was from Switzerland, not France, and that if he turned the music box's handle, an exquisite lifelike miniature bird would pop out. He could tell by the masterful craftsmanship the musical bird box had been made by Jaquet-Droz & Leschot—and not only were the pearls real, so was the gold.

"One of my finest pieces." The man nodded, beginning to sound nervous.

A handwritten price tag dangled from the dainty wind-up handle with *$1,200* scribbled in blue ballpoint pen. Next to the Civil War cavalry rifle hanging over the man's head, the music box was the highest-priced item.

Roan bent down to continue his appraisal, not quite ready to touch it yet, not with someone standing so close to him.

"What brings you to El Paso?" the old man asked.

"Rock climbing," Roan murmured.

"Oh, you must be heading to Hueco Tanks." The man visibly relaxed now that he could peg Roan as an out-of-town climber. "We get all sorts of interesting folk visiting up there. You in some kind of rock band?"

"No." Roan smiled at the man's curiosity. He didn't tell him he was in the same business as he was—antiques—though Roan handled one-of-a-kind rare items and by appointment only. He had sold a Jaquet-Droz musical bird box once. If his instincts were correct, this one would be worth more.

The phone behind the counter gave a shrill ring. The old man excused himself to answer it.

As soon as his back was turned, Roan seized the opportunity. He would touch the box quickly and be done before the man could turn back around. What the shop owner didn't know was that he was a master psychometrist who'd been born with a rare gift.

With the speed gained from a lifetime of training, Roan brought his hands together in an elegant Surabhi mudra, a complex finger lock to help his mind break through the barrier.

Inhaling deeply, he placed his hand on the music box, wrapped his mind around the scrim of time, and pushed past it.

VIENNA

1784

REGINA GASPED WITH PLEASURE as the dainty mechanical bird popped out of the music box and began its slow turn with a sing-song tweet.

She had heard of these new singing boxes but had yet to see one. The handcrafted creature was no bigger than the tip of her index finger, and yet its wings flapped like a real bird. Even the iridescent feathers ruffled with life.

"What a marvelous invention," she said aloud, although she was alone in her room.

She had been in the middle of warming up for tomorrow's concert and waiting anxiously for her music when her maid announced the court official's arrival.

Regina jumped up, at first thinking her sheet music had finally come. She'd been waiting days for the sonata—but it wasn't the new composition. An official stood stiff at the door holding a personal gift from the emperor.

Regina tried to mask her disappointment and gracefully gave the messenger her thanks. Tomorrow she would be playing before the emperor for the first time, and he had continued to extend the warmest welcome to her since her arrival in Vienna.

She could see why Joseph II was nicknamed "The Musical

King." When she had unwrapped the gift she'd found the most exquisite gold music box set with pearls.

As she watched the bird complete its spin on its golden dais, she thought how tomorrow she would be the one on display as society's latest curiosity. She'd already played one concert in Vienna last month, but her second would be a grand affair and her last performance during her visit. To add to the excitement, she would be playing with Mozart.

At this point she didn't know what made her more nervous: playing for the emperor, playing with Mozart, or the fact she had yet to see a note of music.

Mozart was notorious for being haphazard with his time, but she couldn't believe he was waiting until this late hour to deliver their sonata. If it had been any other man, she would have suspected his actions as sabotage, calculated to make her look the fool, but she knew that wasn't the case. He was this very moment urgently composing their duet.

Earlier this morning his messenger had delivered the most hilarious and audacious of apologies, promising she would have the sonata today or Mozart would deliver his slain body instead. He also wrote that when the public discovered she'd only just received the music, her fame would soar to unheard-of heights.

Regina laughed at the note. Mozart was a flamboyant flirt and completely adorable. The truth was he was spread too thin. He performed more concerts than any man in the city and composed various pieces at the same time, choosing creative freedom over the security of a post.

In the short weeks she'd come to know him, she'd seen his full life firsthand: father and husband, a man busy with social engagements, billiards, his beloved pets, and music every day. One day she hoped to have such a life, inventing the rules as she went along.

"I want to live in a world where music doesn't struggle to

exist," he'd told her once, his eyes shining with an otherworldly light. The fact he'd agreed to compose a sonata for her at all still filled her with immense joy when she thought on it. The sun was shining on her with Mozart's attention. Even the prospect that she would barely have time to practice before playing tomorrow didn't detract from her happiness.

Mozart had been the one person she'd wanted to meet during her stay. Her first week in Vienna when she'd attended a party hosted by the educational minister, she recognized Mozart at once without introduction. The shortest man in the room with the blemished skin also possessed the most infectious laugh.

He stopped talking when she entered and rushed forward. "At last, Regina Strinasacchi! Italy's *virtuosa*! I have been hoping our paths would cross."

Regina had heard talk of the great composer, a child prodigy now a man. She didn't know what to expect upon meeting him, but it became apparent within minutes that life drove his genius, for never had she met someone so full of it.

He had a barrage of questions for her, his mind a maze of curiosity. Soon they were laughing like old friends cloistered in the corner away from the crowded room. She was immediately struck with how he treated her as his equal—but then she was a novelty too in the public eye. She'd been paraded about from an early age and lauded as a great violinist, singer, and guitarist from the Ospedale della Pietà orphanage in Venice, the one where Vivaldi had instructed. Her talent had masked her illegitimate birth, and she'd won the hearts of Europe one concert at a time by laying hers bare on the stage. She'd spent the last several years touring Italy, France, and Germany—unheard-of for a woman—and now her arrival in Vienna at the height of her stardom felt like a dream.

By the end of the evening before leaving the party, she gathered her courage and asked Mozart if he would compose a sonata for her to play at her last concert in Vienna.

"Of course I will!" he stunned her by saying. "I'll do even better. I'll play it with you."

⸺

Now, the evening before the concert, Regina resorted to pacing the floor. Her host delivered a dinner tray of ragout, ham, and fine pies, but Regina was unable to eat a bite. The most productivity she'd achieved all day was assisting her maid in preparing her gown for tomorrow's concert: an overly decorated pink confection from Paris that ballooned with too many ruffles.

"I'll look like a wedding cake," she said, holding the heavy gown up.

"A delicious cake," her maid amended with a grin.

Regina smiled without humor. She'd encountered many courters and admirers on her tour, but the reality was marriage would mean giving up her way of life—and her music—a future she couldn't fathom.

The sharp knock at the door startled her.

Regina jumped up, thinking surely this must be Mozart's messenger with the music. If it wasn't, she would officially begin to panic.

The door swung open and Mozart rushed in like the gust from a storm. Regina's maid hovered behind him.

"Forgive me! I am late!" He came toward her as if they had a standing appointment. "Do you hate me? Have I kept you waiting too long? Is that dinner?"

Regina nodded, too stunned by his presence to say anything. She tried to find her voice. "Yes, are you hungry?"

"Famished, but I can't stay." He sat down on the sofa, winded. "I only wanted to hand deliver these myself with my sincerest, sincerest of apologies, Signora." He waved the pages in his hand. "I'm still working out my accompaniment, but never fear, it's going to be the perfect pairing."

Regina sat down beside him, her annoyance at the delay

vanishing as soon as he handed her the sonata. A thrill coursed through her and the pages itched in her hand. She wanted to be alone with the music, to pick up her violin and begin the introduction. She had little time to prepare.

"Now!" Mozart leaned forward, his eyes alight with the passion of having just left his worktable. "You'll find I've made the violin questioning, intentionally so, just like its mistress," he added with a teasing smile.

A bubble of laughter escaped her. "Am I so obviously filled with questions?"

"Only of the best kind," he assured her. "The best kind." He picked up the bird box sitting on the nearby table to study it. "But then life is a question. One we must answer every day."

"Yes. Yes, it is." She gave him a faint smile. Her time in Vienna was coming to an end, as well as her grand tour. At some point she needed to decide the shape of her future. Unfortunately, she didn't have many options. "What if I do not like the answers?"

Mozart hesitated at her confession. "Perhaps I could offer you some advice, as a friend?"

She blinked and leaned forward in encouragement. "Yes, please."

He dropped his voice to a more serious tone, measuring his words. "Do not be cautious, either in life or in music. And never stop performing." He put the bird box down. "My sister did, and I've seen the damage a life without music can do. You have a talent. Play gloriously and your future husband, your children, will happily follow you to the ends of the earth."

His words lit a spark in her heart. They barely knew each other from these past weeks, and yet he had assessed her hopes and fears with the precision of a true friend.

"Isn't that what we all yearn for?" Mozart turned the handle on the music box and the bird popped up. They listened to it chirp and perform its dance.

"A gift from the emperor," Regina told him.

Mozart glanced up and met her eyes with a smile. "What a witty man."

⸺

The next evening the Kärntnerthor Theater was filled to capacity. Rarely had there been such a turnout. Everyone wanted to get a glimpse at Regina Strinasacchi, the current darling of Europe.

Regina, along with her entourage of escorts from Italy, would be meeting the emperor after the concert. She'd spent the remainder of the previous night and all day in solitude preparing for the performance. From what she could tell, Mozart had composed an enchanting sonata for her, though she had yet to hear how the piano would accompany her violin. In many ways tonight would be a complete improvisation. The audience knew it too, and anticipation filled the air.

In her dressing rooms, she received the news that Mozart had arrived along with his piano, a stunning beauty made by Anton Walter. The piano traveled everywhere with Mozart, carried by a group of hired men through the streets. The instrument had only this moment been delivered to the stage.

After the announcement, the minutes flew. Soon Regina was waiting near the curtain with her violin, an immaculate 1718 Stradivarius. She closed her eyes and tried to concentrate on the feel of the wood in her hand.

Mozart took the stage first to boisterous applause.

Regina felt like a bride about to meet the groom for the first time and prayed, yet again, for their music tonight to ring true.

When she walked onto the stage Mozart bowed and clapped. He had never looked finer in his favorite red coat. The fact he was wearing it tonight was a respectful nod to her. He took her hand and they bowed together. The audience applauded louder, ready to see the show.

Regina's eyes slid to Mozart's sheet music sitting at his piano and she let out a gasp.

The pages were blank.

His piano accompaniment had *not* been written. Her eyes returned to his with an astonished look.

He gave her a playful wink. "Do not worry," he whispered into her ear. "I will keep up."

Soon he began to play, and Regina's panic faded as Mozart led the sonata with stunning surety. That night she witnessed his genius, his oneness with the music, which poured from him with perfect incandescence. His piano spoke to her violin in a conversation that had only existed in his mind until this moment. Now he was sharing it with her. The crowd didn't dare to breathe as they listened.

Regina's eyes met his when they reached the opening of the allegro. They both laughed in perfect understanding and played on, unencumbered, and in that moment she believed miracles did exist.

2. THE POCKET WATCH

LOS ANGELES, CALIFORNIA

MELICENT HOPED GOD FORGAVE HER for telling an outright lie. "This lamp has been in my family for generations," she told the appraiser. She could see her brother, Parker, from the corner of her eye giving her a look, but she kept on. "Every year my brother and I would put a sheet over it at Halloween and tell ghost stories by the green light."

Parker crossed his arms, looking ready to disagree. He'd never seen this green lamp in his life. She stepped on his foot to keep him quiet.

"My grandma let me keep it in my room." Another lie—the one grandmother she knew had died when she was four, well before Parker was born. She never knew her father's mother—she never knew her father either for that matter.

"And you had no idea what this was?" The *Antiques Roadshow* representative looked fascinated and gave her an encouraging nod.

"No . . . just Granny's funny old lamp." Not only did Melicent know what the lamp was, but also how old it was and who made it. "Is it worth anything?" she asked tentatively.

"I'll say!" The *Roadshow* representative chuckled and launched into his appraisal. "What you have here is one of the first Tiffany table lamps from the early nineteen hundreds." He pointed out its features with the pen in his hand. "Notice the signature geometric pattern, the alternating bands of monochromatic glass segments, the bronze stand. It's in excellent condition. The last lamp like this one auctioned for . . ."

Melicent held her breath, waiting for the number.

"Fifty-seven thousand dollars."

Melicent was too stunned to respond.

"Fifty-seven thousand dollars?" Parker squealed. "For a lamp?"

The appraiser beamed at the pair of them and shook Melicent's hand. "You have quite a reading lamp there, young lady. Congratulations," he said, signaling it was time to move along and let the next person in line have a turn.

The exhibit hall at the Los Angeles Convention Center had accumulated quite a crowd. Lines snaked all over the enormous space with people waiting to show off their heirlooms to see how much they were worth.

Melicent grabbed Parker's hand and led him away. Her legs felt weightless, like she could run a marathon.

She was holding a fifty-seven-thousand-dollar lamp.

If she could sell it, they wouldn't have to worry about finances for a long time. It would alleviate so much of the pressure they were facing—and she hadn't even appraised the pocket watch yet.

Parker yanked his hand away when they were out of earshot. "Where did you get that thing?"

"Yesterday at the flea market."

"You went to Trading Post again?" he asked in surprise.

"No." Melicent hesitated. "A swap meet in Anaheim."

"You went to Anaheim without telling me?"

A twinge of regret filled her. Ever since their mother passed away, Parker worried about everything. They were more than ten years apart in age—he was only sixteen—and right now he was glaring at her like a parent.

"How much did you pay for that thing?"

"A hundred dollars." Melicent grinned, still in disbelief that she might make a $56,900 profit. A hundred dollars had been a lot of money for her to spend.

She'd gotten the cash last month after finding an antique pen for twenty dollars and selling it for eight hundred on eBay. It's what had given her the idea to go hunting for more antiques.

"I still have to get one more thing appraised," she said, handing Parker the lamp. *Antiques Roadshow* was visiting L.A. for the weekend, and today was her one chance.

"We have to stand in line again? Seriously?" He motioned to the swelling crowd of senior citizens holding their treasures. "Look at all this crap." He gave a nod to the man in front of them holding a bizarre porcelain giraffe.

"Would you watch your language?" Although Melicent couldn't help but agree. The porcelain giraffe was hideous. "I'm sharing the money with you. Can you at least try and act like you're having fun?"

His eyes lit up. "For real?"

"Toward your college tuition, yes." She watched his shoulders droop in disappointment. College was still two years away, but Melicent was already worried about how they could afford it. "Plus the truck you were eyeing."

"Get. Out." His mouth dropped open. The truck he wanted was a fifteen-year-old Dodge Dakota Sport and cost three thousand dollars. It wasn't anything fancy, but it could get him around town and hold his surfboard.

"And the phone," Melicent added wryly. This morning she'd been worried about paying their electricity bill, and here she was agreeing to a car and a cell phone. She let out a laugh. She hadn't felt this good in a long time.

Parker hugged her. "Thank you. Thanks, Mel." He choked up.

Melicent could feel the knot in her throat and squeezed him back. She should have done this sooner, used her talent. Maybe if she had, she could have helped her mother. Fifty-seven thousand dollars could have gotten her better medical care—maybe they could've enrolled her in some kind of experimental drug study. Maybe she would have lived.

Melicent stopped, pushing that dark thought aside, but still it lingered. The truth was she'd always avoided touching old things, fearful of the vivid ideas and images that came to her when she did. She would drop the object like it burned her and cross her arms protectively. It was something she'd been doing all her life—until her mother, Sadie, got sick last year.

The cancer had been aggressive and, in the end, untreatable. After her mother died, Melicent found herself in her mother's house surrounded by all her things, and Melicent wanted to touch everything . . . her mother's clothes, her pillow, her jewelry, all the things Sadie collected . . . the candles, the seashells, the wind chimes.

When Melicent held the objects in her hands, images of her mother's life appeared in her mind like a poignant daydream. Her beautiful mother, young and vivacious, the quintessential California surfer girl from Venice Beach, with long blond hair and blue-green eyes, a Beach Boys It-girl who dreamed of becoming a famous actress one day. Like a story unfolding, Melicent could see her mother's memories and how Sadie almost did achieve her dream. She'd landed the movie role of a lifetime but then gotten pregnant with Melicent and life got in the way—first with Melicent and then with Parker, eleven years apart, both accidental pregnancies with different fathers. No one would be able to tell by looking at them that Parker was Melicent's half brother. Sadie had married Melicent's father young and divorced him two years later. Parker's father had been MIA from the start, the result of a six-month string of dates that had led nowhere. Sadie had never talked about all her almost-never-was moments, the letdowns and the heartaches. And Melicent's heart broke for her mother when she discovered each one. But when Melicent found the old box of baby clothes in the closet, she'd held the blankets and the onesies and sensed how much her mother had loved them. Sadie wouldn't have changed a thing.

Melicent's journey with her mother's possessions had woken up the ability burrowed deep inside of her. Suddenly the odd things that happened to her growing up made sense. As a child, she'd always tried to ignore the sensations when she touched something and saw an image in her mind. She'd explain it away and suppress the encounter.

Now she no longer could. Her ability was growing stronger every day the more she acknowledged it. She found out there was an official name for being able to sense the past in an object through touch: *psychometry.*

The final turning point had come last month when she had gone rummaging at Melrose Trading Post on her one Saturday off from work. She'd picked up an old pen, a Conklin Nozac fountain pen. Before she could put it back down, she knew that the pen had belonged to the author Edgar Rice Burroughs.

In her mind's eye, Burroughs was writing with the pen and Melicent glimpsed moments of his life, like reading a biography about someone while watching him work. Burroughs had been everything from a solider to a ranch hand to a pencil-sharpener salesman before he became one of America's most prolific writers. The pen had been his favorite, the one he wrote *Tarzan of the Apes* with.

Melicent grew up knowing the story of Tarzan, just like every kid, but she had never read anything by Edgar Rice Burroughs, didn't even know his name, and yet now she knew details about the man's life.

She turned the pen over to find his initials engraved on the side: *ERB*. His first wife, Emma, whom he had three children with, had given him the pen as a gift.

Melicent bought the pen for twenty dollars and went home, afraid to touch it again. It was one thing to see moments from her mother's life, but this man was a stranger.

The next evening, she sat at her desk staring at the pile of bills and was struck by the idea of selling the pen. She logged in to her mother's eBay account, relieved to find it was still active. Her mother had often taken to selling odds and ends around the house on eBay to help bring in extra money. Now more than ever, the urge gripped Melicent to try too. Her mother's funeral and remaining hospital bills had wiped out their savings. If Melicent didn't do something soon, she would have to sell the house. The three-bedroom English-style cottage in Venice Beach had been in their family for three generations and was their only asset. It sat on a corner lot and was ringed by giant trees as though it were in a grove. Melicent had spent her childhood climbing those trees. She'd tried to show Parker her secret perches when he was old enough to climb, but Parker was terrified of heights. Melicent hoped one day, if she ever had kids, they could climb her trees too. But that day might never come. Her mother had mortgaged the equity in the house to the point when Melicent could barely make the house payment.

Trying to sell the pen on eBay was worth a shot. So she took a picture of it and posted the auction details:

A Rare Find! The pen that wrote Tarzan of the Apes! *Edgar Rice Burroughs's Fountain Pen, engraved with his initials.*

She didn't know how she could prove the claim to be true, but she decided not to worry about that detail. After mulling over the price, she started the bid at fifty dollars.

By the end of the week, the bidding had climbed to $500 and sold for $825 to a pen collector in Maine.

Melicent carefully wrapped Burroughs's pen in a gift box and included a note about the historical details she knew. Then she mailed it off.

That night she took Parker out for a steak dinner in Santa Monica and told him about selling the pen. She left out the part about how she knew whose pen it was, and Parker didn't seem to care. He was more interested in his top sirloin.

As Melicent watched her brother eat the best meal they'd had in ages, her heart hurt, and she promised herself she would do everything she could to give him a better life.

She took part of the pen money and waited for her next Saturday off from work to go treasure hunting. Now when she picked up an antique, she had a very good reason to not put it down.

⁓

Parker watched Melicent pull a piece of wrapped silk from her purse. "What's the other one?" he asked, invested in their field trip if it meant getting a car and a phone.

"An antique pocket watch." Melicent tried to ignore the wave of nerves hitting her stomach while she waited in a different line. She would have to tell the truth about how she'd found this one. There might be some kind of legal questions or, at the very least, intense scrutiny, which is why she'd had the vendor at the swap meet write on the sales receipt what kind of watch *he thought* it was.

She hadn't told the man he was wrong.

"Did you get that in Anaheim too?"

"No." Melicent shook her head. "Mission Viejo."

"You went to Mission Viejo yesterday too?" Parker shook his head in disbelief. "Your car is barely running!"

Her old Nissan Sentra had two hundred thousand miles on it and was on its last legs. She kept a bottle of brake fluid in her glove compartment for the leak she couldn't afford to fix. "I went to Anaheim and Mission Viejo, that's all." That was all she could fit in one day.

Depending on how much this watch was worth, she may have more places to go—antiques to find and money to make. She was on a mission now.

The line moved forward.

Melicent expelled a deep breath. She was next.

The appraiser spotted her and gave her a wide smile. The man was somewhere in his forties, two decades younger than the last appraiser, and clearly appreciative of the lovely young woman coming toward him. Melicent was wearing faded jeans and a gypsy-style embroidered blouse, and her long hair was knotted into an artful bun and secured by sandalwood chopsticks. The beaded choker around her neck accentuated the eclectic look.

"Hello! Please step forward." The appraiser shook her hand. "What's your name?"

"Melicent Tilpin." Melicent warily eyed the camera crew parked behind him and tried not to panic. How had she ended up in the line with the camera crew?

"Welcome, Melicent," he said. "Is this your brother?"

She nodded. Parker and she shared the same sun-kissed gold hair and hazel eyes, both inherited from their mother. The only difference between the siblings, aside from the age gap, was that Parker towered several inches above her, and she was five nine. He was the one who looked like a giraffe, awkward and not sure of himself.

"So what have you brought us today?"

Melicent held out the pocket watch.

"Well now—" The appraiser suddenly stopped talking as he took it. "Good heavens."

Parker shot his sister a questioning glance.

The man conducted his intense appraisal without a word. When he opened up the case to look at the watch's face, Melicent's pulse sped and she tried to remain calm.

The man glanced at her over the rim of his examining glasses. "Where on earth did you get this?"

3. THE VIDEO

EL PASO, TEXAS

"WOULD YOU LIKE TO BUY IT?" the old man asked Roan. He had finished his phone call and turned back around to see Roan holding the bird box.

Roan set the box down and quickly folded his fingers into a Kashyapa mudra. His hands resembled two tortoises returning to their shells. The finger lock helped him return to the present.

"I could take five percent off," the old man offered.

Roan took a step back from the counter and expelled a short breath. He hesitated, unsure if he could speak yet, and focused all his intention on finding his voice. He had been peering into the past all his life, for as long as he could remember, and over time had developed methods for returning swiftly. It had taken him years to master.

"I'm afraid I can't afford it," Roan answered, his voice hoarse.

"Ten percent?"

"Thank you, but I still couldn't afford it." Roan nodded to the box. "The last singing bird box of this quality sold for a hundred eighty-two thousand dollars in 2007."

The old man's eyes went round and the pen fell out of his hand.

"This one"—Roan motioned—"is worth even more. I'm

fairly certain there's an engraving on the inside indicating it was a gift."

The man looked down at the box in astonishment.

"You'll want to get it into the proper hands and have it auctioned," Roan said as he put back on his gloves. "Christie's in New York would probably start the bidding at two hundred thousand."

"Two hundred thousand? Dollars?" The shopkeeper swallowed and then swallowed again.

"Regina Strinasacchi. Remember that name." Roan took the pen on the counter and wrote *Regina Strinasacchi* on the blank sales receipt tablet sitting beside the register.

"Why? Who was she?" the shopkeeper asked in a high voice, looking ready to faint.

"Joseph II gave this music box to her in 1784, in Vienna. She was also the violinist Mozart composed a sonata for—Sonata no. 32 in B-flat Major." He wrote that down too. "There might be a record." He tore off the paper and offered it like a doctor holding out a prescription.

The old man took the receipt and looked at Roan with wonder, knowing he had been given the gift of a lifetime.

Before he could ask Roan more questions—or thank him— Roan left.

It took Roan a good hour, almost the whole drive to Hueco Tanks, for him to disconnect from the stream of Regina Strinasacchi's memories coursing through him. The pinwheel of sights, smells, and sounds from eighteenth-century Vienna was still circling him, from the pageantry of the clothes seen on a simple walk down the street to the animated talk and scent of spiced coffee spilling out from the sidewalk cafés to the music that lingered in the city's air.

Regina had kept the music box for the rest of her life until her death at seventy-five. Her trip to Vienna and playing with Mozart was a treasured memory, and she took out the bird box during her most sentimental moments of recollection. Her imprint within the object was strong and had offered Roan a clear glimpse of her life.

The year after Regina left Vienna, she took Mozart's advice and married a fellow musician, Johann Conrad Schlick, a talented cellist and the director of an orchestra in Gotha. Her music continued to play a large part in her life, and even after having two children, she performed recitals and composed. In the end she achieved her dream.

⌒

By the time Roan reached Hueco Tanks State Park, he was able to push the bird box and its trove of memories into the back of his mind. He left his car at the campground and hiked into the park to the place he and Stuart had agreed to meet. He waited for several hours, but Stuart didn't show.

Roan called him twice.

The third time he left a voicemail. "I'm here. Let me know if you aren't coming." He hung up and stared at the fantastical rock formations on North Mountain and tried to ease his worry.

Stuart was from London, and they usually rendezvoused to climb two or three times a year. Their last trip had been to Hatun Machay in Peru, and the two men weren't scheduled to meet until next month. But Stuart had called this week and left a message saying that he needed to see Roan right away. The voicemail had been cryptic and strange, and he'd been unreachable ever since. Stuart said he wanted to meet Roan at the spot they first climbed together.

Stuart didn't specify the location, but Roan understood. Their first spot was Hueco Tanks, where they'd climbed four years ago. Why Stuart had relayed everything in code was a question Roan was looking forward to getting answered.

Hopefully Stuart had a good reason for standing him up. He was always traveling in some foreign country, exploring obscure locales with limited cell phone reception. Roan would work on tracking him down when he got back home.

Since he was at the park, he decided to get in a few climbs before he headed back. Hueco Tanks was the bouldering mecca of Texas. The park covered 860 acres and had over two thousand "problems," what boulderers called potential climbs.

Bouldering was climbing with bare hands and without rope, and the climbs were rated by a system of V1 to V17, with 17 being the hardest. Roan had been climbing since he was a teenager, starting with V1s and working his way up until soon he was climbing V9-plus-rated problems, routes only expert boulderers could attempt. Climbing, like the hand mudras, helped him to clear his mind and find balance. It was the only time he could take off his gloves and stay grounded. Today Roan was about to ascend his favorite problem at the park, Terremer—it was also the hardest climb in the park, a V15.

He stripped off his gloves and jacket, wearing a lightweight T-shirt and black Arc'teryx Gamma climbing pants. The pants were his favorite, a four-way stretch fabric with double-weave knees. He took out his climbing shoes from his backpack and wiped them down before putting them on. Then he grabbed his chalk bag and hung it from the hook at his belt along with a small dusting brush he used to clear leftover chalk marks and debris off the rocks. Before chalking up, he did some deep stretches to prepare.

When he put his white-chalked hands on the boulder, the rock was cool beneath his fingertips, but not too cold. The weather was on the warmer side, in the high sixties, a perfect day to climb for early December. A lot of climbers visited the park from November through March, but today not too many people were around. Roan could see a group of college kids in the distance trying to climb a V5 problem. At least he would have Terremer all to himself.

He started his ascent like a graceful spider, the igneous stone solid beneath his grip. His body twisted and turned as he read the rock, finding the hand- and footholds with ease. His climbing shoes forced his weight to the front of his feet and made his toes curl.

He turned his hips on the next sequence to stay close to the wall and set up for the next move. Soon his muscles were straining with each maneuver, and his breath began to come in shorter bursts. As he ascended he took in all the tick marks, chalk holds, and rubber shoe scuffs from previous climbers written like a story left behind. Roan could feel the fierce determination of everyone who had climbed Terremer before him, and it fueled him to keep going.

He climbed like a dancer, his body elegant and lean. No energy was wasted. He performed a tricky crossover arm move that ended with a two-finger pocket hold and soon passed the crux of the climb, the hardest point, to finish the ascent.

At the top of Terremer he stared out over the park and took in the expanse. The climb had invigorated him. He only wished Stuart had made it.

"That was awesome!" one of the kids at the V5 called over to him.

Roan acknowledged them with a salute. Then he made the down-climb to the ground he'd spotted earlier. He checked his cell phone again—still no messages. He called his office to touch base with his business partner, Holly.

"Hey." Holly's voice perked up. "On your way back?"

"In a few hours."

"You got a package today from Stuart. I dropped it off at the warehouse for you. But isn't he with you?"

Roan tried to swallow his frustration. Why had Stuart sent him a package? "He didn't show."

"Well, that was flaky of him." Holly didn't have the highest opinion of Stuart. She was also Roan's oldest friend. "I have some good news," she told him. "I located Faye Young. We spoke. She's in Michigan."

A sense of relief filled him. They had been searching for Faye Young for some time now. His nonprofit corporation, the Heirloom Foundation, wanted to present Faye with a lost heirloom that had belonged to her great-grandmother. "Are you scheduling a flight out?" he asked her.

"This evening." Holly had been busy making these trips for the foundation, which she'd done without complaint, believing in the mission of the nonprofit as much as he did. Before she hung up, she mentioned an interesting video that she'd come across on the internet. "I thought you'd want to take a look at it. I sent you the link."

Roan spent a few more hours climbing and then headed back to the airport. For domestic trips he always flew private, and for this trip had chartered a light jet that sat eight. The cost was worth it if it meant he could avoid busy airports and people. Crowds made him uneasy even with his gloves on.

After the plane took off, he settled in for the two-hour flight back to New Orleans and opened up his laptop to check email. The one from his mother made him grimace.

From: Dr. Jocelyn Matthis, University of Oxford
Please come for dinner. I have some questions for you
on a Bonaparte matter you might be able to resolve.

-M

Roan shook his head. She made it sound like she was next door and not across the Atlantic in Great Britain. He replied with a simple:

Tied up. Soon.

He hit send, knowing that would not please the professor.

He could imagine her at her computer with her reading glasses perched low on her nose, blinking balefully at the screen like an owl.

The next email was from Holly with the promised link. He clicked on it to find recent footage from an *Antiques Roadshow* convention in Los Angeles.

The subject header read: "Psychometrist finds million-dollar pocket watch with the power of her hands!"

Roan leaned forward, now engaged. He launched the video to watch an attractive blond woman standing next to an appraiser while a tall teenage boy hovered behind her. The pair had a California beach vibe about them. The teenager was in board shorts and flip-flops and had a thick braided cuff around his wrist. All that was missing was his surfboard.

The appraiser shook the woman's hand. "What's your name?"

"Melicent Tilpin," she said, her eyes avoiding the camera.

"Welcome, Melicent. Is this your brother?" He smiled, glancing to the boy, and she nodded. "So what have you brought us today?"

The woman held out a gold pocket watch.

"Well now—" When the appraiser took it, he stopped talking. Seconds passed until he said, "Good heavens."

He opened up the dial and peered at her over the rim of his examining glasses. "Where on earth did you get this?"

"At a flea market," she said, crossing her arms, looking nervous.

"A flea market? How extraordinary." The appraiser leaned down to study it closer. "What we have here is an original pocket watch by Abraham-Louis Breguet from 1790. You can see his engraved signature here on the dial. Do you know who he is?"

The woman hesitated and then shook her head no.

Roan could tell she was lying.

The appraiser chuckled. "Only the best watchmaker of all time. This is one of his first, classic 'Grande Complication' pocket watches with a tourbillon, his most precise timepiece. These watches took years to assemble." The appraiser was talking with his hands in excitement. "Very few are in circulation. Most are in museums. The Breguet company usually buys them back when they enter the market. The last one sold for one point five million dollars."

The woman was too stunned to stay anything, then she put her hand to her heart.

"And you say you found this at a flea market?" the man pressed.

"Yes," she whispered. Her eyes welled with tears. Her hands were shaking as she covered her mouth. Her brother put his arm around her.

Roan watched the video, riveted.

"How did you find this at a flea market?"

"Someone was selling a collection of old watches, and I put my hands over them. This one felt special and I knew—" She hesitated. "I feel things with my hands sometimes."

The appraiser didn't know what to make of that. "You're saying you felt this watch was special with your hands?"

She nodded, her expression clearly showing she knew it sounded implausible. "Sometimes I pick up stuff and I can sense things, their history."

"Well, that is something," the man said, trying to make things more exciting for the cameras. "You definitely found a winner! Like winning the lottery, I'd say." He handed the watch back to her. "This might be the biggest discovery we've ever had on this show. You're the one making history."

Melicent looked at the camera, as if remembering the crew was recording her.

The image froze.

Roan stared at her face, seeing the secrets in her eyes. She had just admitted she was a psychometrist to the world. It didn't seem like the appraiser understood.

Roan replayed the video three more times, each time his amazement mounting. He had found someone else like him.

As he watched the clip again, he understood the woman's emotional reaction at discovering the Breguet pocket watch. Years ago, when he found his first antique worth more than a million dollars, he'd experienced the same catharsis at finding something so precious to history it was worth a fortune. That was ultimately what the dollar amount signaled: the weight of an object's worth in time.

Afterward, his life had changed forever.

Roan leaned back and watched the video once more. Without second-guessing his actions, he fired off an email to Holly to have their research team gather all the information they could on Melicent Tilpin. Then he picked up the phone and called the pilot in the cockpit to see if he could reroute their flight to Los Angeles instead of New Orleans.

He had to meet her.

4. THE SNOW GLOBE

CULVER CITY, CALIFORNIA

AFTER FINDING BURROUGHS'S PEN LAST MONTH, Melicent began seriously researching psychometry and was currently reading an excellent book on the subject titled *Mastering Psychometry,* written by Max Woods in the 1990s.

Psychometry technically meant *measuring the soul of things.* Psychometrists had the ability to connect with the memory that resided within an object when they held it in their hands, even reexperience it, and a psychometrist could, by training the mind, tap into any point in history. The world was energy in motion, and every moment in time left an imprinted copy of itself, like a hologram or a recording. Just as a shell was rolled by the waves and held the memory of the ocean, all things in the world recorded the moments that surrounded them. Information was never lost but remained perfectly preserved, and every moment of the past lay dormant, waiting to be rediscovered. Woods even went so far as to say that psychometrists were the archaeologists of the future.

Melicent's eyebrows rose when she read that. Did a lot of people have this ability? Because she'd never heard of it before or met anyone else who did.

The book went on to explain how many psychics relied on their hands to sense the unknown, intuit the future, or track down someone who was missing. They often held personal objects belonging to a person to gather information, but the actual mechanics of psychometry was different. A psychometrist could actually revisit the past.

Impressions or "imprints" could be received as physical reactions, emotions, images, or sound. Usually psychometrists favored one or two sensory channels, and each person had different levels of skill. Some psychometrists had more capability; and the most highly sensitive psychometrists could receive impressions by all four channels to the point where, when they held an object, they became transported to a different time and place in the past altogether. It depended on the talent of the individual.

Melicent read the book's baseline questions in the "Uncovering Your Talent" chapter: *Do your moods swing in a crowd? Do social events leave you feeling drained? Do you sometimes have trouble determining where a particular feeling is coming from?*

Melicent kept reading, thinking a definite *yes* on all counts—*yes,* she was hypersensitive and sometimes weary after dealing with groups of people. She also did sometimes sense or think random things when she shook someone's hand or when she sat down on other people's furniture.

What if furniture could talk? Well, according to this book, it did.

Melicent looked down at her hands, feeling as if they belonged to a stranger. She had found an old pen, a Tiffany lamp, and a priceless pocket watch, objects she could identify simply by touch that were worth more money than she knew what to do with.

The reality was, she had a hard time accepting what had happened—that she had made the discovery by psychic touch or psychometry or whatever she should call it. The appraiser was right. It did feel like winning the lottery, only she hadn't bought a ticket.

Now all she had left to do was to sell the two antiques. At the moment the lamp was in her bedroom and the Breguet pocket watch was hidden under a floorboard in her mother's closet.

Tomorrow she had an appointment with a representative from Breguet at their store on Rodeo Drive. Maybe she would begin to believe this was all real when the money was in the bank.

She glanced at the clock on the wall and grimaced. There was still an hour to go. Why she was at work today when she'd found a $1.5 million pocket watch, she didn't know. Maybe now she could quit her job and try something new. She'd been hovering in an in-between stage forever while she considered the next step in her career. Years ago, when she chose to major in fine arts in college with a focus on sculpture, she hadn't considered how unemployable she'd be after graduation. It wasn't like businesses were lining up to hire sculptors fresh out of school.

For the past four years she'd been working full-time managing The Trove, a high-end gift store in Culver City that sold art, collectibles, and jewelry. She crafted crystal snow globes on the side and sold them at the shop.

She designed and constructed the globes by hand—and they were not the cheesy holiday-themed kind showcasing spooky pumpkins or Santas on sleds. Her globes were exquisite works of art mounted on chunks of granite that evoked the feeling of capturing a daydream.

Inside the glass balls were whimsical cityscapes and microforests and tiny lifelike sculptures. She sold on average one, sometimes two, a month for two hundred dollars apiece. There wasn't a huge market for ornate snow globes, but she loved making them more than anything else. It took her several months to create one, so the profit margin was ridiculously low.

She debated getting out her latest globe to help pass the time. She'd been creating a tiny miniature of Edgar Rice Burroughs sitting at his desk, pen in hand, dreaming up the story of Tarzan with a forest behind him and a boy swinging from the vines on the trees. She'd started the design the day after she found Burroughs's pen, feeling compelled to capture the image in her mind.

She was about to get it out when the door jingled and a customer walked in.

"Welcome" died on her lips when she saw him. Melicent didn't know what struck her first: the fact he was dressed all in black or his raven-like hair. Charisma radiated from him.

When his eyes met hers, they landed on her with such concentrated force she held her breath. He had a look on his face like he knew her and had come to speak with her.

She said "Good evening" and waited for him to say something in return.

He only gave her a polite nod and turned away to browse, keeping his hands in his pockets.

She sat there openly staring at him, more than intrigued. *Musician* was her first thought. *Or an actor.* The man was riveting. Maybe he was an athlete. He looked athletic and was somewhere in his early thirties. He had a self-contained air about him that offset his compelling looks, an intensity that dialed him back from the world and made her second-guess his profession altogether. Whatever he was, he looked out of place.

"Let me know if you'd like to see anything," she finally offered. She looked down at her closed book, wondering if she should open it again and pretend to read.

She glanced up at him from the corner of her lashes as he toured the space. He strolled past the iron wind sculptures from Spain, the batik bags from Indonesia, and lingered over a coral dragon from China she had showcased on a stand. The dragon was one of the stars of the shop next to the exquisite Japanese obis that hung on the main wall. The ornate kimono sashes were over fifteen feet long, and Melicent had displayed them near the ceiling like stunning rivers of silk.

Her mystery customer neared her collection of snow globes, and she waited for him to walk past them too. Instead he stopped and leaned in closer. For several minutes he hovered, looking at each one.

She watched him take his hands out of his pockets. Her eyebrows rose at his leather gloves. Who wore gloves in L.A. in eighty-degree weather? Granted it was December, but it was warm outside.

He began to slip off his right glove one finger at a time. Then he reached out and touched one of the globes with his bare hand.

Melicent watched his fingertips gently trail along the glass before he picked it up. He had beautiful hands, like a pianist. She knew it was rude of her to stare at him so long, but she couldn't look away.

The globe he was holding was the one she'd made when she had to move back home to take care of her mother. Inside the orb was a collection of moonstones precariously balanced on each other—though in reality they were glued together—to create the illusion of stone-balancing art within a water-filled sphere.

"That one's a Zen garden," she said, feeling the need to break the silence.

The man kept holding it while he stared at the rest of her collection. His eyes had a faraway look in them.

She couldn't bring herself to tell him she was the artist. Everything about him unnerved her as the minutes passed. She tried to think of something to say, but then he turned and looked at her, and all the thoughts running through her head retreated out of reach.

Without taking his eyes off her, he walked over and put the globe on the counter. "I'll take all of them," he said. His voice was quiet and husky.

He was standing close enough that she could see his eyes were green and flecked with amber. She couldn't remember the last time she'd found someone this attractive, least of all a customer.

She tried to focus on the conversation, sure she had a blank look on her face. "All of what?"

"All of these," he said, motioning to the globe in front of her.

"All twelve?" Her voice rose in disbelief when she realized what he was asking for. "You want all of them?"

"Yes." Then he added with a little smile, "Please."

She jumped up and knocked over her pen cup, scattering pens and Sharpies across the desk. She almost spilled her tea, too, but his hand snaked out and caught it in time.

"Careful," he said.

Her face flushed in embarrassment and her mind raced with questions.

Why he was buying all her work? Were these gifts? Should she tell him she'd made them? She just couldn't, not when he was buying every single one. The whole situation was confounding. Who dropped more than two thousand dollars on snow globes?

"Do you need these gift wrapped?"

"No. Thank you." He handed over his credit card.

The name on the card said *Roan West*. What did Roan West do for a living, and what was he planning to do with twelve snow globes?

Under normal circumstances she would have made polite conversation during the sale, found out if he'd like to be on their mailing list, and mentioned the upcoming holiday sale. Right now she was too stunned to speak.

Yesterday was shocking enough with the Breguet appraisal, and now an attractive stranger was purchasing all her artwork.

She rang up the sale with a mounting sense of surreality. She had to step out from behind the counter to get each globe. It took her six trips, with one globe in each hand. She tried to stay focused so she wouldn't drop one.

He watched her while she boxed them up. The lull in conversation became an awkward stretch of silence and the tension between them became palpable. Melicent finished nestling all the boxes into two large gift bags and held them out with forced enthusiasm. "Here you are."

Roan West had his gloves back on when he took the bags from

her, but still the brush of his hands across hers had an unsettling effect. His eyes flickered with awareness and he turned away.

She found herself calling out cheerily, "Thank you so much!" when really she felt bereft. Two years of her work were wrapped up inside those bags . . . two years of her life.

When she had priced the globes at two hundred dollars apiece, at the time, she had thought the price was too much, but in hindsight it wasn't enough.

The door jingled shut and her mystery customer was gone—gone with a part of her she could never get back.

5. THE COMPASS

WELL, THAT DIDN'T GO AS PLANNED. Roan scowled at the two gift bags sitting across from him on the plane like a person. He rubbed his chin and let out something between a groan and a laugh, in disbelief that he had just absconded with all of Melicent Tilpin's art.

The reality was he hadn't been able to talk to her. From the moment he walked into the gift shop, he'd been unsure of what to say. She was so much lovelier in person, like a whimsical dancer straight out of a Degas painting.

Seeing her had caught him off balance. He'd watched the YouTube video countless times, studying every nuanced expression on her face and every gesture. But then when she was right in front of him, he'd started second-guessing his urge to meet her.

Did he really want to begin a conversation? Introduce himself and share that he understood exactly how she'd found the watch?

He'd struggled with what to say—until he began to wonder if he needed to say anything at all. Maybe he should remain a voiceless, anonymous customer. She didn't have to know he'd flown all this way to meet her.

Then when he saw her name on the place card beside the

snow globes and her signature on the globes' granite mounts, he had taken off his glove before he could think it through.

When he touched one of the globes a myriad of thoughts filled him. Within the silica, the ash, and the limestone, and after seventeen-hundred-degree heat had fused the quartz, immense sadness lived. She'd made that Zen rock garden inside the crystal sphere to cope with a life out of balance—using her art to help transmute her pain. Then she had tried to sell it because she needed the money.

A deluge of powerful imprints hit him and Roan set the globe back down on the counter, already knowing he had to buy it. He had to buy them all.

Reading the imprints would be the surest way to understand her, he reasoned. Besides, it was always easier for him to touch something than to have a conversation. Having the globes would negate the need to question her at all. He could read the imprints on his own time back home and then decide if he would contact her again.

When he stood watching her box the globes up, he wondered why she hadn't told him she'd made them. Most people would have. She hadn't wanted to sell them either. Her shock and reluctance were obvious. The globes were more sentimental and important to her than she'd realized until she had to let them go.

The crushed look in her eyes when she handed him the bags still burned in his mind—and he began to think maybe he should send them back.

He replayed their encounter in his mind over and over as he stared out the plane window at the clouds. His hand absently took his lucky coin out of his pocket and rolled it across his knuckles in a soothing motion. He didn't know what he wanted to do about Melicent Tilpin. The trip to L.A. had been a distraction, and Stuart not showing up in El Paso had left him with a sense of unease.

He thought back to Stuart's voicemail. All Stuart had said was that it was imperative they meet and that it concerned the group. Roan had no idea why Stuart was trying to involve him.

Stuart belonged to a small international network of psychometrists. Five years ago, when Roan and Stuart first met, Stuart had asked him to join. Stuart was the first psychometrist Roan had ever encountered, and Roan was surprised to hear there was a group—but Roan had no interest in joining. His whole life he'd grown up with his parents drilling it into him never to reveal what he could do. He wasn't about to start now.

Still, Stuart coaxed him into attending one meeting before making a decision. He'd pressed Roan at a vulnerable time, months after Roan's father had passed away; otherwise Roan never would have agreed to go.

Roan had flown to France to attend the meeting, not knowing what to expect.

François Dupuis, an elderly historian, usually hosted the biannual gatherings. The retired widower lived in a charming country house outside of Avignon. The villa was a ten-minute commute to the Ceccano Municipal Library, where François had been an archivist for thirty years.

When Stuart arrived at François's with Roan in tow, François welcome them both warmly and offered them a glass of wine from his cellar. He was a cherub of a man and still spry on his feet at seventy.

Another member, Sun Kim, had already arrived. Roan wasn't sure what to make of the severe-looking Korean woman who greeted them with silent nods. She was wearing pants and a tunic-like jacket, and her silver-streaked black hair was cut short.

François performed the introductions, explaining with enthusiasm that Sun was the best psychometrist he'd ever known. Sun waved off his compliments with a brusque hand, earning a chuckle from the Frenchman. But Roan caught the gleam of laughter in Sun's eyes. It was obvious the two were friends.

The others arrived shortly afterward. Miguel Casal, a tall, soft-spoken Peruvian sporting a full beard and little round glasses, was the leading anthropologist at Pontificia Universidad Católica del Perú in Lima. The group's other member was an archaeologist from India named Gyan Patel, a charismatic man in his thirties. When Gyan met Roan, his intent gaze dropped to Roan's gloved hands.

Roan felt out of place surrounded by two archaeologists, one anthropologist, an historian, and a curt, enigmatic Korean woman who sat surveying them all without a word. Roan had no idea what Sun did.

Stuart fortunately kept Roan's introduction brief. "Everyone, let me preface our meeting by saying I've asked Roan to join our little group, but knowing Roan, he won't. So this is probably the last you'll ever see of him. Right, mate?" Stuart slapped Roan on the back playfully as if they were having drinks at the pub. "I'm afraid Roan doesn't like people. He barely likes me, and I'm his friend." Stuart's outrageousness earned a round of laughter. Only Sun's expression remained unreadable.

Everyone spread out among the sofas and chairs in François's living room. Roan chose a chair farthest from the circle, near the fireplace, and sat back to watch.

Miguel led the discussion. "I brought something that I've been most anxious to share with you."

He pulled out a stone spoon from his satchel and held it up.

"What you're looking at is one of the first compasses of the world. These originated in China and were made of loadstone. The scientists of the time understood that the ore of the stone could find magnetic north."

Next he pulled out a bronze plate decorated with constellations and cardinal points. "This is called a heaven-plate." He placed the plate on the table and laid the spoon in its center. "Now, interestingly enough, before this was a compass, it was first used for divination purposes to foretell the future. But when the diviners realized they could always find north and south with it, the compass was born. If I were to date this piece, I'd say it was Han dynasty. But the true mystery surrounding this piece is that it wasn't found in China."

He looked at everyone, giving his silence a pregnant pause.

"I found it at an excavation in Ecuador buried in thousand-year-old sediment. So not only is there a missing time span of three thousand years—somehow this compass traveled to the other side of the world."

He let that statement hang in the air.

"I have it on loan from the Ecuadorian government for further testing, but I wanted to share it with you because I believe this is an OOPART."

"An oopart?" François asked, looking perplexed. "What kind of word is that?"

"It stands for 'out-of-place artifact.'" Stuart sat forward in excitement. "Something that doesn't belong in the timeline it was discovered in. I've never seen one up close before."

Miguel nodded. "It's a rare phenomenon. But they've been found all around the world." He ticked off a list. "A hammer in Texas, discovered in 1936, was buried in Cretaceous rock. The Dorchester Pot, discovered in 1852, was found in rock that was five hundred million years old. There are the ancient batteries in Baghdad, the nanostructures in the Ural Mountains in Russia. No one's been able to date the iron pillar in Delhi." He looked to Gyan for confirmation. "That could be an oopart right out in the open."

François put on his reading glasses for a better look. "How curious."

"I wanted your help reading the imprints," Miguel said.

Roan listened, his curiosity piqued. He'd never heard of out-of-place artifacts before.

"Give it a go, François." Miguel handed it to him.

François picked it up. Everyone was quiet as François closed his eyes to focus. "I find the imprints to be jarring, like a double exposure my eyes are trying hard to see."

"Exactly!" Miguel pointed at him. "As if it's existed in two timelines, not one."

Stuart took it next and closed his eyes. After several moments he said, "You're right, François, the imprints are muddled. This would take some time to unravel." He offered it to Sun, who was sitting to his right.

Sun took it in her hands and focused on the imprint. Unlike the others she kept her eyes open, gazing inward. "This is from the Qin dynasty, not Han, about two hundred B.C.E."

Miguel's eyebrows shot up.

Her voice was sure as she continued. "It belonged to a man named Shang Yang. He was an architect and used the compass to align buildings, homes, graves. It was a prized tool. Shang received this from his father, who originally used it for divination, like his father before him. They were considered great magicians in their time. The compass was lost with Shang, buried in an earthquake that leveled every town in the province." Her brow furrowed. "I can't see the time after that or before it was found in Ecuador." She was quiet a moment and closed her eyes to concentrate. "The two times are like two parallel imprints running side by side that don't belong to each other. Fascinating."

François clapped his hands softly and leaned toward Roan. "I told you, the best."

Roan gave him a polite smile.

Sun offered the compass to Roan next with a speculating gleam in her eye. "Perhaps our special guest would like to try?"

Roan had no urge to read double imprints from an out-of-place artifact in front of a group of strangers. It sounded like a migraine waiting to happen. "No, thank you." He crossed his arms. His gloves would not be coming off today. Fortunately, Sun didn't press the point and handed it to Gyan, who had little luck with the imprints either.

"After I found this," Miguel went on to explain, "I started looking at the oopart phenomena more closely and began to wonder: What if ooparts aren't random? What if they're connected to each other?"

"You mean a unifying factor?" Stuart asked, intrigued.

"Yes." Miguel nodded, his eyes intent as they circled the group. "If there was, we'd be the ones to find it."

⌒

Roan never knew if the group had decided to pursue Miguel's theory. By the end of the meeting, Roan had graciously declined their invitation to join. He could tell Stuart was disappointed by his decision, possibly offended, and for many months Roan thought their friendship might have come to an end.

It wasn't until six months later that Stuart surprised Roan with a call, asking him to show him how to rock climb. Stuart knew Roan was an avid climber, a boulderer, and Stuart wanted to learn. He said he needed an outlet too. Roan arranged the meeting at Hueco Tanks and had done his best to teach him what he knew.

Roan had been shocked when he'd met Stuart on that trip. Stuart had shadows under his eyes and his jovial smile was missing. He was emotionally hurting on that first climbing trip to El Paso. Roan could feel his pain in the rocks, falling across the stones like a silent shadow.

Stuart had recently lost someone dear to him in a tragic car accident in the rain.

Her name was Nema.

The pain was hard for Roan to ignore. Stuart stamped Nema's memory on every rock he climbed until his heartache covered the mountain like a blanket. This woman was the reason Stuart was climbing. Roan didn't feel they were close enough to admit what he knew from an imprint. So he pretended not to know.

Stuart tried to exorcise his grief by physically pushing his body to its limits. He had a natural talent for the sport too, was incredibly competitive, and soon became even more obsessed with bouldering than Roan.

The men's friendship grew over time and they kept climbing together. As Stuart's expertise began to match Roan's, they sought out the hardest climbs and most dangerous ascents: the Story of Two Worlds in Switzerland, the Burden of Dreams in Finland, and Creature from the Black Lagoon in Colorado, among countless others.

During their trips they kept their private lives separate. Stuart never discussed the other psychometrists either, and Roan didn't ask.

Why was Stuart trying to involve him with the group again after all this time?

Even more perplexing, why hadn't he shown up in Texas?

6. THE HANDLE

WHEN THE PLANE TOUCHED DOWN in New Orleans, Roan breathed a sigh of relief. He got behind the wheel of his black Tesla and put Melicent's bags in the passenger seat. From Lakefront Airport he took Elysian Fields to I10 and exited near the harbor.

He sped down the street since there were no other cars on the road. Tchoupitoulas Street was one of the major industrial corridors that ran adjacent to the harbor's entry points. Only warehouses and yard operations lined Tchoupitoulas, and they were stationed there for efficient cargo transfer to and from the port terminals.

New Orleans had one of the largest harbors in the world. Most of the industrial warehouses clustering the area spanned tens of thousands of square feet, and their loading dock doors could open up to receive an entire cargo container at once. It had been the perfect place for him to move.

Roan pulled into an enormous warehouse lot. He hit the remote to open one of the five bays to the building. The heavy metal door rolled up and fluorescent lights lit the empty cargo bay. He eased the car in and parked, using the bay as his garage.

He'd purchased the warehouse ten years ago. At first he bought the building with the sole intent of storing his most valuable pieces, but then figured seventy thousand square feet could accommodate him as well. The windowless space offered the height of anonymity and privacy, two things he valued most.

Fourteen thousand square feet had already been designated for first- and second-floor offices that stretched along one side of the building. Excluding the loading bays, the remaining fifty-six thousand square feet was wide-open space and had thirty-five-foot ceilings. The entire building was insulated, with concrete blocks and metal panel siding.

Roan had paid twenty-five million outright for the entire lot. It'd been a hefty investment but a necessary one if he was going to continue his work. West, Inc. had earned a global reputation for unearthing some of the most valuable antiques ever to come on the market. Last year, the company, through Sotheby's, had auctioned a royal soup tureen designed for King Louis XV for ten million dollars. Security had always been a priority, and the more discreet West, Inc.'s headquarters the better.

Teaming up with an architect, Roan had carved out a six-thousand-square-foot home and tucked it away in the back corner of the building along with a front door only accessible from the inside.

Roan could never have created such a futuristic home, at least not on the exterior, in a New Orleans residential neighborhood, where every effort went into re-creating houses to look like they were from a previous century. His entire loftlike house had gleaming wood floors and unusual design elements. Glass cutouts in the living room peered like windows into the adjacent dining room and kitchen, and four brilliant stained-glass panels hung on the living room's back wall. They ascended to the ceiling in beautiful arcs and were backlit with strategically placed pin lights to create the stunning effect of sunlight coming in from the outside world.

Aside from the stained glass, there was no other art or decoration in sight.

Except for the flowers.

Roan had vases of roses, daisies, and violets scattered throughout the house that he replaced once a week when he visited the flower market.

He'd found out at an early age that flowers were the most sensitive of all receptors and could hold vibrant imprints for days. The only problem was that when the flowers died, the imprints died with them. But if there was any hint of disturbance in the house, the slightest shift, Roan would be able to sense it right away in the flowers. So he always kept vases of them in every room. They were more reliable than an alarm system.

He took off his gloves and shoes at the door, leaving his things and the gift bags by the entry, and walked through the house, touching all the flowers in every room to read their imprints.

After he inspected the flowers, he headed to the kitchen and opened the refrigerator to stare uninterestedly at its contents. He grabbed a bag of shelled pistachios, seeded crackers, and an unopened jar of Greek tapenade from the pantry. He uncorked a bottle of the Paring, a Bordeaux-inspired blend.

"House," he said to his voice-activated home system, "play Mozart, Sonata no. 32 in B-flat Major."

The sound of the violin filled the air.

Roan headed to the living room, where three sofas took up the center of the room and connected at their corners in a U-shape. They were positioned within a sunken circle that was ringed by three steps leading down to it.

"House, light the fire in the living room. Dim lights, setting three."

The stone gas firepit in the middle of the circle came to life, creating an immediate campfire feel. The lights dimmed to resemble barely-there candlelight.

Roan sank down on the cushions and propped his feet up, drawing sips from the velvety red. As he listened to Mozart and Regina's sonata, he thought the music sounded different. This recording lacked the rich resonance of the original.

It lacked Mozart and Regina, Roan mused, remembering their concert.

He always enjoyed encountering something Mozart had touched, and Roan hadn't had time to linger on the string of memories within Regina's bird box—he'd been too busy looking ahead to his meeting with Stuart and then becoming distracted by Melicent Tilpin.

Melicent Tilpin.

Her name entered his mind like a cloud obstructing all other thoughts.

What to do about her? Did he really want to know to what extent she possessed his ability and start a friendship?

He and Stuart may have become friends over the years, but that didn't have to happen with every psychometrist he met, especially with someone he was so attracted to.

Before he could stop himself, he went to the entry and got one of the Trove gift bags. Holding the handle, he could feel Melicent's emotions when she handed the bags over to him, her jumble of nerves. She couldn't imagine why he was buying all her work and she was so caught up with trying to figure out who he was. Roan was fascinated by her thoughts—she'd found him attractive. He hovered over that feeling a bit longer, until the act of holding the bag handle began to feel like holding her hand.

He let the bag go in frustration and set it aside, no longer compelled to look inside. He didn't need to further complicate his life by getting caught up with a budding psychometrist, no matter how pretty she might be.

He sipped his wine and leaned back on the couch. "House, clear sky, constellations."

The home planetarium screen transformed the ceiling into a night sky illuminated with stars. The Stellarium program was set to show what the sky above New Orleans looked like through a telescope in real time.

Roan found and ticked off constellations in his mind as he brought out his lucky coin from his pocket and rolled it across his hand. He ignored the imprints in the coin and focused his mind on the music. Closing his eyes, he drifted off, riding the strings of the violin and content in the moment . . . stars, a home fire, good wine, and Mozart.

What more could he need?

Perhaps the answer to when he should read the imprints within those exquisite snow globes was never. Maybe it'd be for the best to forget the woman with the pocket watch entirely.

When the sonata ended, Roan got up and stretched. Before he went to sleep tonight, he needed to open Stuart's package. Holly had left it on his desk in the warehouse, and Roan didn't want to wait until the morning.

His office was tucked away in the adjacent corner of the warehouse, surrounded by the thousands of antiques he'd acquired over the years. The pieces sat in the dark, like an army of ghosts he had assembled. Roan knew every imprint.

When he flipped on the light to his office, Stuart's package was sitting front and center on his desk.

Inside the box he found a letter along with a heavy iron key that looked to be several hundred years old.

Roan put the letter aside, deciding to touch the key first so he wouldn't be influenced by what Stuart might have to say. He wanted a clean read of the imprints. He had a feeling it might explain why Stuart had wanted to meet.

The moment Roan touched the key, the memories within it began to tug at him, along with something else, something with a stronger current.

The pull, the sense of imbalance, began in Roan's hands and crept down his body.

Without warning he'd stepped out of sync with rest of the world.

A strange energy wrapped tightly around his hands like a cord and pulled. Then the imprint flooded his mind.

PRAGUE

1489

MIKULAS AND SINDEL STARTED *something they couldn't finish.* Hanus mumbled a curse as he strained to tighten the screw beneath the foliot. His hands were slick with oil from lubricating the gears, and he kept losing his grip on the tools.

The engineering behind the clock was sound. Hanus would concede that much to his predecessors, but the interface wasn't accurate enough. The clock's original builders had tried to do too much without mastering the calculations.

Hanus was a clockmaker, astronomer, and master of the astrolabe, and the one man who could get this clock to do what was expected. For not only did Prague's astronomical clock tell the time, it charted the passage of the sun and the phases of the moon, tracked the zodiac signs, and calculated, every day, the hour the North Star would appear.

The city's grand clock crowning the top of town hall was a true marvel.

Prague was the meeting ground for astronomers across all of Europe, and the clock was a pinnacle of scientific achievement. But its lack of accuracy had become an outrage, and the town council could no longer ignore the crisis.

The councilmen had chosen Hanus from all the other candidates to be in charge of reworking the monstrosity and adding a calendar dial. Hanus was a wizard at both numbers and the night sky. He had studied under Sindel's successor at Prague's Charles University and at the Leipzig University in Germany and graduated from each at the top of his class. Of course he had accepted the challenge.

"What if you fail?" his wife, Catherine, asked him, one night while they lay in bed.

"I will not," he whispered in the dark, kissing her forehead.

If anyone could chart time for both the Earth and the Heavens, Hanus could. He had built his knowledge upon Aristotle's, Ptolemy's, and Hipparchus's theories, and though he would never say it aloud, his expertise exceeded Sacrobosco and Peurback, the authors of the two leading textbooks on astronomy at the university. He'd seen the original geared astrolabes designed by al-Biruni and Abi Bakr from the East and learned the devices' capabilities. Just as he could take apart any lock, a skill taught to him by his father, a master locksmith, so could he do the same with the astrolabe and understand its mechanisms.

Repairing the clock took almost a year. Hanus worked ceaselessly, even moving into the clock tower to work through the night. His son would come to assist him when he wasn't busy with his studies. The boy would bring food and wine along with messages from his mother to stay warm, to eat, to sleep, and to come home soon.

Hanus would laugh at his wife's messages. Catherine knew he would not return home until he was finished. He was time's conductor in the clock tower, directing a symphony of crown wheels, gear trains, and torsion springs. Never had he felt more connected to life and the stars than he did standing in the center of the clock. He even kept the tower key around his neck like a talisman.

"Perhaps I'll never leave here," he said, winking to his son as he drank his wine, "and remain a ghost when I die."

⁓

When the clock bell rang over the city, people on the street gathered and cheered. Even the city councilors were waiting to congratulate him. From that moment on, wherever Hanus went, people tipped their hats to him with the highest respect. Prague was once more the most advanced city in the sciences, thanks to him.

The city councilors hosted a banquet in his honor to celebrate the achievement.

The revelry lasted all night.

The banquet was on the second floor of town hall in one of the grand rooms filled with tables made of wood so thick they looked like giant trees turned on their sides. The tables were laden with a feast of smoked duck, sliced beets, savory pearl barley, spinach garlic pancakes, and cheese mousse.

Hanus surveyed the party with haze-filled eyes. He'd drunk more wine than usual tonight, his cup filled again and again without his asking.

The councilmen sat at the head table away from him, whispering and nodding amongst themselves. The burning candlelight splayed shadows across their faces in ominous patterns, making Hanus wonder if they had heard of his other offers.

When he'd first started working on the clock, word of the repair had traveled throughout Europe. Before he'd even finished, he had received several offers from other cities to construct a new astronomical clock, one as good, if not better, than Prague's. Now that he had achieved the impossible, twice as many offers were arriving for ten times the coin. Hanus was already lining up the opportunities.

Would the council try to stop him?

A worry for the morning, he thought as he tried to brush off his unease. He had done his duty and earned his reward. Catherine sat laughing beside him along with their children, who were watching wide-eyed as jugglers performed with lit torches.

Hanus applauded song after song and drank cup after cup until the evening became a spinning blur. He laughed and looked over to Catherine to find her seat was empty. He didn't remember when she and the children had gone home or why he hadn't gone with them.

Someone had wanted a word, but now he didn't remember who. A vague image returned to him. Had he, like a drunken fool, told the head councilman of his plans to build another clock?

He stared into his cup and a seed of fear began to grow inside of him as he remembered the exchange. He had spoken. He'd done more than that—he had boasted, "I'm the best clockmaker in the world!"

The head councilman smiled through thinly pursed lips. "And Prague is in your debt. But surely you must see that the clock cannot be re-created elsewhere."

"The world needs better clocks, not only Prague." Hanus went to drink from his cup to find it empty.

"Drunken fool." The councilman's eyes narrowed into dark slits.

Another councilman leaned forward, no longer pretending to be civil. "You have not yet responded to our request to hand over your designs for safekeeping. The council demands it!"

"Demands it?" Hanus slurred. "I will not. It is my work." His calculations for the clock he had hidden away in a secret vault under his house. Not even Catherine knew where they were.

He squinted at them, having trouble keeping focus. Suddenly he felt like an animal trapped in the woods and surrounded by huntsmen who meant him harm.

With a glimmer of understanding he began to see the night for what it was: this wasn't a banquet, it was a capture.

A serving girl came to fill his cup again and he waved her off, realizing they wanted him drunk.

He stood, his legs unsteady. "Excuse me," he tried to say, but even to his ears the words were unintelligible.

Outside the hall, he tried to get his bearings. He was so drunk, the two men suddenly gripping his arms barely registered. His head lagged, resting on his chest as they dragged him up the stairs and into the room next to the tower. His last coherent thought was that he wished he had gone home with Catherine.

Hours later Hanus fought to regain consciousness and push past the pain and agony coursing through his body.

He could no longer see.

His mouth was on fire and thick with blood. His abductors had brutalized him and left him to die.

Thoughts circled him. *What have they done to me? I will never see my wife and children again.* He would die alone and the clock's plans would stay buried like hidden jewels no one would ever find.

Helpless rage forged his last bit of strength. His body afire from his wounds, he crawled on his hands and knees to the tower door. He gripped the wall and pulled himself up.

Blind, he reached out in the dark with his hands. When he felt the lock, he took the tower key from around his neck and used it for the last time.

Staggering forward, with muted grunts he found every screw, coil, and dial that could not be rebuilt without him—every piece—and destroyed them all.

When he was finished, he crumbled to the floor, his body too broken to go on. At least the men who had done this to him would never see the clock work in their lifetime. They had failed.

Hanus reached for his tools and grasped the sharpest one to stop the pain. It was time to die.

7. THE BRACELET

ROAN BACKED AWAY FROM HIS DESK, struggling to breathe as he tried to expel the horror of what he'd witnessed. He bent down and put his hands on his knees and heaved in gulps of air. He tried to calm down and brought his hands together into a Ganesha mudra only to find his hands were completely numb.

He began to apply acupressure to all the major pressure points in his hands—the base of his thumb, his wrist, his palm's inner and outer gate, and the heart and lung meridians—until the nerves in his hands started to tingle and wake up like a fiery trail of ants.

This key Stuart had sent him was to the tower of Prague's astronomical clock from the 1400s. The clock master, Hanus, had worn it around his neck until the day he died.

Hanus's violent demise was imprinted in the metal like a permanent black mark. His captors had gouged his eyes out and taken his tongue so he couldn't build another clock or tell anyone else how to do it. Afterward the poor man had gathered his last remaining strength and destroyed his work and ended his life.

Why the councilmen would blind the one person who could restore the clock was beyond Roan. But he also knew that question could never be answered. He could only witness the past as an observer. It didn't always mean he understood the why of things. That was the limitation of his gift.

Even with such a tragic imprint, this key wasn't a normal relic, and what he'd experienced wasn't a normal imprint. There was another element running alongside the imprint within the key, a signature of sorts that Roan immediately recognized.

He'd only touched one other object in his life that had made his hands go numb, and it'd been with Stuart.

They had been on a climbing trip to Colorado, bouldering at the Rocky Mountain National Park. They'd been climbing all week and were due to fly out the next day. They were at the bar at the lodge outside the park having a celebratory drink after tackling two of the hardest V16s in the world, Hypnotized Minds and Creature from the Black Lagoon, when Stuart asked him to hold something.

"I found something at a dig last month I need to get your opinion on." Stuart took out a small box from his bag and opened it to reveal an ornate gold ring.

He placed the ring with great ceremony on the table between them.

Roan kept his gloves on and picked it up for a quick appraisal. "I'd say sixteenth or seventeenth century, a man's ring based on the armorial signet and square bezel set . . . uninscribed with no engraving." He went to hand it back.

"Right. Now gloves off, mate," Stuart said in challenge.

Roan raised an eyebrow. "Here? At the bar?"

"Why not? Afraid it'll interfere with your magic mudra power?"

Roan laughed. Stuart never failed to make him laugh. Their laughter, like climbing, was one of the highlights of their friendship. With Stuart nothing was sacred.

Maybe Roan was as competitive as Stuart, because before Roan could rethink what he was doing, he took off his gloves and held the ring without even doing a mudra to prepare. Within moments he was in Holland in 1633, lost within the intricate memories of the man who had worn it. But unlike a normal reading, while Roan held the ring, his hands began to go numb and a river of ice spread up his fingers.

The sensation pulled him out of the imprint.

He stared at his unfeeling hands, stupefied. That had never happened before. He put the ring back down.

"That was quick," Stuart noted.

Roan tried to revive the feeling back into his hands by rotating his wrists and clenching his palms into fists. "My hands are numb."

Stuart exploded into laughter, his British accent becoming even more pronounced. "Crikey, that's brilliant. This calls for another round. Waitress! Can we get two more, love?" Stuart wiggled his glass in the air at her, motioning her over. "And a basket of crisps?" He turned back to find Roan performing acupressure on his hands. "Come on, man. Let's hear it. Whose ring is this?"

"René Descartes."

"The René Descartes? The mathematician René Descartes?" Stuart was flummoxed. "When I held it all I got was a teacher from Sweden."

Roan nodded. "Because Descartes was in Sweden tutoring the queen when he died of pneumonia in 1650."

Stuart made a long silent "Ah."

"Then the imprint jumps to the present, like a time gap," Roan explained. "You found this in Jordan buried in Cretaceous rock. Your lab technicians tested it several times because it's not possible for a seventeenth-century ring to be buried in rock millions of years old." Roan shook his head, completely perplexed. The Cretaceous period came right after the Jurassic period, and this ring was only four hundred years old. Maybe this was why his hands had gone numb. He put his gloves back on, not wanting to touch it again. "It's an oopart, isn't it? Just like the compass Miguel showed us in France."

"Precisely. Very, very good." Stuart tucked the ring back into its special box. "What I want to know is how these little buggers are jumping through time."

Roan went to open his mouth to say *no,* already knowing Stuart was going to ask for his help, but Stuart cut him off.

"Forget the group," Stuart said. "I know you don't want to deal with those chaps. Let's solve this mystery together. Just you and me."

Roan shook his head. "Sorry, not interested."

"Come on. You're the best psychometrist I know. And you waste all that talent returning heirlooms from the past two centuries? Boring. Grasp the mettle, man. I'm talking about a mystery that spans millions of years." Stuart tried to infuse some humor into their conversation. "We could be the dynamic duo of the archaeological world. You already dress in black."

Roan didn't laugh. Handling ooparts buried in million-year-old rock that made his hands go numb was a risk, for reasons Stuart didn't understand.

"How can you not be interested in objects that are jumping through time and space?" Stuart asked with exasperation.

Roan stared at his friend, realizing he had no choice but to share the truth about why helping him hunt down ancient artifacts was the last thing he'd ever do.

And the easiest way to explain was to *show* him the memory.

Without a word, Roan pulled out his wallet and slid out a flattened piece of plastic from the inside pocket. When he handed it to Stuart it became apparent it was a hospital bracelet. Roan didn't know how accurate Stuart's reading would be, but he was sure Stuart would gather enough information from the bracelet to understand. Roan carried it around with him as a reminder of how he almost died.

He watched the bracelet disappear into Stuart's palm, so he could glimpse the story inside. The incident had happened years ago, before he met Stuart, at Gobekli Tepe, an eleven-thousand-year-old archaeological site in Turkey that had been established as the world's oldest temple.

At the time, Roan had wanted to visit the site and see what he could sense. A German collector he'd sold several antiques to was friends with Klaus Schmidt, the archaeologist in charge of the dig, and Roan managed to get an invitation.

According to modern archaeologists, eleven thousand years ago a structure of Gobekli Tepe's immense size and sophistication shouldn't have been possible. Roan didn't need to touch a single stone to know that its discovery was rewriting history.

When Roan took off his glove and placed his hand on one of the stone pillars, he felt like a light bulb being plugged into a socket and turned on. The imprint pulled him like an ocean current, with such force he became untethered from his body. Then everything went dark.

Later he woke up in a hospital room in Istanbul, where he learned that he'd been airlifted from the dig and treated for cardiac arrest. Both of his parents had flown out to be at his bedside.

The accident changed Roan's outlook on everything.

For months he didn't touch a thing in fear that it would trigger another heart attack. As he picked apart what had happened, he became convinced it was the stretch of time that had been too much. Like a diver in the ocean, he had found his limit, the depth of years he couldn't swim past. So he stopped chasing the mysteries of the ancient past and settled for the world's closer and more well-worn history, never reading anything older than five thousand years. Even with those self-imposed limitations, history was still a vast playground.

That little piece of plastic with his name on it reminded him never to try to touch anything that old again.

When Stuart was done reading the imprints, he nodded somberly and handed the bracelet back. "Right, then. That's that." Stuart didn't mention his oopart research after that night, and he had never asked for Roan's help again—until now.

Roan picked up the letter that had come with the key:

Roan,

Apologies for not showing up in Texas. I'm in more trouble than I thought. I'm sending you something for safekeeping in that warehouse of yours, an original key to the astronomical clock tower in Prague from the 15th century.

Hopefully you're reading my letter before you touch it. I'm afraid the key holds nothing good. What makes this artifact significant isn't its origins, but the fact that it was found buried in 2,000-year-old volcanic ash in Managua, Nicaragua. I know because I'm the one who found it.

It's an oopart, just like Descartes's ring. Any other archae-ologist wouldn't have been able to identify it.

I've been piecing together a unifying theory about these ooparts with Miguel that may have landed us in real danger. Someone doesn't seem to want us to arrive at the answers. Miguel is missing and I'm afraid I'll be next. I need to go into hiding and will call when I can. Please keep the oopart safe.

I'm sorry to involve you, but I don't know who else I can trust.

-S

A myriad of thoughts ran through Roan's mind. Stuart had been in a panic when he wrote the letter. Roan studied the clock tower key on the table and a weary sigh escaped him. He needed to touch the key again to find other imprints and see if it could shed light on Stuart's situation.

He didn't relish having to sense Hanus's life again or endure the numbing feeling that would take hold in hands, but he needed to read every imprint the key held, not only the memories from Hanus's life.

Discordant moments were always the easiest to access and many times masked the rest, but if there was one thing Roan had learned early on it was that time was an objective observer and collected every moment, both light and dark.

Centering himself, he took the key in his hand again. He forcefully pushed past the violence of Hanus's powerful imprint and ignored the nerves in his fingers as they tingled in protest.

Like a minnow in the water, his mind became fluid as he dipped and dived through every layer of memory that had been left by the years.

As he pushed through the centuries, the imprints compressed, until Roan found himself standing in the recent past, in the middle of an imprint he wanted to see.

NEW YORK CITY

TWO WEEKS AGO

STUART HELD HANUS'S KEY WRAPPED in a swatch of silk as he walked through Central Park with Sun. She strode with purposeful steps, her hands tucked behind her back.

"When did it happen?" he asked her.

"His son found him yesterday at home. There was no note. No goodbye. Traces of poison were found in his cognac."

Stuart shook his head in disbelief. "Maybe François didn't want to say goodbye . . . the man was dying of cancer," he pointed out gently.

"François would never kill himself. Never." She had a scowl on her face. "And now Miguel is missing. Why did he go to Australia?"

"Miguel's theory is that the Aboriginal concept of time is the closest to the oopart anomaly," Stuart tried to explain. "The Aborigines believe time dilates, moving seamlessly across the past, present, and future like a circle. Miguel thinks the ooparts might be too."

"Now Miguel might be dead. Like François."

Stuart ran a hand through his hair in frustration. "We don't know that. He's traveling alone in the outback. Give him time."

Sun let out a *tsk* sound in disagreement. "Miguel would not disappear for this long without sending word to his family."

Stuart didn't agree. "The man's divorced. His daughters are busy with college, one in Peru and one abroad in Europe—"

Sun didn't let him finish. "And François would never kill himself, no matter how dire his circumstances. I knew the man much better than you."

"Sun," Stuart said, trying to keep his patience. "We are so close to discovering the answers. Miguel was the one who saw the connection to the circles. Gyan agrees it could be the unifying factor we've been searching for." He stopped walking and held out the key. "Please, I'm begging you. Please help us."

"There is no us." Sun stopped walking and stared at him, a fierce light in her eyes. "Something happened to Miguel and François after they started researching these artifacts. Now you may be blinded by your own ambition, but someone sees our ability as a threat."

Stuart stared up at the sky, feeling helpless. "Don't you think the best way to help find Miguel is to figure out the answers? I'm just as worried as you are, but it's not like we can go to the authorities with this. I don't know what else to do."

"You said you have two ooparts." Sun frowned. "Where's the other?"

"I gave it to Gyan."

"He needs to be warned." Sun continued walking.

"I already have." Stuart hurried to keep up with her. They exited the park and were now on Fifth Avenue. "Please, Sun. Help us find the connection between the ooparts and the circles. I think it could solve this whole riddle."

Sun shook her head. "If you value your life you must stop. Hide the key. Give it to someone you can trust, someone not connected to any of us."

They stopped near the entrance of an apartment building across the street from the Metropolitan Museum of Art.

Sun held back from approaching the doorman. "Who else have you told about your research?"

"Only my friend Roan West, who you met. He was there when Miguel first showed us the compass. He didn't want to get involved."

"He's already involved. Until we find out who is behind this and what happened to Miguel and François, no psychometrist is safe, not even your friend."

8. THE CHAMPAGNE GLASS

MELICENT HAD BEEN GOOGLING ROAN WEST without success. The man didn't exist. There was only one mention of Roan West in an obituary for Robert West, who passed away five years ago from a stroke in New Orleans. Robert West had founded West, Inc., an antiques dealership in New Orleans, in 1997.

West, Inc.'s corporate website didn't offer much information either. Someone named Holly Beauchêne ran the company. She was also on the board of the Heirloom Foundation, along with a history professor from Oxford, Dr. Jocelyn Matthis. Melicent could find no mention of Roan West with the Heirloom Foundation either. The foundation stated it was a nonprofit organization that worked to restore and return lost heirlooms to the original families' descendants. No other details were provided.

RW Antiques was the official name of West, Inc.'s storefront in New Orleans. A picture showed a charming pearl-painted house located on Magazine Street built in the early 1900s. Like so many of its neighbors, the house had been converted into a business. Visits were by appointment only.

The website offered elegant pictures of the showrooms and the house's exterior. Melicent clicked on several links for Magazine Street. More than forty stores lined the six-mile street along with artists' studios and design firms. It was a mecca for home decoration. Only a handful of the antique stores were exclusive, where appointments were recommended or required, and most of the pieces heralded from Europe and previous centuries. RW Antiques had been written up in countless magazines and trade publications, including *Journal of Antiques and Collectibles, Preservation in Print, The Magazine Antiques,* and *Southern Living,* as one of the premiere places for the serious collector.

Melicent squinted at the article she was reading, uncertain. Her mystery customer didn't look like an antique dealer from New Orleans. But then she didn't know what he looked like. She just wanted to stop thinking about him—she'd been obsessing about Roan West, whoever he might be, since he walked out of the shop. Thinking about him was becoming a distraction and kept her from facing the fact that her life had now drastically changed.

Yesterday she'd driven to Breguet's store in Beverly Hills and met with their representative, who had flown in from Paris to appraise the watch. She sat in the back office for more than twenty minutes while he examined every facet under a loupe.

Directly in her sight line, a print of Abraham-Louis Breguet's portrait hung on the office wall, along with the words THE WATCHMAKERS OF KINGS, THE KING OF WATCHMAKERS.

Melicent's eyes kept darting to the picture. Breguet looked exactly like she'd imagined him with his enormous brow and high hairline. His deep-set eyes held a distant gaze and his attire and carriage exuded a gentle grace.

Melicent knew from holding the watch that the man had been born in Neuchâtel, Switzerland, and that the pocket watch was one of his favorites. He'd made it during one of the happiest times of his life, while living in Paris before his wife died. For a glimmer of a moment Melicent had seen his workshop at Quai de l'Horage, the worktable lined with his tools, his view from the window to the Seine, his desk with stacks of handwritten orders from patrons, along with the registrar book that kept account of every record.

Breguet had taken the watch—hidden in his breast pocket—to Switzerland after he escaped the French Revolution and the guillotine. He had gifted it to a family in repayment for their help during those years before he returned to France, and Melicent felt how difficult that decision had been. Giving the watch away had set the course for its long journey from Europe to America over a tide of centuries. Louis would be overcome to learn that his beloved pocket watch had been found and, in essence, returned to him.

"The last original Breguet timepiece to surface came from the private collection of a noble family in England," the French representative said, bewildered as to how one of the most treasured watches in the world had been lost at a flea market in Anaheim. He acted as if she had been the one to put it there.

When the representative offered her $1.8 million, every muscle in Melicent's body seized. She sat there frozen, suspended for an endless moment, feeling disconnected and far away. Then she heard herself say yes.

The company kept the watch and wired the funds to her bank account right then.

When Melicent walked out of the store, she looked around, turning in a full circle, suddenly feeling like an astronaut who had landed on another planet, a world where she was no longer struggling or stressed. She was free to live a different life.

She had almost two million dollars in her bank account—an account that had had four hundred and twenty-nine dollars before today.

Her whole body was shaking with a heady rush of emotion. She thought about calling Parker, but he was staying over at his best friend BJ's, which was just as well. She needed time alone to process what had happened.

Where did they go from here? If time equaled money, Breguet had just given her all the time in the world.

⌣

When she got home, the house was empty. She looked around her mother's cluttered living room, at the threadbare sofas draped with decorative printed quilts to cover the stains. Sadie had been a master at hiding their secondhand furniture and worn walls with colorful art and plants.

Every inch of the house held her mother's memory—and the fear of losing those memories, of having to say goodbye to their childhood home, had been keeping Melicent up at night. Not having that threat looming over her felt surreal. They could keep the house her mother had loved so much. The bank wouldn't foreclose. Melicent could pay off her student loans. She could walk into a car dealership and buy a new car that didn't break down every other week. She could get Parker a new car too. Forget the used truck. She'd get him a brand-new car that would last him well through college and beyond.

"Mom, I did it," she said to the empty room. Her voice sounded hesitant. She didn't quite believe it yet.

The house answered with a heavy silence.

Melicent didn't know if her mom could hear her, if she knew they'd be all right, and a sob escaped her. Soon she couldn't stop crying. She cried harder than she had at the funeral as the ball of stress and worry inside her uncurled like a clenched fist.

After the tears were gone, she was emotionally spent. A pang of hunger hit her—she couldn't remember the last time she'd eaten. She jumped up, deciding to call her favorite Thai restaurant. Tonight she'd splurge.

She went to the refrigerator in the garage to get a bottle of champagne. Champagne had been her mother's drink of choice, and Sadie had always kept several bottles chilled for entertaining. The labels were nothing fancy—or even more than fifteen dollars—except for one or two bottles that had been in the fridge forever.

Melicent looked at the selection and picked the Moët. She sensed her mother had bought it for a special occasion. Sadie hadn't known what it would be, but she'd wanted to be ready for it.

Melicent swallowed, becoming emotional again, and brought the bottle to the kitchen. She wasn't a champagne drinker, but today was monumental. She popped the cork and poured a glass.

Holding her mother's favorite champagne glass brought on a cascade of memories from birthdays to baby showers to friends' milestones and Sadie's one big break as an actress. Those moments coursed over her like a bubbly river of happy thoughts. Her mother might be gone, but Melicent could embed one more memory into her mother's champagne glass. She would add another celebration to the stem and commemorate the day Abraham-Louis Breguet changed their lives forever.

After today nothing would ever be the same.

She raised her glass in the air and said softly to the empty kitchen, "Thank you, Louis."

9. THE GIFT

ROAN ARRIVED TO NEW YORK IN THE MORNING, to overcast gray skies and a nipping wind. At Teterboro Airport he reserved a car and driver for the day to take him into Manhattan.

From the imprint in Hanus's key, he was able to identify where Sun lived. He'd seen clearly in his mind's eye her building right across the street from the Met. The fifteen-story co-op looked like it had been built in the 1920s.

Stuart must have been desperate to have gone to New York to enlist Sun's help. Miguel was missing and François was dead, and Sun thought both were connected to their research with the ooparts—now Stuart couldn't be reached. Things were much worse than Roan had imagined. He needed to see Sun and find out what she knew.

He didn't have her phone number to schedule an appointment. But given the circumstances, maybe it was better if he arrived unannounced. She could be a factor behind Stuart's disappearance. He didn't know anything about the woman.

After Roan tried to meet with Sun, he would fly on to London and see what he could find at Stuart's apartment. Stuart had always extended Roan an open invitation to stay at his place whenever he was in town and had shown him where he kept a spare key hidden in his garden. Roan had never taken Stuart up on the offer. He hoped the key was still there.

When he got out of the town car the doorman in front of Sun's building greeted Roan with a tip of the hat. Roan went inside and approached the concierge behind the desk. "Could you please call up to Sun Kim and tell her Roan West is here?"

The man behind the desk said, "Certainly, sir," and dialed. He spoke quietly into the phone. "There's a gentleman here, Roan West, to see you. Shall I send him up?" His eyes flickered over to Roan. "Very good, ma'am." The man hung up and looked at Roan and the small box he was holding in his gloved hands. "She'll be down in a moment."

Not two minutes had passed when Sun stepped from the elevator. She looked just as she had five years ago, and her eyes landed on Roan with the force of an arrow. Her gaze fell to the box he was holding.

"Shall we walk?" Sun inclined her head, clearly not wanting to discuss their business in front of anyone, least of all the concierge, who was eyeing them. She did a pivot and went outside without waiting to see if he would follow. She was no more than five foot three, a foot shorter than him, and still Roan had to hurry to keep up. "What's in the box?" she asked.

So much for cordial hellos. Roan's curiosity about the prickly woman was increasing. "Stuart's oopart. I assume you know why I'm here?"

"No. Did he ask you to come?" Sun had no idea Roan knew the entire conversation she'd had with Stuart in Central Park.

"I'm here on my own accord. Stuart's in trouble. Or maybe you already knew that?"

Sun stopped walking. For a minute she didn't say anything. "How did you find me?"

"With this." He held up the box holding Hanus's key.

Sun raised an eyebrow. "From an imprint?"

"Like I said, I'm here to help Stuart. He's been unreachable."

"For how long?"

"Three days."

Sun said something under her breath in Korean that sounded like a swear word. Then she turned around and marched back toward her building. "Come inside then. We have much to discuss."

⁓

They rode the elevator in silence to the fifteenth floor, where Sun had a corner unit. Roan walked inside to find a gorgeous view of the Met from the living room. The rooms had gleaming mahogany floors, and a dining table that sat close to the floor was the only furniture in sight. A ring of flaming-red embroidered silk floor cushions circled the table instead of chairs.

"You sit," Sun ordered. "I'll bring tea," she said, and disappeared into the kitchen.

Roan assumed she wanted him to sit on one of the cushions. He took off his coat and folded it into his lap. He looked around the spartan space, wondering what Sun did for a living. She was still a total enigma.

An enormous antique Korean screen hung on the main wall like a fresco. The six painted panels portrayed a magical scene of wildlife being chased through a forest and over the ocean by hunters wielding bows and arrows. As Roan studied the masterful brushstrokes and vivid hues, the urge gripped him to touch the panels, but he knew Sun wouldn't appreciate the gesture.

"Third century," Sun said from the doorway. "From a burial chamber in Silla." She came toward him holding a tray. She placed a porcelain cup in front of him that looked more like a bowl and sat down across from him at the table.

The fragrant smell of barley in the tea rose with the steam, making him want to drink it. Yet he hesitated, unable to discern if Sun was friend or foe.

They studied each other for a long moment. Roan refused to

look away from her commanding stare. Was she trying to intimidate him?

She finally asked, "Why did you not join us after you came to France?"

"Because I like to work alone."

Sun's hooded eyes glinted with intensity as she considered him. "I understand. You're a busy man. Pine Ridge, St. Joe's, Manzanar, Minidoka."

Roan crossed his arms, the tea forgotten as she began listing the sites he'd been working on with the Heirloom Foundation.

"So many dark spots in this country's history to shed light on . . . the Japanese internment camps of World War II, the Native American massacres, the government boarding schools. The United States has a complicated history. I believe your work started with the sugar plantations in Louisiana?"

Roan pursed his lips, not saying a word. Sun had done her homework on him.

She measured his reaction as she continued, "West, Inc. sold over fifteen million dollars in antiquities last year, and yet you spend most of your time giving away heirlooms for free. Anonymously. How noble."

Roan couldn't tell if she was mocking him or not. Tracking down lost heirlooms and giving them back to those families who were the victims of the darkest times in history had become his passion and made him feel like he was doing something purposeful with his life. He didn't need to explain himself to her.

He tried to steer the conversation back to the matter at hand. "I came here for Stuart, to find out if you have any idea what he's involved in. I'm trying to help him." Roan still didn't understand what it was Stuart had discovered about the ooparts. Stuart had mentioned to Sun something about "the circles" and finding a connection. But Roan wasn't about to reveal that he knew that much from an imprint.

Sun gazed at him hard. This was some kind of bizarre test. She was sizing him up.

"How old do you think I am?" she asked. The question caught him off guard and she answered before he could. "Seventy-eight. Maybe in thirty years you'll learn how not to need gloves. And maybe in twenty you'll learn how to be polite to your elders."

Roan let out a short laugh. Sun was beginning to remind him of his mother. He never would have pegged her as being in her late seventies. She looked closer to sixty.

"My years have taught me many things, and my instinct is telling me you can be trusted. Whatever has happened to Stuart is connected to the research the group was doing. Miguel is also missing, and poor François is dead from an apparent suicide, which I think was staged."

Roan could see the emotion in her eyes, hear the strain in her voice. These men were her friends.

"Two psychometrists halfway around the globe from each other, and something happened to them weeks apart," she said. "Now Stuart is gone too. I'm afraid we'll be next." She reached over and opened the box Roan had brought.

Roan tried to warn her. "I wouldn't touch that—"

Sun picked up Hanus's clock tower key and closed her eyes, sitting immobile like a statue for a long moment. Then she set it back down and let out a tsk. "I really don't like handling things from the fourteen hundreds . . . too much brutality," she said with distaste, and sipped her tea.

Roan could only stare at her in amazement, wondering how she had read the imprint without being affected.

She went on. "This key may be an oopart, but I don't think the answers lie in its imprints. Miguel believed the ooparts were not random anomalies. He recently discovered a connection between ooparts and crop circles."

"Crop circles?" Roan's eyebrows shot up.

The circles Stuart had been talking about with Sun were *crop circles*?

What Sun was saying was so unexpected, it threw him for a moment. Roan didn't know much about crop circles, except that there had been wide public interest in them in the nineties, followed by a Hollywood blockbuster film that ended with an alien in theatrical makeup. Their mystique diminished when two men, a pair of "crop circle artists," came forward and confessed that they had been traveling to different countries for years and creating them overnight. The media officially declared the phenomenon a hoax and over time crop circles faded from the public eye.

After his mother moved to Oxford, Roan had been surprised to learn that Great Britain, particularly the area around Wiltshire, continued to be the crop circle mecca of the world, well after the two artists had officially retired. Crop circles still occurred every year around the globe, with dozens of circles appearing in Britain alone. Only a handful were ever acknowledged as being made by an actual person or a group while the rest remained shrouded in mystery. But the phenomenon had been going on for so long, not many people paid attention to them.

He asked Sun, "How are crop circles connected to ooparts?"

"I haven't seen their research. I don't have the answers." Sun nodded to Hanus's key on the table. "But someone doesn't want these ooparts identified. And who better to do so than us?"

Roan shook his head, unable to make sense of it all. He needed to go to London and see if Stuart had left any clues at his house that could give them some insight. "What about Gyan?" Gyan had Stuart's other oopart, René Descartes's ring. Roan might need to pay the man a visit.

"He's in India with his family. Stuart warned him to be on guard." Sun gave him a contemplative look. "You must be careful too. You're a target as well."

A feeling of anger prickled inside him. "Because I came here?"

"Because we must assume someone is going after all psychometrists," Sun said, her face unreadable. Then she reached into her pocket and pulled out a long thin box that looked like it might hold a necklace. She slid it across the table to him as an offering. "We need to trust each other, Roan West."

Roan stared at the box, not quite willing to take it. It was true he didn't trust Sun. He couldn't imagine what she was giving him.

Sun handed him her card with her phone number. "There is a psychometrist in Korea I must warn," Sun told him. "She was planning to join the group this year. She is young and inexperienced, which makes her even more vulnerable."

Roan immediately thought of Melicent Tilpin back in Los Angeles. She was all those things too. Then there was the YouTube video, announcing that she was a psychometrist for all the world to see.

Would the people who were after Stuart's group find her in the minefield of the internet? Holly had and sent him the YouTube link, which meant others could find it.

Roan took Hanus's key with him and Sun's mystery box. They agreed they would be in touch if either of them received news from Stuart.

⌒

As Roan headed to the airport in the back seat of the town car, he pulled out his lucky coin and ran it back and forth across his hand as he contemplated his next move.

He couldn't stop his train of thought from landing right where he didn't want it to—before he flew to London he needed to return to Los Angeles and actually talk to the woman he was trying so hard to forget. He needed to warn Melicent Tilpin she was in danger.

10. THE DOORKNOB

MELICENT WAS ON THE LAST CHAPTER of *Mastering Psychometry* and had gotten caught up by Woods's account of all the archaeological mysteries in the world that were waiting to be solved: the giant stone spheres of Costa Rica, the Nazca lines, the megalithic jars in Laos, the Sajama Lines of Bolivia, Stonehenge, the Great Pyramid. The list was long and Woods believed many of the answers could be found through psychometry. He pointed out how the technology archaeologists were using was getting better with time and that as a result everything their machines dated kept getting older. The accepted timelines of history didn't match up anymore. It was like getting a new coloring book of the history of the world and being told it had to be colored all over again. Woods believed psychometrists could help fill in the lines. The knowledge was there, buried and waiting.

The front door jingled.

"When were you going to tell me?" Tish, the owner of The Trove and Melicent's boss, rushed in with excitement.

Melicent blinked and looked up. She'd lost all track of time. "Hey, I didn't hear you come in." She slipped the psychometry book under the register.

Tish came toward her with an astounded look, waving a

newspaper in her hand. "Is this you?" She slapped the paper down on the counter.

Melicent read the headline of an article in the Arts & Culture section of the *L.A. Times* in disbelief. "Woman Sells Priceless Pocket Watch Back to Breguet." Next to the article was a picture of the Rodeo Drive storefront and the French representative she'd met, smiling for the camera and holding up the watch.

"Is this you?" Tish asked again. "You sold a pocket watch for almost two million dollars?"

"Oh my God" was all Melicent could say, feeling out-of-body when she found her name.

> Melicent Tilpin, a Los Angeles native, found the Breguet pocket watch at a swap meet in Anaheim. The timepiece was a noted favorite of Abraham-Louis Breguet and became lost sometime during the French Revolution.

"I know! Answer me! Did you sell a watch for two million dollars?" Tish was beside herself.

Melicent quickly skimmed the rest.

> Ms. Tilpin sold the watch back to Breguet, which has estimated its value to be close to two million dollars. The company is very pleased to have an original Breguet, made by the man himself, returned, which makes the pocket watch priceless in their eyes.

This was a nightmare.

"Yes," Melicent whispered. She hadn't been ready to share the news with anyone, least of all her boss.

"When?" Tish demanded.

"Yesterday." Melicent shook her head in disbelief that she'd made the paper. She read the article again.

"And you haven't told me yet?" Tish put her hands on her hips.

"I haven't told anyone. I'm still processing it." Melicent was beginning to feel annoyed. Tish had a way of thinking Melicent's life was her personal business. They had been roommates and good friends in college. But the dynamics of their friendship had changed when Tish began to officially pay Melicent for her time.

"Tell me everything! Start at the beginning." Tish sat down next to her. "What are you going to do with the money?" she asked, catapulting over the part about wanting to hear the story. "I mean, you could start your own gallery. You could go into business for yourself. You could even partner with me."

Melicent's eyebrows rose at that. She had no urge to partner with Tish. "I don't know my plans yet," she hedged. "It's still kind of all sinking in."

It'd been only a few days since the *Antiques Roadshow* appraisal, and Melicent had already decided that she wouldn't use her budding ability to sense anything else. Now that she and Parker had more than enough money, she didn't want to go antique hunting for a while. Part of her didn't even want to dwell on what she'd done. In the aftermath, it still felt like a dream.

"Well, think about it. Seriously. I could use a partner. I'm practically getting an ulcer running this place."

Melicent frowned at that. *She* was running this place. Melicent had been store manager for almost four years, since opening day. Melicent and Tish had both been art majors at UCLA. Tish's parents gave their daughter The Trove store as a college graduation present. Melicent got flowers from her mom on graduation day—and yet Tish always complained she wished her mother were more like Sadie, quick to hug, laugh, and invite the world over for dinner. The irony was that Melicent's mom was the struggling actress, the cliché L.A. waitress juggling auditions and night shifts while living paycheck to paycheck. Tish's parents were Hollywood producers, the kind who had the best parking spaces on the studio lot. Tish pitched the idea of managing the store to Melicent while Tish traveled to find the art to fill it with. At the time the proposal sounded like a fabulous idea. But the reality was Melicent was a workhorse. She was in charge of running the store and handled the payroll, advertising, and accounting. She usually put in six days a week and had only one part-time assistant to cover for her, while Tish breezed in and out whenever she wanted.

Tish turned to the sales receipt book and began flipping the pages. Melicent knew her friend didn't mean to be dismissive, but still it stung. It also astounded her that Tish wasn't asking the real question—would Melicent quit her job?

"Wow, you go, girl. You sold all your snow globes?" Tish sounded more shocked over Melicent selling the snow globes than getting two million dollars. She looked at the sales receipt again. "To the same person?"

A flutter hit Melicent's stomach thinking about it. "Some guy came in and bought them all." *Some guy* was putting it mildly. Tish would have flipped over her customer and been all over him trying to get his number, flirting in her yoga pants and sexy hoodie. Meanwhile Melicent hadn't even been able to tell the man she'd made the globes—not that it mattered.

Melicent checked her watch. "Can we talk about this later? You're covering for me, remember? I've got a parent-teacher conference for Parker."

"Oh, that's right." Tish sounded so put out. Melicent's irritation returned tenfold. She'd had the school meeting on the calendar for weeks. She could literally quit her job right now and leave Tish in the lurch. The one thing holding her back was her loyalty. Melicent put on a tight smile and grabbed her purse.

Before she left, Tish called out to her brightly, "I still want to know the story behind this sale." She tapped the paper. "And think about that offer!"

Melicent didn't respond, already knowing that, just as Roan West had taken all her artwork from The Trove, soon she wouldn't be there either.

⌒

When Melicent arrived at Parker's school, all thoughts of Tish and the shop evaporated as Parker's homeroom teacher ushered her into the principal's office and took a seat too. She had thought she was having an end-of-the-semester parent-teacher conference, but instead they'd marshalled her in for an official sit-down meeting.

"Miss Tilpin, I'm afraid we have a problem." The principal got straight to the point.

Melicent sat up straighter and clutched her purse in front of her. Her anxiety level rose as the principal sighed painfully. He seemed like a kind man. He was somewhere in his sixties, completely bald, and had aviator bifocals on that made him look like he was from the seventies.

"Parker has been skipping school." He dropped the bombshell. "He was caught trying to leave campus yesterday and received detention. We spoke to his afternoon teachers, and it seems that this has been going on for some time."

"Skipping school?" Melicent shook her head in disbelief.

"He leaves at lunch," Parker's homeroom teacher added. "We were going to have him sit in on this meeting today, but he's left again."

"To go where?" Melicent all but yelled. She couldn't fathom that her brother had been doing such a thing—was doing such a thing. "Where is he right now?"

"We don't know." The principal looked down at the student

file in front of him. "His friend BJ has been skipping too. As you know, leaving campus is a serious offense. And Parker will be receiving Fs this quarter in his last three periods."

Melicent nodded slowly, overwhelmed. She was going to strangle her brother when she found him. Forget the new car, the kid was grounded.

The principal and homeroom teacher exchanged looks, both uncomfortable. "Miss Tilpin, we're taking into account that Parker has been through a lot this year with his mother's passing." The principal added, "As have you." His eyes were sympathetic.

"But that's still no excuse," Melicent said, sounding shorter than she meant to be. She didn't know what made her angrier, the fact Parker had been skipping school with BJ or that he'd lied about it. And not only had he been missing the majority of his afternoon classes by sneaking off campus, he wasn't even on the debate team, which was where she thought he was spending his time after school.

What the hell was he doing?

By the time she was done with the meeting, she could barely remember what else had been said. All she knew was Parker would have to do summer school at the end of the year if he hoped to be a senior next year. He also had some kind of community volunteer hours to do, starting in January. Melicent had basically agreed to everything to keep her brother from getting expelled.

When she left the principal's office she was so livid she was shaking. She drove straight to BJ's.

No one appeared to be home. Melicent marched through the backyard, past the garage, to the back room where she could still remember BJ and Parker playing when they were little kids.

When she walked in, the space looked like anything but a kids' playroom. Piles of empty beer cans were scattered around several guitars and beat-up amplifiers. Junk food wrappers littered the room and an ashtray filled with cigarette butts sat next to a bong.

Her eyes landed on Parker. He and BJ were frozen, not sure what to hide first.

"This is what you've been doing instead of going to school?" she bellowed.

Parker and BJ jumped to their feet. Parker stammered, "It's not what it looks like."

"Are you kidding me?" Melicent was so furious she couldn't even think straight. "You're skipping school to get high and drink beer? What am I, stupid?"

Parker's face hardened with anger and he crossed his arms.

Melicent was too mad to care, flat-out yelling. "Did you think no one would notice?"

Parker looked like he wasn't going to answer her, then he shrugged. "Yeah."

That took the wind from her anger and she could feel a big ball of emotion rising up to choke her. Suddenly Melicent felt like the worst sister in the world—the worst guardian—because what Parker said was true. She hadn't noticed.

BJ had family problems, the kind that had made Sadie try to get Parker to hang with other kids more than once. BJ's parents wouldn't notice or care if their son was skipping school. But Sadie would have noticed—if she were still alive. And she would have stopped it, much sooner than this.

Parker had been left alone, fending for himself ever since their mother had gotten sick. He'd put up a brave front, a silent front, coming and going and never making a demand. But now Melicent knew how fragile that front had been.

Melicent couldn't say another word. For the first time she was witnessing the depth of her brother's pain, the damage it had done, and the moment overwhelmed her.

BJ sat huddled in the corner. Melicent had known BJ most of his life and had babysat him for half of it. She gave him a cutting look. "*This*"—she made a circular motion with her hands, indicating the room—"*this* is over." She turned back to Parker. "We're leaving. Now." She marched out.

Parker followed behind without a word.

⁓

They drove home in stony silence. Parker's new cell phone binged in his pocket. He had the good sense to ignore it.

Melicent finally spoke. "I don't know what the hell you think skipping school and sitting in the back of a garage is going to accomplish. You're just lucky—" She stopped and bit her lip.

"What? That Mom's not here?" His voice caught.

Again the phone dinged. Parker didn't pull it out of his pocket.

Melicent mentally berated herself. God, she was an idiot. "The bottom line is you're doing summer school at the end of the year to make up those classes."

"Whatever." He sounded petulant.

Ding ding ding. The phone was making too much noise to ignore.

"And no more hanging out with BJ. I'm serious."

Parker didn't say anything, until he asked, "Am I still getting the car?"

"No. I don't know. Don't ask me right now," she flip-flopped, trying to focus on driving. "First you have to get a job."

"Didn't you just sell a watch for like two million dollars?"

"*You* need to learn responsibility! *You* need things to do besides getting stoned in a garage!"

Parker let out a pained sigh.

She tried to dial her anger back down. "Isn't that café on Washington hiring? Something part-time, a few hours a week after school to help you readjust. I swear it'll help."

"Help what? To miss Mom less?" He crossed his arms over his chest and looked out the window, his eyes suspiciously bright.

Melicent hesitated. "No. Nothing will help with that."

Parker's phone started emitting another string of sounds. "Jesus!" he exploded. He pulled it out. "What is going on?"

Melicent let out a sigh and turned into their subdivision. She had no idea if how she was handling Parker's situation was right. As she drove down her street, she absently waved back to several neighbors who were out doing their lawns and to Mrs. Mercer, who lived across the street. The little old lady was in the middle of her afternoon power walk. Sadie had been a friend to everyone within a three-block radius. Many people living on this street had been a lifeline during the last year, delivering meals, dropping off groceries, and driving Sadie to the doctor when Melicent couldn't get off work.

Parker put on his earphones and was busy reading texts. His fingers started flying as he texted someone back. Then he clicked on a link.

"Holy shit," he said to whatever he was watching.

"Watch your language." Melicent took her eyes off the road for a moment to give him a stern look.

"Sorry, but you're going to freak," Parker said with wide eyes. "You're on YouTube."

"I'm on what?" She had no idea what he was talking about. "Why on earth am I on YouTube?"

He unplugged his headset and played the video he was watching. Her voice came through loud and clear on the phone's speaker.

"And what's your name?"

"Melicent Tilpin."

The blood rushed to her head as she listened to herself talk to the appraiser at the *Antiques Roadshow*. She'd signed a release to possibly be on a future show, but she hadn't expected to be streaming on a YouTube channel within days.

"Sometimes I pick up stuff and I can sense things, their history."

Her voice filled the car. In a daze, Melicent pulled into their driveway and hit the button to open the garage door.

"There's like ten thousand views on this already," Parker said.

"'Psychometrist finds million-dollar watch with the power of her hands.' You're, like, famous."

"What? *Antiques Roadshow* called me a psychometrist?"

"This isn't from *Antiques Roadshow* . . . it's on some psychic investigator's YouTube channel."

Her mind was spinning. First the newspaper and now she was on some wacko's YouTube channel racking up thousands of views?

"Some dude uploaded it the day we were there."

"You're saying that's been on YouTube all week?"

"Tori and Stephanie saw it and texted me. They recognized us."

Melicent could barely park the car. Her whole body was quivering. She felt naked, exposed. Anyone in the world could watch that video.

Parker asked her, "Did you really sense those things with your hands?"

Melicent couldn't answer right away. "Yes. It's hard to explain." She'd been grappling her whole life with how to explain the random thoughts and sensations that filled her when she held something for too long.

Maybe because Parker was still smarting over the day's events and her anger, he didn't ask her to talk about it.

Melicent turned off the car. Before she could say anything Parker got out and slammed the door. She got out too. Her mind still reeling, she unlocked the garage door to the house and went to turn the doorknob.

When her palm touched the knob, an ominous feeling wrapped around her wrist like a snake, along with a sharp sensation.

She jerked back with a startled cry.

"What? What's wrong?" Parker was standing behind her.

"Nothing, I . . ." she trailed off, staring at the doorknob in confusion.

Parker opened it for her with an impatient twist and huffed inside.

Melicent stood there a long minute, afraid to touch the door again. Her hand still tingled from the shock she'd received.

A man—a stranger—had touched this doorknob and left behind a malevolent thought so corrosive, it felt like venom.

11. THE LANTERNS

THAT NIGHT MELICENT DOUBLE-CHECKED all the windows and doors, making sure they were locked. She stayed up late, listening to every creak and noise from the house. In bed, she tossed and turned. Every time she almost fell asleep, a clear image of the intruder's face formed in her mind. He must have been a potential burglar, scoping out the neighborhood for unlocked doors.

Tomorrow at work she'd look into getting an alarm system. She mentally put it on her to-do list, and when she woke the next morning, the doorknob incident seemed less scary in the light of day. Their subdivision had dealt with prowlers before, and there was a neighborhood watch. She'd let them know to be on the lookout.

Everything would be fine.

Before heading to work she dropped Parker off at school, now that BJ wasn't giving him rides anymore.

Parker looked out the window with a stoic air the whole way.

She glanced over at him. "I have to close the shop tonight, so I'll be home late. How are you getting home?" The subtext was *no rides with BJ*.

"The bus. Maybe I'll get mugged."

"Parker."

"What? Until I get a car I'll be on the streets."

"You're not *on the streets*. When you prove to me you're going to try hard at school and show results, then you get a car."

He rolled his eyes. "You won't even give me my driver's license."

"Because you don't need it yet. I don't want you driving someone else's car without me." Melicent tried to reason with him. She kept his license with hers in her wallet. While he was sixteen, he only drove her car when she was with him. "And I mean it. No skipping."

"I'm not stupid." He got out of the car in front of the school and slammed the door.

She rolled down the window. "There's leftovers in the fridge!"

He swatted his hand behind his back, embarrassed by her calling out to him in front of other students. A group of nearby girls giggled.

As Melicent watched him go inside the school a wave of self-pity descended on her. How did she handle a rebellious hormonal teenage boy who hated the world because his mother had died and now he was stuck with an inadequate sister?

If anything happened to her then he'd have no one.

She tried not to question that morbid thought and why it entered her mind—she was only twenty-seven. But the garage incident had shaken her. She couldn't help feeling deep in her gut that the man had come for her.

If something happened to her, she needed to make sure Parker would be provided for. Melicent harbored a fear that the Breguet company would one day come and demand that she give them back the money from the pocket watch. Perhaps it was irrational, but the sale still seemed too good to be true.

Maybe she should get life insurance. Her situation was unusual, and it would be one more layer of protection for Parker.

She stopped by the AAA office on her way to work and got the application. She'd been a club member for years, primarily for their towing service since her car was always breaking down. When she held the life insurance application in her hand that same feeling of dread rose up and threatened to overtake her again.

Why had that man been in her garage? The question circled around in her head like the buzz of a fly that wouldn't go away.

As she drove to work, she considered the idea that maybe they should leave L.A., at least for a while. She could disguise it as an extended vacation, a celebration of the pocket watch sale. Tonight when she got home she'd pitch the idea to Parker and let him choose where to go. They both had passports. They could fly anywhere the day after school was out for the winter break, which was less than two weeks away. She'd be free from the shop as soon as she gave Tish her two-week notice.

They could leave town and become anonymous until the watch story died down. In the meantime, she'd schedule an alarm installation for the house and change the locks. Maybe she'd also buy pepper spray, or a Taser, or both.

When she pulled into her parking spot behind The Trove, she was more determined than ever to quit her job right away.

⁓

Tish all but melted down over her cappuccino when Melicent informed her that she was leaving. It was their busiest time of the year. Melicent tried to appease her by saying she would handle interviewing the candidates and that Tish could meet with the contenders. Tish still took the news hard and huffed out of the store, not mentioning her offer to partner with her again.

Melicent remained determined to gracefully maneuver her exit by the end of the two weeks. She decided to focus on organizing the inventory in the back room and tried to shut off all of the worries running through her mind.

She pulled down an enormous box from the top shelf, already

knowing what was inside. Last year Tish had come back from Nepal with three dozen paper lanterns. The rectangular shapes had vibrant mandala patterns painted on them with intricate designs.

"Made from the finest Lokta paper!" Tish had said, as if that would make it easier for Melicent to turn around and sell all thirty-six.

Perhaps guilt over giving Tish her two-week notice before the holidays made Melicent open up the box and figure out how to showcase the lanterns. She spent the remainder of the day creating a fantastical display in the store window by stringing all the lanterns up and interlacing them with pin lights, wind chimes, and paper windmills.

Creating the window display became a welcome distraction, and random thoughts and images came to her as she handled the lanterns. She saw a Tibetan nunnery surrounded by the majestic cloudscape of the Himalayas—and a woman, the lantern maker, who was somewhere in her fifties and dressed in the traditional red robes of a Tibetan nun with a shaved head. The woman's eyes shone with serenity and her hands were gentle as she fashioned the paper lanterns' frames. That peaceful energy had been affecting Melicent all day like a soothing balm.

Now it was almost eight o'clock in the evening and time to close, but at least the display was done. A collection of lanterns hung from the ceiling like its own little galaxy.

Melicent stood on the ladder and stretched to hang the last one as the door jingled.

She turned around at the sound and her smile faltered when Roan West walked in.

Seeing him again literally threw her off balance—she wobbled and slipped.

His hands shot out and grabbed her by the waist to keep her from falling. "Easy there."

She let out a strangled yelp and gripped the top of the ladder with one arm, trying not to crush the lantern.

"Let me," he offered, and took the lantern from her so she could climb down.

A jumble of thoughts hit her at once: he was back, his hands were on her waist—and his eyes were just as mesmeric as she remembered.

"Oh my gosh. I'm so sorry," she stammered. That was twice now that she'd done something clumsy in front of him. She put on her brightest smile, inwardly cringing at how fake it must look. "Welcome back to The Trove!" She sounded like Tish. "How can I help you?" she asked politely, hoping he couldn't tell from her face that she'd been Googling him.

With a faint smile Roan turned to the window display. "These are quite beautiful."

"Thank you. They're from Nepal," she said, and then ran out of words.

Roan pulled off the glove from his right hand, all the while still holding the lantern she'd almost crushed. He placed his hand on the paper and waited.

Melicent stood watching him, unsure of what he was doing. It looked like he was listening to a heartbeat.

Should she say anything? Tell him the price?

His eyes were staring off into the distance with an unfocused look for a full minute.

"Dolma Ling," he finally said.

"What?"

"These weren't made in Nepal. They were made at the Dolma Ling Nunnery and Institute at Dharamsala."

She stared at him blankly.

"In the Kangra Valley in northern India, by a Tibetan nun named Yangchen Metok." He gestured to the wall of lanterns she'd just spent hours hanging.

Melicent gaped at him. *Yes. Yes,* she knew that name. It'd been in her mind all day. But this was crazy. How did he?

Then he stunned her by saying more. "She arrived at Dolma Ling nineteen years ago, after a twenty-eight-day trek over the Himalayas. When she got there, she couldn't read or write. Now she is one of the elders helping the younger women." He sounded so sure of the facts, like a narrator at a museum exhibit. "She makes these lanterns in her spare time, often reciting prayers while she works." His gaze was hypnotic as he held her eyes and challenged her to disagree with him.

All the air had been let out of her lungs. She couldn't catch her breath because she knew everything he'd said was true.

How did he know about the lanterns? Tish didn't even know they were from Dolma Ling, and she was the one who'd bought them.

Dumbfounded, she watched him reach up and hang the last lantern on its hook. He turned to her. His eyes softened at the confusion on her face and he asked, "Can we go sit somewhere and talk? Maybe next door?"

There was a wine bar next door with an open patio. Feeling dazed, her eyes went to the clock. It was after eight—they were now closed. She had a sinking feeling this little stunt he'd pulled with the lanterns was only the beginning. Roan West had plenty more to say.

⸺

They each ordered a Pinot Noir and took their glasses to a table outside. Melicent noticed he had his gloves back on. She had so many questions but didn't know where to start. She couldn't wrap her head around what was happening. Not only had he come back, he shared her ability.

He searched her eyes. "We should probably start by introducing ourselves." Then he said, "Melicent Tilpin."

Her name was the last thing she expected to hear from his mouth. "How do you know my name?"

"From the *Antiques Roadshow* video on YouTube. 'Psychometrist finds million-dollar watch with the power of her hands,'" he recited the caption. "Have you seen it?"

"Yes," she whispered. He had seen the *Antiques Roadshow* video. "When—when did you?"

"Before I came here."

"Came here now or came here the last time?"

"The last time."

"From where?" She crossed her arms. Somehow this had turned into an interrogation.

"New Orleans."

Her face burned. So West, Inc. and RW Antiques in New Orleans were tied to him. He was a collector. She tried to quickly put the pieces together. "Were you trying to get involved with the watch transaction? Be like a middle man or something? Because I already sold it."

Roan shook his head. "No. I wanted to meet you."

"You're saying you came from New Orleans to meet me?"

"Yes."

That simple confession made her heart jump. He came all the way to L.A. to meet her? The warmth in his eyes made her feel like they were suddenly on a date.

She reached for her wine and almost spilled it. Roan's hand snaked out and caught the glass as it wobbled. She gritted her teeth in annoyance. She'd been clumsy all her life, but her penchant for spilling things was rising exponentially around him.

He surprised her by saying, "I bet you were left-handed as a child and your teacher made you switch to your right."

Her eyes widened.

"Am I right?" His eyes searched her face with a faint smile.

Melicent didn't know what to say because the crazy thing was she *had* been left-handed in preschool, and in kindergarten her teacher had coaxed her into changing hands.

But how did Roan West know that?

"Your hands are at war with themselves." Roan swirled his wine while he studied her hands. "Your natural dominant hand is your left, but you were taught not to trust that instinct, so you use your right. It's the same with psychometry. It's best to read an imprint with your nondominant hand, your receptive hand. The problem is you don't know which hand that is anymore. I'm guessing you can't quite control how and when you get an imprint."

"Is that why you wear gloves? You're a psychometrist?" While they'd been sitting there she couldn't stop staring at his hands. "You get information from touching things?"

"So do you." He tipped his glass to her.

She found herself confessing. "Not very well. It's random. Sometimes it's like soft static, sometimes I get clear images and a string of thoughts." Roan West had gotten way more information from those lanterns than she had. It was obvious he was much more trained. The man wore gloves for Christ's sake because he was so good. The whole situation was mind-boggling.

She clarified, "So you saw the YouTube video and came out to meet me. And yet, you didn't say anything about any of this last time?" He hadn't even muttered a hello. He'd only bought all her snow globes.

Suddenly a realization dawned. He had bought her artwork knowing it was hers.

"Did you buy my work to read the impressions like you did with the lanterns?" she asked him, incredulous, already knowing the answer. Now it all made sense, and her anger sparked. "That's what 'psychometrists' do, right? Read objects?"

The look in his eyes became guarded.

She leaned forward. "Did you spy on me?"

"I didn't spy on you. I only read one."

"You read one?" She gaped at him.

"The one I picked up *in front of you* at the store. I haven't touched any of the others—I promise. They're still in the boxes."

"What did you see? In the one you touched?" She held her breath.

"Your mother." Roan's voice softened. "She told you there'd be no more treatments. You moved back home that week, breaking up with your boyfriend to do it. The snow globe was something you worked on late at night."

Melicent's heart grew hollow. He had gotten all of that from touching her work? Tears pooled in her eyes. Never had she felt so infringed on before.

"How dare you," she whispered.

"I'm sorry." He looked like he meant it. "I didn't mean to intrude."

She shook her head, unable to process that he'd seen intimate details of her life. That's what he'd been doing when he'd held the globe in the store and she'd sat there watching him.

She stood up, overcome with emotion.

"Wait." He reached out and grabbed her hand to keep her from leaving. "I know you're upset. I understand and I am sorry. I'm telling you this so you'll believe me. Please, I really do need to talk to you about something important. It's why I flew back."

The feeling of his hand in hers was like a magnetic pull, a not entirely comfortable one. She tugged her hand away and sat back in her chair, crossing her arms and legs defensively. She actually did want to hear whatever he had to say.

"Go on," she dared him. "I'm listening."

12. THE WINEGLASS

ROAN WAS TRYING HARD to do damage control. When he shared that he'd read the imprint in the snow globe, Melicent had transformed into a vengeful sprite straight out of a Tolkien novel, an enraged Lady of the Golden Wood ready to make him pay for his trespass. For a moment she had looked ready to throw her drink in his face.

Her artwork had been *for sale,* he wanted to remind her, and sitting out there in the open for anyone to touch. How could he have known it held such private memories? He hadn't even shared all of the intimate details he'd learned from touching it: When Melicent's mother became ill, Melicent moved out of her apartment in Culver City, at the same time ending the two-year relationship she'd had with her boyfriend, Walt. Roan had learned all he needed to know about her bozo ex. Walt was a pastry chef and the guitarist for an up-and-coming local band, a man-boy, full of energy and drive and wonder, a real Peter Pan. Melicent and Walt never fought, were never annoyed with each other, their lives had blended harmoniously—until her mother got sick. Roan had seen their relationship's demise play out. Walt didn't know how to deal with Melicent's tears or depression, and her life was suddenly "bringing him down." Terminal cancer was a definite downer. He said she had changed.

It was a rude awakening for Melicent to learn how shallow their relationship was. When she was packing to leave, Walt made her reopen all the boxes to make sure she wasn't sneaking off with one of his prized books or overpriced kitchen appliances. His pettiness and insecurities were embedded within his things, and she assured him she didn't want anything of his. In her heart she didn't want him. All she wanted was for her mother to get well.

Melicent's mother put on a brave face as she underwent a valiant battle against the cancer, but in the end it was a battle she lost. Melicent finished the globe Roan had held during the most difficult moments of her mother's passing, in the pockets of time between the tears.

It'd been wrong for him to touch it, but he hadn't known when he'd picked it up how personal the memories would be. He understood why she wanted to sell it, because somewhere in the recesses of her subconscious she wanted to let the pain go. Memories lived in possessions, but most people didn't realize just how much. Melicent never expected anyone to recognize the pain within her work. How could she, when she didn't herself? Roan had not only exposed her wounds, he had exposed her, holding up a mirror with his words.

Things were getting off to a bad start.

He tried to explain. "I didn't mean to infringe, I promise. I came here to tell you there's a group of psychometrists who share the same abilities."

"You're kidding." Her brow furrowed. "People like us?"

The *us* made him pause. He studied her face, wishing he didn't find her so compelling. His fascination with her was complicating matters.

He shook his head. "A group of archaeologists and an historian." *A dead historian,* he could have said, but refrained. "I'm not a part of their group, but my friend is, and he's missing." He watched her eyes widen in shock as he tried to explain. "They've been researching rare artifacts only psychometrists can identify, and someone might be trying to interfere with their work. I came here to tell you that anyone labeled as a psychometrist could be at risk. If I've seen that YouTube video of you, then they could have too. I wanted to warn you."

Melicent didn't say anything for a long moment. She looked terrified. He regretted having to alarm her like this, but she needed to be aware of what was happening.

When she spoke he could detect the shakiness in her voice. "You flew all the way from New Orleans to warn me about what's been happening to this group of psychometrists?"

"If these people who are going after my friend's group think you're a psychometrist, they may come after you, too. I can't have that on my conscience." He waited for her to ask him something else, anything. Instead she sipped her wine, lost in thought. It made him question her, "Has anything out of the ordinary happened since the video came out?"

"You mean besides selling a watch for almost two million dollars and ending up in the *L.A. Times*?" She finished her wine, looking anxious to leave. "Thank you for letting me know. Really. I'm sure everything will be fine." She licked her lips, nervous, and gathered her things. "Sorry, but I have to dash."

What he'd said had struck a chord. He could tell. She was already afraid.

"Listen." He leaned forward and lowered his voice. "I know you don't know me, and I know this all sounds crazy, but that pocket watch got you on YouTube. You don't know who could've seen it."

"You did." She tried to joke but failed. They stared at each other for a suspended moment.

"Take my card." He held it out. "If anything happens, please call me, day or night. I'm going to be in town a few more days. I'd like to talk again before I leave."

She took it, trying to downplay his warning. "And do you

plan to read the rest of my artwork and let me know what other private moments you can see?" Her eyes flashed with anger again. He still wasn't forgiven for reading the imprints. "Or maybe there's something else you'd like to buy? Like three dozen lanterns from Dolma Ling?" She tossed her hair back with a defiant flick.

Roan let out a surprised laugh. "I won't read the others." He met her eyes. "And I'll think about the lanterns."

"Goodbye, Roan West." She said his name pointedly even though he'd never said it. She must have remembered it from the store. Her eyes trailed over his face, his gloved hands, and then landed on the wineglasses. She raised her gaze back to him. "Thanks for the wine. Don't touch my glass when I'm gone." She gave him a sharp look and walked away.

Roan laughed to himself, feeling firmly put in his place. "I won't!" he called out, watching her leave.

Maybe he *would* go buy all thirty-six Dolma Ling lanterns. The look on Melicent's face would be worth it.

He stared at her wineglass across the table—and dammit if she hadn't known how tempted he was to take off his glove and touch the stem to see what she'd been thinking. He hadn't touched a woman's wineglass in years, and although the temptation was strong, he would never go back on a self-made promise.

When Roan had first started seriously dating in his early twenties, he used to reach over and touch his date's wineglass all the time to read her mood and gather what information he could to improve his chances of having a good evening. But his wineglass reconnaissance always backfired on him, because most of the time the imprints he picked up from the glass had nothing to do with him or what he and his date were talking about. . . . The woman had broken up with her boyfriend and was looking for an escape, another was obsessing about how many calories were in her Merlot, another kept wondering what Roan and her future children would look like, another was in a deep depression, hated her life, and thought Roan was boring as hell.

Roan had run the gamut of emotions and judgments to the point that he debated whether he should stop dating altogether. He'd complained to Holly about the wineglass imprint fiascos, and she'd chastised him for spying on "those poor unsuspecting women." She said it served him right. He would never find anyone by using his gift in such a devious manner. Her reprimand stung, but she was right, and Roan never touched a woman's wineglass again.

The women he'd dated never knew about his ability, and he preferred to keep it that way. It was usually easier if he took off his gloves when he was with them and tried to tune out the sea of imprints surrounding him. The problems always arose when he'd have to touch something of hers and then he'd get caught with a thought or a feeling he'd rather not know—and God forbid if he held her hand. A hand-to-hand connection with a person always gave him the most powerful read of someone's thoughts and feelings.

The one time he'd wanted to reveal his ability had been a disaster. He thought Gianna might have been the one to start a lasting relationship with; at least he'd been ready to try. She'd even moved into his place, slowly at first—a toothbrush, a change of clothes, then a drawer full of clothes, then half of the closet was hers—until all of her things had migrated and they were talking about whether it would make sense for her to sublet her apartment.

When Roan finally told her that he was a psychometrist, he'd made the mistake of holding her hand when he did, feeling all of her confusion, judgment, and distrust—and then deceit when she tried not to let those feelings show on her face. The hurt hit him harder than he expected, and he ended the relationship.

The breakup hadn't been pretty. He let Gianna take all of the furniture when she moved out, even though most of it was his. He didn't want to revisit any of the memories embedded there.

He bought all new furniture and over time emotionally recovered. That'd been almost two years ago. Gianna was the last woman he'd taken his gloves off for, and he'd never allowed anyone to get close since.

He couldn't imagine attempting a relationship with another psychometrist. Not only would he have to worry about holding her hand, he'd have to worry about her holding his.

The problem was that was exactly what he wanted to do with Melicent.

With a frustrated swipe at his glass he finished his wine and left. If Melicent didn't call the day after tomorrow, he would visit the shop one more time—to say what, he wasn't sure. He couldn't leave L.A. without her believing she was a potential target. He'd stay here two days, and then he had to go on to London.

⌣

The boutique hotel Roan checked into nearby in Venice Beach had funky graffiti art on the walls outside and surfboards mounted above the sofas in the lobby. The hotel clerk at the check-in counter glanced twice at Roan's gloved hands while he filled out the registration form.

"You from up north?" the girl asked, popping an enormous gum bubble.

"Something like that." Roan was used to the question and had stopped caring years ago. His gloves were like oxygen and he couldn't go without them—especially in hotels, the Grand Central Station of imprints.

When Roan got to his room, he opened his bag and took out the box Sun had given him. He finally had a block of time to analyze the gift. He only hoped it wasn't another oopart.

He sat down at the small desk and placed the box on the table. He took off his gloves and laid them aside. His hands joined together in an intricate Manipura mudra, a fire mudra, performed to increase courage and mental will. Before taking any kind of known risk, Roan always performed this mudra—and touching Sun's present was a definite risk. He had no idea what memories lay in store or why she had given it to him.

When he lifted the lid, he found a fan made of carved lacquered bamboo.

With the care of a surgeon he opened it up to reveal an exquisite painting of a sapphire dragon, a white tiger, a red phoenix, and a black turtle circling a yin-and-yang symbol.

He rested the fan in his hands and closed his eyes, feeling his mind begin to slip between the folds. He was about to meet the maker of this masterpiece.

WONJU, KOREA

1949

"WHY IS THE DRAGON BLUE?" Sun watched her grandmother finish painting the dragon's scales. The meticulous brushwork had taken her all morning. Sun had sat and watched every delicate dab and stroke.

"This is the Blue Dragon of the East, the noblest of animals. It brings good fortune on its wings and is the head of the four symbols."

The fact that her grandmother answered meant it was all right to speak while she worked. "And the others?" Sun asked.

A turtle, a phoenix, and a tiger, along with the dragon, circled a vibrant swirling yin-yang emblem in the center of the fan. Sun knew the circle represented balance, day and night, male and female.

"They are the four guardians of the world," her grandmother explained, "standing at the four directions, protecting the fifth, the center. The most powerful point in nature is always the center."

Sun nodded. Her grandmother had used the five cardinal colors—blue, white, red, black, and yellow—to represent not only the five directions but the five elements of wood, metal, fire, water, and earth. Even Sun, at the age of eight, could see that this fan was perfectly balanced.

Her grandmother went back to finishing the painting. Sun could tell from her faraway look not to ask another question.

Sun's grandmother had been born into a family of *seon jajang,* master fan makers. The trade had been in her family for more than six generations, dating back to the late Joseon kingdom. She'd grown up in Jeonju, the seat of fan making in Korea. Her childhood home, an original Joseon *hanok* wooden house with an elegant, sloping slate-tile rooftop, was as old as their trade and was tucked away off a cobblestone lane in the center of Jeonju.

From an early age her grandmother had been taught to make both styles of fan, the round open-faced fan, the *dandeon,* traditionally meant for women, and the folding hand fan, the *hapjukseon.* Sun knew making each fan required a hundred and fifty steps, and that a paper fan made of *hanji,* from Korea's sturdy mulberry tree, could last more than a thousand years.

The fans of her grandmother's family had been held in graceful hands at ancient court and had weathered the years—even the thirty-five years of Japanese occupation that ended with the close of World War II. Over time Jeonju had become a melting pot, with more people arriving every year as the county kept expanding. The bustle of increased trade made Korean fans prized by foreigners abroad as well.

Sun knew all this not because her grandmother had told her, but because Sun loved to touch her grandmother's fan-making tools, the hammers, stones, and knives her grandmother had brought with her from Jeonju. Sun's grandmother had married into a family who imported and exported goods from the industrial town of Wonju. And as Korean custom dictated, the daughter left her family to join the husband's.

Sun's grandmother gave away the fans she made once a year for Dano Festival, the fifth day of the fifth lunar month, when everyone across the country gifted fans to their loved ones, particularly to the elderly and the children, to prepare for the coming hot summer months. This fan had taken her grand-mother many months to create.

Sun watched her grandmother paint the last brushstroke and place the fan on the shelf to dry. Now that her grandmother had finished the final image, the Blue Dragon, Sun slid open the lattice screen door and slipped outside to play.

The family lived on the outskirts of Wonju near Chiaksan Mountain in a large country house that had an apricot tree, a cherry tree, a vegetable garden, two pigs, and a chicken. The forest started at the edge of the garden and led up the mountain like a blanket of green, where ancestral tombs dotted the hillsides and an ancient Buddhist temple, Guryongsa Temple, sat in the center.

Sun loved to wander through the fields, touching the dome-shaped relics and laying her hands on the stones. When she did, she could often hear the voices of the past and sometimes see them like ghosts performing shadow puppet plays.

One day when she came home from her adventures, her grandmother gave her a stern look. "Who goes knocking on the door of the deep, deep mountain?" she asked, reciting the line from an ancient song.

Sun glanced down at the floor, afraid her grandmother would be angry. "I was only touching the stones. They tell me stories if I listen long enough." Sun balled her hands up into fists, worried she'd said too much.

Her grandmother beckoned to her. When Sun sat beside her, she said with a grave tone, "Perhaps you've been gifted with the sight."

Sun shook her head, adamant. She knew all about the *mansin,* the shamans, powerful women who could talk to spirits and call the dead down from the heavens to communicate with the living. Her grandmother and mother sometimes visited the village *mansin* to receive divinations or make offerings to the ancestral gods. And once when her grandfather was ill, her entire family held a *kut* where their *mansin* came to the house with several other assistant *mansin* to perform a ceremony to draw the illness out. The event had scared Sun to death, with the women clanging cymbals and beating drums as they called on the spirits. Sun shook her head in refusal at the thought she might be one of them. To be a shaman was a hard road and meant living on society's edge. "I only see old things. That happened before."

Her grandmother took her hand and squeezed it in understanding. "Good" was all she said, and they didn't speak of it again.

In the spring, for Dano Festival, Sun's grandmother surprised her by giving her the dragon fan as a gift. Later that day, her grandmother and mother went to visit their *mansin* to give offerings to the ancestors. When they returned, Sun could see her grandmother was distraught.

From that day forward her grandmother stopped making fans and working in the garden. Instead she took to her bed. No one would tell Sun why.

Sun made an effort to be the one to bring her grandmother tea and then take away the cup when she was finished, for the sole reason to hold the cup and try to understand what had happened.

One day she sensed more than saw it. The *mansin* had given her grandmother a divination of the darkness that was to come.

Sun dropped the teacup with a gasp and heard her mother call out a strict reprimand from the kitchen at the sound of broken porcelain on the floor. But when Sun met her grandmother's dull, defeated eyes she understood.

A war was coming.

Sun's grandfather always said that after World War II ended, Korea was a person broken at the waist. Split at the 38th parallel with a communist north and democratic south, the capital cities of Pyongyang and Seoul became bitter brothers. That break between the two sides had been festering for five years. In Russia, Stalin refused the UN's attempt to reunify the country. He wanted a communist foothold in Korea, just as the Americans wanted a capitalist one. The impasse mounted until finally the wound was rupturing.

Within days North Korea advanced south to reunite the country, but it quickly became a massacre. They gathered up anyone they believed to be fighting for the West.

Sun's family didn't know what to do—leave their home and make their way south toward Pusan with the river of refugees or wait in Wonju and see what would happen. Soon Seoul fell and the North Korean army was taking over the whole country. Wonju was at a major crossroads, and there was no way the city would be spared.

The South's Republic of Korea regiments were rounding up everyone in Wonju they thought might be aiding the North. Sun's father traded with China, which was North Korea's supporter, along with Russia. Sun's father also traded with other countries, but that didn't matter. To the South Republic's eyes, he was a communist sympathizer.

Officers came and took him away one night for interrogation. Sun watched her mother scream and plead, her knees on the floor, begging them to have mercy and change their minds, but they wouldn't. They demanded that Sun's brother, Jin, her only sibling, come join the southern regiments to prove the family's loyalty, and they took him with them. He was only thirteen.

Sun's grandfather died in his sleep the same week, unable to recover from the shock of losing his son and grandson in one night.

Days later the North Korean army swept through Wonju, occupying the town as well as every village, all the way south toward Pusan. The North wanted to punish its southern brothers and they were brutal in their occupation. It wasn't until the UN and American forces arrived in full force that the invaders were driven back.

The tall big-nosed warriors from America struck hard and pushed back the North toward the Chinese border. When Western forces crossed the 38th parallel, it enraged China and woke their dragon.

In October the Chinese entered into Korea like an ocean, with wave upon wave of men. They moved in the night, in total stealth, coming in like a shadow tide, and attacked.

With this new turn of events, Sun and her mother and grandmother waited for months in fear, unsure what to do. Now that Sun's grandfather, father, and brother were gone, the house was a skeleton whose brittle bones were about to break. The women began to make plans to leave Wonju and head south as soon as the harsh winter lifted. Until then, they kept hope that either Sun's father or Jin would return. Because if and when the women did leave, the family would no longer know how to find each other.

Soon the decision was taken out of their hands when a Chinese group settled three miles north of Wonju and began attacking down the riverbed. The thunderous barrages of artillery never ceased as more military arrived every day. The women packed what they could carry on their backs and stole away in the middle of the night.

Sun tucked her dragon fan into the folds of her blanket, and she crossed the threshold of her home for the last time. She turned back and looked at all their belongings.

In the silence she could hear the house saying goodbye.

Sun wanted to believe she would see these walls again, and she prayed one day that she and her family could return to their lives before the war. But instead that night they walked right into a skirmish on the hills where the Chinese had the high ground.

"Sun!" Her mother put her arms around her as they ran to the bushes for cover.

It was a moment Sun would remember forever—right before the bullet hit.

Her mother's body jerked, exhaling from the shock, then she was no longer holding her. She'd fallen back from the force of the bullet.

Sun dropped to the ground, clutching her mother's body. Her grandmother knelt beside her, grabbing them both. Their cries were masked by the relentless barrage of gunfire all around them. For hours they stayed huddled together, holding Sun's mother in their arms until the battle moved over the ridge to the west.

Sun was unable to speak. Shock had robbed her of the ability. They would have to leave her mother's body to find shelter, to hide, but they had no means to bury her, so Sun covered her with her blanket.

Only her grandmother was alive. The old woman was barely holding on, her head bowed in defeat. Her spirit had been wounded beyond repair. Her family was gone. All but one.

The old woman's frail hand held on to Sun's as Sun led her deep into the forest and up the mountain where the caves might offer protection. Sun found a hidden alcove between the rocks and she laid down their pallets. They had no water, no food, but for the moment they were safe.

She helped her grandmother to lie down and then she nestled beside her.

Her grandmother's hand reached out and clasped hers, giving her the faintest squeeze, just as she always did when Sun did something right.

"Do you remember the story of Princess Bari?" her grandmother asked, her voice weak.

Sun nodded. Her mother had told her the story many times at night before going to sleep. Bari was an ancient princess who lived long ago in the time of the three kingdoms, born the seventh daughter of a king who wanted sons.

Her grandmother mustered up the last of her strength in order to continue. "When she came into this world her parents did not recognize how special she was, and she was banished." Her quiet words filled the cave. The walls were listening. "Years later when they were dying she came back to help heal them. She traveled to the sacred realms beyond this world to find magical water to restore their life. In return she was granted exalted status, but Princess Bari chose to remain in the otherworld to help guide the dying to the next life."

The tears that slipped from Sun's eyes were silent. With each word she could feel her grandmother's life ebbing from her.

"You're my Bari," her grandmother whispered, her voice growing fainter. "You could lead me there . . . to your mother and grandfather. I could forgive myself for leaving you if you took me there." She kissed Sun's hand. "Please take me there. Then go back to Wonju."

Those were her last words. Sun could feel her grandmother's spirit being pulled away like a kite caught on the wind. Sun held on tightly to her grandmother's hand, determined to go with her.

Her grandmother was wrong—she wasn't Bari, a courageous princess able to lead her to the netherworld, she was a scared girl, unwilling to be left behind in such a desolate place.

As her grandmother's spirit departed, Sun gripped her hand harder and closed her eyes. A force pulled her up and out of her body until she was floating, looking down on the mountain like a bird in flight.

Sure she was dying too, Sun told her life goodbye as she ascended beyond the web of fear and hate the war had created— She was free.

A brilliant light approached, growing bigger and brighter like a newborn star. As the light drew near, a feeling of incredible joy bloomed in Sun's heart.

She looked to her grandmother, who now stood radiant beside her.

Sun's mother came forward, surrounded by a shimmering light. Sun had never seen anyone so beautiful. Her mother embraced her and placed Sun's hand on her heart.

You must go back.

Sun protested. She couldn't imagine returning, not now. But her mother persisted, guiding her away from the star's light.

You still have much work to do. We will be waiting.

Her mother led her away and let go of her hand. Like a curtain falling, Sun floated back to earth, feeling as if she were a stone sinking to the bottom of the ocean.

The coldness woke her up. Sun didn't need to reach out to touch her grandmother's body lying beside her. Her grandmother's spirit was gone, leaving behind an empty husk. The vivid memories of Sun's journey to the other side still circled around her. The feeling of immense love had not faded. Sun yearned to go back, but she didn't know how and knew she couldn't.

Gunfire and explosions sounded in the distance. Only now Sun didn't feel afraid like she had before. Her mother had sent her back.

Sun covered her grandmother's lifeless body with her blanket. The cave would be her burial place. She climbed outside and moved as many rocks as she could to seal the opening so her grandmother's remains wouldn't be disturbed. Then Sun made her way back to Wonju because her grandmother had told her to return home.

Halfway to town, Sun sat down on the side of the road, too tired to walk any more. She took her grandmother's fan from her pocket, her one possession left in the world.

The paint dazzled in the sun, making the dragon's scales seem alive.

Sun closed her eyes and fluttered the fan as the tears made a trail on her cheeks.

A car was heading down the road. The driver slowed and came to a stop. A foreign soldier got out, his eyes filled with concern as he squatted to ask her questions with words Sun didn't understand. She knew she looked pitiful, covered in dirt and blood, her thin frame emaciated.

The man went to the truck and returned with a canteen of water and a bar of some kind of food wrapped in paper. Sun tried to stand up to take it but was too weak to rise.

The man put his arm around her and helped her. From his touch, fleeting images and thoughts passed through Sun's mind . . . his grandmother mailed him care packages from a place called Virginia . . . he wanted to go home . . . his job was to pick up children on the side of the road and take them to the shelters in Wonju for the hundreds of war orphans found sleeping among the rubble. Now she was one of them.

Sun closed her grandmother's fan and tucked it inside her shirt, letting it rest against her heart.

13. THE TALISMAN

ROAN SET THE FAN BACK on the desk and folded his hands into a compassionate heart mudra, the Hridaya.

Sun had given him her touchstone, the object that carried her most important memories. The fact she had entrusted him with the fan was so humbling, so astounding, Roan didn't know what to think.

A well of emotion rose within him. He could still smell the war, the dead burning, the smell of napalm and its ammonia-like aftereffects. The acrid odor filled his nostrils and lingered in the hotel room even though he knew the scent only existed in his mind.

He had touched many relics from the past whose imprints of war had taken him to battlefields, but Sun had experienced those atrocities firsthand. She had lived through war's worst circles of hell and witnessed its annihilating force, witnessed it destroy the love that bound families together and send children to walk through the world alone.

Sun had been such a child.

An orphan of the Forgotten War, she'd heeded her family's words and strived to live, forging her path through sheer, unstoppable will.

Sun Kim had lived a monumental life. Where Roan made

sense of his gift by looking to the past and returning lost heirlooms to their descendants, Sun had looked to the future, saving children. Roan had seen through the imprints in the fan how, when she became older, she left the orphanage in Wonju and used her gift to raise money to build a network of orphanages. Her company, BariHome, saved children orphaned by war, not only in Korea but around the globe. Sun had estimated that more than two hundred million orphans were lost in the world—an unfathomable number—with every day seeing six to ten thousand more children without homes. Sun was one of the global warriors leading the fight.

The knowledge of her life and the last seventy years had been encoded into the fan, because Sun always kept it tucked in her breast pocket. The fan was her talisman.

Talismans were powerful objects, embedded with the owner's essence, their thoughts and emotions. The longer a talisman was worn, the stronger the imprint.

This fan wasn't a gift: it was a book of her life she had loaned him, and she expected it back, that much was certain.

Roan possessed such a talisman too, his lucky coin, which he'd kept in his pocket for almost twenty years. The coin technically wasn't even a coin—it couldn't buy anything—and it wasn't made out of gold or silver but hardened plaster that had been enameled. He couldn't imagine giving it to a stranger.

His coin was the original model Augustus Saint-Gaudens had made for the gold Liberty coin. Minted in 1907, the twenty-dollar gold Saint-Gaudens Liberty coin was revered as the most beautiful coin ever made in the United States.

Roan knew the history by heart. Saint-Gaudens had been a prolific sculptor and was personal friends with President Roosevelt. Roosevelt believed only Saint-Gaudens could make a truly remarkable coin, something that would rival the coins of Europe and ancient Greece. The president, without obtaining congressional approval, hired the artist outside the Mint. There was much resistance, particularly from Saint-Gaudens's archrival, Mint artist Charles Barber.

The plaster model in Roan's possession was the coin's original three-dimensional model in high relief, the finished masterpiece Saint-Gaudens envisioned. Lady Liberty stood poised in flight in front of the Capitol, holding a torch and an olive branch to symbolize peace and enlightenment, the rays of the sun blazing behind her.

Saint-Gaudens gave this plaster coin to President Roosevelt for his approval, and the president bellowed in triumph when he saw it, "This is the one!"

Roan didn't need one of the gold coins this model had made. This piece of plaster was far more valuable. His model coin held all of the stories. It held Saint-Gaudens's passion, his drive, and the joy from his studio sessions as he sculpted Lady Liberty, working with Hettie Anderson, who he proclaimed was a goddess and the most beautiful model he had ever seen. Hettie was a rarity, an African American model, who could pose for hours with perfect concentration, and she'd held Roan's lucky coin in her hand as well.

When Roan found it at a swap meet in Virginia at the age of ten, he'd been fascinated by the drama. The challenges the most beautiful coin in America faced in order to meet the world had been substantial. The image on the coin needed to be obtained at press with one strike, but Saint-Gaudens's coin required nine. Roan could hear Roosevelt's fist pounding on the desk of the Oval Office as he shouted, "I want this coin! Even if it takes you all day to strike only one!"

Saint-Gaudens's coin went into production, but Saint-Gaudens died of cancer in 1907, the year the coin was released. Saint-Gaudens never saw the final result. In order to mass-produce it, the Mint had to use a model set in lower relief—but even slightly altered, it was still lauded as the most beautiful coin the Mint ever made.

The gold coins from Saint-Gaudens's original model were now worth millions, and Roan's was perhaps worth even more. He always kept the coin tucked away in his pocket as a reminder that the real worth of an object could never be measured by money.

He fingered the coin in his pocket now, reassured to feel it there, and guilt consumed him for judging Sun so harshly at both of their meetings—first in France years ago and then in New York. He'd taken the look in her eyes for arrogance when really it was strength.

He hadn't known her at all.

Roan returned to the Hridaya mudra, and he could feel his thoughts centering as the enormity of what Sun had done hit him. She'd opened the window to her life and invited him in to see all her years tucked within the fan. She needed his trust, so she had sacrificed her most treasured possession to gain it.

Anyone who possessed their ability had been marked as a target. Sun had given him her fan to help Roan understand that he was entrenched with her in this fight. She had given up her secrets because she desperately needed his help. She needed an ally and had chosen him.

14. THE TREE

THE FIRST THING MELICENT did when she got home from the wine bar was put her hands on the house's front and back door to try and sense if the man had returned.

She stood with her eyes closed, waiting for a new sensation—anything. She could still feel the man's hold on the knob, his intention to harm them, to harm the house. She let go, more unnerved than ever, and hurried inside and locked the door. The alarm technician was scheduled to come tomorrow, but now tomorrow seemed too long to wait. She tried to assure herself they'd be fine for one more night.

She could hear Parker upstairs in his room, and she called up, "I'm home!"

He didn't answer. In the kitchen a pile of his dirty dishes sat in the sink. Melicent was too keyed up to nag him to come down and wash them. Her mind kept returning to Roan's warning. After the initial shock, the reality was beginning to sink in that he'd really flown from New Orleans to tell her she was in danger.

She checked again to make sure all the doors and windows were locked. Then she went over to her desk and turned on the computer. Logging into her email, she found the YouTube link Parker had sent her. When she clicked on it, the views had climbed to twenty-five thousand. *What the hell?*

"Parker!"

He didn't answer. Then she yelled his name so loud he had to acknowledge it. His door opened and he came to the top of the stairs. "What?"

"Come downstairs. We need to have a serious discussion."

His whole body radiated defiance as he stomped downstairs and plopped on the couch. "What did I do now?"

"Nothing. It's me," she said, rubbing her forehead. "I haven't been honest with you about something." Parker perked up now that this wasn't going to be another lecture about school. She pointed to the YouTube video on the screen. "I really did find those antiques with my hands by sensing the past. I am a psychometrist."

There, she said it.

Her brother gave her a nonplussed look. "I know. You got like two million dollars for it and you're still not getting me a car."

"Oh my God, you're impossible. Can you forget about the car for one minute?" She wanted to scream but tried to stay calm. "Some guy came to see me today to warn me that I might be in danger because I am being publicly labeled a psychometrist."

"What are you talking about?"

"Because of this stupid video." She pointed to the computer. "People are looking for people who have my ability."

"Your *ability*? What are you, Wonder Woman now?"

"No, I'm not Wonder Woman." She sighed. This wasn't going well. "But I did sense the history of those things. How do you think I found the watch?"

He mimicked her—"You sensed it"—and he air-quoted her to boot.

"Okay. The point is he came to warn me about it."

"Because he's a psycho who saw the video."

"He's not a psycho," she snapped, exasperated. Yes, Roan West was a complete stranger. But something about him made her want to trust him. They had shared the lantern memory. She hadn't imagined that. "What I'm trying to say is, we both need to be on guard for anything that seems odd or suspicious." She debated telling him about the garage doorknob.

"So how long have you been like this?" he asked her. "Able to sense shit with your hands."

"Watch your language." She pointed her finger at him.

He rolled his eyes. "How long?"

"I don't know. A while," she said, unable to be more specific. Technically it had been her whole life, though the instances had come in spurts. "When Mom got sick it got stronger and . . . after she passed away I couldn't stop . . ." She didn't finish explaining but jumped ahead. "And now I'm on YouTube." She made a gesture to the computer. "So we need to be alert."

"Alert." Parker air-quoted her again.

"Yes. Alert," she said shortly. "Can you please do that for me?"

He gave her a sullen look. "And the car?"

"Enough about the car!"

"You're the one who just got two million dollars, and I'm riding the bus. What the hell, Mel?"

"Show me you're back at school and get your grades out of the toilet and then we'll talk."

Parker glared at her like what she was proposing was unreasonable. He stormed back up the stairs and slammed his door.

That hadn't been productive.

Melicent swiveled in her chair to look at the computer screen. Just seeing the YouTube video on some psychic investigator's channel gave her chills. There had to be a way to take the thing down. It wasn't from *Antiques Roadshow* or connected to their show whatsoever. Someone with the camera crew or a person nearby in line must have recorded it and shared it.

She fired off an email to the address listed for the channel. If they didn't take it down, should she hire a lawyer? She couldn't have this *National Enquirer*–esque video of her and "the power of her hands" on the internet forever. Why had she even said it in the first place, on camera? What had she been thinking?

She spent an hour online researching what to do when someone posted a video of someone without permission—because she definitely hadn't signed a waiver for this. She clicked on various articles and read about public versus private places, "reasonable expectations of privacy," commercial usage, and infringement. It all sounded murky and in the end didn't give her a clear-cut answer. With a sigh she gave up for the evening and shut off the computer.

She grabbed her purse and the accordion folder where she kept all their important paperwork and headed upstairs. She needed to fill out the life insurance application and double-check their passports. More than ever she felt the urge to get out of L.A. Tonight she'd start planning the details, maybe book the tickets.

Finding the watch was beginning to feel like a burden, not a gift. Now they might not be safe.

When she passed by Parker's door she almost knocked and went in so they could talk some more. She raised her hand but then dropped it. Parker didn't understand. And if she tried to get into it more, he'd start to think she was crazy. There was only one person who grasped what she was going through—and she couldn't stop thinking about him either.

Tomorrow she'd call Roan and ask to see him again and share her concern about the intruder. Tonight she'd been too off balance about the snow globe to open up. But tomorrow she would invite him over so he could touch the doorknob too. He seemed to be so much better than her at reading objects.

Hadn't he proved that with the snow globe?

Talk about skipping over small talk and the get-to-know-you stage. She'd been so livid with him, but looking back, she also knew her anger wasn't fair. Her work had been for sale, out in the open for him to handle. And he promised he'd only touched one when he realized the private memories tucked within it.

Maybe she would ask if she could refund him for all the globes and get them back? Though at the moment Roan reading imprints off her artwork was the least of her problems.

She needed his take on the doorknob because the more she placed her hand on the knob and tried to reread the imprint, the more she couldn't let go of the feeling that man had specifically come to her house because of her ability. He had tracked her down after seeing her on the internet—just like Roan West.

When Melicent went to sleep that night, she dreamed of the lantern maker. She could hear the woman reciting a Buddhist prayer, and images of the lantern maker's life accompanied the words. Memories flickered through the dream like a pictograph whizzing by too fast. The woman's voice grew louder, expanding with a powerful resonance, and an explosion of sound—like a glass window breaking—woke her up.

Melicent opened her eyes to find thick smoke in the room, surrounding her in a fog. The acrid smell burned her nostrils and she gagged for air.

Frantic, she made her way to the door and grabbed her purse and the file folder sitting on her desk, instinctively knowing she might never be coming back.

She ran to Parker's room through the smoke-filled hallway and saw flames licking up the staircase.

"Parker!" She ran to the bed and shook him, but he was listless. "Parker!" She rocked him hard. "Get up!" She wrapped her arms around him and tried to sit him up.

"What are you doing?" he mumbled in a groggy voice, his eyes half-closed.

"There's a fire! You have to wake up!"

She opened the bedroom window and threw her things down into the front yard. She rushed back and put her arms around Parker's middle to pull him to his feet.

They made it to the window, where she forced his head outside to get air. The fire was crawling down the hallway. Soon it'd be in the room.

The tree by Parker's window, an enormous old camphor with thick knotted branches, was their only chance. Sadie had been wanting to trim all the trees in the yard for years, afraid that several might damage the house, but she couldn't afford the expense. Now Melicent was thankful her mother never did.

Parker was becoming alert as the brisk December ocean air hit him from outside and he began to cough, clearing his lungs.

"Reach for that branch, Park. Hurry!" Melicent leaned him forward so he could grab on to it.

Parker resisted, coming to his senses. He looked down at the thirty-foot drop to the ground and froze in terror. "No, you go first."

"No. Go. Now!" Her voice brooked no argument. They had seconds, and she wasn't going first.

His body shaking, Parker reached out for the branch while she held him steady. "I can't. I can't . . ." He quivered, his fear of heights paralyzing him.

"You can do it, Park! I got you." Melicent tried to support him with all her strength and forced him out of the window.

He clutched the branch, like a cat afraid to move.

"Crawl! Crawl to the trunk."

The fire entered the room. Parker glanced back, petrified when he saw the flames.

Melicent yelled at him. "Parker! Listen to me. You have to get to the ground! It won't hold us both!"

But he reached for her instead. "Meli! Meli!"

"Parker, climb. I need to you to keep going." She could feel the heat burning her back.

Parker looked around, hysterical, and slid backward toward the trunk. His room was now a gulf of flames that was almost at Melicent's feet.

The bed caught fire. Melicent had to jump out of the window before Parker could reach the trunk. The branch bent downward, threatening to snap.

Parker cried out as the branch bowed. Melicent hugged the tree in a moment of panic, but then she felt the strength within the wood beneath her fingers, and the sting of the bark was a relief on her skin. This weathered tree had stood beside their home like a guardian her entire life. She had climbed the branches almost every day of her childhood. It would not break on her.

Melicent closed her eyes and clung to it. "Park, keep going," she said, breathing out. "We're going to be fine." For the first time she believed it.

Parker scrambled to get off the branch. When his weight transferred to the trunk the branch swung back up.

The sound of sirens came from a distance, but the whole house was already engulfed in flames. The firefighters would have nothing to save. If Melicent's dream hadn't woken her up, they wouldn't have survived either.

When she reached the ground she hugged her brother to her. They clung to each other, watching the house burn. A sense of certainty filled her that she would never be able to explain: those paper lanterns she'd spent all day hanging and then dreamed about had somehow saved her life.

15. THE HOUSE

MELICENT AND PARKER SAT TOGETHER in the back of the fire department ambulance, blankets draped around them, taking oxygen. The police had arrived too. Melicent stared at the ruins from the fire and listened to the investigator explain how the fire burned the longest and reached the highest heat at the point of origin. She closed her eyes, unable to listen to the man go on about V-patterns, electrical systems, and gas pipes. They had brought in their arson dog and found the point of origin in the garage by the water heater right near the door.

Her eyes began to water. *The garage. Arson.*

But then she'd already known. After putting her hand on that doorknob she had sensed how malicious the man's intent had been, and now this stranger had made her home a crime scene.

He had burned down her house with her in it.

The investigator explained there would be forensic testing, insurance inquiries, and legal considerations. For the house, there were structural and safety issues as well. They had a whole team collecting evidence and taking photographs and video.

Melicent was calm as she listened, or maybe it was shock. She could feel Parker trembling and put her arm around him and squeezed him tight.

"Do you have any idea who would want to do this?" the

investigator asked. "Have you noticed anything strange the past couple of days? Any signs of forced entry?"

Parker looked at her. The conversation they'd had earlier tonight was in his eyes. He had scoffed at her then, not knowing she'd been trying to warn him—just as Roan had tried to warn her.

"Yes," she admitted, her voice a whisper. She felt Parker stiffen beside her. "I came home the other day and something seemed strange in the garage. When I touched the doorknob . . ." She trailed off, unsure how she could explain it.

"When you touched the doorknob?" the man prompted, busy taking notes.

"I could tell someone had recently been there."

"Because it was unlocked? Or the lock was broken?" he asked, to clarify.

"No—I—something felt wrong. Like a strong hunch. Like something was out of place."

The investigator nodded. He understood hunches all too well in his line of work. "We found accelerant in the garage hidden under the water heater near the door," he said, "and faint trails of gunpowder spread throughout the ground floor inside the house."

"Gunpowder?" Parker spoke up.

He nodded. "There were trails along the floor paneling to spread the flames."

Melicent covered her mouth, her whole body shaking. That man had gone inside her home and laid down gunpowder?

"Ma'am, can you think of anyone who would want to do this?"

She shook her head, a sense of numbness setting in. She didn't know the intruder, didn't recognize him, but she'd sensed the impressions he had left. Her whole body began to shiver.

Parker was the one who spoke up. "My sister recently sold an antique pocket watch for a lot of money. It made the papers and got on YouTube. Maybe some crazy person saw it?"

The man nodded. "Might be a motive." He wrote that down too. "Do you two have a place to stay tonight?"

Parker nodded. "Yes, sir."

All their neighbors had descended on them like a little army. They were huddled together in their robes on the front lawn, there to help in any way they could. Jim and Ruth Mercer lived right across the street and had already insisted that Melicent and Parker spend the night. The couple had offered them the guest room for as long as they needed it.

The investigator gave Melicent his card and got her cell phone number. He would let her know when the house was released and keep her apprised of the investigation. He said to call him if she could think of anything that might help their efforts.

Melicent stared at the destruction, overwhelmed. Tomorrow she'd contact Sadie's homeowner's insurance—if her mother had any. She didn't remember seeing it in the accordion file. One of the neighbors had brought the folder and her purse over to her after finding them in the yard. They were the only things she had left besides her car, which was parked on the curb in front of the house. She'd been avoiding using the garage ever since feeling the doorknob. She also needed to tell Tish she wouldn't be in. She needed to call Parker's school too.

Then she stopped. Did her to-do list even matter now? Someone had tried to kill them. Would he try again?

Melicent didn't know what to do. If this was about the two million dollars, she didn't want the money. She'd give it back.

She stared at the car. Roan's card was still inside. She'd stuck it in her cup holder when she left the wine bar.

"I'll be right back," she mumbled to Parker, and got out of the ambulance.

"Where are you going?" Parker asked in panic.

"Just checking the car. I'll be back in a minute." She padded down the sidewalk, suddenly conscious that she didn't have shoes on and underneath the blanket the EMT had given her she was in her nightie. She didn't own any clothes anymore.

Every object tied to her life was gone, every memento, keepsake, work of art, and photograph, belonging not only to her but to Parker and their mother. Their computers, their hard drives and files wouldn't have survived the fire either. A lifetime of "saves" had been obliterated in one night.

Their home held more memories than she could imagine. Her grandparents had bought the house after they'd married in the early sixties. Sadie had spent her entire life inside those walls, born and raised under one roof. The master bedroom was still full of all her things—and the boxes, good God, the boxes— Melicent had planned to sort them after the new year. Now all her mother's treasures were lost. The house, which had been the keeper of the memories, had been destroyed.

Melicent stumbled under the weight of the loss, and when she reached for the car door a sob welled within her. She heard the sound from far away as if her ears were under water. She opened the door and sat down in the car, finally allowing the full force of her anguish to come out. She put her head on the dash and wept.

After several minutes she pulled herself together and found Roan West's card. She needed to tell him about the man who had done this.

16. THE CIRCLES

ROAN COULDN'T IMAGINE how Miguel and Stuart had linked crop circles to the ooparts. After taking a shower he got out his laptop to research crop circles in more depth. He clicked on one of the most popular crop circle databases in England, which had a huge library of aerial photography. The site had cataloged photos for the past twenty-five years and gave an overview of the phenomenon.

The average circle was two hundred feet across, though some spanned up to a thousand feet. Many of the circles showed up on farms with gently sloping hills. As Roan clicked through the pictures, he became more and more spellbound. He'd never looked at crop circles up close before. The geometrical designs were stunning in their intricacy and held a timeless, poetic grace.

He read that the circles usually formed overnight without fanfare, during the summer months before harvest. The full grandeur of the designs could only be viewed from the sky. Most circles were created during the shroud of night, sometime within a span of six to seven hours—though a few had miraculously appeared during the day in minutes. One notorious circle in 1996 nicknamed the "Julia Set" appeared near Stonehenge during the day, according to eyewitnesses and Stonehenge security guards.

The field next to the busy highway and ancient monument had been clear all day and then suddenly, within minutes, everyone noticed an exquisite design had miraculously materialized. Even more incredible, the design was an arrangement of 149 circles in an intricate fractal pattern representing the Julia set, a complex mathematical formula.

Roan made a note of the other crop circles researchers had flagged. They were significant because they showed the circles could not have been made by any known conventional methods. The Milk Hill crop circle in 2001 appeared in full glory one night over the hills of Pewsey Vale. The enormous design was approximately nine hundred feet wide, the length of two and half football fields, and curved in an intricate spiral that divided into six sections that contained 409 circles inside of them. The Milk Hill circle was the Empire State Building of crop circles. No one could fathom how any person, or group, could create such a masterpiece within hours, in the dead of night and under wet and windy weather conditions, and yet the circle was fully formed by dawn—a brilliant work of art lit by the morning sun for all the world to see.

In 2000 the Picked Hill circle, a fractal sunflower pattern, was also flagged. The design contained forty-four spirals and fourteen concentric rings. 44 divided by 14 equaled 3.142, better known as pi (π). The design was near impossible to draw on paper, much less in a field at night.

Were the circles messages? Written in a language based on math?

One circle was a replica of a DNA strand and another appeared in the fields next to the Chilbolton Observatory, with pixelated squares that were almost identical to the pattern of a binary code sent up into space in 1974 with the purpose of contacting other life-forms. To anyone analyzing the pixels on the field, the design read like a reply.

The database showed the marked differences between fabricated circles, which were crudely created by someone with tape measures and "stomp boards" that crushed the plants, and the geometry was far from accurate. The other circles, the unexplainable ones, were geometric masterpieces. Their creations left plants unharmed, lying on their side. Those circles remained just that: unexplainable.

One crop circle researcher, a pilot who had devoted his career to documenting the circles from the air and on the ground, believed that the way the world was turning its eyes from these unexplainable masterpieces was a phenomenon in itself. Like clockwork, dozens of new circles appeared around Great Britain each summer from April to August. No two circles were ever alike. Some circles' geometric designs were so confounding and impossible to create that they would spark renewed widespread public interest. Then the science-hoax argument would start and quickly stalemate all over again.

Roan clicked on the links to all the aerial photos of crop circles from the present year. The designs were stunning geometric-like mandalas. The more he read, the more Roan found himself sliding down the rabbit hole of something he didn't understand. Now it was almost three in the morning and he couldn't sleep.

Why did Miguel and Stuart think the ooparts were connected? Crop circles were fantastical enough. How did the two tie together?

When his cell phone rang, disrupting his thoughts, at first Roan thought it was Stuart. Only a few people knew his private number. "Hello?"

"Roan? It's Melicent Tilpin."

Roan sat up, suddenly alert. She sounded strange and he could hear the quake in her voice. Something had happened.

He launched out of bed. "Are you all right?"

"Someone set my house on fire—my mother's house." Her voice broke, her words spilling out in a tangled rush. "A stranger came to my house. I felt the doorknob . . . I saw him—I think he may come back. I need your help. I need to protect my brother."

Roan was already getting dressed and throwing his things into his bag. "Are you safe? Where are you?"

"Our neighbors' right across the street. I'm sorry to call so late. I don't know what to do."

"I'll be right there. I'm nearby." Roan's mind was already in the zone, looking ahead to carve out a plan. The fire had to be connected to the group and the ooparts. There was no question in his mind.

Once whoever did this discovered that Melicent had survived, would they come back again?

"You need to be out of Los Angeles before the six A.M. news reports on the fire. I can make that happen."

"Leave town? With you?" She tripped on the words.

"We'll talk about the plan when I get there. Come out when you see me. Bring your brother."

"Wait. You don't know my address."

"I know your address, Melicent." He couldn't help the soft edge that found its way into his voice. She'd been easy to find. Anyone else who was looking could find her too.

17. THE WRISTBAND

AFTER MELICENT HUNG UP, she tried to calm the adrenaline still coursing through her. She was sequestered in the Mercers' guest bathroom. She splashed water on her face and took several deep breaths, her body still shaking from the shock of the night.

The Mercers had finally gone back to sleep after Melicent encouraged them. The elderly couple was distraught too but needed to rest. They gave her and Parker a change of clothes, fresh towels to shower with, and an invitation to help themselves to anything in the kitchen. Parker had showered first and then Melicent. She'd brought her cell phone into the bathroom so she could talk in private. She thought Parker would be asleep from exhaustion, but he was sitting on the guest bed and waiting for her with his arms crossed.

"Who was that you were talking to?"

"A friend." Melicent hesitated, not sure how else to explain Roan West. She sat down next to him and hoped her brother wouldn't be freaked out by what she was about to say. "Park, I need you to trust me."

"Of course I trust you." He sounded offended.

"The fire tonight . . . was meant for me."

That statement lingered in the air. He frowned at her. "Because you found the watch?"

"No, because of how I found it." She put her hands on her legs in front of her. "My friend thinks whoever did this may come after me again. He wants to help us."

"How do you know he didn't start the fire?"

"Because I saw the face of the man who did."

"When?" Parker gaped at her in disbelief. "You saw him at the house?"

"No. In my mind when I touched the doorknob to the garage."

Parker covered his face with his hands, looking like he might break down and cry. "I don't believe this, Mel."

"I know. I'm sorry. I can't control what I see or when I see it. But I also can't ignore it anymore." She reached out and touched his knee. "We need to go. My friend's coming to pick us up right now."

"The psycho?" He looked at her, appalled.

"Would you quit calling him that?" she said, trying to keep her voice down.

Parker glared and lowered his voice too. "Fine! Then *you're* the psycho. What about the Mercers? We're just going to run off in the middle of the night?"

"We'll leave them a note."

"And go where?"

"I don't know. Anywhere but here. We need to leave town." She nodded to the accordion file where their passports were. "I was already planning on it. I was going to tell you."

Parker stared at the accordion file in shock. He was about to say something but then changed his mind. "What about the investigation? The house? Won't it look suspicious that we're skipping town?"

"I'll call and tell them we didn't feel safe in L.A. because of the arson and are staying with a friend out of town."

"A friend you don't even know." Parker was practically choking on the words. "He could be a serial killer, a complete wacko. And we're getting into his car like a bad eighties movie?"

"Parker. Roan is like me. He's here to help us."

"What do you mean *like you*?" He air-quoted her.

"Would you stop doing that?" She swatted his hand. "He can sense things with his hands. Even more than I can."

"How do you know?"

"Because he proved it." Everything Roan had said about her and her mother from touching the snow globe was not only true but true with a specificity that still astounded her. And what he'd done with the lanterns was on a whole other level.

"Well, he's got to prove it to me." Parker crossed his arms. "Or I'm not going anywhere."

"Fine! Ask him when you see him." She threw up her arms in exasperation. "But we're leaving. Now."

Parker looked ready to challenge her. But when she opened the guest room door and motioned for him to go, he did.

As he walked past her he whispered, "I hope you know what you're doing."

She turned off the guest room light and quietly shut the door. She hoped so too.

⌒

Across the street, the violent remnants of the fire stood etched against the night shadows. What was left of the house had been cordoned off. The doors and windows were gone, leaving only a blackened half-standing frame.

It was three thirty in the morning, still the dim hours before dawn. But Melicent knew the person who had done this would return to assess the aftermath. She didn't want to be anywhere on this street when he came back.

The Mercers, when they woke, would see her note on the entry hall table. She'd written: *Thank you for the clothes. A friend came to pick us up and we'll be staying with him. Talk soon.*

When Roan drove up in front of the house, relief rippled through her. He'd come. She turned the bottom lock of the

Mercers' front door and pulled it shut. Parker stood stiff beside her, an unwilling participant, and gave her a disapproving look she ignored.

She hurried down the walkway to the car with her brother one step behind. Roan motioned for her to get in, but Parker stepped in front of her.

"No, you get in the back," Parker said protectively, and he opened up the front passenger door.

Melicent muttered under her breath and hurried into the back seat to hear whatever her brother was about to say.

When Parker got in the two men assessed each other.

Roan finally offered, "You must be Parker."

"I am." Parker was eyeing him like this was all Roan's fault.

"Thanks for getting us." Melicent spoke up, meeting Roan's gaze in the rearview mirror.

"You're not hurt?" He searched her eyes and she shook her head, the trauma of the night still a cloud around her.

Parker announced, "Before we go anywhere I want proof."

"Proof of what?" Roan turned to him.

"Of everything!" Parker raised his voice, becoming emotional. "My sister says you can do what she can do, only better. It's why you're here. To help her. So prove it!"

Roan met Melicent's gaze again in the mirror.

Parker crossed his arms. "We're not going anywhere until you prove it."

"Fine." Roan pulled off his right glove. "Give me your wristband."

Parker's hand went to his left wrist on reflex. Melicent knew her brother never took the leather cuff off. She doubted he'd hand it over.

Parker stalled by asking, "Why?"

"You want proof. I need to borrow it. I'll give it back." Roan put the car in drive and started driving.

Parker gripped the dash. "Wait! I said—"

"I know. But I suggest we do this on another street and not in front of your house." Roan turned the corner and found a spot several blocks down on a side street. He shut off the car's ignition and gave Parker his full attention. "Now," he said, holding out his right hand like a magician about to perform a trick, "the wristband."

Melicent almost spoke up to warn her brother that he may not want to hand it over. After what Roan had discovered from touching her art at the store, no amount of money would make her give him her jewelry.

But Parker surprised her by slipping it off.

"Thank you." Roan held the wristband with surprising gentleness and closed his eyes. After a moment he opened them again and looked at Parker closely, a hint of surprise on his face. Then he said, "You got this in Hawaii. Your mother gave it to you. A woman was selling these at a gift stand where you had lunch. Your sister was there." Roan's eyes glanced to Melicent in the back. She met his eyes in the mirror, holding her breath. He was looking at her, like he was comparing her to how she'd been all those years ago. He dropped his gaze and focused on the wristband again. "The trip was a splurge, a surprise present from Sadie for the three of you. The owl carved into the leather is an 'aumakua, a family guardian in Hawaii. The woman selling it said it would bring you luck, and you never take it off."

The car was quiet. Parker was listening with bated breath. That trip was one of Parker's happiest memories.

Roan jumped forward in time and announced, "You've been skipping school . . ."

Parker snapped out of his daze and crossed his arms, defensive again. "Did my sister tell you that?"

". . . to go to the cemetery," Roan finished his sentence.

Both Parker and Melicent were stunned into silence.

"You bring your mother flowers. Carnations because you can't afford anything else. You talk to her, clean the headstone, some days you cry, some days you lie on the grass and read books. Some days you just sit, wondering if death would be easier." He fingered the wristband. "You thought about digging a hole beside her grave and burying this with her because you don't feel lucky anymore at all."

Tears pooled in Parker's eyes as he listened to Roan go on. The intimacy within the car became stifling.

"You don't want to burden your sister. You think her life will be better without you, and you've been planning to run away. That's why you were at BJ's that day, to finalize your plan. He has a cousin up in Michigan you were going to stay with until you found work. Once you had the car—"

"Enough!" Parker yelled. "Enough." He grabbed the wristband back and held it in both hands with a sob, bowing his head.

"I'm sorry—" Roan began, but then stopped.

Melicent was too stunned to say anything. The bottom of her world had given way. Parker had been spending all that time at the cemetery, and she'd assumed the worst.

He was going to run away. *From her.*

"Just drive," Parker said, his voice sounding small. With those two words he was giving Roan permission to help them.

Roan put his glove back on and started the car. They drove in silence. Melicent was too dumbstruck by Parker's confession to make sense of what was happening until Roan asked, "Do you have ID?"

"Sorry?" she asked, her mind blank.

"Do you have identification? Can you fly?"

She nodded and then realized he couldn't see her in the dark. "Yes. To where?"

"New Orleans."

Parker was staring straight ahead, vacant. What had happened tonight was too much. He'd passed the brink.

Melicent was barely functioning herself. In one night her entire life had been stripped away. She looked out the front window. There were few cars on Lincoln as they drove to LAX. She watched the road stretch out like a black band between the headlights, unspooling infinitely in the dark.

18. THE WINDOW

"IS IT MAGIC?"

Roan looked up from his coffee to find Parker studying him. They were at the Atlantic Aviation terminal at LAX, reserved for private planes, and sequestered in the corner of the lobby with coffee, waiting for their plane to fuel. Melicent had stepped away to the ladies' room, leaving Parker and Roan alone.

"No," Roan said with a faint smile. His proof in the car had fired up the sixteen-year-old's imagination. "I don't control anything. I only see it."

Parker glanced down to his coffee cup as if it held better answers.

Roan could tell Parker wanted to talk but didn't know how. *What an earnest kid,* Roan couldn't help but think now that he'd read him. Roan hadn't expected to feel so overwhelmed holding his wristband. Without warning he'd gotten tangled up in all the joy, sadness, and pain inside it. Parker had worn that leather band every day for six years, and it held a trove of memories; jewelry always did—the more worn, the denser. That wristband had been a time machine, showing Roan the last years of Parker's childhood, before his voice had deepened and become a man's. Parker was still a boy stretched inside a tall frame, a little boy afraid of heights, afraid of the dark, a boy who loved his mother and missed her very much.

"I'm sorry about your house," Roan offered in a quiet voice. He understood the power of home and through the imprints had witnessed Melicent's desperate attempt to save theirs. Helpless anger filled Roan at whoever had done this to them.

Parker nodded, trying to appear strong. In that moment he looked so much like Melicent it was uncanny. The two siblings shared Sadie's fair coloring and same delicate features.

Roan would have loved to touch something of Sadie's to learn what had happened to Parker and Melicent's father. Who was he? Why wasn't he in the picture? Then Roan shook his head at himself. He had no right to be sifting through their past. Melicent and Parker's family dynamics were none of his business.

His eyes strayed across the lobby, watching Melicent return to their seats. He felt a tightening in his gut, unable to ignore his growing attraction to her. His eyes swept her body, for the first time getting a good look at the bizarre floral sweatpants and jacket set she was wearing, no doubt borrowed from her elderly neighbor. It looked like sportswear a senior citizen would wear—a tiny one. The pants were too short and the faux-velvet jacket hugged her rib cage. When she walked he caught a glimpse of skin at her waist.

He met her eyes. She was watching him watch her. They stared at each other for a lingering moment. Roan wondered what it'd be like to kiss her.

She slid into the leather seat next to her brother. Roan could see Parker picking up on the tension between them. Roan's mouth twisted in consternation at the whole situation. Suddenly his life had become incredibly complicated.

They sat quietly until Melicent said, "I'd like to pay for our airfare."

"Please don't worry about it." Roan tried to brush aside her offer.

"But it's too expensive."

"Really, it's not a problem. I've been finding and selling watches my whole life." It was why they were waiting in a terminal that looked like a hotel lobby instead of standing in line with the rest of LAX.

Her lips pursed in a frown. He hadn't meant to sound cavalier, but it was true. He shook his head at himself for coming across wrong, something he seemed to do with her too easily, and he pulled out his cell phone to check email. Holly should have finished up her meeting with Faye Young and delivered the heirloom for the foundation. As he scrolled through his inbox he could feel Parker scrutinizing him.

The boy asked, "Why are you really helping us like this? Flying us in a private plane? Who does that?"

Roan could have told him helping people was what he did—although usually they were dead. He exercised his ability by returning lost heirlooms to their original owner's descendants. But the truth was ever since he'd seen that YouTube video, Melicent Tilpin was a comet that had come streaking across his world. Was he rescuing her or chasing her? Maybe both. And now he had her inquisitive sixteen-year-old brother to handle.

An intent light shone in the boy's eyes and Roan could tell that nothing but the absolute truth would fly.

He tried to explain. "My good friend in England is a psychometrist. He's part of a group of psychometrists who are researching out-of-place artifacts."

"Out of what?"

"Out-of-place. They're called ooparts." Roan reached into his bag and took out Hanus's key. He dropped it into Parker's hand. "Like this one."

Parker held up the key with a frown. "Looks like an old key to me."

"Because it is." Roan's eyes slid to Melicent's, then he took the key back and returned it to his bag. "But to a psychometrist we can sense the dual timelines running through it. These artifacts shouldn't be in the time and place they've been found, and there's no explanation as to why."

"So these psychometrists are trying to find the explanation?" Melicent asked.

Roan didn't offer the key to Melicent, knowing the last thing she needed was to sense Hanus's lifetime. "My friend Stuart's trying to tie the ooparts together and find a unifying factor."

Parker frowned. "So how many people are in this group?"

"There were six. But now two of them are missing and one is dead," Roan said bluntly. After the fire, Melicent and Parker needed to know what had happened to the others.

Parker was speechless. Melicent's hand covered her mouth in a quiet gasp.

Roan looked at them gravely, his eyes settling on Parker. "That's why we're taking the plane."

After they boarded and took off, Roan checked his watch—six A.M. Right on schedule. They were in the air as the morning news began. Whoever set the fire was probably still in L.A., but the arson had done its job, hiding the identity of whoever was behind it.

Before Roan had picked Melicent and Parker up, he'd parked two blocks away and walked to the house and circled the perimeter. There had been no door left to touch and find the imprint Melicent had mentioned. Roan would have given anything to hold it.

But he'd placed his hands on the trees and replayed the scene of the fire.

A man had stood, hidden in the shadows, watching the house catch ablaze. He wore a hoodie up over his face, looking like a jogger in the cold. As the fire spread, the man hesitated and began to throw rocks at the bedroom window. When one shattered it, he ran off.

Through the window Roan saw Melicent get up and run out of the room and across the hall. He saw her through another window on the other side of the house. It was Parker's room.

She threw her things into the yard and rushed to get her brother out. Parker didn't want to go. He was too afraid. Somehow Melicent forced him. They made their way down and collapsed on the grass, heaving in air and hugging each other.

Roan stayed with the imprint. His mind was so honed he was standing in the moment.

The firefighters came and then the police. Roan stood in the center of the memory as they tried to save the house and rush Melicent and Parker to safety.

He watched Melicent get oxygen and a blanket. Then he followed her as she walked to her car. She opened the car door and got in, crying alone in the dark. She found his card and clutched it in her hands.

Roan sat beside her in the shadow of the past, wanting so much to comfort her. But these moments had already happened. There were no imprints left for Roan to investigate.

The man in the hoodie had not been a jogger. Roan desperately wanted to know who he was and how he was connected to them.

Too many questions were flooding his mind.

He folded his fingers into Vyana mudra to help his tension release. At least Melicent and her brother were safe with him thirty-five thousand feet up in the air. They were sitting on the other side of the aisle, staring out their window as the clouds moved past, no doubt thinking about their circumstances and the bombshell he'd dropped on them at the airport by telling them what he did.

Parker was the one who broke the silence. "So what now? We just hide out in New Orleans?" His eyes went to Melicent. "Skip school the rest of the year?"

"I'll call the school. We need some time to figure this out." Melicent was trying to stay strong for both of them. She looked over to Roan.

He asked her, "You said you felt the doorknob and saw him. What did you see?" She had touched her door and gotten an imprint. Right now this arsonist was the only lead he had to finding Stuart. This person had to be connected to Stuart's disappearance.

She hesitated, glancing at her brother. "He wasn't from here. He came to L.A. to find me . . ." She glanced at her brother again.

"What did he look like? How old?" Roan asked, trying to get her to dig deeper into the memory. "Close your eyes and try and reimagine it."

She did as he asked and soon let out a shuddering breath. "Brown hair. Forties? Tall. He had a baseball cap on and sweats and a canvas bag across his shoulders. Like an army duffel. He came to burn down the house." Her voice caught. She looked at him. Her devastation grabbed at his heart, and Roan immediately felt guilty for asking her to see a painful moment again.

Roan unbuckled his seat belt and moved over to join them on their side of the aisle. He sat across from her. "Hey, listen to me," he said gently, putting his hands on her knees.

She looked at him in surprise. The connection between them was like a running current, growing stronger every minute. "You two are going to stay in New Orleans, where you'll be safe. I'm going to find out who's behind this. Think of your time there as a short trip." He would deposit them at a hotel downtown near the warehouse. Holly could watch over them while he went to London.

Melicent nodded, defeat and despair on her face. In that moment Roan wanted nothing more than to hold her hand. For the first time the barrier of his gloves frustrated him. He wanted to take them off.

19. THE GIFT BAGS

AFTER THE PLANE LANDED IN NEW ORLEANS, Roan drove Melicent and Parker straight to their hotel, the Westin on Canal Place. He chose it because it was near the warehouse and also the hotel had a mall next door. Parker and Melicent had no clothes and would need to buy the bare necessities while they were there.

Melicent was adamant on paying for the hotel room and got Parker and herself two rooms that connected. Roan made note of their room numbers so he could order flowers to be delivered to them as a precaution.

"I'm going up," Parker said, subdued, and took his room key from his sister. "Thanks for helping us," he added to Roan, and then turned to Melicent without meeting her eyes. "See you later. I'm going to sleep."

With a troubled look Melicent watched her brother leave and then she turned to Roan with a sigh.

"He'll come around." Roan had felt firsthand how much Parker loved his sister. Whatever misunderstandings stood between them wouldn't last long.

"I still can't believe he was going to run away."

"He's a complicated kid" was all he could say. "Give him time.

You've both been through a lot. Why don't you go get some rest?" he suggested. "I'll come back late this afternoon."

"You're coming back?" she asked in surprise.

He searched her eyes. "You didn't expect me to just drop you off at a hotel and not come back?" Her cheeks became flushed and he added, "I want you to meet Holly, my business partner. She's going to look after you while I'm gone." He watched her face fall in disappointment. She had no idea how expressive she was.

"Where are you going?"

"London—tomorrow. Only for a few days."

"To look for your friend?" She crossed her arms with a thoughtful frown.

"The sooner I find out what happened to him, the sooner you two are safe." He took a step back to leave.

"Wait." She grabbed his hand. "Thank you. For bringing us here. For everything."

He could feel the warmth of her hand through his gloves. He raised her hand and kissed it—something he'd never done to anyone before—and walked away.

                   ⌒

When Roan got home he took a long steaming shower. He should have gone straight to bed to catch a few hours of sleep. Instead he came back downstairs and sat on the sofa, staring at the Trove gift bags.

He needed to return them to Melicent. The sooner the temptation to touch her artwork was gone the better—because now he wanted to read the imprints more than ever. She was becoming an obsession. He wanted to know her.

Maybe he would ask if he could keep one globe—the one he'd already handled. The others he would give back, upholding his promise not to touch them. But the snow globe with the rock garden he'd already held. So if he touched it again now, he wouldn't be breaking his word. There was nothing else to see. He'd already read all the imprints.

Before he could second-guess what he was doing, he reached in, took the snow globe out of the box, and leaned back on the couch. He rested the globe on his chest and closed his eyes. The weight of the rock rose and fell with each breath as he held it in his hands.

His breathing calmed as his mind sifted through all the memories he knew were there, like a movie he wanted to watch again. Two people besides him and Melicent had touched this globe before: one person was a customer from The Trove—a woman preoccupied by her twins fussing in their stroller. She had considered buying it as a birthday present for her mother but put it back down when one of the babies started screaming.

The mother left the store with a harassed look and an apologetic smile to Melicent. "Thanks, I'll come another time."

Melicent was behind the register, her hair knotted into a twist with wooden chopsticks, just like in the YouTube video. She was bent over the counter working intently on another snow globe.

She looked up with a smile and waved. Sunlight streamed through the window, framing her in a luminous light.

Roan was captivated. He could watch that moment a hundred times. He finally left the imprint and moved on to the next.

The other person who'd handled it was the woman Melicent worked for, Tish. Tish had held the globe for several minutes, gazing at it with a critical eye, thinking it wasn't that good. Tish's imprint was a long raveling thread holding a lot of history—and baggage—between the two women.

Tish was the one who had offered to let Melicent sell her artwork at the store, and she gave Melicent one small shelf in the back corner. The arrangement was that Melicent could keep all the profits from anything that sold. But Tish regretted making the offer. In her mind the crystal globes mounted on chunks of granite took up valuable space.

Who would want to buy this? was all Tish could think. She'd picked up the rock garden snow globe, all the while wondering how she could steal the shelf back.

Roan grimaced at the bitter taste in his mouth and moved past Tish's negative imprint, impatient to get to Melicent again. He adjusted his fingertips on the glass sphere as if fine-tuning an instrument until he was able to capture her.

Melicent sat at her desk in her bedroom, creating the sculpture. She liked to do a little bit at a time late at night. Her eyes were focused on the task, but her mind was far away as she constructed the miniature rock garden. She was in her pajamas, boxer shorts and a wispy camisole, her hair splayed over her shoulders, with tendrils falling forward as she leaned closer to the desk. Roan felt like a voyeur watching her, his mind's eye so focused on the moment he could have reached out to touch her.

It was the first time an imprint had ever frustrated him—because he wanted it to be real. He'd learned early on as a child imprints could never replace the present. The singularity of the present was what gave "the now" its power, but he'd also never wanted to choose an imprint over reality before.

He watched her work until he drifted off to sleep, and his hands stayed wrapped around the crystal globe, cradling it, like it was the most priceless possession in the world.

20. THE PEACE PIPE

THE KEY TO GETTING ROAN WEST TO TALK, Melicent noticed, was to ask him about history. In the fifteen minutes they'd been in the car together, Roan had regaled her and Parker with all kinds of historical trivia, painting a vivid picture of New Orleans as a city steeped in time, a grand melding of cultures, and a living doorway to the past. "The biggest small town in the world" had the country's oldest public market and the first cathedral in North America. Tennessee Williams had lived next to Gumbo Shop, and Mark Twain had had his fortune read just down the street when he was a Mississippi steamboat pilot before the Civil War.

The other thing she noticed about Roan was that he sometimes talked about the past in the present tense, describing events as if they were still happening. It was disconcerting. She'd never heard another person do this.

"Thomas Jefferson tries to buy New Orleans and Florida from Napoleon in 1803 for two million dollars. Napoleon doesn't answer the offer. So James Monroe goes over to Paris and raises the price to ten million." Roan was driving them through the French Quarter, giving them a play-by-play commentary on the history of the city.

"Instead Napoleon shocks everyone by announcing he'll give

up the entire Louisiana Territory, an expanse of fifteen states extending from Florida all the way to Canada, for fifteen million. After the math is said and done, New Orleans is basically bought for seven dollars." This fascinating discussion of New Orleans was the most Roan had said since they'd met. As they toured through the French Quarter in his car, the last twenty-four hours began to recede in Melicent's mind like a distant nightmare. But the fire had happened, and now Roan had decided that she and her brother were his responsibility.

He'd even sent flowers to her hotel room. When the bouquet had arrived that afternoon, her first thought was that he was trying to make a romantic gesture.

The card simply said, *To brighten up your room. R.*

The gift had been so surprising, but when she knocked on Parker's door to deliver the jeans and T-shirts she'd bought him at the mall, she'd been stunned to see that Roan had sent Parker a beautiful bouquet as well.

A swift stab of disappointment hit her. The flowers weren't a romantic gesture. The man simply liked giving flowers. But then she'd already determined Roan was odd. Maybe it was a condolence gesture since they'd lost the house—a fact she was trying hard not to think about. The shock would be with her for some time before she was ready to face the reality.

Roan was busy explaining to them how Napoleon had never come to New Orleans, but that uptown streets were named after his battles, and one of the few first copies of his death mask was housed in the Cabildo Museum.

"What's a death mask?" Parker asked, perking up in the back seat.

Roan glanced at Parker in the rearview mirror. "It's the mold of someone's face cast on their deathbed. Napoleon's mold was stolen, so historians are unable to determine which mask was cast from the original mold and which is a copy. The two top contenders are the masks in the Musée de l'Armée in Paris and the one at the Musée de Malmaison."

"So if you touched them, would you know the answer?" Parker asked.

Roan didn't hesitate before saying "Yes."

"Did you ever touch something that was Napoleon's?" Parker wanted to know.

Melicent tried not to roll her eyes. Parker was full of questions for Roan, but her brother hadn't said two words to her since the dramatic revelation that he was planning to run away. Granted they hadn't had a moment to sit down and talk, but the silent treatment was beginning to wear on her.

"I did more than that. I found something." Roan's eyes had a gleam in them, remembering. "His sword."

"Whoa." Parker leaned forward.

"I was your age. His insignia was engraved on the hilt. It had been damaged and was illegible, but I still knew. He commissioned the sword to be made after his campaign in Egypt."

Melicent glanced over at Roan from the corner of her eye, surprised he was continuing to be so talkative. If she didn't know better she would swear he sounded nervous—like he was talking to fill the silence. Something had happened to him during their afternoon apart. She focused on listening and used it as an excuse to study him. He was wearing black jeans and a cotton stretch long-sleeved T-shirt that made him look athletic. She had to admit that his gloves looked sexier when he was driving.

Roan caught her assessing stare. She cleared her throat and looked back out the window as he continued with his story. "The sword disappeared—like so many of Napoleon's possessions did—when he was imprisoned by the English. We took it to a laboratory that dealt in advanced metalwork testing, and they were able to show the insignia under the right microscope."

"You sold it?" Melicent asked. She couldn't imagine touching something that belonged to Napoleon and sensing his past. The man had controlled entire continents and the lives of millions.

"For how much?" Parker chimed in.

"Parker!" Melicent craned her neck around to give him a look. "That's rude."

"What? I'm not asking his salary. It's Napoleon's sword. Chill."

"One point two million dollars," Roan answered.

Parker frowned. "That seems low."

"Oh my God," she said to her brother. "Would you stop?"

"No, it was low," Roan agreed, clearly trying to defuse the tension. "At the time, my dad was worried that a public auction would garner too much media attention. So we sold it to a military antique collector in the States. Four years later, when I was twenty, another of Napoleon's swords came up for auction from the Bonaparte family. The sword was appraised at one point six million but it sold for six point five million and became one of the highest-selling antiquities of all time."

Parker whistled and everyone fell silent.

Melicent crossed her arms and looked out the window again, feeling a weight pressing on her. Finding Breguet's watch had garnered attention—a lot of attention. She hadn't had time to see where else the story had circulated besides the *L.A. Times* and YouTube. Not that she wanted to—it'd only unnerve her more. That video had made her a target. There could be dozens of articles about the pocket watch, and here she was hiding out in New Orleans.

They left the French Quarter and took Decatur Street, which soon turned into Magazine Street. As they drove down the winding road filled with restaurants, shops, and bars, she thought the vibe felt a lot like Culver City's walking district or SoHo in New York, which she'd visited once with a friend in college.

When Roan pulled into a small drive next to one of the houses, Melicent received a momentary jolt. Seeing RW Antiques days after clicking on every available picture of it was unreal.

Not once had she imagined she'd be visiting the house, let alone soon.

The pearl-colored exterior was even more charming than the pictures on the website. A delightful winter garden of pansies and petunias surrounded the wraparound porch and steep patio steps led to the entrance. The entire house was raised high off the ground, in traditional New Orleans fashion, to safeguard it from flooding.

On the way to the front door she caught Roan taking off his right glove and trailing a hand over the tips of the flowers with an intent look on his face.

Without slowing his stride, he put his glove back on in one smooth motion before buzzing the front door. The intercom sounded. "Holly, it's me," he said.

A few moments later the front door opened and a silvery-blond woman stepped out. She was in her thirties and dressed in an elegant pencil skirt and silk blouse. She'd accessorized the look with dramatic jewelry, a brass cuff and ropes of pearls around her neck, and a touch too much makeup.

"Roan! I—" Her smile faltered when she noticed he had brought people with him. "Why hello." A professional mask fell into place and she stepped back to welcome them inside. "I didn't realize you were bringing clients today." Her Southern drawl was pronounced.

Roan ushered them in. "They're not clients. They're visiting from L.A. Melicent and Parker Tilpin, I'd like you to meet Holly Beauchêne."

The announcement of Melicent's and Parker's names made Holly's mouth drop open. "Oh my Lord. You're from the You-Tube video." She looked from Melicent and Parker to Roan in disbelief.

"You saw it too?" Parker asked.

"I'm the one who showed it to him," Holly said, sounding like she wished she hadn't.

Everyone stood in the foyer for an awkward moment. Melicent watched the silent exchange between Holly and Roan and could hear the unspoken words: *Why did you bring them here?* And his *It's a long story* look. It was obvious Roan and Holly had a close relationship to enable that kind of nonverbal shorthand.

Roan excused himself and Holly for a few minutes and they went to the office to talk. They didn't shut the door all the way, and Melicent could hear every word bouncing off the hardwood floors and the old house's thin walls—how she and Parker were connected to what was going on with Stuart and how he needed Holly to watch them while he was in London.

Holly's voice rose. "You're leaving? And you want me to watch them?"

Melicent couldn't help but cringe. Holly sounded horrified. Melicent felt like going in there to tell her not to worry, she wasn't about to stay in New Orleans and be babysat.

Holly shut the office door for privacy, muting their voices. Melicent shook her head and tried to tamp down her annoyance. She moved as far away from them as possible and turned her attention instead to the showrooms.

She wandered from room to room, much like Parker was doing. But unlike her brother, who was picking up the merchandise, checking the price tags, and making whistling noises, she kept her arms crossed with her hands under her elbows.

At this point she was afraid to touch anything. Every piece of furniture and collectible in this house had a story to tell or Roan wouldn't have brought it here, from the Viennese silver spice boxes to the grand chandelier from Bohemia to the fifteenth-century embossed bowls from Nuremberg.

Melicent moved past an inlaid gaming table and drop-front secretaire that looked like they had graced a castle in Europe. Who were the last people to own these treasures? Her hand almost reached out to touch the gaming table but instead she walked on.

The next room held a beautiful assortment of table clocks: porcelain sculptures from Italy, vase clocks from France, and an ornate Roman chariot where the clock was the wheel. On the wall a painting from Prague had a clock embedded into the canvas as part of the picture. The room made her smile. Of course Roan would collect unusual clocks.

She finished touring the showroom and stepped through the last doorway at the end of the hall.

The chill hit her first and then the coldness of the air turned invasive, as if invisible fingers were trying to touch her bones. Melicent wrapped her arms around her middle with a twinge of apprehension.

Four long tables were draped with black tablecloths. The antiques on the tables were tagged with lot numbers instead of price tags, and many items had a page of typed or handwritten notes tucked beside them. The collection looked Native American and featured everything from beaded ceremonial dresses and matching moccasins to feathered headdresses, musical flutes, and handmade dolls made from hides.

Melicent placed her hand on her chest to calm her heart and ease the sense of dread spreading through her. She had to know why this feeling, this concentration of sadness and loss, was in the room.

Making a conscious decision to use her right hand instead of her left, she picked up a small handmade horse from a cluster of toys. If Roan was correct, her right hand was her more receptive hand and would be the best one for reading an imprint.

Immediately she felt a tug and closed her eyes to follow the animal's trail through the darkness, to hear the story of a boy who had to leave his beloved toy behind.

Little Deer was one of thousands of children rounded up by the U.S. government, wrenched from his family, and sent to live in a Native American boarding school. He was forbidden to speak his language; his glorious black hair was shorn off; he could no longer walk freely; he had to march. He wore the same uniform day in, day out.

Little Deer's memories resounded in the toy horse, along with his fear, his confusion, his shame. On the table along with the horse were toys belonging to other children, handmade by their grandmothers, which had to be left behind and were only seen again in the summer months when the children were allowed to return home.

Melicent could hear the sounds of their laughter silenced, feel the brutal push against their spirits to stifle their light. At school the teachers called Little Deer uncivilized and a savage. He was beaten with horse cords and sticks, and when he ran away the punishment was much worse.

Melicent was trapped in the dark memories, no longer in the room. Like a sleepwalker she put down the horse and moved to the next table, and reached out to touch one of the wooden pipes decorated with banded feathers.

First she heard the words "Hetchetu welo," *it is indeed a good day,* spoken so clearly, like the man speaking was standing beside her. Then a torrent of imprints hit her.

The images came like a stampede from the last evening this pipe had ever held smoke. It'd been passed around with great ceremony by the tribe's medicine man, Yellow Bird, but the ceremony had been interrupted by the arrival of a cavalry of soldiers.

The soldiers were escorting another band of Sioux and their ailing chief, Big Foot, whom they were arresting. The pipe held the fear of that night and the following day as the soldiers rounded up every weapon from every tepee.

The killing started when a soldier's gun went off and shot a deaf man who was resisting the soldier because he couldn't hear the orders.

Within seconds the panicked troop fired at the crowds and into the tepees, forever burning that winter day red with blood.

Men, women, children were shot like animals while they tried to run.

"Melicent, let go!"

Melicent could barely register that Roan was shouting. The grief had eclipsed her.

His arms wrapped around her, rooting her back to the present. She dropped the pipe on the table with a clatter and buried her face in her hands. Her legs were about to buckle as her whole body shook from the annihilation she'd witnessed. The pipe had showed her the memories of the hundreds of men, women, and children who had died.

"I didn't know." She choked the words out.

Roan stroked her hair. "I'm sorry. I should have shut the door."

Parker came rushing to the doorway with Holly right behind him. "What happened? Mel?" he asked, alarmed.

"She touched something," Roan said firmly. "Give us a minute."

Melicent was too devastated to care that she was making a scene. The room was spinning; her sense of gravity was gone. The muscles in her stomach cramped and she thought she might be sick.

"Please give us a minute," he ordered, sounding short. Holly ushered Parker back to the front of the store.

Roan took both of Melicent's hands and rubbed them between his, the friction of his gloved fingers hot on her skin. "Melicent, listen to me. You've had a shock. I'm going to show you a finger position to help calm you. It's called a mudra."

Melicent shook her head, unable to make sense of what he was talking about.

He took both of her hands and molded them together. Then he joined the tips of her little finger and ring finger and pointed everything to the floor. Both his hands controlled hers as he sculpted them into the intricate hand position.

"Focus on the feeling of energy flowing out of your body, through your hands and to the floor." His voice sounded sure. She didn't question what he was telling her to do. His hands became anchors around hers, rebuilding the floor she was standing on.

Her breathing began to slow and she could feel her pulse calming as he kept talking.

"Focus on your hands and your breath. That's it. In and out . . . breathe in and out." He stood with her, continuing to cup her hands and adopting the same stance until they were breathing in unison.

Through his breath and body, she could feel him giving her his strength. A powerful bond had been forged between them and she began to understand why he was helping her. She was starting out on a path, one that he was far, far ahead of her on, but they both shared the same ability, and he understood its dimensions and pitfalls.

Within minutes she could feel her equilibrium returning. She opened her eyes to find Roan watching her. He lifted a hand and trailed his fingers down the side of her face.

"Better?"

"Yes, thank you," she whispered, her voice hoarse. She looked down at her hands, still keeping them locked. "What is this?" She raised her arms and studied how each of her fingers were connected. It'd actually helped.

"The Shakti mudra. Think of it like meditative yoga for the hands. Shatki is the *essence of power* gesture. You use it when you need to rebalance your energy quickly."

She nodded, even though she secretly hoped she'd never need to use it again. She looked down at the pipe lying innocently on the table. "What was it I saw?"

"December 29, 1890. The massacre at Wounded Knee, South Dakota. Many of the things here belong to the Lakota Sioux who died that day."

Melicent wrapped her arms around herself and shivered. She

looked down at the tables, at the children's toys, unable to hide her repulsion. "Why are you collecting such things?"

He glanced back at her with surprise. "I'm not. I'm returning them. These are heirlooms that belong to the descendants of those who survived." Roan stared at the tables, an intense light entering his eyes.

"But the memories they hold . . ." *Who would want them?* was the question she wanted to ask but didn't.

Roan picked up the pipe Melicent had touched. "This medicine pipe has been passed down by the Lakota for generations and holds infinite stories. The tragedy at Wounded Knee is only one imprint. Your mind went to the most violent one—and the last. But this pipe has celebrated the sacredness of every day and every life on earth for hundreds of years. It holds the Lakota's history and is much too important to stay lost."

He held it out to her, explaining its design. "The four ribbons represent the four corners of the Universe. The eagle feather tells us the four are truly one—one spirit, *the Great Spirit*—and our thoughts should soar higher than an eagle. And these twelve feathers," he said as he moved his hand across the line of dangling feathers underneath, creating a rippling effect, "are the cycles of the twelve moons." He looked down at the pipe. Melicent could tell he'd seen every memory it held.

Then he said something in Lakota.

Goose bumps rose on her arms. He had spoken the words that were embedded in the pipe. "What does that mean?" she whispered.

"*Only the hands of the good shall take care of it and the bad shall never see it.*" Roan sat the pipe gently back down on the table.

For a moment she couldn't say anything. The weight of the room was pressing on her. She wanted to leave, but couldn't, trying to understand. She turned to him. "So you've been finding these lost heirlooms of the Lakota?"

"I work in groups, periods of time in history, geographical

location. There are other collections at the warehouse. Holly's focusing on returning these right now, so we moved the Lakota artifacts over here." He led her out of the room and closed the door.

Melicent frowned, realizing, "So *this* is the Heirloom Foundation, the nonprofit organization that returns lost heirlooms to people?"

His eyebrows rose. "You know about the foundation?"

"I looked up West, Inc. and it's linked to Holly's name." She signaled to the closed door. "So this is the other half of your business?"

He nodded. "I try to give back in small ways. I can't just make money off of what I do."

A flush of shame hit her. She'd never once considered using her gift to help others. Granted, she was nowhere near Roan's level of expertise, plus he'd been finding relics his whole life. But suddenly she felt embarrassed—by everything—by her assumptions of him in the beginning, how she'd judged him for leading a life of wealth and privilege. He was a lone psychometrist willing to face the darkness to help lost treasures find their way home. The poignancy swallowed up her heart. Roan was unlike anyone she'd ever met.

After they left the back room, Roan finished the introductions between Melicent and Holly. Melicent didn't know what to make of Roan's partner. Holly Beauchêne wasn't the warmest person, and Melicent had a hard time seeing past the facade. Holly was too polished, too poised—too Southern. Not a speck of makeup was out of line, not a hair out of place. A woman who used that much hairspray must have issues.

What in the world did Holly and Roan have in common? A love for antiques?

Melicent wasn't sure if she could like her, but right now she was too dazed to worry about it. Roan whisked her and Parker back into the car. Soon they were dining at a restaurant in the French Quarter, under vaulted ceilings and slow-turning ceiling fans, and looking at the picturesque view of Royal Street from the patio doors. Thankfully the traumatic memories from the heirlooms had begun to recede into the back of her mind.

Roan recommended they all order the restaurant's signature gumbo. Melicent smiled vacantly during the waitress's culinary trivia talk about how "in New Orleans the Holy Trinity is two parts onion, one part celery, one part bell pepper, and garlic is 'the Pope.'" Melicent must have *tourist* written all over her face.

After the waitress left she asked Roan, "So does your psychometrist friend in London help you with the foundation?"

Roan shook his head. "Stuart and I met through my mother. We're rock climbing buddies."

Parker jumped into the conversation. "No way! That's so cool. You rock climb?"

"I like to boulder," Roan said.

"Wicked." Parker was impressed. "That's where you don't use ropes, right?"

Melicent looked at Roan, wide-eyed. "Isn't that dangerous?"

Roan shrugged. "On certain ascents. But I've been doing it since I was a kid."

"Where do you climb?" Parker looked utterly fascinated. Roan was quickly becoming his new favorite person.

"All over. Stuart and I meet several times a year and take turns picking the spot . . . trying to one-up each other on finding the hardest climb. We were supposed to meet in Texas and he didn't show."

Melicent could see his worry. She hoped his friend was all right. "We want to go to London with you."

"We do?" Parker turned to her in shock.

Melicent shot him a look that told him to keep quiet. "I want to know what's going on with this psychometrist group. I can't just sit and wait in a hotel room."

"You're not going." Roan shook his head.

"I am going," she said adamantly. Roan leaned back in his chair, crossing his arms.

Parker chimed in, "I don't want to go either."

Melicent turned to Parker in surprise. "Why don't you want to go to London?"

Parker shrugged, looking weary. "I just want to stay at the hotel and sleep."

Melicent's heart sank. She understood why he wanted to be alone. They were both processing losing the house in their own way. But the thought of staying cooped up in a hotel room while Roan tried to figure out who had destroyed her house was downright torturous to her. She needed to go. That Parker didn't want to was a complication. "You can't stay at the hotel by yourself," she said as the waitress came and delivered their gumbos. "You have to come with me."

Roan reiterated, "You're not going."

Parker ignored him. Her brother knew her well and could tell she was dead set on going. Parker pointed out, "Two or three days at a hotel is nothing compared to summer camp, and I've been doing that for years. Please? I promise I'll stay put."

Melicent mulled over the idea. Parker had been doing summer camp for years and had been left alone at the house for a weekend too. She knew he'd be okay. The unspoken question was, *No running away?*

She searched his eyes. "You promise? You're sure you'll be okay?"

Parker nodded. "Can I do pay-per-view while you're gone?"

"Oh my gosh, people, you're not coming with me!" Roan erupted. The frustration in his voice was comical.

"Yes I am," she threw back, ignoring the sound of Parker snickering into his gumbo.

"You're not going," Roan said for the fourth time. "Am I talking to a wall?"

"Why are you being so stubborn?"

"Why are you?"

She tried to make him see reason. "I'll just get my own plane ticket and meet you over there."

They stared at each other, at an impasse. Melicent had to admit, she was enjoying the argument. It was waking her back up, making her feel alive again. Their mental tug-of-war felt primal, like a circling dance.

She spelled it out clearly for him. "This is my life. I need to be in control of it. To do that I have to find out what is going on. I need to go with you. I refuse to stay here and be babysat." *By Holly,* she wanted to add but didn't. Roan's business partner hadn't seemed too thrilled by the idea either.

Roan let out a pained sigh and ate his gumbo. Melicent watched him, noting his gloves were still on. He must never take them off.

Ignoring her food, she waited for him to look up at her. She'd eat when she won the argument. The fierce determination in her stare communicated without words, *I'm going and there's no stopping me.* To drive it home she sat up straighter and flicked her hair behind her in defiance. His eyes flashed in response and she knew she'd won.

"Your gumbo's getting cold," he said, then he added, "And it's freezing over there. You'll need a winter coat."

Melicent nodded, triumphant, and looked down at the decadent bowl filled with seafood, okra, and a perfect scoop of rice in the center of a thick, dark roux. She should have been ravenous but instead her stomach was a jumble of nerves.

Tomorrow she was going to London.

21. THE DOLL

THE NEXT MORNING ROAN SAT behind the wheel of his car and watched Melicent leave the hotel lobby with a small overnight bag. She had a bright purple winter parka in her hands and a long muffler. He was pleased to note she'd bought a pair of winter boots.

She walked in front of his car, fully aware he was watching her, and flicked her hair back behind her shoulders in that alluring way of hers.

Roan mumbled to himself, "This was a bad idea." He couldn't believe he'd let her talk him into coming. She was a complete distraction. He'd never been so hyperaware of someone before. It'd be so much simpler if she had stayed at the hotel while he focused on finding Stuart.

When she got in the car there was a moment of silence, then he asked, "Are you sure Parker will be okay on his own?" Roan had no problem if she wanted to change her mind about going. Then maybe he could sleep on the nine-hour flight to Heathrow.

"It's only a few days. And he wants some alone time. I'm going." She stared at him, determined.

Roan's eyes traveled over her face. She looked just like she had in his favorite imprint, framed by the sunlight. His resistance was starting to melt. Right now he wanted nothing more than to lean over and kiss her. Instead he put the car into drive with a sigh and drove them to the airport.

"Thank you for the flowers," she said. "It was a sweet gesture, but . . ." *But odd,* is what she was getting at. "You didn't have to."

"I wanted to." He hesitated, abashed at having to explain. "They read the room better than anything."

"What do you mean, read the room?"

"Flowers are the most sensitive imprint holders. The imprint's gone when they die, but while they're alive they pick up everything around them."

"So you're spying on me with flowers?" she asked with an incredulous voice.

"God, no." He choked out a laugh. "I'm not spying on you." He may have replayed the imprint of her making the snow globe countless times in his head, but that was one imprint. "I'm not planning to touch the flowers unless I have to. It's for peace of mind. What if something happened to you two at the hotel while I'm not there? How would I know or be able to find you?"

She didn't respond and he glanced over to gauge her expression. Her eyes were bright with emotion. It was the last thing he was expecting.

"Jesus, Melicent. I'm sorry."

"No." She stopped him. "It's just . . . thank you. For caring. I haven't been able to think straight since the fire," she confessed. "I'm sorry if I overreact or jump to the wrong conclusion." She rubbed her forehead.

Roan glanced over at her again. She looked more tired than she let on. "Have you gotten any more news about the house?"

"No." She shook her head and he watched a shadow fall on her face. "I checked in with the investigators this morning. They have nothing."

Roan's thoughts returned to the man in the hoodie. Why had he done it? How was he involved with the ooparts? He hoped London offered answers.

They finished the rest of the drive to Lakefront Airport in silence. They checked in and were escorted to the plane, a Gulfstream GIII that sat eight. When they got on board, Melicent took the second seat on the right. The configuration was a single row on each side of a center aisle. Roan took the seat across from hers.

The pilot stuck his head out of the cockpit to greet them and said they'd be taking off shortly. The galley was fully stocked and they were welcome to help themselves.

"And we have your special request," the pilot said, winking, and went back up front.

Melicent turned to Roan with questioning eyes. "What special request?"

Roan went over to the little galley. "Even though we're about to fly out, you can't come to New Orleans without having Café Du Monde in the morning." He poured them each a coffee and brought over a cardboard box. Inside were decadent-looking pastry puffs, shaped like squares and liberally dusted with powdered sugar.

"The beignet," he said, offering her one.

Melicent looked touched by the gesture. The expression on her face made him glad he'd made the request. He watched her savor the rich chicory coffee and French doughnut. She put away not two but three of the squares along with two cups of coffee. They were well in the air and at cruising altitude when she finally leaned back, done with breakfast. "Thank you. That was so delicious."

There was a lull of comfortable silence. For a moment their worries on the ground were at bay.

"You know—I have a question," she said. He looked at her expectantly and waited as she tried to find the words. "Who helped you? When I touched the pipe, you helped me come back. Who helped you, when the same thing happened the first time?"

Roan thought back to the first time an imprint had swallowed him up whole. He'd been twelve. Through the years he'd tried to block the whole experience from his mind, but when he thought on it, it still felt like yesterday. "My mom. I touched the wrong thing and she found me."

His mother had found him unconscious, unable to speak or move. She and his father rushed him to the hospital. The doctors couldn't find the cause and thought it was a seizure, but his mother knew he had touched something so horrible it had shut his body down. She searched his room until she found the object.

"What was it?" Melicent whispered.

Roan barely heard the question, lost in the memory. "A doll I found at a flea market. It was beaded, made of hide, from the Old West . . . or so I thought." He smiled bitterly. "I'd started wearing gloves the previous year and preferred to read imprints in private away from people. I took it home and that night I got it out in my room."

He swallowed, unsure if he could describe what had happened. He'd never tried before. "Up until then it was more like a game to me, peering into the past like a spy through a window. I would go looking for old, unusual things at flea markets with my dad. He was always on the hunt for treasure and had grand schemes to open up a family business."

"West, Inc.," she said.

Roan looked at her and gave a faint nod. "But this was different. This doll held so much despair it choked me." He shook his head, trying to brush past the worst of it. "That night I was delirious, trapped in the imprint, talking in my sleep. My mom thought it was a bad nightmare, but then I went into a coma for three days. I was in the hospital. My father stayed by my bedside while my mother went to the library to figure out what the doll was. She was able to trace it based on my sleep talking. She wanted to find its history so she could explain it to me and bring me back."

"What was it?" Melicent hesitated. "The doll?"

"The doll had belonged to a girl named Henney," he said. His voice still caught when he said her name even after all these years. "Her mother had made it for her. Henney was a girl brought by ship to New Orleans in 1800. She was from a small village in Africa. Captured by slavers and thrown on a boat with strangers for seventy days. She used to dream of dying in her sleep." His eyes met hers. "My mother spent days researching the U.S. Customs slave manifest historical records, trying to find her. Henney was separated from her family, sold to a plantation." Decades later, Roan could feel the same feeling of bleakness well up inside him, threatening to take over. He could never forget Henney. He brought his hands into a soothing Yoni mudra, joining his thumbs and index fingers to redirect his energy.

Melicent's eyes went to his hands in question.

He held his hands up to her, keeping his fingers locked in the position. "That was the first time we tried the mudras. My mother was desperate to help me expel that memory. She would sit there with me and hold my hands in the positions, with my fingers in hers, breathing with me."

"Like you did with me," Melicent said, her eyes soft with understanding. She knew how it felt to be lost within a life that was not your own.

"Then I came back." Roan released his hands from the finger lock.

"Your mom sounds like an amazing woman."

Roan gave her a half smile. That was one way of describing his mother. That doll was the beginning of the end for Roan's parents' marriage. They separated the following year because of the incident. His parents didn't need to see a marriage counselor to figure out Roan was the reason they could no longer stay together. They couldn't agree on what was the right course for their son and his extraordinary gift. Roan's mother wanted him to stop peering into the past altogether, while Roan's father thought his son "had been put on this earth for a reason," and they needed to allow his ability to flourish. In the end, the solution meant living in separate houses with joint custody.

"Was that what made you start the Heirloom Foundation? The doll?"

Roan looked over at her and shook his head. He didn't know how to explain Gobekli Tepe, and he didn't want to get into too many details. "I was in Turkey visiting an archaeological site and touched something very old—too old—and I couldn't find my way out of the imprint. I don't know if it was the time span, the imprint itself, or the power within the site. But it felt like drowning. Afterward the whole experience made me reassess my life, my gift, everything. Our time here is finite, and I wanted to make mine count for something, something more than myself. It's always moved me how so many memories from generations of a family can exist in a single object. It became a passion of mine to find the lost ones."

She nodded in understanding. "How do you return them? How does it work?"

"I trace the imprints back to the original owner. Once I have that information, Holly and I work with both a genealogist and an online investigator to track down the descendants. After they're located, Holly usually writes to them first and follows up with a phone call saying that a lost heirloom of their family has been traced back to them." Roan smiled. "Many times they think it's a scam at first, too good to be true. But Holly has her ways."

Melicent gave him a faint smile.

"If it's a rare or high-value item, she flies out and hand delivers it. Otherwise we use a private courier and arrange a delivery time."

His most recent recipient, Faye Young, was the rightful owner of a high-value heirloom that was part of the Lakota collection. Roan had insisted on Holly hand delivering it. Faye was the great-granddaughter of Edith Brown, a Lakota medicine woman who was the keeper of the winter count, her tribe's recorded history.

The winter count was a piece of animal hide that looked like a blanket. Every winter the tribe would capture the essence of their year in a picture and paint it on the hide. The symbol represented the whole community and their recorded history. Edith's great-grandmother had been the keeper of the winter count, and her tribe's hide stretched back hundreds of years.

All Faye knew was that the foundation had traced the artifact back to her family and was returning it to the rightful owner. As a proud Lakota descendant of the Sioux Nation, Faye planned to donate the winter count to the Sioux Indian Museum in Rapid City.

Holly had sent Roan a picture of Faye beaming to the camera as she held up the hide. When Roan stared at Faye's picture he could hear the echo of the Lakota's blessing. "Hetchetu welo," *it is indeed a good day.* The picture had filled Roan with a deep joy that wasn't entirely his own but also Edith Brown's. Edith's last hope before dying was that her people's record would not be lost.

"Returning heirlooms gives me a satisfaction that no amount of money can," he said. "Heirlooms keep the stories alive."

Melicent seemed to grasp what he was saying. She was leaning forward, listening intently with her elbow on the seat rest. "How did you become so good at reading things?"

Her question surprised him again. He wasn't used to anyone asking him about his ability. Even his mother had stopped years ago. He tried his best explain. "Growing up in New Orleans was like a wonderland, a training ground, being able to walk into any corner antique shop and pick up a bona fide piece of the past." He had held a cornet of Joe "King" Oliver's, Louis Armstrong's mentor, and heard the music; he'd touched the fence around Jackson Square and seen the hand of Micaela Almonesta Pontalba, the "Baroness of New Orleans," who conceived the cast iron design in 1851 after returning from France broken-hearted. He'd met Degas in his mind when the painter came to visit his cousins in 1872, and he overheard the conversation between the pirates Jean and Pierre Lafitte and Andrew Jackson at the blacksmith shop when they agreed to aid in the War of 1812 in exchange for their pardon.

"I saw what New Orleans was like before the city changed hands from the Spanish to the French to the Americans. I saw the settlers, the immigrants from Germany and Ireland building the channel by hand. I saw the slave rebellion."

New Orleans had been named the most haunted city in the country, the place where they said the dead and the living slept side by side with barely a wall between them. Through the imprints Roan had walked down the steamboat wharfs, visited the slaughterhouses, and watched the white flags from the plantations being raised on a pole beside the river to call the doctor when someone was sick. He visited the room where Étienne de Boré discovered how to granulate sugar, an invention that would change the city forever. Even without his ability Roan couldn't imagine living anywhere else. The city was his domain and he knew every inch of it, through every century.

"Is that why you wear gloves? To keep control?"

Roan looked down at his hands. Most of the time he forgot he had gloves on. They'd become like second skin. Today he was wearing his thinnest tactical Under Armour gloves. He owned countless pairs and brands, each for different activities. These were best for working at the keyboard.

"I don't want to wear gloves," she added.

"I didn't suggest it."

"But it helps you." Melicent considered him. "So you don't touch anything you don't want to."

Roan stared back her, seeing the concern in her eyes, and he could tell she was wary of what challenges might exist for her further down the road if she fully exercised her power.

The gloves did help him because, unlike most psychometrists, Roan could feel every imprint, from any time, with excruciating detail to the point the boundaries of the years blurred. Most psychometrists were limited with the information they could retrieve from an imprint. But Roan was a pure receiver with the rare ability to be transported into the memory. He'd stood in the past as the future's witness. There was no way he could explain some of the imprints he'd seen or the deep marks within history, gouges left by hatred and cruelty, over beliefs, power, and greed. Roan had witnessed tragic moments, the annihilation of life, from both world wars and the countless other conflicts that stretched further back. He'd seen how history was doomed to repeat itself until humanity acknowledged the deep connection between every living being. That was the true war, the war that never ended, and it had taken Roan many years to learn how to live in such a world. The gloves were his armor.

"You won't need gloves," he assured her, and he leaned toward her across the aisle, until their faces were a breath apart. He could see the pulse at her neck speed up. He wanted to touch her. He had since he'd walked into the store in L.A.

Here was a woman who shared his power, who'd begun to experience the thresholds that could be crossed. He'd never been able to have this kind of intimate conversation with anyone before, not even Stuart. He found himself wanting to share his world with Melicent and invite her in.

He searched her eyes. "I only touch what I want."

She met his gaze with a challenge. "Then do it."

Those three words unraveled his good intentions. Their lips came together in a lock, the connection between them tightening like a twisting coil. He could easily forget everything right now, where they were going, the why, the danger. His hands came up to frame her face with surprising tenderness, and it made them both pull back in surprise.

No words were needed. Now was not the right time. They made a silent agreement not to take the kiss further.

"You should get some sleep," he suggested.

"Right." Melicent nodded and leaned back in her chair. She closed her eyes but after a moment said, "About my snow globes. Did you really only touch the one?"

"Just the one."

"But you saw a lot more than what you told me, didn't you?" She pinned him with her eyes, knowing it was true. Then she surprised him by saying, "I get to touch something of yours. At your house."

He laughed, not sure he was willing to concede to that demand. "I'll think about it."

She shook her head and closed her eyes again. "I will. You owe me."

The retort died on his lips because he knew she was right. He had intentionally peered into her life without permission and seen things no one else knew, like a voyeur—or worse, a Peeping Tom. He would be lying if he said he wished he could undo the moment, because he wasn't sorry. What he'd done was more intimate than the kiss they'd shared. The problem was he wanted more.

As he watched Melicent doze off, he pulled out his lucky coin and rolled it across his knuckles back and forth in a soothing motion. His thoughts strayed to Stuart. Why hadn't he called? Who was after them? The group was being targeted one by one because of their research, and Roan needed answers. He wasn't sure what he would find at Stuart's home. He only prayed his friend was safe.

LONDON

ONE WEEK AGO

STUART WENT TO PAY FOR THE FLOWERS and wondered if he was overdoing it. He bought five arrangements on the brink of blooming. The shop owner promised they would live a long time. He hoped so—he didn't want to have to keep shelling out for daisies.

That morning at the post office he'd paid a fortune to express mail Hanus's key to Roan. Afterward he passed by the flower market on his way back to his flat, just as he did every morning, only this time he went inside. Roan had mentioned on one of their climbing trips how flowers were the best imprint holders. If it had been any other person, Stuart would have thought he was joking. But Roan didn't joke. He was also the best psychometrist Stuart knew.

Nestling the flowerpots in his carrying basket, he hurried back to his place two blocks away. Notting Hill in the morning was always a flurry. The breeze carried an inviting scent of roasted coffee and fresh-baked bread from the bakery down Portobello Road, but Stuart didn't stop.

Once he arrived home, he set the flowers in strategic positions, a pot in each room. Then he took his laptop and a rolled-up map and went to the built-in bookshelf behind the sofa. The shelf swung open when he found the secret latch, revealing a wall safe inside. The safe was a hidden gem, an architectural delight, and the place where he kept all his valuables.

Right now the safe only held his laptop and the map. He locked them inside, closed the outer cabinet, and moved the sofa closer to the bookshelf for good measure to hide the spot even more. Then he grabbed his keys and left.

After he'd gone, the flowers watched the room like a silent witness and the stillness stretched through the minutes. It wasn't until the day was done and the last sliver of sunlight had left the curtain's edge that the lock in the door jimmied and turned—only it wasn't the sound of a key.

Two men in ski masks and black attire stepped inside, blending in with the shadows. They used high-powered penlights to pierce the darkness as they searched the house, opening every cabinet and drawer with painstaking precision, careful not to leave a trace.

The sound of the key at the front door made them kill their lights.

When Stuart walked in, the larger of the two men grabbed him from behind and held him in an arm lock, clamping his hand over his mouth.

"Where are the ooparts?"

The other man shut the door behind them with an ominous click.

22. THE FLOWERS

ROAN KEPT HIS HAND on the daisies and expelled a shaky breath. He was deep in the imprint, trapped by the violence of the moment. He winced as he watched the man at the door punch Stuart in the stomach, doubling him over. Stuart struggled for breath, unable to talk.

"What is it? What happened?" Melicent asked, but her voice sounded muted and faraway to Roan's ears. He was trying to glean every bit of information he could from the flowers.

He'd found Stuart's spare key hidden in the faux rock in the garden. When he walked into the townhome, he'd been alarmed to find all the flowers. Stuart had been afraid enough to put an arrangement in every room.

He'd left them for Roan to find—of that Roan was certain.

Roan hadn't needed to touch a single flower to feel the disturbance in the air; the residue of hostility lingered like an electric charge. The flowers held the imprints in vivid detail.

He closed his eyes, needing to see every second. His focus was so sharpened, the present and the past fused together and he was standing beside Stuart in the memory.

The man at the door's voice was laced with a Hindi accent. "Where is your computer? And the artifacts?"

Stuart gasped for air. "Not here."

The large man squeezed Stuart's arms together behind his back and pulled him up. Stuart cried out in pain as the man punched him in the gut again. "We don't believe you."

Stuart pleaded, "I swear. I swear."

The man at the door put a hood over Stuart's face.

Stuart struggled, screaming in panic. His captor gave a swift jab to his temple, causing Stuart to crumple to the ground, unconscious. The man took out his cell phone and made a call.

"We have the package but not the goods. Possibly New York like you thought." He listened. "Yes, sir." He hung up and turned to his friend and switched to speaking Hindi.

They went back and forth in quiet voices as they waited by the blinds at the front window. The big man picked Stuart up and swung him over his shoulder. They slipped outside, disappearing into the night like two shadows that had never been there at all.

—

Roan opened his eyes and released his hold from the flowers to find his hand was shaking. He'd just witnessed Stuart's kidnapping.

So many thoughts raced through his mind at once. Stuart had bought the flowers on the same day he express mailed the key to him. Then the men had come for him.

Who had they called on the phone?

They wanted Stuart's research and the ooparts—and they believed someone in New York had them.

Sun.

Melicent interrupted his train of thought. "He bought the flowers for the same reason you did, didn't he? What did you see?"

Roan turned to look at her, unable to speak, and shook his head, his mind in a panic. He needed to call Sun and warn her, but first he needed to see if what Stuart had hidden was still there.

He hurried to the bookcase and found the latch.

"What are you doing?" Melicent watched, mystified, as the bookcase swung open like a cabinet to reveal the safe.

Roan closed his eyes and thought back to the numbers Stuart had used to open it: 81-2-81. He replicated the combination and the safe's door opened. The laptop and map were still there. "This is what the men were looking for."

"What men?" Melicent's eyes couldn't have been any rounder as she watched him take the laptop case and the poster tube and close the safe back up again. She had her arms crossed and her hands tucked in beside her. Roan could tell she was afraid to touch anything. *Just as well,* he thought. The hostility in the room was sickening.

Roan set the laptop and map down on the table. "I'll be right back. I want to check the bedroom. Watch the door. If it sounds like anyone is coming, don't make a noise and come get me."

Melicent nodded, cupping her mouth with shaking hands.

Roan tried to hurry. He didn't want to risk the men coming back. But when he walked into Stuart's bedroom, he stopped in shock.

The bedroom was a disaster, the bed a tumble of sheets and clothes, the nightstand littered with a collection of empty scotch bottles. Women's items filled two dressers—perfume, jewelry, hairbrushes, and makeup—all in piles like a rummage sale.

Roan had stepped inside a dervish. This wasn't an ordinary messy bedroom. This was a psychometrist's room, chock-full of memories. Roan didn't have time to touch everything to unravel what had happened, but he could feel Stuart's pain all around him like a time capsule filled with grief.

The restaurant menu sitting on the dresser drew his eye. It wasn't a take-out menu, but an actual menu with a leather-like vinyl cover and gold embossed letters. It had no business being there.

Roan quickly performed a Ksepana mudra to release the negative energy permeating the space so he could get an objective reading. He needed to capture the imprint quickly.

When he picked up the menu, both sides of it opened like a window.

⌒

Stuart was sitting in the back corner of the dimly lit Italian restaurant at a table for two, watching the rain. Rivulets ran along the glass pane and obstructed his view. Even though hard sheets were coming down outside he'd kept their plans for the evening.

A bottle of champagne sat on ice. The ring was in his pocket, and the words were memorized.

After he proposed to Nema he planned to serenade her in front of all these fine restaurant-goers. He was going to sing "Purple Rain" by Prince and had already tipped the waitstaff. The humiliation was worth it to watch Nema laugh and flash him that *I can't believe you did that* look.

He'd already asked Miguel to be his best man. Miguel was the one who'd introduced them two years ago, somehow knowing Stuart would find the archaeologist from Wales irresistible. They began dating shortly after.

Stuart had been boasting to everyone, including Nema, that she was going to be his wife one day. Now he was ready to make good on that promise.

He sat at the table for hours.

He tried calling her, convinced she'd gotten caught up at work. He ordered dinner to go and brought the menu with him so they could play restaurant at home. He promised the manager he'd bring it back. They were regulars.

The manager said of course and sent him on his way. But

when Stuart got home to a cold, empty house without any lights on he began to grow afraid.

The call from the hospital came minutes later as he stood in the kitchen. Stuart couldn't grasp what he was being told.

A fatal car accident in the rain. Blocks from the restaurant.

The voice on the other end of the line destroyed him. Stuart laid his head on the counter and the menu became his pillow as he wept.

She'd been on her way. To him.

⌇

Roan held on to the imprint . . . *Nema*. With blinding clarity, he understood Stuart's quest to unravel the ooparts' mystery. Stuart was trying to make his way back to Nema—to stop that day from happening. Stuart didn't want to see the imprints of the past, he wanted to *go back* to the past, for her. Somewhere along the way he'd gotten tangled up with the wrong people, who were now trying to stop him instead.

Roan took out his cell phone, pacing the room as he made a call to Sun. He needed to warn her about the men coming to New York and tell her what had happened to Stuart.

Melicent's safety in London was in question too. The men who'd taken Stuart had to be connected to the person who'd set fire to her house. He should never have brought her here and exposed her like this in the open. It had been a stupid and irresponsible thing for him to do. Stuart's abductors could even be watching the house right now. Melicent should have stayed in New Orleans with her brother. He needed to extricate her from this nightmare.

The call to Sun went straight to voicemail.

He expelled a frustrated breath. "Sun. You need to get out of New York." He hesitated, not willing to say anything more in case someone else listened to the message. He added, "I'm keeping the fan safe until I can return it."

He hung up and looked around the bedroom, a helpless feeling overtaking him. His friend was out there somewhere in desperate need. Roan couldn't go to the police—no one would believe him. His best course was to dig into Stuart's research and leverage what he found. He also had one of the ooparts as collateral. The men had been looking for Hanus's key and Descartes's ring.

Roan had the key and Gyan had the ring.

Gyan could well be the person behind all of this. The men who'd taken Stuart had been speaking Hindi.

Roan turned to find Melicent in the doorway. She was surveying the room, taking in the disarray.

"Let's go." He took her hand in his without thinking. The touch of her palm hit him like a jolt and his fingers wrapped around hers. Adrenaline coursed through him as he led her to the living room. "When we go outside, stay hidden behind me. If I tell you to run, run. Don't wait. Get in the first cab that you can and we'll meet at Paddington station."

Melicent nodded, trying to stay calm.

He dropped her hand and put his gloves back on, then he grabbed the laptop and map and led her out the door and locked it, all the while scanning the street.

Right now he needed to get her somewhere safe—somewhere out of London where he could study the laptop and the map while he figured out his next step in finding Stuart.

There was only one place he could think to go. He just hadn't intended for Melicent to have to meet his mother on this trip. Jocelyn Matthis wasn't the easiest person to handle and she would have a million questions for them both—questions he wasn't willing to answer.

23. THE PICTURE FRAME

THEY TOOK A TAXI FROM NOTTING HILL. Melicent knew Roan had seen something distressing while touching the flowers at Stuart's, that much was obvious. Now she was kicking herself for not touching the flowers too. She'd come to London for answers, but she'd frozen when she stepped inside the house. When she tried to ask Roan what he'd seen, he became evasive. He was brooding and staring out the cab window.

"Where are we going?" She finally broke the silence.

"Oxford."

"Oxford University, Oxford?"

He looked over to her. "My mother's a professor there. We'll stay the night with her."

"Oh." Melicent silently gulped. They were on their way to meet Roan's mother?

She remembered coming across the name of an Oxford professor in her initial online snooping—Dr. Jocelyn Matthis—who was on the Heirloom Foundation's board of directors. She was also a distinguished historian. Melicent never imagined the woman might be his mother. Dr. Matthis either must have kept her maiden name or changed it after the divorce.

The idea of meeting her made Melicent's stomach flutter with nerves. The scene at Stuart's had been unsettling enough, now she was about to meet the mother of her potential boyfriend—if they survived this.

Melicent wanted to ask who the men were that wanted Stuart's laptop, but she didn't want to get into it in front of the cabdriver. Plus, she was pretty sure Roan would sidestep the question. The man was forming the habit of trying to protect her.

She sighed and looked out the cab window, unable to marvel at the fact that she was in a taxi in London, a city she'd always wanted to visit, with a man she'd love to get to know under normal circumstances. But nothing was normal anymore. Her previous life was gone, and she still wasn't ready to revisit that pain or accept the loss.

Right now, there was nothing more she'd rather do than reach over and hold Roan's hand again and enjoy a simple cab ride. But Roan didn't hold hands, and his were once again encased in thick leather. She'd seen the surprise on his face back at Stuart's when he'd taken her hand without putting his glove back on first. And it'd occurred to her that he was afraid to hold her hand—or anyone's hand for that matter. Someone had hurt him in the past, broken his trust, and he was afraid to let anyone do it again.

She didn't know how she knew that truth. Either it was her ability assisting her, or woman's intuition, or both. Whatever the reason, Roan's gloves were back on, and she wasn't sure when they were coming off again.

She tried to distract herself by looking out the window at the city as they headed to the station. When she thought of London, she hadn't expected to see all the canals or boats in the water. The atmospheric waterways looked like havens tucked within the city, surrounded by Victorian warehouses and charming waterside restaurants.

When they reached Paddington station they had some time before their train, so Melicent asked to go to platform one to see the Paddington Bear statue. She couldn't pass through Paddington station without seeing it. As a child she'd sat on her mother's lap reading about the little bear from Darkest Peru.

Seeing the life-size statue of Paddington sitting on his suitcase gave her the impulse to touch the sculpture. Perhaps she could sense an imprint from the artist who had made it—or even the author, Michael Bond. The writer must have come to see this work of art inspired by his stories. The bronze statue would be the first object she'd intentionally tried to read since the toy horse and the peace pipe. Paddington Bear seemed like a good place to start.

"You don't want to touch that," Roan warned her, breaking her concentration.

Melicent turned to him, her hand in midair. "Why, is there a negative imprint in it?"

"No, there's a piece of gum stuck to the side of the hat." He nodded.

Melicent leaned down to look, and sure enough there was a sticky wad of goo right where her hand had been about to go. "Thank you," she said wryly. Perhaps the universe was trying to tell her something.

Roan gave her a smile that didn't quite reach his eyes; his attention was now fixed on something else.

Melicent turned to see what he was looking at and caught sight of the little girl, no more than five years old. She was standing alone like a scared animal afraid to cross the road as tears streamed down her face.

The little girl was lost.

Roan was already walking toward her with purposeful strides, taking off his right glove as he approached. Melicent hurried to follow.

Roan bent down on one knee to match the little girl's height. "Hello, have you been looking at Paddington? I was just showing him to my friend here." He motioned to Melicent behind him, who found herself nodding and smiling to alleviate the girl's fear.

The little girl looked at them both through her tears.

"My name's Roan and this is Melicent." Roan held out his bare hand for a proper handshake, and the little girl shook it. "We're visiting from out of town. Do you know the story of Paddington?"

Melicent stared at their joined hands in fascination. Roan had his other hand by his side tucked in some kind of mudra.

The little girl nodded. "He's a very brave bear from Peru who loves honey."

Roan continued to hold her hand. "I bet you're as brave. Do you know where your mother is?"

"No, and I've gone all over looking. We're visiting my auntie who just had a baby."

"Would you like me to try a magic spell to find her?" he asked her. The little girl nodded vigorously. He said, "All you have to do is count to ten and picture your mother in your mind. Can you do that?" Roan continued to hold her hand while the girl counted. Melicent had no idea what he was doing.

"Did it work?" the little girl asked when she was finished.

"Absolutely." He took out a pen and notepad from his bag and began to write. He tore off the piece of paper and handed it to her. "Take this paper over to the policeman at the end of the platform. See him over there?" Roan pointed out the man in uniform. "Show him the paper and he'll call your mommy for you."

"Is this really mummy's telephone number?" The girl looked at Roan in wonder. "Are you from Hogwarts?"

"Something like that." He winked at her. "Now hurry on. I'm sure your mother's worried."

Without saying goodbye, the little girl took off running through the throng of people to the policeman at the end of the platform. Roan stood up and put his glove back on and waited until she handed the note to the officer. When the officer took the paper and began to call the number, Roan turned away.

"Let's go." He walked in the opposite direction and disappeared into the crowd.

Melicent hesitated, riveted by the sight of the little girl taking the officer's phone. The expression on the girl's face transformed from one of fear into a portrait of light when she heard her mother's voice.

Melicent felt a pang in her heart as if it had been broken and then repaired at the same time. Roan had helped the little girl find her way home.

⌒

Melicent didn't say a word for most of the hour-long train ride to Oxford. She stared out the window as the train sped through suburban London and left the industrial sprawl for a picturesque English countryside.

The depth of Roan's ability was beginning to boggle her mind. He had scanned that little girl like a hard drive, expertly extracting the precise information he'd needed.

How had he retrieved the mother's phone number? Had he replayed a memory of the girl hearing or seeing it? And what was the mudra that he had made with his left hand?

She noticed Roan read imprints with his right hand too, which meant he was left-handed. Maybe her ability would have been more developed by now if she had not suffered a lifetime of second-guessing which hand to use. Would she ever be able to perform such a feat?

If Roan thought her silence unusual he gave no indication. Or perhaps he understood. He had his eyes closed; his arms were folded with one hand on his face and two fingers against his forehead, casting shadows on the frown on his face. His gloves were back on.

Melicent used the time to study him while he napped. His

large frame barely fit in the space. This was a man who'd been reading imprints since he was a small child, peering into the nooks and crannies of the past. If he held her hand, could he go back and see her life? Press rewind and return to any time? Was her biological body just a sum of information, a walking accumulation of every moment she'd ever experienced, collected and encoded? Is that all DNA was?

Roan opened his eyes and caught her gaze. They looked at each other for a suspended moment. "What are you thinking about?" he asked.

"*You.*" She watched his eyes widen in surprise. They were sitting together like any other couple on a train, a hand's touch away, an inch from a kiss. She wanted to know about his life. "When did you realize you had your ability?"

"When I was five."

Her eyebrows rose. *That was young.* "How did it happen?"

"My parents and I were on a family vacation to Disneyland and we stopped at an outdoor flea market. My mom was rummaging through boxes of books and my dad was browsing a stall of musical instruments." He got a faraway smile on his face as he remembered. "I tugged on his pant leg and asked him who Roy Rogers was."

A surprised laugh escaped her.

Roan caught her eyes. "My father laughed too. He said, 'The King of the Cowboys a long time ago.'" Roan extended his hand, showing her. "I had my hand around the neck of a guitar that was propped up on a stand, and I told him, 'Roy Rogers's name was really Leonard Slye. This was his guitar before he was famous.'"

Melicent was hanging on to every word. How she would have loved to see Roan at age five reading the imprint of Roy Rogers's guitar.

"My father knelt down and asked, how did I know? And I

said because of the story in the guitar." Roan met Melicent's eyes. "My dad asked me to tell him the story. So I told him how Leonard had moved from Ohio to live with his sister, Mary. He was shy but he tried out for a radio show. I knew all these things up until the time he was playing for the Rocky Mountaineers, the years before he became famous and changed his name."

"What did your dad think?"

"He was so flustered." Roan chuckled. "He bought the guitar for forty dollars. Then we went and found my mom. I told her too in the car. They didn't know what to think. My dad read a biography on Roy Rogers and confirmed all the things I knew about Leonard Slye in the 1920s and thirties. When we got back home to New Orleans, he found a guitar salesman who restored historic guitars. The restorer found 'L. Slye' had been written on the back of the neck and then polished off. A collector bought it from us for ten thousand dollars."

"Wow. So that was the beginning of West, Inc., Roy Rogers."

"Roy Rogers." Roan nodded. "My dad had been a struggling accountant up till then. He began taking me to antique fairs to see if what had happened with the guitar was a fluke. It wasn't. After that my parents rearranged their lives around my gift."

Now Melicent was about to meet one of those parents. Anticipation trilled through her.

⌒

When they arrived at Oxford rail station, Melicent stepped onto the street and looked around in wonder, never once having imagined she would be in Oxford, England. The first thing she noticed was the sea of bicycles parked by the station.

Roan guided her by the elbow past the taxis. "The house is close, just a half mile, near the university."

They walked toward the city center. With each step, the architecture began to transport her to centuries past, the curvature of the stones offering up a glimpse of their yesteryears. She found herself yearning to create a snow globe to capture the magic in the air.

"They call it the City of Dreaming Spires," Roan said. "The university was founded in the eleventh century. It's the oldest English-speaking university in the world. Some of the greatest minds have come here to study . . . Stephen Hawking, Indira Gandhi, Tolkien, Margaret Thatcher, Aung San Suu Kyi . . . Edwin Hubble." A little smile hovered on his lips with Hubble's name. "These buildings witnessed it all."

Melicent followed one step behind Roan, watching him stride down the street. He seemed energized by being in Oxford and knew his way around. In fact, he looked at home. She asked him, "What does your mom teach?"

"Cultural history."

She fell into step beside him. "The history of cultures?"

"Not exactly. It's more the study of beliefs and ideas across the world through time. Cultural history dissects how the past defines the present, everything from art, food, clothing, objects, customs, values, religion. It draws on anthropology and philosophy as well."

"Sounds serious."

"My mom's a serious lady." He gave her a rueful smile as he led her past an array of cafés and bars and a quaint-looking sign that said 17TH CENTURY HOTEL. They turned down a lane leading to a pocket of residential houses.

"Did you tell her we were coming?" It was almost evening and her stomach was grumbling. She didn't know what time zone her body was in anymore.

"Not exactly. I did leave a message."

So they were just showing up to his mother's without an invitation? That didn't sound good.

"All these homes were built in 1850 and have been beautifully restored," Roan said out of the blue. He motioned to the charming street like a polite realtor.

She couldn't help but wonder if he was getting nervous.

When they arrived at the Victorian townhome she watched him fish out his own keys from his pocket and unlock the door. He flipped on the lights and stepped aside to let her in. "She's probably tied up with a lecture. I'll see what I can cook us up for dinner."

Melicent's eyebrows shot up. He was going to cook for her?

He hung up their coats and beat a hasty retreat into the kitchen. Seconds later he called out, "Wine?"

"Yes, please." Never had a glass sounded more inviting. Here she was crashing his mom's house without an invitation. Was Roan going to tell his mother everything that was going on? Were they all going to powwow together over Stuart's laptop?

She rubbed her nose, knowing it was surely red from the cold. And she was still standing in the entry hall like an idiot. So much for Roan's abilities as a host. He'd vanished on her as if he was embarrassed to have brought her there.

She hung her muffler on the peg next to her coat and left her boots by the door. When she wandered into the room off the hall, the first things that struck her were the number of books and the musty smell from the dust.

The room held a dizzying array of wall-to-wall bookshelves that were filled to capacity with thick volumes and intimidating-looking tomes. Melicent skimmed the titles closest to her: *The Complete Works of Plato, The Histories of Herodotus, The Meaning of Relativity* by Albert Einstein, and *The Structure of Scientific Revolutions* by Thomas Kuhn. Merely reading the titles fatigued her. Along with the immense number of books, artifacts in glass cases were scattered about and a cluttered desk sat in the corner.

She'd just wandered into Dr. Jocelyn Matthis's study. If an historian could be compared to a mad scientist with a laboratory, this room would definitely fit the bill. Instead of beakers and vials it was words and relics. There was also something incredibly intimate about the space. There were no pin lights for the glass displays and the books all looked well worn and used—like they'd been read too many times.

Melicent turned toward the desk, and a lone photograph on the shelf caught her eye. At first she thought it was a picture of Roan, but it was his father. He had glasses on, his black hair was blowing in the wind, and his head was thrown back in laughter. The shot was a close-up, taken on a mountaintop with a ledge of rock and clouds visible on each side of the frame.

Melicent studied his profile. The jawline, the aquiline nose—everything about him was Roan. She reached out and picked up the metal frame to study the photo more closely.

The moment she held the picture in her hand she heard the music.

The song sounded far-off, playing in the distance. Then it began to gain resonance, like a radio in the room, and she recognized it as "Unchained Melody" by the Righteous Brothers.

Oh, my love, my darling, I've hungered for your touch

A long, lonely time . . .

Images and thoughts cascaded over the music. They'd been woven into the melody. Roan's parents had gotten married in New Orleans. It had been a boisterous celebration with a wedding parade down Bourbon Street and a second line brass band. The next day they'd flown to Mexico City for their honeymoon. Jocelyn had taken the photo of Robert right as the sun was rising on top of Popocatépetl, the most active volcano in Mexico and one of the highest mountains in North America. They'd camped overnight to catch the sunrise. Within the silence at the summit, they could feel the rumbling energy of the earth. There had not been an eruption since 1947, but they thought there might be another in their lifetime. They both agreed Roan was conceived that night.

The imprints within the frame poured into her. Melicent didn't know how long she stood there until she turned to find Roan standing in the doorway with two wineglasses in hand. Embarrassment flooded her cheeks and she put the picture frame back down.

"Your father's picture," she said, stating the obvious and realizing she'd just witnessed some very personal memories.

"Yes." He came toward her to offer her the wine.

She murmured her thanks and turned back toward the picture, still unbalanced from the deluge of information it had imparted. "Have you touched this?"

Roan stared at the picture of his father and shook his head. "I don't touch my parents' things. It'd be infringing."

He hadn't meant to say it as a reprimand, but still she could feel a fresh flush on her face—she had infringed. It hadn't been intentional, but she'd seen private moments. Every anniversary Jocelyn would play "Unchained Melody" to hear her wedding song. It's why the photo was so full of the music.

Melicent could feel the lingering emotions from the imprints squeezing her throat, taking away any words she might have said. Instead she took a sip of the wine. After reading the imprints, it felt like the lines of Jocelyn's life and her own had momentarily blurred, and the wedding song was an echo in the room that would never fade.

Roan had a closed look on his face. "They were complicated. They divorced when I was thirteen." It was obvious he didn't like talking about it. "Some people aren't meant to be together even if they want to be. Life gets in the way."

Melicent looked up at him and realized he wasn't just talking about his parents. She set her wine down and took a step toward him. "I disagree."

His eyes darkened. "Melicent," he said in warning.

Ignoring the caution in his voice, she took the final step and kissed him, their mouths twisting in the dance that had begun on the plane and never stopped. His gloved fingers slipped around her waist and traveled up her back.

It was the sound of the front door opening that broke them apart.

Jocelyn Matthis stood in the foyer looking exactly as Melicent had imagined her, only now her hair was silver and her glasses were bigger. In her college years Jocelyn had been a philosophy major, a cutting-edge feminist, a wild child of the sixties and seventies, and then a wife in the eighties. When she'd gotten married she'd had cat-eye glasses and black hair, cut spiky short like Annie Lennox.

Jocelyn's sharp gaze took in the two of them, the wineglasses, the picture frame of her late ex-husband set ever so slightly off from where she had placed it last, and the stamp of the kiss on their faces.

"Why, hello." She raised both eyebrows and set down her briefcase. She shrugged off her coat. "When I asked you to come to dinner, Roan, I had hoped for advance notice." Jocelyn said it so cordially, Melicent couldn't tell if she was upset or not.

"I left you a message," Roan said.

"Well, I lost my phone. So I didn't get it." Jocelyn came forward, her hand already extended to shake Melicent's. "And you are?"

Roan spoke up first. "This is Melicent Tilpin, from Los Angeles."

"It's a pleasure to meet you, Melicent. And I bet you two were at Paddington station." Jocelyn didn't wait for confirmation and marched straight into the den and turned on the TV. "I'm sure they're airing it on a loop. It's the feel-good story of the day. Lord knows we all need one."

Roan and Melicent followed her into the den to catch the news story already under way. A female reporter stood beside the Paddington Bear statue.

"Is Sirius Black alive and well? A little girl from York seems to believe. Today, five-year-old Anna Montgomery was lost in Paddington station, where she said a man in all black from Hogwarts cast a spell to find out her mother's phone number and wrote it down on a piece of paper, allowing Anna to be reunited with her family. Anna's parents could not be more grateful to the mysterious stranger. Perhaps there is magic somewhere in the world."

Melicent watched the TV in fascination. They'd made the news. She looked at Roan and he gave her a little smile.

"So I take it that was you?" Jocelyn asked in exasperation, although she already knew the answer. "Roan, you shouldn't take risks like that. What if you had been identified? How could you have explained it?"

"No one saw me." Roan brushed off her concern. He took out his cell phone and opened up a tracking app. "And it says your phone is somewhere here in the house."

"Of course it is." She rolled her eyes. Roan tried calling it. She shook her head. "I'm sure the battery's dead. I'll never find it."

Roan smiled. "Always the pessimist."

"Realist. Now, tell me exactly what's going on. You can explain everything while you're cooking. And please put on some house slippers. The floors are chilly." Jocelyn sounded like a general, ordering them about. She brought two pairs of guest slippers from the entry hall closet and returned to her study to reset the photograph where it had been before. "Welcome to my home, Melicent. I'm sorry I wasn't here to greet you personally."

Melicent watched Jocelyn through the doorway and couldn't help but detect the censure in Jocelyn's voice that silently conveyed, *Don't touch my things.* Roan's mother knew he wouldn't dare touch the photograph. A blush rose in Melicent's cheeks.

If Melicent hadn't held the photo beforehand she would have been intimidated by the woman, but all she could think about was how incredibly lonely Jocelyn was underneath her brisk demeanor.

"So tell me what on earth is going on—start at the beginning." Jocelyn turned off the lights in her study, leaving Robert West's portrait to sit in the shadows with eyes that seemed to continue to see.

24. THE MAP

ROAN ATE WITHOUT TASTING A THING. At this point he barely remembered cooking the pasta. He tried to focus on the conversation at the dinner table as he brought his mother up to speed about Stuart, their failed meeting in El Paso, and the mysterious oopart delivery.

He underplayed everything, not revealing Stuart's abduction or Melicent's involvement. That would take all evening and require another bottle of wine between them. He could tell his mother had questions for him, too, about Melicent, the first person he'd brought to her doorstep. When they were out of this mess he could figure out what to do about his growing feelings for her. He didn't have to touch Melicent's wineglass to know that she was equally affected.

When they were done eating, Jocelyn turned on the TV to catch the evening news and Roan turned to Stuart's laptop, booting it up. Fortunately, he didn't need a password to log on. Stuart had been careless, but then he'd also thought his computer would stay locked up in his safe.

The three of them sitting at the dinner table with the TV on and Roan at the computer looked strangely domestic. Roan couldn't begin to guess what Melicent was thinking. The trip must have taken a surreal turn for her—here they were in Oxford having a spaghetti dinner with his mother in a dusty, cluttered Victorian house, while a stiff-upper-lip British news anchor went on about world events. Melicent probably thought Jocelyn rude for preferring the BBC over visiting with her. Then again, maybe after reading the imprints from the picture frame, Melicent understood that his mother didn't do small talk. He also should have warned her that Jocelyn was addicted to the news—specifically the BBC or CNN. The TV was always on.

One of the top stories tonight was about three dozen whales that had been stranded on Tysfjord's beaches in northern Norway. A female reporter was commenting, "Whale-watching season may have ended for the rest of Europe, but orcas abound in Tysfjord every winter through December, when the whales follow schools of herring into the fjords. However, this year something has gone amiss. The whales are ending up on the shores, scientists say, due to geomagnetic disruptions from solar storms."

Roan and Melicent both watched the report, and Roan couldn't help but think the ooparts could be categorized as a geomagnetic disruption too. They were just harder to find than a whale on a beach.

Roan turned back to the laptop and scrolled through Stuart's files. It would take time to go through them all.

Jocelyn was eyeing him. "So what exactly was Stuart working on with these out-of-place artifacts?"

Roan looked up from skimming the most recent project file. "From what I can tell, he's been tracking every oopart ever discovered . . . recording the time and place they originally existed in and when and where the objects were rediscovered. It's as if they're jumping through time."

Jocelyn gave Roan a stern look. "How is that possible? Jumping through time?" She peered at him over the rim of her glasses, looking every bit the discerning professor. "*What* are they? What are ooparts?" She even lowered the TV volume to hear the answer.

Roan hesitated. He'd been studying the mechanics of time all his life, but when it came to ooparts, he didn't have a clear picture of the phenomenon yet. The subject was the Bermuda Triangle of the archaeological world. Like crop circles, ooparts were either brushed off as a hoax, explained away, or ignored. But Stuart had dedicated the past several years to solving the riddle, and it had begun for him with Descartes's ring.

So how was a ring from a man born in France in the late 1500s found in Jordan buried in Cretaceous rock?

He glanced between the two women—Melicent was waiting for his answer too, and he attempted to explain. "Our physical reality is made up of 99.9 percent space. Our bodies and everything around us are, in essence, the leftover .1 percent, organized within a vast sea of energy. These out-of-place artifacts are jumping in and out of the electromagnetic boundary between our .1 percent and that space. If the ooparts on Stuart's list are legitimate anomalies, then the question becomes, have they been jumping into new locations and timelines with intention? Or is it random?"

Jocelyn nodded, pensive. Through Roan's ability she and her son had learned a long time ago that the impossible was possible.

He went on. "These ooparts could even be the result of a time-traveling experiment in the future. Right now we don't know. Which seems to be the question Stuart is trying to answer." Roan glanced back to the computer, toggling between files. Stuart had been unable to correlate all the ooparts' timelines together to find any pattern.

"And you say he's unreachable now?" Jocelyn asked.

Roan nodded, a knot in his stomach. He couldn't bring himself to tell her Stuart had been captured by the men who wanted his research. Jocelyn was the one who'd introduced Stuart to Roan in the first place; he was a family friend. Jocelyn had met the unorthodox archaeologist, a pioneer who paired psychometry with archaeology, and invited him to do several guest lectures for her students at Oxford. After Stuart's first lecture, she'd called Roan, insisting he had to meet him.

Roan had been surprised by the suggestion, knowing her and his father's opinion of allowing anyone to know about his abilities. It was the one thing the estranged couple had always agreed upon. Only Holly knew about his gift. His parents had kept Roan sheltered for most of his life.

Roan flew out to Oxford and sat in on a lecture to hear what Stuart Alby had to say. The outspoken Brit used his psychometric ability to survey archaeological sites, attempting to assess what had existed in the past at a location and what may be buried there. His success rate was good enough that he had earned a name in the field and worked with clients across the globe. He called what he did "intuitive archaeology."

Roan watched him explain with glee to a hall of rapt Oxford history students how reading bones was his specialty. He held up a femur to the class with a dramatic pause. "I can pick up a bone and gather the general facts of a person's life. I may not always get it right, but I get it right enough times to count. Because bones," Stuart said, "can tell you anything."

Roan listened, amazed that he had not only found another psychometrist, but a psychometrist who enjoyed the notoriety of being one.

"Using intuitives at digs," Stuart said, pointing to himself, "is a fringe idea and usually scoffed at by academia—the word *psychic* is even more taboo—and yet here I am at Oxford talking to you chaps, so I can't be too batty." The lecture hall broke into laughter. "Only one renowned archaeologist in Canada, Dr. Norman Emerson, from the University of Toronto, has ever officially shared his findings while working with a psychometrist on his digs. That was with George McMullen. Emerson and McMullen worked closely together for decades until Dr. Emerson passed away in the late seventies, but they had many successes."

He gave them an engaging smile. "I have found Byzantine

ruins, lost mosaics, buried columns, hidden statues, and even a stone labyrinth all with the power of my hands and my mind." He held up his hands to make his point. "Now, I love all the gadgets and technology just as much as the next archaeologist. I work with magnetometers, aerial thermal imaging. I rely on light detection, geophysics, and X-ray fluorescence spectroscopy. But there's something I can do that ground-penetrating radar simply can't, and that is to sense the ghost ship of the past that is sailing all around us." He opened his arms wide. "So don't be afraid to hop aboard."

The lecture ended to roaring applause. Roan introduced himself after the last student left. The instant camaraderie and connection between them was the start of a friendship that cemented quickly.

"My God. I hope he's all right." Jocelyn's eyes were bright. She got up to clear away the dishes. Melicent jumped up to help, but Jocelyn brushed aside her attempt.

Melicent abandoned her place at the table to study the laptop too and pulled up a chair right next to Roan, making a loud noise in the process. She pointedly ignored Roan's questioning look and leaned in to study the screen.

Roan could feel his mother's eyes on them. Jocelyn was wondering how in the world Melicent factored into all of this—a question he didn't want to answer.

He got up and opened the poster tube Stuart had hidden with his computer. Inside he found a map of the world with specific sites on every continent marked with bright yellow Xs. He unrolled it on the far side of the dining table. Melicent and Jocelyn joined him to look at it.

"So these Xs are all the ooparts he's sure about?" Melicent asked. There were over three dozen Xs circling the globe.

He noticed the frown on Melicent's face. "What is it?"

"I don't know." She blinked several times and rubbed her eyes to clear her vision.

Jocelyn noticed. "You must be tired. Why don't you both look at this with fresh eyes in the morning? How long will you be staying?" she asked him, appearing hopeful.

"Just tonight," Roan answered. "I've arranged for us to fly back to the States in the afternoon."

"And is it one or two bedrooms?" she tried to ask with non-chalance.

Only Roan could tell his mother was struggling to sound casual. Then he watched with fascination as Melicent's face bloomed a solid pink. Between her and his mother acting like Mary Poppins it made him want to laugh. "Two, please."

"Of course. Let me make up the beds."

"I'll help." Melicent hurried to follow her.

He watched the two head up the stairs. Melicent was saying, "You have a lovely home."

"I wouldn't say lovely. I haven't dusted in years."

Roan shook his head to himself as they disappeared. Poor Melicent. Not many people tried to strike up conversation with the prickly professor.

Jocelyn had bought the house ten years ago when she first moved to Oxford, intending to stay in England for good. When she crossed the ocean, Jocelyn left her previous life in New Orleans behind. Roan was always the one who had to travel to see her. And she preferred not to know if her son was still using his abilities. She'd made her stance on that clear after Turkey. She believed that Roan's gift would one day kill him.

His mother might not approve if she discovered Melicent was like him—even worse, Melicent had peered into the private recesses of her life.

He'd stood riveted in the doorway watching the expressions on Melicent's face as she experienced the imprints within the picture frame. He would have loved to ask her what she'd seen, but that wouldn't be fair to his mother. Melicent had overstepped by touching that photograph—but she hadn't thought about the consequences. That kind of understanding and foresight could only come with time and experience. Creating boundaries was something she would have to learn.

Roan sighed and went back to studying the computer and the map, trying to understand what it was that Stuart had discovered. And he couldn't ignore the feeling festering inside him that if only he'd helped when Stuart asked him years ago in Colorado, then his friend wouldn't be missing now. Stuart had shared his findings with the wrong person.

Roan was anxious to hear back from Sun. He also needed to find out more about Gyan. Gyan might be the key to all of this. He looked back at the list of files still left to go through.

A file named "Circles" made him sit up straighter with an edge of excitement. He'd just found Miguel and Stuart's research on crop circles.

25. THE BOOK

"ARE THESE YOUR BOOKS?" Melicent recognized the titles of Jocelyn's work on the guest bedroom bookshelf. Jocelyn had authored two theoretical history books, *Chasing History* and *The History of Time.* A dozen copies of each were perched on the shelf.

"Those would be mine," Jocelyn said dryly, busy making up the spare bed.

"May I?" Melicent asked.

"Of course." Jocelyn gave her a tight smile and went to the door. "There's fresh towels in the bathroom and bottled water downstairs. Please help yourself. Good night."

That was the extent of the conversation. Jocelyn was not in the mood to visit. All Roan's mother probably wanted to know was how Melicent knew her son and if they were sleeping together.

At this point Melicent was too tired to worry about what Jocelyn thought of her. She was too tired to even shower. She could do that in the morning.

Instead she brushed her teeth and changed into her pajamas. In New Orleans she'd bought long underwear and a long-sleeved shirt to match, the kind that could be worn under ski gear. Thermals had seemed the best bet for England in December, and she was glad she'd gotten them. The house had a frosty nip to it, just like the professor.

She crawled into bed with one of Jocelyn's books and for a moment simply enjoyed the luxury of the feather comforter. Then she reached over for her purse on the nightstand and grabbed her cell phone to call her brother.

He answered on the first ring. "Hey, you okay?"

"That's funny." She smiled. "I was calling to ask you the same thing."

"How's London? Did you find anything?"

"Some. I'll fill you in when we're back. We should be there by tomorrow night. You staying put at the hotel?" she asked, unsure whether he would think her return was a good thing. The truth was that ever since she'd discovered her brother had been planning to run away she didn't know what to say to him.

For a moment neither said anything.

"Mel, I'm sorry."

She expelled a breath, feeling tears coming on. *There.* He'd finally opened a door to discuss it. Of course he'd waited until she was thousands of miles away.

"For what? Planning to leave me?" Her voice broke.

"It wasn't like that." He pleaded, "I didn't want to be a burden to you, for you to have to take care of me."

"Was I complaining?"

"You didn't have to. I knew you didn't want to come back home. I knew how much you were struggling. Then Mom died and we were gonna lose the house—"

"Were you even going to get in touch? Let me know you were safe?"

"I hadn't thought that far ahead." His voice wobbled and he broke down. "I just miss her so much."

Warm tears slipped from her eyes. "I miss her too, Park," she whispered.

"I'm sorry," he said.

"I love you. We're going to stick together." Nothing more needed to be said. When she returned they could begin to rebuild their lives.

After they hung up, Melicent closed her eyes, suddenly feeling alone and far away, like a planet out of orbit hurtling through space. She wanted to go back with Parker and be in their mother's home. She wanted to make snow globes and run Tish's shop, even though on some days it drove her crazy. But none of that was possible anymore. The fingerprint of her life no longer matched what it used to be. Parker was all she had left, and Roan had unknowingly helped tear down the invisible wall that had stood between them, which she hadn't known existed.

In the months before and after her mother's funeral Melicent had sought out her mother's things and touched them for comfort, worn Sadie's favorite sweater, handled all her treasured knickknacks sitting out on the countertops and tables. But Melicent had never once thought to touch Parker's things—to sense how he was on the inside. Roan had held her brother's wristband and learned more about him than she had in years. What if she had thought to reach out sooner, to connect with him on a deeper level, to look past the surface? Maybe Parker wouldn't have felt like he was such a burden.

Roan knew how to look beyond the facades people wore to get to the inner truth. He'd seen past her facade, on that first day when he walked into the shop. He'd seen her. And he knew her.

She replayed their last kiss in the study, wondering what he thought, how he felt. She wished she knew.

And why hadn't he mentioned her involvement in this whole situation to his mother? Or that she was a psychometrist too? Melicent was following his lead by staying mute on those details. But doing so stung. Jocelyn must be assuming she was some starry-eyed groupie. The whole idea put her in a foul mood.

With a sigh she opened up Jocelyn's book *Chasing History* to see what Roan's mother had to say about the subject since her son had been doing it his whole life.

The first chapter, "The Future of History," began with Jocelyn making the claim that the seat of recorded history would transfer to the realm of neuroscience, genetics, and physics. Current recorded history was selective and subjective, "the argument without end," but it was objects that held the objective past—with no judgment, no bias, no editing, no censure. The past was a pure, simple recording, and she believed future historians, "futurians" as she called them, would one day be able to decipher history much better.

Talk about facades. Jocelyn Matthis had perhaps the biggest facade of them all. One of the most respected historians in the world had a son who could rectify any historical discrepancy and yet she could never come forward with the findings because she couldn't explain her source testimony was alive and well. Dr. Matthis's tour de force through the past wasn't a scholar's quest for knowledge but the result of a mother trying to help her son.

Her book delved into history's discrepancies to show how historical narrative oftentimes went astray. There were the easy examples: how Napoleon wasn't short but of standard height and Marie Antoinette did not infamously say "Let them eat cake!" Another queen did a hundred years before her. Jocelyn also took great care in pointing out historical "ghosts," not ghosts in the literal sense but within written records. Ghosts were the opinions of scholars that had been passed down but were never challenged. The danger was that a ghost could become accepted as a commonplace fact. Jocelyn wanted to expose as many historical ghosts as possible because she believed, "when someone realizes the foundation of the floor beneath their feet has cracks, they will look closer at the ground they are walking on."

The more Melicent read, the more she couldn't help but feel every word on the page was the result of a struggle, a struggle to reconcile the mechanics of time with the human experience. Jocelyn had been trying to keep up with Roan by researching what he was holding and where he was going with his mind. Along the way she'd begun to see history's flaws in a glaring light, how fragile and subjective it was, how the past was shaped by the beliefs of the present and then used to form the beliefs of the future. Even Herodotus, "the Father of History," was the first to admit he was only recording what he'd been told. Jocelyn had become an historian's historian by default, not by choice.

Robert West believed Roan had been born for a higher purpose and that his ability needed to be nurtured. All Jocelyn saw was her little boy struggling, unable to shoulder the past like Atlas holding the weight of the world.

With that thought, an image popped into Melicent's mind. *Atlas.*

She sat up, realizing what it was about Stuart's map that had been bothering her. She got out of bed and hurried downstairs.

By the quiet of the house—and the silence of the TV—she could tell that Jocelyn had gone to sleep. She found Roan still sitting at the dining table with Stuart's laptop. He looked up when she entered and his eyes traveled over her leggings and nightshirt.

She took a step forward, feeling self-conscious in her silk winter thermals. Roan had surely seen sexier pajamas than this.

He closed out the file of whatever he'd been looking at on the computer. "Couldn't sleep?" he asked, keeping his voice quiet.

"No. I thought of something," she said in a hushed voice. "It's about the map."

Earlier when she'd seen Stuart's map, the Xs had drawn her attention but they'd seemed off, like a painting that was warped. Her artist's eye could see those Xs formed a shape.

"Would it be possible to re-create the markings on the map but put it into 3-D? So it's on a globe?"

Understanding dawned in Roan's eyes and he turned back to the computer. Within minutes he'd transferred Stuart's oopart coordinates onto a virtual globe of the world. They didn't even have to rotate it to see the partial geometric patterns taking shape.

But that was where the progress stopped, with a broken net of lines and partial figures. Melicent's shoulders fell in disappointment. That hadn't been helpful.

Roan was frowning at the map, lost in thought.

She offered, "Well, it was worth a try. Good night." She hesitated and waited for him to look up, to see that right now she wanted to reach out to him.

When he did look at her she could see the distance in his eyes—his mind was somewhere else entirely. She couldn't help but take it as a rejection. An invisible barrier stood between them again. He was caught up in Stuart's research. Now was not the right time. She would not be initiating another kiss.

She was also done with facades, including her own. So she told him point-blank, "The next time we kiss, I want your gloves off. Period."

Without waiting for a response, she went back up the stairs, letting his soft "good night" fall behind her back.

26. THE FILE

AFTER MELICENT'S SURPRISE announcement and exit up the stairs, Roan had trouble returning to Stuart's research. Before she'd come downstairs, he'd been reading the file on crop circles, and the map he and Melicent tried to create tonight had been a step in the right direction. He was on the brink of a discovery. He could feel it.

He forced his attention back to Stuart's notes:

> Makers of crop circles are masters of geometry. There are never any errors in their work, either in form or measurement. There are no footprints left behind, no broken stalks, and when the crop circle appears in a field of flowers, the flowers are never crushed but perfectly preserved. The precision within the technique is surgical.
>
> Even more perplexing, the designs have grown in complexity over the years, comprising intricate spirals, fractals, and knots with interlocking triangles, pentagons, hexagons, dodecagons, and other geometric shapes.
>
> The labyrinth is an important design element as well—the circles have a tendency to create a mazelike pattern within the design.

Roan studied the aerial photography imported into the file. He could make out a labyrinth in many of the designs. But Roan knew there was a marked difference between a labyrinth and a maze. A labyrinth had only one path to take, and there were no false ends to become lost in like in a maze.

In cultures around the world labyrinths were considered to be the enchanted path the mind walked in order to arrive at the answer at the center. Throughout the centuries and no matter which religion, walking the labyrinth was considered a path of meditation.

These circles were laying down labyrinths.

Stuart's notes accompanied the images.

> Over ten thousand crop circles have appeared to date in almost every country, with the majority unclaimed, conjured by a group of silent artists. The circles' designs have not once, ever, repeated themselves.
>
> The circles, like ooparts, are found near many ancient, sacred sites. They also form near water. Scientists believe that the ground near aquifers holds a greater electrical charge.
>
> Crop circles leave a magnetic charge in the soil where they appear. Using a microscope, biologists have discovered tiny micron sphere-shaped particles of iron attached to the stalks. These microscopic magnets seem to be remnants of some kind of energy source.
>
> The ooparts, when measured with the same instruments, show an altered magnetic field too.

Stuart had underlined that last part. Roan frowned. He'd never touched the grass within a crop circle, but he could attest that ooparts felt magnetically charged. Stuart had drawn a correlation.

The partial shapes the map formed in 3-D hinted that the

ooparts formed a larger geometric design, but it wasn't complete. Roan couldn't help but think he was overlooking something.

Knowing sleep was out of the question, he made himself a cup of Earl Grey and drew the curtains in the dining room. He wasn't used to being in rooms with windows, and he found them disconcerting. The feeling he was being watched kept circling around him, and he tried to brush the sensation off. It didn't help that there were no flowers outside due to the cold.

After closing the blinds and setting the house alarm, he sat back down at the table with his tea to study Stuart's map. There had to be an answer here he wasn't seeing. He'd never been so confounded by an artifact before, and now there was an entire collection of them spread across the globe.

He went back to the crop circle photos and enlarged the picture of a labyrinth circle found near Cellé, France, in June 2014. The longer he gazed at it, the more the image began to remind him of tree rings within a trunk.

The labyrinth had two openings on the outer edge. As Roan's eyes traveled the path to its center he thought too how ooparts existed in two time periods. In essence they existed in two places—

Roan stopped, gripped by an idea.

Two places. When his eyes landed on the labyrinth's center he found the answer.

He went back to Stuart's spreadsheet and entered in a new set of coordinates for each oopart onto the 3-D global map.

So far they'd plugged in the coordinates where the ooparts were last found, not where they originally came from. The objects in essence existed *twice* and at two locations.

That meant two points on the map, not one.

Only a psychometrist would have been able to find that original coordinate. Together Stuart and Miguel had pinpointed each oopart's city and country of origin.

Excitement rose within Roan and a feeling of momentum took over as he entered the new data points. Goose bumps trailed over his arms and up his neck when he watched the geometric shapes complete themselves on the map. The labyrinth had just unlocked the secret.

The connecting lines between all the ooparts with their twin sets of data points transformed the map of the world into a dazzling array of geometric perfection. All the lines crisscrossed and intersected each other to form intricate shapes within shapes in an arrangement of circles, triangles, diamonds, and starlike pentagons. It was like looking at the inside of a kaleidoscope.

"My God," he whispered. Roan couldn't begin to process what he was seeing. These seemingly random ooparts actually had perfect symmetry and coherency between them as they jumped through time.

The ooparts, like the crop circles, were a mathematical equation. Roan couldn't help but see the connection—one of the ooparts was a ring that belonged to the man who had married geometry and algebra and created a coordinate system to locate any object in space, including on a map.

René Descartes.

René Descartes also believed geometry was the language of the universe.

Roan stared at the computer screen with wonder. The image formed by the ooparts' coordinates looked like one giant crop circle imprinted on the Earth.

27. THE SONG

MELICENT WOKE UP early and stayed in bed, snuggling under the down comforter to read the chapter in Jocelyn's book on ancient silk weavers. In Japan, ancient weavers believed a thousand stories could exist in a single thread. Threads were woven together and sometimes broke, but they always remained. In that way too, so did the past remain forever a part of the tapestry of life.

Jocelyn's words somehow brought comfort to her. Even though her possessions and the physical links to her past were gone, her memories would always be a part of her. They were the threads of her life.

Melicent held the book to her chest and closed her eyes, feeling her first goodbye to the house she grew up in riding on the exhale of her breath.

She brought the book with her downstairs after she had showered and changed into jeans and a cable-knit sweater. She found Roan and Jocelyn at the table, watching news from the States on CNN.

Jocelyn stood up with a brisk "Good morning. Coffee and toast?" She was already heading to the kitchen to get it.

"Please." Melicent sat down at the table.

Roan looked preoccupied and asked in an absent tone, "Did you sleep well?"

"Very." In fact, she couldn't remember the last time she'd slept so soundly.

Jocelyn returned with coffee and a thick piece of brioche bread with butter and set out jams and marmalade.

Melicent signaled to the book on the table. "Are you sure it's okay if I take it with me?"

"Of course." Jocelyn was flattered but still dubious. "Are you sure you want to read it? It might be a bit hard to get through." Roan snorted at that and his mother playfully whacked his arm. Jocelyn informed her, "He has yet to read one of my books."

Melicent's mouth dropped open. She looked at Roan. "You've never read her work?"

Jocelyn didn't look the least bit bothered. "I'm afraid it would only frustrate him."

Roan smiled. "My mother is long-winded."

Jocelyn laughed out loud at that. It made her look years younger, and Melicent caught a glimpse of Jocelyn from years before.

Reading the book seemed to be an ongoing joke between them. Jocelyn turned to Melicent. "You don't have to either. I have thick skin."

"No, I'd like to. I'm . . . beginning to have a deeper appreciation for history." Melicent left it at that.

Jocelyn gave Melicent a prim look, obviously thinking her newfound appreciation for history was because of Roan.

Maybe Roan *was* to thank. If he had never come to Los Angeles, Melicent wouldn't know anyone who shared her ability, much less what that ability looked like if it were nurtured over time.

She sneaked a peek at him from under her lashes as she ate. He was watching the TV, looking troubled by the news.

The reporter was saying, "Tonight in New York City, we're outside a residential building across the street from the Metropolitan Museum of Art where a fire broke out hours ago on the fifteenth floor."

Jocelyn put her hand to her mouth. "My word."

The footage showed the corner windows on the building's fifteenth floor engulfed in flames. The blaze shot up like a pinnacle to the midnight sky. London was five hours ahead of New York, so it was still the middle of the night in the States. The street had erupted in pandemonium with firefighters on the scene and police cordoning off the area. The reporter said, "As you can see, firefighters are hard at work containing the flames. We've received no word yet if there are any victims."

Melicent's stomach turned. All the memories of her mother's home came flooding back along with the sheer terror and panic of that night. For a moment she thought she might be sick.

After the news report ended, Roan became even more quiet. By the time they were gathering their things to head back to London to catch their flight, he'd retreated so much into his head, he barely said goodbye to his mother.

Jocelyn wrung her hands together with worry. "Are you sure you're going to be all right? There's nothing more I can do to help?" She must have sensed that there was a lot Roan wasn't telling her. Melicent was beginning to feel the same way.

Roan shook his head with a distracted air. "I'll be fine. I'll call you soon," he promised and reminded her, "Get a new phone."

Jocelyn saluted him with a smile, unable to hide the fact that she was bereft he was leaving. "Check in with me tomorrow, please? I want to know the minute you hear from Stuart."

Melicent came forward and gave her a big hug, surprising all three of them with her warmth. But Jocelyn needed a hug, a proper hug, the kind that made her feel better for having gotten it.

Jocelyn stiffened in response like a cat, then she relaxed and returned the gesture. "It was lovely to meet you." She had a softer look in her eyes.

"You too, Dr. Matthis," Melicent said, but Roan's mother

insisted she call her Jocelyn. Melicent nodded and patted her purse. "Thanks for the book."

———

Now she and Roan were on the plane, well over the Atlantic, and Melicent was reading while Roan ignored her. He'd barely said two words since they'd taken off. They might as well have been on separate flights.

The plane sat twelve. Two rows of six seats on each side of the aisle faced each other like two long sofas. Roan was sitting across from her, several seats down, as though they were total strangers. The flight was ten hours—ten torturous hours. They'd taken off at two P.M. and were arriving at six P.M., though it'd feel like midnight when they landed. Doing the math made Melicent's head hurt. She wasn't sure if she was still jetlagged or about to be.

When Roan stood up to stretch, he surprised her by joking, "Maybe if you keep reading, the book will perk up."

Melicent cocked an eyebrow at him. "So you're talking now?"

He sighed in regret, sounding like he meant it. "Yes, of course. I'm sorry. I have a lot on my mind." He sat down next to her but didn't say anything for a long moment. He stared at the floor. Then he said, "I didn't want to say anything in front of my mom. But the fire that happened in Manhattan on the news . . . I know who lives there." He turned to look at her. "It's a psychometrist in Stuart's group."

Melicent's heart dropped.

"She's the person I called to warn. I've been to her place before."

"Oh my God." Tears welled in Melicent's eyes and she blinked them back. These people, whoever they were, had come after this woman too.

Roan ran his fingers through his hair in agitation. "I want you to stay with me at my place—you and Parker. I'll have Holly bring him from the hotel in the morning. It's the safest place for you right now." His words wrapped around her like a warm embrace. She nodded in acceptance. "Good," he said, relieved. "We'll get through this," he vowed solemnly.

They stared into each other's eyes. A bundle of emotions were swimming inside her. Then he surprised her by tugging off his glove and brushing the hair away from her face in a tender caress. "About that special request you made last night." He took off his other glove and his hands framed her face.

His kiss was tender and full of promise. She pulled away, their lips still hovering near each other. She asked him the question that'd been on her mind. "Why didn't you tell your mother I'm a psychometrist?"

"Because I wanted her to like you," he admitted with a smile. "She doesn't approve of me using my ability."

Melicent made a silent *Oh*. She hadn't considered that Roan cared what Jocelyn thought of her. The thought pleased her, and she held on to it. She'd take as much normalcy as she could get right now.

Roan slipped his gloves back on and stood up. "After you went to sleep last night I made an incredible discovery." He brought over Stuart's laptop. "I plugged in a new set of coordinates, where the ooparts originated from, and came up with this."

When he showed her the computer screen with the new version of the map, Melicent gasped. It was the most beautiful creation she'd ever seen, an exquisite work of art. "The ooparts made this?" She could barely speak. What in the world were they looking at?

"Your idea last night led me to it." Roan was just as riveted. "It's like a mathematical key."

"Unbelievable," she whispered. The map looked like a beautiful mandala.

"The group's theory was correct. The ooparts aren't random."

"Then what are they?" She looked to him. "*How* did they make this?"

Roan shook his head. "I don't know."

She could tell he was determined to find out. They looked at the map for a long time in silence, marveling at its perfection, and awe filled her. She couldn't begin to process this discovery. Where did they go from here?

"Can I touch the oopart you have?" She felt like she could handle the key. When he'd shown it to her at the airport, she'd been too shell-shocked by the fire to want to touch it.

Hesitation crossed his face. "You don't want to, trust me. There's a memory that'd be hard to see."

Melicent swallowed her disappointment but nodded, letting go of her request. After what happened in New Orleans, she wasn't ready to experience such despair again.

Roan closed the laptop and put it aside. "Why don't we study this more later? I was up all night with it." He went to the galley, poured them each a glass of white wine in an elegant stemless glass, and brought over a charcuterie board that had been prepared with assorted cheeses, baguette slices, fig jam, and Marcona almonds.

She took a sip of the crisp sauvignon blanc and selected a piece of aged Gouda to nibble on while her thoughts returned to the key. "I do want to read the key's imprints at some point," she told him. She couldn't be afraid of finding negative memories forever. "How do you get past the bad imprints to find the others?" She'd seen his notes for the Lakota collection, how he was able to unravel multiple imprints in an object from various times. She didn't understand how he did it.

He considered her question before answering. "It's like layers in an ocean. You have to swim through each memory with your intention. Your mind becomes fluid, moving around the moments. You decide how fast you swim, how far, in what direction, and when to stay. . . . Take the wineglass you're holding." He nodded to the glass in her hand. "There are countless imprints embedded there. Try and focus until you can see the last three people who held the glass before you."

Melicent looked at the glass in her hand with surprise.

"Do a mudra to prepare, whatever one feels the most empowering. Deepen your breath. And remember you are in control as you encounter the memories. Sometimes it can be hard to push past a negative one. It just takes focus."

"Is that how you find people for the Heirloom Foundation? Through the water method?"

He chuckled. "Yes, something like that." He took her hand and kissed it. She was coming to love when he did. Roan leaned back, closing his eyes. "I need to take a nap if that's all right."

Melicent could tell he was exhausted. She watched him fall asleep and the guarded look on his face slowly melted away. She studied his gloves, which were back on his hands, and wondered when he started wearing them and at what age. He was so experienced at reading imprints and he'd already taught her so much. She mentally sifted through the small collection of mudras that she'd learned and settled on the first one Roan had shown her, the Shakti mudra.

She went to put down her wine, almost knocking the glass, but then caught it before it spilled and grimaced. Her clumsiness was the result of being out of step with herself. Maybe she'd been out of step for a long time. Her mother used to tell her that cynicism was born from a fearful heart and, looking back, Melicent had not wanted to acknowledge her extraordinary ability. She'd stifled her gift. It'd taken her mother getting sick to wake her up, to force her to embrace her inner power and reexamine who she was. Now she was living in a world where not only was the past touchable, but it was trying to communicate through these strange artifacts. She could either run from this new world or embrace her ability and try to understand it. That started one imprint at a time.

Expelling a deep breath, she settled her hands into the mudra and closed her eyes.

When she was ready she picked up her wineglass and tried to read its history.

The first imprint came quickly: A lead singer from a band she didn't know was on tour in Europe and the man had last used the glass to hold his red wine. He spent most of the flight composing a song for his next album with his acoustic guitar.

As much as Melicent tried she couldn't get past the singer's imprint to anyone else's. After several attempts she felt the start of a headache and gave up. Roan made it sound so much easier than it actually was.

She finished off her wine in a salute to the artist and made a mental note to buy the band's latest album when she was back in the States. The song was quite good. She closed her eyes, softly humming its tune.

She must have dozed off because when she opened her eyes her ears were popping as the plane made its descent.

Outside the plane window the lights of New Orleans were glittering jewels, and the cityscape crested against the Mississippi like a moon. Its nickname "the Crescent City" had never seemed more appropriate.

When the plane touched down the account manager of the charter company overseeing their flight was waiting to greet them along with a customs official to check their passports and welcome them back.

"Was the trip business or pleasure?" the customs official asked them.

Roan tilted his head toward Melicent with a wink. "Introducing her to my mother."

Melicent would have laughed out loud at the audacity of the statement if it wasn't technically true.

They got into Roan's car and headed downtown. Roan seemed recharged after the flight. Neither of them said a word during the twenty-minute drive. Melicent stared out the window, feeling the magic of New Orleans come to greet her. Tonight she was going to see Roan's home.

But her anticipation peaked and plummeted when he pulled up to a warehouse that looked like it was straight out of a slasher film.

This couldn't be where he lived.

Roan punched a code into his cell phone and one of the warehouse's bay doors opened and he pulled in. Melicent got out of the car, mystified, and he led her inside.

"Where are we?" she asked. Her voice had a hollow ring as it bounced off the metal walls.

He gave her a smile. "I live here. In the back."

She'd imagined him living in a house similar to the one on Magazine Street, not an industrial storeroom. "How long have you lived here?"

"About ten years." He led her down a long corridor toward the back of the building that ended with a nondescript door.

Ten years in a windowless warehouse was a long time. She couldn't fathom why he would choose to live in such a place—until Roan opened his front door and said, "House, lights on."

It was like stepping into another world, from the dramatic gray stone walls made of enormous slate slabs jigsawed together to the vaulted ceilings and stained-glass panels that were lit from behind like windows. All the rooms were divided by freestanding walls made of opaque glass tiles, and a sculptured metal staircase led to a hallway upstairs. The innovative design aesthetic took her breath away.

She couldn't believe something so exquisite could exist inside such an ugly box. Melicent turned to him, speechless. She could tell he was waiting for her reaction and managed to say, "It's gorgeous."

He smiled. "I don't have many visitors."

It made her wonder who Roan's friends were. So far she had only met Roan's partner. His relationship with Holly seemed to run deep, and Melicent couldn't help but wonder at their history together. It wasn't that she was jealous, but she did feel a twinge of insecurity. The two were close and Holly hadn't come across as the warmest person. In fact, Holly had been downright horrified that Roan had brought her to New Orleans. Now Melicent was practically moving in. Granted the situation wasn't normal.

Melicent would make a concerted effort to get to know her. Maybe eventually Miss Southern Living would warm up.

Roan set their things down and took off his gloves, touching the flowers in the room. Satisfied by whatever he did or didn't feel, he turned to her with a smile. "Would you like a tour?"

She nodded, staring at his hands and realizing that he wasn't going to put his gloves back on. But then why would he? He was home. She swallowed, her throat suddenly dry.

She followed him through the living room. Behind the first glass wall was a wide-open kitchen with gleaming stainless-steel appliances and long stretches of marble countertop and an island in the center.

Roan showed her the list of numbers on the refrigerator door. "There's a grocery and a restaurant delivery service I have an account with, so whatever you need, just order it. And feel free to use anything you'd like to cook. I won't mind."

Roan had made the offer innocently. Still her cheeks colored with embarrassment. Did he know from reading the imprint of the snow globe that her ex-boyfriend had been a chef? Walt had hated her using anything in the kitchen. Their biggest fight had been over a hand mixer. They'd broken up during the time she made the rock garden. Maybe Roan had seen everything, but the idea that he knew intimate details of her life didn't bother her like it had before.

Next to the kitchen was a breakfast room filled with indoor plants, a mixture of blooming bromeliads and philodendron vines that thrived in luminescent light. "The laundry room is upstairs and there's a computer room back here with a scanner, printer," Roan was explaining, "and an exercise room with some weights and equipment. . . . Feel free to use anything. My office is in the warehouse."

So basically he'd built a self-contained universe he never had to leave. All that was missing was other people. He was also talking like she'd be staying here alone without him, which didn't make sense. Of course he'd be here.

He led her upstairs. "House, lights on, second floor." The lights in the hallway turned on. "I'll show you how to activate all the voice controls."

"But I can just turn on the lights by hand, too, right?" she clarified, nodding to the light switch on the wall right next to him.

He actually laughed at that. "Yes, of course."

He just chose not to touch the light or power switches, not even in his own house. Everything electronic was hardwired and controlled by a state-of-the-art voice-activated computer system.

He moved down the hallway. "There's two spare bedrooms. I thought Parker could take this one." He opened the first door and then the next. "You can have this one."

Both bedrooms were elegant with queen beds and minimalistic art on the walls. Decorative Japanese screen lamps made of wood and rice paper sat on the night stands, giving the rooms a tranquil feel.

"Thank you for letting us stay," she said, touched by his generosity.

Roan brushed off her gratitude with a hint of embarrassment and continued down the hall to the end door. "There's a special room I want you to see." The door had an electronic keypad for a lock and he entered in a long code.

A nervous bubble of laughter rose within her and almost escaped. With a line like that she hoped it wasn't his bedroom.

When he opened the door and she walked inside, all the laughter inside her died. She couldn't believe what she was looking at.

28. THE COLLECTION

"I CALL IT THE TIME ROOM." Roan smiled because he wasn't joking.

Melicent stood beside him speechless. He was beginning to relish the moments when he surprised her. He didn't question the fact that he wanted to show her the gallery tonight. There might not be another time.

He'd spoken with Sun on the plane while Melicent had slept. She'd gotten his message. Sun was in Korea, making sure the young psychometrist who'd been about to join the group was safe. She believed it was impossible that Gyan was involved in Stuart's kidnapping or the fires, but Roan needed to make that judgment for himself. He had to meet with Gyan.

Gyan also had Descartes's ring, and Roan needed to hold it again. He believed it could be the key to understanding the map.

Sun agreed to arrange a meeting for him. The challenge was that the man lived in India.

Melicent wouldn't like being left behind, but Roan had no choice. It was too dangerous for her to go with him. She and Parker could stay at the warehouse while he was away.

He'd decided not to tell her his plan. He didn't want to ruin their one evening alone together. In the morning when she woke up and Holly arrived with Parker from the hotel, he'd already be gone. A twinge of guilt circled around his mind but he pushed it aside. He wanted this night with her.

"After you," he said, motioning for her to go ahead of him.

A cast-iron staircase spiraled down to the ground, creating an observation deck above. The gallery had a high ceiling and took up the whole back corner of the warehouse. It was the largest space in the house, two times the size of his living room.

Roan's private collection was filled with the creations of the pioneers who had sought to understand the mechanics of time. Roan had been collecting timekeeping inventions all his life in his quest to understand the force that had shaped him. The room held every kind of clock and device imaginable from the earliest sundials to the world's tiniest atomic watch. Roan knew all of their stories and considered their creators to be his friends. He often came to this room to clear his mind.

They descended the staircase and first Roan showed Melicent a stunning collection of obelisk shadow clocks, water clocks, and sundials from ancient Egypt, China, Babylonia, and Greece that varied in sizes. The pointed pillar of the tallest shadow clock ascended to the ceiling, and the largest sundial was a gorgeous copper plate raised on a dais as big as a park fountain.

He picked up a smaller metallic sundial, one of his favorites, with intricate astronomical and zodiacal carvings. "It was the Babylonians who first divided the day into hours, minutes, and seconds. They were magnificent astronomers and could look at the stars and know the time to the nearest fifteen minutes."

He motioned to the little carved owl sitting within the center of a tubelike contraption. "Here we have the clepsydra. This particular water clock may well have been the world's first cuckoo clock, made by the Greek mathematician Ctesibius, an imaginative fellow. He invented the pipe organ, too."

"And this?" Melicent asked in a hushed tone, taken by the collection. She pointed to a more complicated-looking sundial.

"In the thirteenth century, Abu Ali al-Hasan al-Marrakushi invented a dial to finally measure equal hours throughout the day. Before that the length of an hour depended on the time of year, and they were never the same." Roan led her to the next table. He had set up the room to progress from the oldest time-keeping pieces to the newest.

"And what about this quill? Why is this here?" Melicent signaled to the ornate quill pen and inkpot.

"This mighty quill," Roan said, picking it up with a smile, "took away ten days from the world. It belonged to Pope Gregory XIII, who in 1582 decided the calendar had to be fixed because the year was too long. So he informed Europe—which in his mind meant the world—that they had to lose ten days all at once. It was better to get it over with just like that." Roan snapped his fingers. "With this quill, he signed an edict that after Thursday, October 4, 1582, it would be Friday, October 15." Roan thought about the headaches this decision had caused. "All of the countries were in an uproar, feeling very cheated." He put the quill back down. "It took Britain two hundred years to finally change their calendar."

Roan slipped his hand in hers, savoring the feel of her palm against his. Her hand fit perfectly and he could sense her wonder and excitement in her touch.

Tonight felt like a first date. Instead of walking through a park, they were strolling through a room of clocks. It made him want to laugh and a feeling of serenity struck him.

Next they moved to a collection of maritime watches that looked like steampunk brass contraptions, with assorted wheels and gears. "Having the correct time became vital to seafaring. It allowed sailors to calculate an exact longitude," he explained. "So in 1675 King Charles established the Royal Observatory at Greenwich on the River Thames. Sailors would set their watches before a sea voyage, but no matter how hard they tried, the watches couldn't keep accurate time at sea. Then John Harrison came along and perfected the chronometer." He showed her. "I have one of the originals he tested on a voyage to Jamaica."

Melicent bent down to study it, keeping her hand tucked in his.

"He was a fascinating man, a self-taught watchmaker from Yorkshire who was also a carpenter. John Harrison went up against the whole astronomical society to revolutionize maritime timekeeping."

Roan knew every one of the scientists, mathematicians, and philosophers in this room. They had all stood on the shoulders of the giants who had come before them, allowing the next generation to come closer to unraveling the mystery of time.

He found himself confessing, "Sometimes when I'm in this room, my ability doesn't feel like a burden anymore."

Melicent's eyes were bright. She squeezed his hand in understanding.

It made the words pour from him as he tried his best to describe time's evolution. "First it was ships, then it was trains that made towns and cities want to synchronize with each other. Next came airplanes, and Universal Coordinated Time was created, connecting countries on a bigger scale. Starting with the Industrial Revolution, time became 'public time.' Overnight people didn't have time to themselves anymore because suddenly time equaled money. Technology made everything speed up."

He showed her one of the last tables, filled with the most modern timekeeping gizmos and gadgets. "Now we have fast food, speed dating, instant delivery, instant everything, with twenty-four time zones around the world synchronized to the vibration of a cesium atom. The smallest clock in the world is the size of a grain of rice."

He showed her his atomic clock, which in fact looked smaller than a grain of rice.

"And time's shortest interval is no longer the millisecond, the microsecond, or the nanosecond. It's picoseconds, femtoseconds, and attoseconds, a quintillionth of a second."

He turned to face her. "So you see, *Time* has its own journey alongside ours. It runs through our bodies and affects everything we do." He trailed his finger from her ear to the pulse at her neck and felt her shiver. "Even our brain has its own clock." His fingers traced a line from her neck up to her forehead and drew a lazy circle. "The suprachiasmatic nucleus, a twenty-thousand-cell cluster no bigger than a pea."

Still holding her hand, he led her to a single watch displayed under a glass case. "There's one more thing I want you to see." He took great pleasure in watching her face startle with surprise when she leaned in to study it.

"You have a Breguet." She looked at him in astonishment.

The pocket watch was one of Abraham-Louis Breguet's first. Roan would never sell it, not when he had the watchmaker to thank for leading him to Melicent.

He took both of Melicent's hands in his and their fingers folded together like a perfect braid as he leaned down to kiss her.

⌣

If the mind dreams twenty-four hours a day and the world records it, Roan wanted this moment to never end, the feeling of Melicent against him, their bodies entwined.

In all his mental travels through time, he had been privy to countless love stories. He'd been an accidental voyeur to the passions of the heart, the triumphs, the joys, the sorrow, the longing. He'd heard the poems—good grief, the poems embedded in centuries of parlor room writing tables.

What if he allowed his and Melicent's love story to be told? What if they left their imprint behind for a future world to find?

Objects held on to the love that never died. Lovers lived on through their rings, their lockets, their picture frames.

Their picture frames.

His parents had had such a love, until he'd come between them. It was the one regret of his life. He'd witnessed their bitter separation as a teenager and would never wish that heartache on anyone. He also never thought he'd find a person who could understand him or touch his heart until Melicent.

After they made love they lay in each other's arms. Melicent rested her head on his chest and their hands playfully came together to create mudras.

"I love your hands," he said. Her hands were truly beautiful, delicate yet precise. The hands of an artist. She tried to mirror his gesture and laughed at her clumsiness. "The Kalesvara." He showed her. Their fingers curved, resting palm-to-palm to create a heart shape.

"What does the name mean?"

"Lord of time. It's an ether mudra to ground you in the moment." Their hands came together again, and he started massaging her palms in an upward motion, finding each of her acupressure points. He could feel two tiny knots in her palm. "Do you know we carry knots in our hands like our shoulders?" He tried to work the kinks out. Her face startled when he zeroed in on the nerve bundle. "The major meridians terminate at the tips of the fingers. You should give your hands a workout every day. Practice the mudras. They'll help. I promise."

He took her left hand and made it cross his at their wrists. Then he lined up the backs of their hands and wrapped each of their fingers together except their ring fingers, which came down to touch the tip of the thumb.

"Which one is this?" she asked, fascinated.

"The Fearless Heart." He kissed her.

Their hands still joined, they made love again, their bodies becoming a part of each other, and their minds touched, melding together.

They held each other, not wanting to dispel the magic, until sleep came to draw a blanket around them.

Melicent smiled and closed her eyes and in that moment looked like Botticelli's *Birth of Venus* with her hair spread out on the pillow. Roan brought his fingertips to her cheek in a light caress and watched her fall asleep.

Soon their evening would come to an end and leave an imprint on the pillow. Tomorrow would be a new day, one that would bring consequences when Melicent woke up to find him gone.

When Roan knew she was sound asleep he touched her hand in farewell. Then he got out of bed, quiet as a whisper, and began to pack.

He was going to see this nightmare with Stuart through to its end and make sure Melicent would never be harmed again.

29. THE NOTE

ROAN'S NOTE RESTED ON THE BED. Melicent read it in disbelief. Her mind rejected every word.

> Melicent,
> I'm sorry.
> It's too dangerous for you to come where I'm going. I need for you to be safe.
> Touch anything of mine in the house that you'd like. A promise is a promise.
> My Breguet is yours.
>
> Always,
> Roan

She sat on the edge of the bed, needing a moment to breathe. Angry tears pooled in her eyes. He'd gone without her. Without waking her. When had he decided? How could he have not said anything? Where the hell had he gone?

He'd snuck out in the early hours like a bad morning after. She knew that hadn't been his intention. He thought he was protecting her, but still it cut her to the quick.

Yes, the situation was dangerous—for them both. Psychometrists were missing, maybe dead, and her and another woman's house had been burned down. Now Roan had charged off like some kind of misguided knight. And he'd signed his note that she could have his Breguet—*like a will,* was all she could think.

Because he didn't know whether he was coming back.

Overwhelming fear clawed at her. She ran to fish her cell phone from her purse and called him. Of course he didn't answer. "Roan, it's me. Call me back. Now." She hung up and tried again. "I really can't believe you just left! And all I have is a note? A note?!" Click. Again she dialed, her anger at a full boil. "If you don't get back here I'm touching everything you own!"

Her fingers redialed his number. She couldn't believe she was leaving these crazy voicemails. She knew she sounded insane. But dammit—"Call me. I'm serious." Nothing she said conveyed her feelings or the thoughts running through her head.

He wasn't going to call her. Even worse, he thought it was for her own good.

There had to be something she could do. She wasn't about to just sit there while he risked his life finding Stuart. She closed her eyes and tried to focus on the note in her hands, hoping to pick up an imprint, any bit of information as to where he might have gone. It had to be possible. Roan had pulled a phone number out of thin air for a lost little girl. Maybe she could discover his next steps with this note.

She closed her eyes, centering her attention on the paper. Minutes passed as she tried to pick up a sensation. She began to feel Roan's emotions emanating from the page: his guilt, his anxiety, his conviction. His love.

He'd written the note without his gloves, knowing she would hold the paper in her hands. He wanted her to feel his heart behind the words and his intentions behind his actions.

He'd left her behind because he loved her.

She took that kernel of truth embedded in the page and allowed it into her heart, and her anger defused like a storm at sea suddenly calm.

She called him one more time, resolve in her voice. "Wher-ever you are, whatever you're doing, I need you to be safe too. I want to help, however I can. I'm here." She hung up and buried her face in his pillow. His scent was woven into the cotton like it held its own memories. She had to believe he'd return. This new life she'd been thrown into didn't make sense without him.

Her hand trailed across the place where he'd slept, the con-tours of his body now a lost shadow on the sheet. Their time to-gether played in her mind and washed over her body like a wave. Last night hadn't been a dream. They had shared themselves with each other, and it had meant as much to him as it did to her.

Cocooned in the memory, she lingered there and then tucked it away in her mind. She got up and slipped on the shirt that he had tossed in the laundry basket yesterday. The tail hung mid-thigh and the arms devoured her but she didn't care. She still wanted him on her skin to keep their connection alive.

She went downstairs to the kitchen to make coffee before her shower. Holly and Parker would be there in an hour.

Roan might have hidden her away in his home like some trea-sure, but he didn't know her well enough yet if he thought she was going to just sit around and wait. She might not have the full scale of his abilities, but she did share his gift and she didn't want to be afraid of it anymore. She would use this time alone while he was gone to get stronger.

Banging cabinets around in the kitchen, she was too busy muttering to herself, "Just what century does he think he's from?" to hear the front door open.

"Mel?" Parker said, hesitant.

Melicent whipped around to find Holly and Parker in the doorway. Melicent's hand flew to the opening of Roan's shirt at her chest to make sure the buttons were closed and her face turned beet red.

Things were, in this case, exactly how they looked.

Holly and Parker were each holding a grocery bag. Holly had

a startled expression on her face that she tried to mask, but Roan's business partner was clearly taken aback. "Good morning," she said, setting the bag down and facing the counter to unpack the food.

Melicent looked around the kitchen wondering if there was someplace where the floor could swallow her up whole. She scooted around the island to cover up her bare legs. "I thought you two weren't coming until ten."

"Obviously," Holly said, which made Melicent blush brighter. Holly went to the drawer with the coffee makings, the one Melicent hadn't tried yet, and she began to put on a pot with lightning-quick efficiency. It was clear she'd done it many times. "I'm supposed to show you two the lay of the land, how to come and go, though Roan left word that he'd prefer for you to stay put until he's back."

What else did Roan say? Melicent was dying to know, but she had too much pride to ask. He hadn't told Melicent where he was going or when he'd be back, and Melicent didn't want to know if he'd divulged that information to Holly. It would cut too deep if he had and bring back that irrational insecurity she'd been wrestling with. She didn't want to compare their relationships, and she hated herself for having these feelings. It was petty and small-minded and not like her at all.

Melicent tried to sound nonchalant. "Yes, he told me."

"Why don't you . . . get dressed and then we'll go over everything," Holly suggested with a hint of frost in her eyes.

Melicent turned to Parker, who was still staring at her with a dumbfounded look. "Hey, Park, let me show you your room," she said, and walked out of the kitchen with as much dignity as she could muster. Holly stayed behind with the coffeepot.

When they reached Parker's room upstairs, he scowled at her. "So you're together now?"

"Yes . . . no . . . I don't know." Melicent ran her hand through her hair. "Can we talk about this later?"

He put his hands up in a truce. "I'm not gonna judge, though Holly didn't seem too cool with it."

Melicent had noticed. Holly's pursed lips and raised brows spoke volumes. Melicent had no idea where she stood with Roan's business partner.

Parker put his duffel down and crossed his arms. "So what did you find out in London?"

Melicent noticed the lines of worry on her brother's face. He looked older and tired, and her heart hurt for him. His life had fallen apart along with hers.

"Stuart's place had been broken into. But we got his laptop and research. We made a discovery." Melicent didn't know how to explain the oopart map. It'd be easier if she just showed it to Parker. She wondered if Roan had taken the laptop with him.

"That's it? A laptop?" Parker was looking at her, horrified. "So what now? We're just stuck here in Roan's Batcave while you wear his clothes?"

Melicent put her hand over her mouth, trying not to laugh. Parker hadn't meant it as a joke. He was clearly upset. "Look, I don't know what the plan is yet. We need a little more time."

"For what? And where's Roan?"

Good question. She didn't know that either but didn't want to admit that she was floundering as much as he was. "Roan's following up on a lead and he'll be back soon and we'll figure out our next step. Okay?" She put her hands on his shoulders, feeling the anxiety radiating from him. "The important thing is we're safe and we're together. We'll get through this," she promised, giving him a hug. He nodded and hugged her back.

It was a start.

She hurried to Roan's bedroom to get her clothes, knowing Holly was waiting downstairs. She could shower later. She gave her hair a quick brush and debated applying a little lipstick from her travel bag and then rolled her eyes at herself. Holly might be all done up, but Melicent wasn't going to actually attempt to look good for her.

The smell of French roast was filling the house. Melicent looked around Roan's room while she changed, taking it in for the first time. Roan didn't have many personal effects out in the open. She wasn't about to refuse his invitation to touch his things, but she also wouldn't take advantage of the offer either. She'd find one object to read, just one. Like he'd read her snow globe, she would see what it could tell her about his life. Then she would put it away and find out the rest directly from him.

⌒

When she arrived back down to the kitchen, the awkwardness with Holly still hung in the air.

"Coffee?" Holly offered her an already poured mug like a hostess.

Melicent took it with a murmured thanks and added cream. "Thank you for taking Parker to the store and bringing him over."

Holly waved her hand with a polite smile. "It was no trouble. I'm afraid Parker did all the shopping. I wasn't sure what you liked."

Melicent stifled a grimace. She bet Parker got all his usual instant and frozen food favorites.

"Roan said to help yourself to anything in the pantry." Holly opened up the double doors to show her the organized shelves. Melicent was beginning to feel like Holly was a flight attendant showing her the plane. "So!" Holly smiled brightly. "What do you do in Los Angeles?"

Melicent's eyebrows rose. Holly had said it casually, but Melicent couldn't help but feel like this was the start of an interrogation. "I make snow globes," she said, deadpan.

"Pardon me?" Holly's eyes widened and she leaned forward in confusion.

"I said I make snow globes." Melicent was purposely trying to ruffle Ms. Perfect's feathers.

"The kind that you shake?" Holly tried to clarify.

Melicent nodded slowly and tried hard not to laugh. "Mmm-hmm." She was sure Holly didn't know what to think of her now.

"How fascinating. I've never met a snow globe maker."

"Roan bought a few. Maybe he'll show you them." Melicent was quickly running out of things to say. She sipped her coffee, savoring the rich overtones.

Holly sipped hers too. "Listen," Holly finally said, clearly getting to the point. "Roan is like a brother to me. We've known each other forever. I know the situation here is unorthodox with what is happening with you and Stuart and all . . . but no matter what the outcome of all this is"—she waved a graceful hand across the kitchen—"just please don't hurt him. Roan is very special."

Melicent could see the absolute sincerity in Holly's eyes, and for a moment she got a peek behind Holly's careful veneer. Melicent met her gaze head-on, not shying away, and allowed her to see the same sincerity. "That is the last thing I would ever do. You have my word."

30. THE RING

ROAN USED HIS TIME on the plane trip to Bengaluru to study the oopart map in closer detail. Before he left New Orleans he'd transferred the file to his own laptop and left Stuart's computer behind in his office at the warehouse. During the flight he had an uninterrupted block of time to analyze it.

Was the map a message? A sign? That humanity was not alone in the universe? Or was it simply nature's signature, left behind by the ooparts' movements across time, like the intricate pattern of a snowflake? Roan understood how nature found cohesion through geometry. Geometry could be seen in everything from the spiral of a seashell, a tornado, or a hurricane, the fractals of a leaf, a beehive, the mandala of a spider's web, down to the perfect symmetry within a crystal under a microscope.

Were the ooparts' beautiful geometry simply a natural pattern?

Roan studied the map again. It couldn't be coincidence that the map's grid lines aligned with ancient sites. He could easily pick them out: Stonehenge, Avebury, Giza, Easter Island, Angkor Wat, Machu Picchu—Gobekli Tepe. They all landed on the map's geometric lines, connecting each other.

By the time Roan's flight landed in Bengaluru, he was no closer to finding answers, and when he got off the plane, he felt farther away from home, Melicent, and his life in New Orleans than ever.

Melicent had left him countless voicemails and he had not listened to any of them. There was nothing he could do right now to change his course of action. Ever since he'd unlocked the map, his whole life had come into sharp focus. He felt in his bones that he could unravel the mystery of the ooparts. He needed to understand what the map meant almost as much as he needed to find Stuart and keep Melicent safe. Hopefully coming to Gyan's would shed more light on the situation.

Roan had traveled to India a few times before, and it had always been to Delhi, where he would take a sleeper train to the ancient city of Jodhpur in northwest India, his favorite place to go searching for relics. Jodhpur was a hub, with antiques arriving from the ancient port of Kochi and the World Heritage site of Jaisalmer, a city where Roan had found not only Indian treasures, but Chinese, Arab, and European as well.

Arriving in Bengaluru, however, was a different experience altogether. Bengaluru was a city stretching its arms to the future. The cosmopolitan center was the IT portal of India, the country's Silicon Valley.

Gyan worked for the Ministry of Culture and the Archaeological Survey of India, which focused on the conservation and preservation of monuments around the country. He helped oversee the Bengaluru office. It had been an hour-long taxi ride from the airport for Roan to get to his house. Gyan and his family lived in a villa in Palm Meadows, one of Bengaluru's most popular residences, where the entire grounds looked more like a resort getaway.

Sun had been trying to reach Gyan and arrange a meeting between him and Roan, only to be informed by Gyan's wife, Aadira, that Gyan hadn't been home for three days. She'd been away in Mumbai with her parents, helping her sister prepare for her wedding. Gyan had called her saying that he had found Stuart and promised to call her the next day. But he never did and he never came home.

They had a three-year-old daughter.

Roan didn't know what to expect when he arrived at Gyan's. Aadira answered the door. The young woman's eyes were swollen from crying and she was beside herself with worry. Gyan was still missing. She was desperate for answers and willing to help Sun and Roan in any way. Sun had returned to New York to deal with the fire after making sure the young psychometrist in Korea was hidden and safe. She'd been reaching out to all of the contacts in their network to see who else, if anyone, Stuart and Miguel had involved in their research. So far she had not found a lead.

Aadira showed Roan around the house. The three-bedroom luxury condominium had marble floors in every room, a black granite kitchen, and ornamental teakwood doors and matching window frames.

"Here is Gyan's home office." She flipped on the lights.

When Roan walked in, he stopped in shock. Descartes's ring was sitting on the desk. Why had Gyan left the oopart out in the open?

Roan needed to touch it, but first he wanted to inspect Gyan's other things. He knew that handling the ring would make his hands numb. "Where did your husband get this?"

Aadira hovered in the doorway. "Stuart sent it to him for safekeeping," she said, confirming what Roan already knew. "The ring was sitting on his desk when I returned yesterday."

After touching several of Gyan's personal effects—particularly by holding his pen and his phone—Roan could confirm that Gyan had been truly worried for Stuart and Miguel and that he had done neither of them harm. Gyan had been passionate about the oopart research and was trying to find out what had happened to François, Miguel, and Stuart. That was where the trail ended.

Aadira put her hand over her mouth and gripped her stomach. "Something has happened to him, too. I know it. He would never . . ." She couldn't go on.

Roan didn't know how to comfort the poor woman, and it was obvious she knew nothing except that her husband was missing.

"Whatever you and Sun can do to help find him," she whispered. "Please excuse me." She left the room to be alone in her grief, giving Roan the respite he needed to examine Descartes's ring.

Roan formed his hands into a Surabhi mudra, one of the most powerful mudras in his arsenal. The mudra helped to cut through any barrier that stood between a person and their desires. Right now he desperately needed to understand the ooparts' riddle and find Miguel, Stuart, and Gyan. He held the intention in his mind.

Then he took a deep breath, like a diver preparing to go deep in the ocean for a long time without air, and he picked the ring up.

LEIDEN, HOLLAND

1633

THE BOOK OF THE WORLD didn't feel so inviting today. Descartes wished he'd stayed at home.

He had ventured out into town to hear the gossip at the tavern and gather what news he could of Galileo. Word had reached Leiden that the scientist had been summoned to Rome for trial. The iron arm of the Inquisition had been making threats for some time now and had finally followed through.

Shock continued to ripple through Europe as the tribunals of the Roman Inquisition made an example of Galileo, a warning to all who thought to push the boundaries of accepted science. Even the French Parliament had passed a decree forbidding anyone to criticize the works of Aristotle. The punishment was death. Heretics continued to be burned along with women who were declared witches. Descartes had escaped to the Netherlands in search of greater tolerance and to avoid prying eyes as he worked. For he believed the old adage: *Bene vixit, bene qui latuit,* he lives well who is well hidden.

Descartes's deep-seated fear stemmed not only from the fact that he had come to the same conclusions as Galileo, that the Earth did indeed revolve around the sun, but from what else he'd found. In his quest to marry algebra and geometry, he had made several startling discoveries about gravity, trajectories, the rotation of the Earth, and the movement of the solar system around the sun.

For the past four years, Descartes had been compiling his research into a book that, when published, would expand the realms of physics and metaphysics in exciting new ways. He had chosen to write the work in French and not Latin so that everyone could read it, including women. He was planning to title the book *The World,* but now, with Galileo's trial, he wasn't sure if he'd ever be able to publish it.

Descartes refused to follow in Galileo's footsteps. The Frenchman had his freedom, his daydreams, and no financial worries thanks to his family's wealth. Galileo was Italian, a staunch Catholic, and in the good graces of the Pope. Still the poor man was being convicted and fined, and every copy of his book *Dialogue of Galileo Galilei* was being burned in Rome. Descartes shuddered to think what his own fate might be. Nothing was as dangerous as men who were robbed of their reputations that had been built on false ideas. And the view that the Earth was the center of the universe was false.

But Descartes had also learned early on that he could not change the world, only himself. Now he had to make a vital decision: what to share of his work and what to keep secret.

He kept waiting for word that Galileo would be pardoned, so that he too could move forward and publish. But when Galileo's yearlong trial in Rome ended with the Italian being sentenced to house arrest for the rest of his life and his work being censored, Descartes had his answer. His research could never be shared.

For a week Descartes debated whether to burn every word. Each night he would sit by the fire with his wine, the pages of *The World* a hand's throw from the embers. He would stare at the flames, their curling fingers beckoning him. He had found the equation for understanding everything that the world was built upon. He had found the mathematical unity between the Platonic solids, the geometric building blocks of life.

Could he destroy such a miracle?

He could not.

So instead he made a secret copy, rewriting his words in a code no one could understand. Then he burned the originals containing his precious theorems.

From that day forward he would be more careful. He would become a nomad, a stranger, traveling from village to village. He would never stay in one place for long. Indeed, he would become the hermit philosopher at the winding staircase, an image his good friend Rembrandt had painted. He and the artist had often spoken of the struggles to capture the unattainable in their work, Rembrandt in the two-dimensional plane, Descartes in the third. Descartes would bury his secret and limit the discoveries he shared to findings that fit within accepted mathematical boundaries. He would keep his secrets and cherish his freedom.

The world wasn't ready for a mathematical proof so pure it could only be divine law. For even though his discovery was not mysticism or magic or alchemy, it offered an understanding of creation, an understanding that Descartes believed lived deep inside the hearts of all men.

31. THE CAVE

ROAN PUT DOWN THE RING and tucked his hands into a Kashyapa mudra, forcing himself back to the present, only to find his fingers were numb as he'd expected. He closed his eyes, feeling dizzy. He'd just been thrown out of seventeenth-century Leiden and he was jetlagged to boot. It was a heady combination. But he'd seen Descartes's unpublished work, *The World*, and he now understood how Descartes's discovery of geometric unity held the key.

The point of unity on the oopart map was the center, the single point where all the geometric symbols converged. That was the answer to the map: *the center*.

Goose bumps flowed over him as he realized what that meant. "Oh my God. It's a labyrinth," he said aloud to himself, and opened up the map. They were meant to walk the path outlined on the oopart map to its center.

He enlarged the image to see where the center point of the ooparts' design landed.

Naica, Mexico.

He took out his phone and dialed Sun, who was waiting for his call. Exhilaration coursed through him.

She answered on the first ring. "Is there any word from Gyan?" she said.

"No." He heard her soft exhale. "But he left behind Descartes's ring. It holds the key." Roan tried to contain his excitement and explained, "Descartes discovered an equation that unifies geometry. He was also *the* master of the compass, the man who enabled the world to find any point in space on a map. These ooparts are connecting to each other to form a labyrinth. We're meant to walk the path to the center."

He heard her gasp in understanding. The most powerful point in nature was always the center. "Where is it?"

"Naica, Mexico. Hold on." He plugged that name into the search engine on his phone to see if the internet could shed any light on its significance. A long list of articles appeared, and they stunned him into silence for a moment. *Giant Crystal Cave Found in Naica, Mexico.*

Calm descended over him as he looked at pictures of an underground cavern filled with crystals towering more than thirty feet. "Sun? That's it. The Crystal Cave in Naica, Mexico, has the largest crystals in the world."

Crop circles had been the guideposts to deciphering the map. Now Roan understood where it all led: to an ancient crystal vault buried within the Earth.

"I can meet you there," Sun insisted. "We should go together. I'll take the first flight out."

"All right. I'll work on getting us access inside." Roan had no idea how to do that or what they'd find once they got there, but he knew in his heart he had to go.

The ooparts had laid down a labyrinth for him to walk.

32. THE BEADS

WHEN MELICENT FOUND the Trove gift bags tucked away in Roan's living room, for a split second her old life in L.A. came flooding back.

So much had happened since the day she'd watched Roan, a stranger at the time, walk out of the shop door with her snow globes, and now here she was standing before them in his home. For a moment it did feel like time travel.

She put her hands on each box to see what she could sense—and could tell Roan had gotten out just the one globe he'd already touched. His imprint was all over it.

She had yet to touch anything of his. First she'd wanted to explore the house and find the perfect object. Roan's place was like a maze, filled with more rooms than she'd expected.

"Who has a planetarium in their living room?" Parker asked in amazement, checking out Roan's computerized system.

Who indeed? Melicent picked up the antique decorative telescope in the corner of the room and discovered that it had belonged to Edwin Hubble. The impressions of Hubble flew through her mind: the astronomer had been a strong athlete—loved basketball, the high jump, and boxing. He'd served in both world wars and liked to adopt a British accent, a pipe, and a cape to appear more accomplished. He was also one of the greatest astronomers of all time, the first to discover that the universe existed beyond the Milky Way. Roan had found this telescope at an estate sale in Oxford while visiting his mother—Hubble had been a Rhodes Scholar at the University of Oxford—and Roan's home planetarium was an homage to the man who had shown the world the cosmos.

The telescope inspired her, just as the rest of the house inspired her. Seeing Roan's Time Room made her not only want to embrace her ability, but master it. She wanted to travel through the centuries and taste the years. One day, she wanted to be able to hold a child's hand and help her get home. She wanted to find lost heirlooms and touch peace pipes without being afraid. She wanted to learn how to hold anything and see the light.

⌣

By that evening the urge to touch something of Roan's and peer into his life had taken hold of her. From her previous research on psychometry she'd read that, to obtain the strongest imprint, it was ideal for the object to be either a piece of jewelry, a person's keys, a lock of hair, or a wallet—something someone would have had on their body for long periods of time. The more personal the object, the more magnetized it would be by the individual.

When Melicent found the Mardi Gras beads in the little wooden box on Roan's dresser, she knew right away that she had found the object she wanted to read. The necklace had sentimental written all over it.

For a moment she hesitated, feeling as if she were about to open Roan's diary or read his mail without his permission. Then she reminded herself she did have permission.

She sat down on the center of his bed and crossed her legs into a meditating position. Closing her eyes, she brought her hands into a Bhramara mudra like Roan had taught her to increase her concentration. She held the finger stance for a long time. When she was ready, she picked up the beads and Roan's past opened inside her mind like a flower.

NEW ORLEANS

1989

ROAN HAD NEVER TRIED TO CATCH anything before. Every year at the parade, beads, stuffed animals, swords, and doubloon coins would sail over his head. This year, Roan raised his hand and caught a pair of beads right as Dolly Parton went by on her float.

He could have sworn she winked at him.

The necklace had been flying right at him, glinting in the sun like rainbows. The translucent beads were made of heavy plastic that felt more like glass. The man on the float who had thrown the necklace had been drunk and was going through a nasty divorce, but Roan tried to ignore that imprint. Maybe he would give the necklace to his mother—or on second thought, maybe not.

His parents had been fighting a lot lately and they'd almost not gone out today, but his father had pointed out it was tradition. Roan's family went to Endymion every year, New Orleans' brashest and friendliest Mardi Gras parade, named after the Greek god of eternal youth and fertility. Endymion had the biggest floats, the brightest floats, and the best marching bands that went through Mid-City all the way down Canal Street to downtown.

Roan's parents had good friends who owned a house on Orleans Street where they would always host a huge potluck party before the parade with chili, potato salad, and fried chicken. There was liquor for the adults and outside along the streets vendors sold cotton candy, wigs, sunglasses, and caramel corn from carts for the children.

"Hey, you're that weird kid."

Roan turned to find three boys gathered around him. He recognized the boys from his school. They were in seventh grade, one year ahead.

The tallest of the bunch jabbed him in the shoulder. "Yeah, my little brother told us all about you. You're like a freak. What's wrong with you?"

The boy who'd jabbed him was Billy Crump, the older brother of Tommy Crump, the official bully in Roan's class.

Roan looked down the street to the corner where his parents were. They knew he'd made his way down the block through the crowd to get caramel corn from the street vendor.

Roan let out a pained sigh. The first time he'd talked his parents into letting him venture out on his own and now he was going to return looking beaten.

What a crappy Mardi Gras.

Roan could just imagine the reception at his parents' friends' house. His mother would become hysterical and his father would demand to speak to all the boys' parents that night, driving to each of their houses to have a serious talk on the porch while their children shot nasty looks at Roan and his bloody nose. Roan would be the laughingstock of the school by Monday.

Roan put his hand back in the pocket with the beads and stared at the boys. He was only eleven, but he'd taken to keeping his hands in his pockets all the time. Roan tried to skate through the situation, just like he usually did whenever he had to interact with other kids, by not saying a word.

Billy Crump took his silence as a personal insult. "Get him."

Before Roan could react, all three of the boys grabbed him and hauled him off to the park's grassy area away from the crowd.

They threw him on the ground and began to punch and kick him all over.

Roan curled up defensively in a ball, his arms coming up to protect his head on reflex. They were going at him full force— hit, whack, kick.

The pain went on forever, though it'd only been a few seconds until he heard a girl scream.

"Get off of him!" The girl grabbed one of the boys from behind and punched him full-on in the face.

Another boy received a hard kick to the chest. Tommy's brother stopped hitting Roan and turned around to find his friends were down.

Roan lay on the grass, riddled with pain but also frozen in disbelief at this unexpected turn of events.

Holly Beauchêne was standing over him like an avenging angel. Roan didn't know her at all, had never said a word to her before. She was in the seventh grade with Billy and lived in one of the great mansions on St. Charles Avenue. Her dad was even friends with the mayor. Roan had no idea why she was standing up for him.

Tommy's brother said, "Get lost, Holly. This is between me and the freak."

"You're an idiot, Billy." Then she kicked him, too. Billy hit the ground next to his friends, who were nursing their wounds. Holly looked down at them. "My daddy taught me how to kick any boy's ass. Now y'all better get out of here before I really get mad."

Billy's friends got up and ran. Billy hesitated a second longer. Then he saw the measured look in Holly's eyes and cut his losses. No one messed with Holly Beauchêne.

When the three were gone, Holly turned to Roan. "You okay? You look a real mess." She helped him stand. "Billy's a jerk." Holly snapped open her purse and pulled out a dainty handkerchief. The white lace linen was the kind of girly item

Roan would have expected to find in Holly Beauchêne's purse before today.

"I'll get it all bloody," he protested.

She shrugged. "I have plenty more."

When Roan held her handkerchief a myriad of thoughts and emotions sifted through him. Unhappiness existed inside Holly's perfect world. Her parents fought all the time while she tried to block out their anger and bitter words. She was the only child of a loveless marriage, between two of the oldest old-money families in the South, who had the kind of wedding that was written up in the society page and had cost a fortune. But after the glamour faded, the husband and wife realized they didn't care for each other that much anymore. Holly was her parents' one saving grace, their Southern Belle princess, only she didn't want the title. Instead she escaped into books and her imagination. Holly's favorite things were her home, a historic playground and the place that fostered her daydreams, and her cats, Bruce and Lee, her best friends.

"Why are you smiling?" Holly asked.

Roan shrugged. He couldn't well tell her he thought the names of her cats were funny. "The way you handled Billy. Thanks."

"Here, stand still." She dabbed at his bloody nose and the cut on his cheek, which had started to swell. "You're going to have a black eye," she said, matter-of-fact.

"Great. My parents are going to freak."

They looked at each other and smiled.

"I've watched you at school, you know," she surprised him by saying. "You're different. You seem . . ." Holly trailed off, looking unsure.

"Weird? Strange?" Roan tried to help her out.

"Special," she settled on. "Why do you always keep your hands in your pockets?"

Roan hesitated, surprised that she'd noticed. He'd never been asked to explain himself before to anyone besides his parents, and certainly not to another kid. But Holly was different. Roan felt an innate trust in her—not to mention she had basically saved his life. His parents had drilled it into his head that he should never talk about his ability, but for the first time he wanted to confide in someone.

He wanted a friend.

So he told her, more than he'd ever told anyone. And the worst day of Roan's young life suddenly turned out to be the best.

They sat on the grass eating caramel corn and talking as the marching bands went past, their horns blaring a glorious New Orleans hello. The trumpets and tubas created a wall of sound that pushed through the parade line.

From afar, Roan watched the St. Augustine Band play a synchronized masterpiece. The musicians wore white gloves and looked invincible in their uniforms as they marched.

Roan thought, *Maybe gloves are what I need.*

Holly listened to every word he said without interruption. She didn't appear to be shocked by his secret. In fact, she asked Roan if he could come to her house the next day and tell her some of the stories behind her favorite antiques. He said sure.

When Roan came back to Orleans Street with a bloody nose and a black eye his parents had a meltdown, and they threatened to pull him from school altogether. But Roan insisted he could handle the bullies. And he did. With Holly's friendship, no one dared to taunt or tease him. Because of Holly Beauchêne, Roan had been given a free pass, allowing him to get through school unscathed. Holly became his best friend and the keeper of his secret, and Roan kept those Mardi Gras beads as a reminder of that fateful day, and of how sometimes a guardian angel came in the guise of a friend.

Melicent let go of the beads. Never had she experienced a memory so vivid, so powerful before. For a split moment she'd been with Roan and Holly on the grass, her heart heavy and uplifted all at once.

She'd peered into the recesses of a beautiful friendship and witnessed its beginnings. Melicent had seen the real Holly behind the outer face she presented to the world.

Melicent didn't know the rest of their story, but she didn't need to. All of her insecurity and questions about Holly had been erased by one memory. Melicent loved that little girl who'd taken on Billy Crump and shielded Roan from everyone else. Holly had seen his gift, recognized his fragility, and become his protector. No wonder Holly had taken Robert West's place at the helm of West, Inc. after he died. No one else could.

33. THE CLOCK TOWER

ROAN HAD GIVEN HOLLY AN ALL but impossible assignment: get him and Sun inside the Crystal Cave. The problem was the cave was located a thousand feet below the Earth's surface and was not open to the public.

Cueva de los Cristales was controlled by Peñoles Mining Company along with their Naica mine operation. The Naica mines had been in business since 1910 and had Mexico's most productive mining for lead and silver. The company kept the Crystal Cave separate from the mine, and the area was restricted to a team of scientists.

Holly had been keeping him apprised all day. After several strategic calls, starting with the head of the National Museum of Anthropology in Mexico City, who they had worked with on the return of a Mayan sculpture, she had managed to get the head of Peñoles on the phone.

Roan answered his cell right away when he saw it was her. "How did it go?"

"It's going to cost you."

"How much?"

"For a million dollars you can have a private tour, no questions asked."

"Good," Roan said without hesitation. "Wire the money."

"Good? Have you lost your mind? What on earth is down there that's worth a million dollars? It's not like you can bring anything back."

For Roan, reaching the cave transcended any dollar amount. Every antique he'd ever found, every treasure he'd unearthed and sold was enabling him to make this journey. "It's going to lead to me to answers about Stuart . . . about me, our ability. Everything. There's no price tag for that."

Holly was silent for a moment, then she said, "I'll text you when it's done and give you a contact at the site."

"Thank you. Really." He couldn't have done this without her.

"Thank me by getting to the bottom of all this with Stuart." The stress was evident in her voice. "Where are you right now?"

"Stuck in the back of a cab on my way to the airport."

He'd used that time to research more on Naica. The city of Chihuahua was the closest place to fly into. He called his charter company and booked a Gulfstream with a private bedroom to fly him direct. Flying from Bengaluru to Chihuahua on the fastest jet with a king-size bed had also cost a small fortune, but he desperately needed uninterrupted sleep. At this point he was so exhausted he was slurring his words, and he needed all his strength for whatever awaited him in Mexico.

When Sun had insisted on meeting him there, Roan hadn't said no. He might need her help. He'd never touched ancient crystals before.

By design, crystals were powerful mediums of nature, the integral force behind watches and computers, making the modern world sing. They also held the most precise imprints, second to flowers, like a pure recording. But unlike flowers, which died within days or weeks, crystals remained for millennia.

Roan wasn't sure what would happen when he touched a crystal that held imprints spanning half a million years. He wasn't sure he could survive it. All he knew was that the ooparts' labyrinth lead to the Crystal Cave, and Melicent would never be safe until he found out why.

He emailed Sun the name of the motel where they would meet in Saucillo, which was a small town south of Chihuahua close to the mine. Roan had been the one in charge of getting them into the cave, and Holly had not let him down.

Before Holly hung up, she surprised him by saying, "I think you should call Melicent."

Roan didn't say anything at first. "How is she?"

"Upset, from what I can tell, though she's trying to hide it. I would be too. Not the smoothest move running off like that. Don't pull a Gianna on her."

He could feel Holly shaking her head at him. She had helped him weather all of his previous failed relationships. "Believe me, I'm not." His feelings for Melicent were totally different from anyone in the past. But he couldn't reveal that he'd left Melicent because the trip was too dangerous, or Holly never would have helped him. "I'll be back soon and work everything out."

He was almost to the airport when his phone rang again. He didn't recognize the number and answered, thinking it was his contact for the cave.

Stuart's voice was the last thing he expected to hear.

"Stuart? Where are you—"

"Listen. I can't talk right now." Stuart cut him off, out of breath. "I just managed to get free. Can you make it to our meeting place? I'll explain everything there. Can you meet me tomorrow?"

"Stuart—wait. I read the flowers. I've got your computer and the map. Are you hurt?"

"Oh my God, thank you . . ." he said, his voice weak. "Thank you."

"Who took you? Is Gyan with you?"

"I'm alone. I don't know who they were." Stuart broke down,

becoming emotional. "They had me in an abandoned warehouse at the Isle of Dogs. They got a phone call and left and never came back. I was able to escape."

"Where are you now?"

"I'm still in London."

"Can you get to Mexico by tomorrow?"

"Mexico?"

"The ooparts lead to Naica, Mexico. We've found the answer."

⁓

After the wire was sent, Holly texted Roan telling him how to get in touch with the operations manager of the cave, Oscar Gonzales.

When Roan called the man, Oscar had no idea who Roan was or how he'd obtained permission to get inside the cave. All Oscar had been told was to provide the tour and to be discreet. Roan and Sun would meet him at the mine tomorrow afternoon after all the scientists had left for the day.

"Are you both in good health?" Oscar asked over the phone. His voice was gravelly and his English was laced with a thick Mexican accent.

"It's going to be three of us," Roan corrected him. "My . . . brother will be there too."

"Is he in good health? It's hot as hell down there. Even with a special life-support suit and gear, you can only remain in the cave for forty minutes. Without it, fifteen minutes or you're dead. *Comprende?* So your tour will be short."

Roan had read about the challenges the cave's explorers had faced. Not only was the Crystal Cave a thousand feet underground, it was situated on an ancient fault line directly above a magma pool. Because of its location, the temperature stayed at a steady 120 degrees with 90 percent humidity. Those conditions had created the perfect environment for the world's largest crystals to grow, with one towering more than forty feet tall and weighing fifty-five tons. The giant Crystal Cave resembled a real-life Fortress of Solitude, even more magnificent than anything imagined for Superman.

The cavern had gained the attention of biologists, geologists, crystallographers, cave scientists, and space exploration experts from around the world. They came to Naica to see what secrets the crystals could reveal about ancient life on Earth and its relationship to the universe. But none of them was a psychometrist.

Roan was about to collect a whole other set of data.

⌒

Roan slept the entire flight, suspended above the clouds and oblivious to the turbulence as the plane arched across the globe at eight hundred miles per hour. He awoke shortly before landing in Mexico and performed the same series of deep stretches he always did before climbing. Nervous energy trilled through him at the thought of the journey he was about to make. He ended the session with a powerful Bhairava mudra, the mudra of fierce determination.

When he stepped off the plane in Mexico, he could have been anywhere, in any time zone; the world had begun to feel that small.

There was no meter in the taxi to Saucillo. The old man driving him negotiated in advance the fare for the hour-and-a-half ride south through the desert.

The rusted Toyota Corolla blared mariachi music from the speakers the entire way in a rich symphony of horns, strings, and a chorus of men that filled the car and spilled out through the open windows.

Roan closed his eyes, feeling the December sun on his face

and the whip of the desert wind as the car raced down Highway 45 through northern Mexico. The long stretches of farms passed by him like a stream.

They drove through the city of Delicias and soon after reached Saucillo, a town of eleven thousand. Roan was meeting Sun at a motel near the town's center. They would see Stuart tomorrow at the site if he could get there in time. Roan had emailed him the oopart map, showing him just how they'd arrived at their destination.

On the way to the motel, the taxi drove past the town square, where a charming clock tower stood, and Roan smiled. It was either the perfect welcome or an ominous sign. Hanus had died in a clock tower, and Roan had the man's key in his bag next to Descartes's ring.

Roan thanked the driver and got out of the car, grabbing his duffel. The motel he was staying in was a three-story redbrick building with bars on the windows. The restaurant next door had a hand-painted welcome sign with a cow on it saying FLAUTAS and TORTAS.

The people of Saucillo were eyeing him as he walked to the motel. They seemed to wonder what the tall stranger wearing gloves and all black was doing there.

When Roan checked in, he found that Sun had already arrived. He went upstairs to drop off his things before meeting her. His spartan motel room had a white tile floor, a double bed, a scuffed-up old dresser, and a loud mini-fridge. That was it, but at least everything was spotlessly clean.

He had several messages from his mother's home number on his phone. She must have realized he'd gone off the radar. Like Melicent's voicemails, he ignored them. Talking to either of them right now would make him second-guess his decision to be there altogether. He couldn't allow his emotions and attachments to make him change course. He had less than twenty-four hours until he was in the cave.

All his life Roan had felt like an astronaut, out of place in the world as he launched into the inner depths of the past. Tomorrow would be his hardest journey, but a journey he had to make. Whatever he discovered in that cave would be the collateral they could use against whoever was targeting them.

Roan didn't know what answers he would find tomorrow. But as he'd come to understand since the age of five, when he'd first held Leonard Slye's guitar and seen the man's life, anything was possible.

34. THE KIMONO

"IS THERE ANY CHANCE I have your ability too? Because that would be seriously awesome," Parker called out from the breakfast room. He was sitting at the table reading something from the internet on his phone. "This article says technically everybody has it, because we're all electromagnetic transmitters and receivers, or whatever, but some people's brains are hard-wired to be better at it. Like yours. Which to me is mind-blowing because well . . . you're you."

"Ha ha, very funny." Melicent rolled her eyes. She put a bottle of sparkling water on the table and went back to the kitchen.

"Ooh, this is creepy." Parker read, "'Since the brain doesn't immediately die with the heart, a psychometrist could attempt "neuro-residual recollection" and read a dead person's last thoughts.'"

"Very creepy. I won't be doing that," she said from kitchen.

"How about tactile telepathy?" he called out. "Reading people's thoughts in general by holding their hand. Can you do that?"

Melicent returned with two dinner plates without answering. She and Roan had done it once with each other, but she wasn't about to share that with her brother. "Can we eat and save the twenty questions for later?"

She had heated up one of the many frozen pizzas Parker had bought when he and Holly went to the store. It seemed surreal that they were basically homeless and had taken over Roan's house when he wasn't even there.

She glanced at Parker. Maybe this would be a good time to discuss something with him that'd been on her mind. "Listen, I want to talk to you about the house. What if we donate the land to the city and build a park, in Mom's memory?"

She'd been trying to figure out what to do with the property. The arson investigator had notified her the case was officially cold and the house was being released back to her. They'd sent her the fire report and she had pulled up the pictures online. She didn't want to show them to Parker. It was best if he didn't see the aftermath. There wasn't enough of the house to restore, and she wouldn't have wanted to rebuild it even if there was—not after the memory of the fire and the man who'd set it. That night would forever haunt her, even more so if she returned.

But she also didn't want to discard all the beautiful years they'd had growing up. The house had been Sadie's childhood home too. Melicent wanted children to climb their trees again, and what better way than to clear out what was left of the house's frame, lay down new grass, and build a playground? The corner lot was the perfect location for a neighborhood park.

"We could name it Sadie Park."

Parker's eyes were bright when she finished outlining the plan, and he agreed. Her heart lifted knowing that he thought it was a good idea.

"Maybe we should move here, to New Orleans," Parker said. "It's not like anything's keeping us in L.A. anymore. I can finish school here."

It was a good sign that he was thinking of school again. Right now he was officially on family leave because of the fire, but he'd have to go back after the holiday break. New Orleans could be a fresh start for both of them.

She mulled the idea. "What would I do for work here?"

"Don't you have like two million dollars?"

Melicent laughed. "You keep saying that, but I still want a career."

"Become an antique hunter like Roan. Have you seen all the stuff in the warehouse? It's insane."

She had to admit that returning lost heirlooms sounded like a fascinating job. Maybe she could work with Roan for the foundation. She hadn't been back in the warehouse yet, and after dinner Parker talked her into going on a tour.

When they flipped the switch, the lights turned on like the sun, illuminating the space, and her mouth dropped open.

Roan's world stretched out before her, filled with the thousands of stories he'd collected.

"He's like Indiana Jones turned hoarder." Parker's voice carried across the warehouse as he headed toward the back. "Check out all these candelabras. It's so Goth."

"Don't touch anything," she called out to him. Melicent wasn't an appraiser, but she could see that many of these pieces could grace a museum.

The storefront on Magazine contained only a fraction of what Roan owned. The warehouse was filled with racks of paintings, ancient maps, temple doors, furniture and chandeliers, figurines and iconography from around the world, all organized by some sort of system Melicent couldn't decipher.

She wandered through the rows, her arms crossed with her hands tucked under them. It wasn't that she was afraid to touch anything, she told herself, there was simply too much to choose from.

Along the back wall were built-out offices and individual storage rooms. When Melicent opened the first door and stepped inside, she was greeted with the same hollow feeling she'd had in the back room of the Magazine storefront. She almost closed the door and left the room alone, but instead she forced herself to walk inside and turn on the light.

When the lights came on she gasped with pleasure. The room was filled with Japanese kimonos displayed on oversized hangers that stretched out the arms to showcase the graceful T-shaped sleeves. Each gown had a matching obi and was made of heavy silk in vivid hues of red or gold. Cascading images of cranes, flowers, or cherry blossoms trailed over the fabric in delicate patterns. Many kimonos were paired with a *tansu,* a wooden wardrobe chest, or a *kyodai,* which was a dainty mirrored vanity with an array of tiny drawers and cabinets. Some of the sets had all three pieces. The whole room felt like an exhibit at a museum.

From the lot numbers and the pages of notes next to each she knew right away that she'd found another collection for the Heirloom Foundation. Like the Lakota collection, these antiques weren't for sale. Roan was planning to return them.

The first kimono was a dramatic white-and-black silk with red poppies brocaded at the hem and shoulders. When Melicent touched the gown she was greeted by memories of loss so strong they felt like rain.

A woman named Emi Tanaka had been the last person to own this kimono and the tears were hers. Emi was an American, whose grandparents were Issei, first-generation Japanese who had come to California from Japan and settled years ago. Emi didn't speak Japanese, but she treasured her grandmother's *tansu, kyodai,* and *kimono.* Emi had planned to give her bridal set, called a bride's *yomeiri-dogu* in Japanese, to her daughter, Mary, one day.

Emi's plans for the future ended with Pearl Harbor. The day after the attack her family's bank account was frozen. Hysteria gripped the nation over anyone who looked Japanese. Within two months, the government issued instructions to Emi and her family informing them that they would be relocated to a military camp somewhere.

They would have to leave all their belongings, their pets, their cars and first go to the Santa Anita racetrack in Los Angeles, which was the closest temporary detention center. Rumors of barbed wire and armed guards were already flying. Emi couldn't imagine what it would be like. They said that people were sleeping in horse stalls.

She didn't know how long they would have to stay at the racetrack before they would be shipped to a camp. They were being constructed in California, Arizona, Colorado, Wyoming, Utah, and Arkansas—ten camps to hold the entire Japanese American population, 120,000 people. No one was given word if and when they could ever return home again.

The week before Emi received her relocation orders, her husband was taken in for questioning. The FBI came and knocked on their door and took him away without warning. All the family knew was he was to be sent to a different camp, a special camp for interrogation. Emi's husband was a schoolteacher and also wrote for the local newspaper. The U.S. government was rounding up all the Japanese American professors, journalists, and community leaders to ensure that they weren't spies.

Emi packed the one suitcase she was allowed to bring while her daughter watched. Mary was only three. Emi opened each drawer of her *tansu* and looked at all of the things she couldn't take with her. She laid her kimono on the bed. The poppies spread across the blanket like a field of flowers, and she let her daughter's hands touch the gown for the first and last time. Then Emi carefully hung it back up in the closet.

The story within the kimono ended there when Emi dimmed the lights of her bedroom, took her daughter's hand, and left with their one suitcase. They both were dressed in their Sunday best. Emi's parents and in-laws would all leave together, walking out of their homes and into a new, dark world without hope. Emi never returned or touched her things again.

⌐

Melicent lifted her hand from the gown, her heart heavy. She read through the notes Roan had made for Emi's *tansu, kyodai,* and *kimono.* Roan had found Emi's treasures and he'd charted the imprints, enabling him to track down her descendants.

Emi, along with her entire family, had been imprisoned in Manzanar, a camp located at the foot of the Sierra Nevada in California, until November 1945. After four years in captivity, they were released. They had no home, no money, no place to go. Their property had been taken, all their possessions gone.

Emi's daughter, Mary, was now eighty-one, a retired nurse who lived in San Francisco. She had one daughter and three grandchildren. Emi had died fifteen years ago.

Melicent walked through the room, the kimonos watching her like silent women. Their voices were woven into the silk. She read every page of Roan's notes for every *yomeiri-dogu.* He had worked hard to find the women who were the rightful owners of these heirlooms, and he was attempting to rebuild the bridges between mothers and daughters, grandmothers and granddaughters that had been destroyed by the war.

Melicent finally understood Roan's mission for the Heirloom Foundation. Roan was trying to help mend the wounds he encountered throughout history, the forgotten wounds, the buried wounds. Roan wasn't a collector, he was a healer.

There were more rooms like this one sequestered in the warehouse, filled with the dark stones of the past Roan had overturned. When she was strong enough she would visit them all.

Now that she was trying to connect with her ability, she was touching life for the first time, looking under its skin and seeing all its facets, shadows, and light. She wiped tears from her face that she hadn't felt fall and left, shutting the door. Her heart ached too much to stay.

Right now she only wanted to be with the man who had built this room and found these treasures. Where was he? Was he safe? The questions wouldn't leave her mind.

She had left Roan so many messages, but she knew he wasn't going to call her back. He had continued on the journey without her. He may have taken his gloves off with her for one night, but in his heart he had put them back on.

35. THE COIN

ROAN CAME OUT OF THE SHOWER to discover his phone, laptop, and wallet had been stolen. His duffel bag had been rifled through, but nothing else was taken. Saint-Gaudens's model coin was still in his pant pocket and the ooparts were in the secret pouch in his travel bag.

The irony didn't escape him. The thief had missed not one but three priceless items and taken everything that was expendable.

Roan put his hand on the room's doorknob and could see the thief clearly: a twelve-year-old boy, a local, who had been tipped off by his uncle that a wealthy tourist was staying there. They had instructed him to get his wallet, cell phone, wristwatch, and whatever else he could find that looked valuable.

The boy had squatted outside, waiting for the sound of the shower, and picked the lock with ease. His father and uncle ran a chop shop outside of Saucillo that brought in stolen cars within a three-hundred-mile radius. They were experts at breaking into anything.

Roan sat down on the bed and rubbed his eyes. So much for locking the door. It was going to be a hassle to replace his passport and get money wired, but he'd deal with that headache after the cave. Right now a stolen ID seemed inconsequential, and no one could access the information in his phone but him.

At least he wouldn't be tempted to call Melicent and hear her voice. He also wouldn't continue to feel guilt while watching the number of voicemails from his mother rack up. Neither of them would approve of what he was doing.

His father might.

Was that why he was pushing himself so hard now? To find out if his father was right? Had his gift been worth the demise of their family? Tomorrow he hoped to find out.

He changed and met Sun downstairs in the courtyard. She looked just as she had in New York in her tunic jacket and pants. Roan felt a wellspring of emotions when he saw her. If Sun hadn't given him her fan, she would have remained a stranger. He might have even suspected she was behind the psychometrists' disappearances. But Sun inherently understood how vital it was they trust each other, and she had foreseen the best way to do that.

How different his world might have been if a psychometrist like Sun had been his teacher. He'd lived his whole life closed off from people, even from his parents, if he was honest. But Sun had opened a door and pushed her way in.

"Shall we walk?" she asked him.

She took off without waiting for an answer, just like she had on their first meeting in New York, and the moment began to take on a dreamlike quality. Roan might be a four-and-a-half-hour flight from New Orleans, but today was the farthest he'd ever been from home. And tomorrow would be the equivalent of sailing off the edge of the world.

He and Sun made their way toward the town square right as dusk finished its fall. Near the church a dance rehearsal was under way. A dozen couples were spinning and weaving in complex patterns while onlookers clapped, and a little girl in fairy wings ran around them. The sleepy town was an assortment of old pickup trucks, men with cowboy hats, and colorful buildings nestled between the hills. Roan and Sun passed a flamenco studio and a bright purple painted restaurant on the corner.

Roan brought Sun up to speed on his conversation with Stuart, who was en route and meeting them tomorrow afternoon at the site. He'd been able to book a flight to Chihuahua in time.

"Does he know who is behind this?" Sun asked. Her arms were crossed and she had a worried frown on her face.

"He doesn't. They were keeping him in a warehouse off the docks on the Isle of Dogs. He managed to get away when the guards left."

"Or they let him get away."

The same thought had crossed Roan's mind. He studied Sun's closed expression, her face unreadable, and yet, after holding her fan, Roan could read her expression better than anyone. She was gravely concerned.

"I'm sorry about the fire," Roan offered. They had yet to speak of it. "Have they discovered anything?"

Sun waved her hand with a dismissive air, not wanting to discuss it.

When they reached the gazebo in the square, Roan knew it was the time to give the fan back. He took the box out of his pocket. Her eyes flashed in response.

"Thank you." Roan tried to convey the depth of his feelings, his voice solemn. "I'm honored you entrusted this in my care."

Sun took the box with a nod and it disappeared within the voluminous folds of her jacket. A guarded look remained in her eyes, an unspoken question. He had not given her anything yet in return. Her absolute trust in him was not guaranteed—and he needed it if he was going into a cave of ancient crystals with two ooparts in hand.

Roan had brought his coin with him for that purpose. Handing it to her was in essence handing her a book of his life.

He never thought he'd share his lucky coin with anyone, and now he was about to give it to a seventy-eight-year-old psychometrist, in the middle of a desert in Mexico. Life never ceased to amaze him.

Sun took Saint-Gaudens's model coin in her hand and gazed at it, her eyes turning inward.

Roan looked up at the stars beginning to blanket the sky and waited patiently for her to read the imprints. His eyes landed on a nearby lamppost. It was a striking design with two sculptured lions on top, each holding a light and facing away from each other.

The pair of lions made him wonder what Melicent was doing right now, what she was feeling after his desertion—what she had found of his to touch.

He missed her.

He'd made the wrong decision by leaving her behind. He'd shut her out, just as he did to everyone who got too close, no matter how noble his intentions. And he made a vow that no matter what happened tomorrow he would come back to her.

Sun shifted and opened her eyes, finished with the coin. She handed it back to him and folded her hands over his gloved ones. Sun now knew intimate details about him, the thoughts and feelings he had carried in his pocket for so many years. But strangely enough, he didn't mind. He felt free.

"Your greatest fear is time," she said with startling precision. "The immensity of it, its vastness, its weight. Time has given us our power and yet time stopped your heart."

Roan found himself holding his breath as he listened to her go on.

"The Earth is billions of years old and our lives are less than a century. Every new century is built on the ruins of the old, adding to the weight of our collective memory, like gravity. What will the memory of your life be? What will be its weight?"

Her eyes brimmed with understanding.

"Cosmic time is something we all search to understand. In ancient Korean philosophy we believe in the cosmic year. One year of the universe is 129,600 years on Earth. One month of the universe is 10,800. Our recorded history is less than a week, and our own story begins in the final seconds. This whole life is but a blink in cosmic time. We all want to feel like there is a reason behind the time we live in. Our ability makes us more aware. It's why we're here." She motioned to the desert. "Why we followed Stuart and Miguel on this journey. The ooparts are speaking to all of us."

Roan took the coin back and put it in his pocket. "Why aren't you ever afraid of what you might see?" he asked.

She measured her words. "Because I cannot pick and choose what to see, just as I cannot choose the time I lived in. So I must see it all." Roan knew she was talking about her childhood, the war and the deaths of her family. Sun stared into his eyes with certainty. "But if there's one thing my life has shown me, there is a place beyond the world that pain and darkness cannot reach. After you experience that place, you can touch anything."

36. THE LAPTOP

THE SOUND OF THE PHONE RINGING in one of the warehouse's offices was incessant. It wouldn't stop. After four rings and a delay for voicemail, it started up again.

"Should we get that?" Parker yelled to Melicent from the opposite side of the warehouse.

"I don't know." Melicent shut the door to another room filled with heirlooms she'd been investigating and followed the sound.

When she turned on the lights to the office, the ringing stopped. She went inside, sure the caller would try again. A brilliant ruby Persian rug covered most of the floor and a smaller circular rug in the back corner looked like a meditation mat. Melicent walked over to the desk made of contemporary chrome and glass and saw Stuart's laptop. She'd found Roan's office.

When the phone rang again, she picked it up abruptly. "Hello?"

"Hello? Who is this?"

Melicent recognized Jocelyn's voice right away and cringed. "Dr. Matthis—Jocelyn. I'm so sorry. You surprised me. It's Melicent."

"Why are you answering Roan's office line? Is everything all right?" She sounded frantic. "I've been trying to reach him all day."

"Roan's . . . not here," Melicent hedged.

"But is he all right?"

"What do you mean?" Melicent was getting alarmed by Jocelyn's tone.

"I couldn't sleep last night, worrying he might do something foolish again to find Stuart. He had an incident before where he touched something he shouldn't have."

"What do you mean he touched something he shouldn't have?" Melicent asked, all the while thinking *He has done something foolish*—he'd gone off without her.

"Roan had a heart attack," Jocelyn said flatly. Melicent's breath caught as Jocelyn went on to explain what had happened at Gobekli Tepe. How Roan believed it was the age of the stone that had triggered it.

"He told me about Gobekli Tepe," Melicent said, "but not that he almost died."

"I'm sure he'll be livid for my telling you. Do you know where's he gone? Why he's so unreachable?"

Melicent tried to focus on answering Jocelyn's string of questions, still reeling from the revelation of what had happened in Turkey. "Roan's gone off to find Stuart. I don't know where he is and he isn't returning my calls either."

The words began to bubble out of her. Melicent didn't question the impulse to tell Jocelyn everything—starting with the Breguet watch and *Antiques Roadshow*. She wanted Jocelyn to know the whole story.

By the time Melicent had gotten to the YouTube fiasco, Jocelyn couldn't have sounded more shocked. "You mean, you have the same ability?"

"Not as strong as Roan, but yes." Melicent could hear the wheels turning in Jocelyn's mind.

"I see" was all she said.

Melicent's voice held a slight tremor when she recounted the fire and the imprint of the man who had set it. She explained how Roan had helped them and then they'd come to London. Roan had picked up another ominous imprint in Stuart's house. After that Melicent knew he'd started keeping things from her. "A psychometrist in New York had her home set on fire too. It was the fire in Manhattan on the news. I don't know if she's okay."

"My God. I can't believe he kept me in the dark about all this."

Melicent felt a twinge of guilt that she'd gone against Roan's wishes and told Jocelyn everything—but dammit, he'd gone against hers too. Where was he?

"Do you think he went to New York?" Jocelyn asked. "To see if this other psychometrist is all right?"

"Maybe Holly knows." It had been the one question Melicent had been loath to ask. Even though she no longer harbored the same insecurities she'd had when it came to Roan's childhood friend, it would still hurt if Roan had confided in Holly and said nothing to her. Melicent was planning to pin Holly down for more information in the morning, but now it couldn't wait. Jocelyn thought so too.

"That's it. I'm flying over there," Jocelyn said. "I'll book an early flight this morning and be there by tomorrow." London was six hours ahead, so although it was eight P.M. in New Orleans it was two A.M. in England.

Melicent hung up and sat down in Roan's chair, feeling as galvanized as Jocelyn. If Roan thought he could exclude them and go off by himself to save the damn day, then he had another thing coming. She wasn't going to sit there and wait either.

She picked up the phone and called Holly, who answered on the first ring. "Roan? What are you doing back? The tour's not until tomorrow."

Melicent hesitated. Well, she'd just gotten her answer. Holly knew exactly where Roan had gone. It stung, but not as much as she thought it would.

"Holly, it's Melicent."

"Oh." Holly sounded flustered. "What are you doing in Roan's office?"

"The phone kept ringing, so I answered it. It was Jocelyn trying to reach Roan." Melicent could sense Holly's unspoken question: *Why were you in the warehouse?* But Holly didn't say anything.

"Here's the deal." Melicent found herself adopting Holly's no-nonsense style. "Jocelyn is worried that Roan's going to have another incident like Turkey," she said, showing Holly she knew more about Roan than Holly thought. "He's not returning either of our calls. I'm seriously worried too. Where is he?"

Holly became flustered. "Look, Roan is on a trip, investigating something for Stuart, and he'll be back. I'm sorry he hasn't called you yet. If it means anything, I did tell him to."

Melicent was surprised to hear that and used it to press her point. "Can you at least tell me where he's gone? Please. Jocelyn is getting on a plane right now she's so frantic."

"Well Dadgummit," Holly muttered, sounding more Southern than ever.

"I'm pretty sure you know Jocelyn well enough that you're going to have to tell her where he is."

Holly sighed. "He's in Naica, Mexico, at the Crystal Cave. I have no idea why. You know Roan. He's so secretive. But it's got the oldest or the biggest crystals in the world—I had to pull serious strings to get him inside. He said it would help him find Stuart and the answer to everything, whatever that means."

At Holly's words Melicent sat there frozen, unable to move. She knew what Roan was planning to do. Her eyes watered and a feeling of helplessness filled her. Roan had discovered something within the oopart map that led to the cave, and then he'd kept it from her. He was going to risk his life to find out what happened to Stuart and why someone had tried to kill her. It's why he had written her that note, why he'd given her the Breguet.

He didn't know if he was coming back.

Holly was busy saying how Roan would be back soon.

"Holly." Melicent stopped her cold with her voice. "Don't you see? It's why he won't talk to me or Jocelyn. He's going to try and *touch* the crystals and read the imprint."

⁓

By two A.M. Melicent couldn't sleep; she was too filled with anxiety. After their phone call earlier, Holly had been keeping her abreast. Holly couldn't reach Roan either, which wasn't a good sign. She was making arrangements to get them to Naica as quickly as possible the next day. Jocelyn was in the air and would land in New Orleans before noon.

By morning, Melicent crawled out of bed to get ready. Parker was still asleep. He had talked her into letting him come with them, and she'd agreed. She understood how it felt to be left behind.

She went downstairs and made coffee. The inviting aroma helped her wake up. She took a cup to the computer room behind the kitchen and sat down at Roan's computer to research the Crystal Cave.

When she clicked on the pictures that came up, the images of monstrous selenite pillars boggled her mind. That was where they were going?

The more she read, the more she wondered how Holly had gotten Roan inside the cave. The Crystal Cave was off-limits to the public and even to the miners from Peñoles. The entrance was locked away behind a great steel door, and anyone who went inside needed to wear a special suit packed with ice. Even with the ice suit, humans couldn't survive the heat or the 90 percent humidity for long. The dangerous conditions were almost the equivalent of going to the moon.

Melicent heard Holly's car pulling into one of the cargo bays and went to the warehouse to meet her.

Holly gave her a brisk greeting and headed into Roan's office. "I left word with Roan's contact at the cave for him to call right away when he arrives for his tour this afternoon. I stressed it was urgent." Her cell phone rang.

Melicent sat down in Roan's chair, watching Holly pace as she talked. Jocelyn was due to arrive in two hours, and they'd be rendezvousing at the airport to fly by charter direct to Naica. From what she could gather, Holly was on the phone with the head of Peñoles, talking him into letting them use his private airstrip.

Holly had painted their arrival as a simple late addition to the tour, a flighty mistake on her part in her efforts to coordinate the group, and she cajoled him into not only letting them use the private airstrip next to the mine's entrance, but into having a representative ready on the ground to escort them to the cave, where they would join Roan and Sun's tour before it began. The goodwill that accompanied a million-dollar purchase went quite far.

Melicent turned to Stuart's laptop sitting out on Roan's desk. She wanted to find where Naica fell on the oopart map.

When she opened it, the screen immediately powered up. Using the touch pad, she scrolled through the files to find the map. As her hands rested on the keyboard, an ominous feeling began to circle her wrist and coil up her arm like a snake. Her throat constricted and her heart sped as a whirlwind of imprints entered her mind. *This can't be true.*

She couldn't take her hands off the computer. The thoughts and images were coming hard and fast at her, each one like a physical blow.

Stuart had intentionally planted his computer in the safe for them to find. There was a spyware program on it to track the laptop and view its activity from a remote location.

Stuart had been using the tracking app to monitor Roan and

know where he was at all times. He'd also planned to steal Jocelyn's cell phone and use her tracking app too, knowing Jocelyn and Roan had their phones linked.

Roan hadn't touched this laptop without his gloves on, or he would have felt the same calculating intention.

The thoughts from the keyboard continued to bombard her. Suddenly everything in the world seemed upside down. The man they'd been trying to save was at the heart of the darkness. She took her hands off the keys with a cry.

Holly hung up the phone. "What is it? What happened?"

Melicent looked at Holly, her whole body sickened. "It's him. . . . It's him," she could only keep repeating. "He's the one."

"Who?" Holly stared at the laptop in confusion, trying to catch up. "Whose computer is that?"

"Stuart's." Melicent tried to voice what she'd felt, what she'd seen, but she couldn't. She'd just met the man who set her house on fire. "He's behind all of it."

Melicent had seen Stuart's face clearly for the first time, and she recognized him. The man in the imprints was the man in her nightmares.

"What are you talking about?" Holly had become frozen.

The words tumbled from her in a panic. "Stuart's after Roan. He lured Roan with the disappearances, the threats—they were all to get him to decipher the ooparts. He needed Roan to figure out the connection because no one else could."

"You're saying it's all Stuart?"

"Yes." Melicent could barely get the word out. "Everything was planned." She shook her head, her mind in a fog, unable to believe it. She'd seen the moment Stuart locked the laptop in the safe. He'd created a show to fool Roan and he'd calculated the outcome. "He staged his own kidnapping so Roan would save him. He put flowers everywhere to record the violence."

Holly put her hand over her mouth. "But that's insane."

Melicent nodded. It was beyond insane. The man had hired thugs to beat him up. "But it worked. Roan's doing exactly what he wants."

Melicent's emotions were clouding her ability to see further than that. She needed to touch the laptop again to try and sense more details, but she wasn't sure she could stomach ever touching it again. "Roan needs to touch this—he needs to see."

Holly nodded, shell-shocked. "We'll bring it with us."

It was much harder to break the news to Jocelyn. Jocelyn couldn't believe Stuart would commit such atrocities. She had been the one to introduce Roan to Stuart and encourage their friendship.

"Why would he do such a thing?" Jocelyn thought Melicent was somehow wrong. "It's just not possible. You have to be mistaken."

Melicent, Parker, Holly, and Jocelyn were on the plane en route to Naica. Parker was sitting beside Melicent and surprised her when he reached out and gave her hand a squeeze in reassurance. The love and care in his touch wedged a knot in her throat, and she squeezed back.

Jocelyn asked her for the hundredth time from across the aisle, "Are you sure you couldn't be confused?"

Melicent was trying hard to keep her patience with Roan's mother. If Stuart was so incapable of doing harm, as Jocelyn believed, then somewhere along the way he'd become capable.

Melicent was grateful that Holly didn't question her judgment or seem to doubt her. But then Holly had worked with Roan every day, for years. She knew the power of an imprint and the information it could impart.

Melicent looked out the plane's window at the clouds. The imprints from Stuart's laptop were still swimming in her mind. She'd seen glimpses of him in Jordan, when he'd found his first oopart. He'd begun to believe there might be a way to travel through time, to not only witness the past but to actually go back to the moment. He began to study every theory he could on time travel—wormholes, cosmic strings, time gates and ladders. Stuart was trying not only to read time but to bend it. He'd become demented in his obsession. She thought back to the moment she'd stood in his bedroom, how disturbed she was by what she'd seen.

This man had taken everything away from her, and now he might take Roan, too. The thought was too much to bear.

Holly made a call to the ground. "Thank you so much. We're due to land any minute." She grew still. "I see. Then we'll join them shortly." Holly hung up and any semblance of a smile left her face. "They're already there."

Jocelyn put her hand over her mouth, becoming more upset. "He won't touch the crystals. He knows he can't survive it." She was talking more to herself, her voice faraway.

Melicent knew Jocelyn was reliving memories of Turkey. Melicent had already noted with surprise that Jocelyn had her old wedding ring on and was twisting the ring back and forth on her finger. After touching the picture frame, Melicent had been privy to the solemn pact Jocelyn and Robert had made with each other. Their marriage might have ended, but they had promised each other that they would protect Roan as long as they lived.

Holly didn't offer Jocelyn words of comfort. Perhaps because she knew Roan too well. Like Holly, Melicent wasn't sure if Roan would touch the crystals or not. Throughout Roan's life his gift had brought him to the brink of understanding time's force in the world, but the deepest answers had always eluded him. If those answers were waiting in the Crystal Cave, he might take the risk.

Melicent understood the temptation. If she were Roan, if she had lived his life, she might do the same. Her thoughts returned to the picture frame and Jocelyn and Robert's last fight in Turkey, and she found herself agreeing with Robert West. Roan had been put on this earth for a reason, and the ooparts had led him to Naica.

Roan's one mistake was that he hadn't taken her with him.

37. THE MINE

OSCAR GONZALES HATED HIS JOB. There was no escaping the heat in a sweltering control room one thousand feet below ground, even in the antechamber with fans running at high speed. He had thought this oppressive sauna would at least help with his weight problem, but his girth had not shrunk in the five years he'd been operations manager at the Crystal Cave.

Today he was in a terrible mood, partly due to the lunch his wife had packed him earlier: an apple, three celery sticks, and half of a tuna sandwich with a speck of mayonnaise. Now he was starving and ready for dinner but had to stay after hours to give a tour to some wealthy tourists who were friends with the president—of the company or of Mexico, at this point it could be either, because only a select number of scientists were allowed inside.

The tall man in black and the little Asian woman were an odd pair. They were probably space engineers from NASA; the strange ones always were. The tall man's brother was running late and due to meet them any minute.

Oscar finished shaking the man's hand and gave him a pained smile.

Why me?

Roan pulled his hand away from Oscar's and put his glove

back on, feeling satisfied. Oscar Gonzales had no idea why they were there. The poor man just wanted to go home and have dinner.

Oscar snapped his fingers and pointed at him, remembering. "A woman named Holly something called. She said she was having trouble reaching you and for you to call her when you got here."

Roan smiled and nodded. He had no intention of calling Holly; he didn't need the distraction. They were waiting outside the mine's main entrance for Stuart to arrive, and their tour guide was growing antsy.

Oscar checked his watch and rubbed his hand across his face in frustration. They'd been waiting almost thirty minutes now.

"He'll be here," Roan insisted. He'd come too far to leave Stuart behind. This was Stuart's discovery, and he deserved to be in the cave as much as they did.

Sun was staring off into the distance with her arms crossed. "Here he comes."

From afar they could see the car kicking up dust as the taxi made its way up the mountain.

Roan could make out Stuart sitting in the back seat, and a rush of relief hit him. After witnessing the attack at Stuart's house, he thought he'd never see him again.

Who were the men who had taken him? And where were Miguel and Gyan?

Oscar hurried to greet the taxi and help Stuart out of the car. Stuart had his right arm in a sling and looked like he hadn't showered or slept for days. His face was haggard, with deep circles under his eyes.

Oscar herded Stuart toward the doors, anxious to begin. "Good, good. Come, come. We've been waiting."

"Sun?" Stuart stopped short when he saw her. "How . . . ?"

"I found her through Hanus's key." Roan didn't have time to explain.

Stuart looked at Roan in amazement. "Looks like you found a lot of things." He motioned to the building. They had so much to talk about, but right now Oscar was hurrying them inside to sign in with the guard at the front desk.

"Have you heard from Miguel or Gyan?" Sun asked, her face grave.

A pained look came over Stuart and he shook his head. "It was only me in the warehouse. What's happened to Gyan?"

"He's missing too," she told him.

"My God." Stuart couldn't have looked more taken aback.

"He left the ring behind," Roan said. "It's what got us here." There was so much Roan needed to discuss, but they couldn't talk freely in front of Oscar, and right now they didn't have time. This hour was costing them one million dollars, essentially $16,666 per minute. It was the most expensive block of time he'd ever purchased.

Oscar led them into a conference room for their orientation, where he opened up a large wall closet and started handing out the safety gear. "Without the proper suits you would have only ten minutes—fifteen at most—in there. With the ice suits you'll have forty-five."

The ice suits were really two vests and a caving suit that went over both of the vests. The inner vest had hand-size ice packs sewn inside, and the outer vest protected the ice. They were also given respirators that blew frigid air, as well as protective boots, gloves, and a helmet with a headlamp. The getup looked close to what an astronaut might wear.

Oscar struggled to put on his gear as well, the fabric of his suit straining against his middle. For now Roan kept his gloves on, though soon the time might come to take them off. He helped Stuart zip up his suit.

"Did you bring the ooparts?" Stuart asked him.

Roan took out Hanus's key and Descartes's ring from his bag and handed them over. Stuart opened his satchel. Roan froze when he saw Miguel's oopart, the Chinese compass. The spoon and heaven-plate were in Stuart's bag.

"Where did you get that?" he asked Stuart.

Stuart hesitated before answering. "Miguel gave it to me."

Stuart was lying, he could tell. A cold feeling washed over Roan—why did Stuart have Miguel's compass? Miguel would have taken the oopart with him to Australia. The fact that Stuart had it now didn't make sense.

Roan met Sun's eyes. He could see the same question in them. *Why is Stuart lying?*

"Let's go, people!" Oscar corralled them toward the back door. "It's a twenty-minute drive down the main mineshaft. We'll be a thousand feet under. *Vamanos.*" He led them down a hallway to the backside of the building where a row of fifteen-seat passenger vans was waiting.

Oscar hopped into the driver's seat of one of them. Sun took the seat next to him and Roan and Stuart climbed into the back. Roan's mind kept circling around Miguel's oopart. There was only one way Stuart could have obtained it. He'd been with Miguel in Australia. Everyone thought Miguel had gone by himself, that he'd disappeared in the outback. But Miguel hadn't been alone.

Suddenly everything began to shift into a different light. What other secrets was Stuart keeping?

The van entered the mineshaft and began its near-vertical descent. Oscar did his best to play tour guide. "The cave you are going to see is one of the great wonders of the world. It was discovered in 2000 during an excavation for the Naica mine. Scientists are petitioning the Mexican government to have the cave designated as a UNESCO World Heritage site to protect the crystals for future generations. These crystals are very fragile, very rare. So please be careful where you walk. The chances of there being another cave like this anywhere else in the world are next to none."

Roan knew there was no other place like it on Earth.

Stuart leaned toward him and dropped his voice. "All the way here I kept looking at the map you emailed me. And I could see how for years I've been traveling along its grid lines. I went to Easter Island, Machu Picchu, Giza, Paracas, Stonehenge, so many sites with the ooparts, thinking it would trigger something, anything. And here you found the center of the whole maze. Well done."

"It's not a maze. It's a labyrinth," Roan explained. "The crop circles gave me the answer."

"So Miguel was right."

And Miguel should be here was all Roan could think. Miguel's oopart was here, but Miguel wasn't. What had happened to him in Australia?

Stuart was amped up, not entirely himself. "What if this labyrinth's center is a doorway to other times, other dimensions?"

Oscar had been following the conversation and looked at them in the rearview mirror. "What kind of scientists did you say you were?"

"Psychometrists." Stuart gave him a brazen smile. Oscar nodded, clearly baffled.

Roan glanced down, surprised to see his suit lighting up in the dark. He had thought the plastic plates attached to the fabric on his shoulders and knees were simple reflectors, but these suits had working lights built into them. It magnified the fact they were heading deep underground into another world.

～

When they arrived at the cave's entrance Oscar parked. The area was well lit with floodlights, and Roan could see the shadows of the road behind them leading away like an ant trail.

Oscar opened the enormous steel door to the anteroom of the cave, and the temperature shot up from 95 to 110 when they stepped inside. A big thermometer was mounted on the wall next to a clock.

Everyone put on their helmets and Oscar passed out bottled water. "Drink. You're going to sweat out every bit of moisture you have in you. When you come back, drink more."

Oscar turned and led them upslope toward a glass door to the entrance of the main chamber. "I'll be waiting here inside the control room. Once I open this door you'll be hit by heat that is going to feel like an elephant slamming into your body and sucking all of the water from your cells."

"Don't mince words, mate," Stuart tried to joke, but his eyes were wide with anticipation.

"You will have thirty-five minutes to explore and ten minutes to get back. No more. When your time is up, I'll come to the door and call you. I suggest you do not go far. The crystal beams are fragile and easily scratched by a boot or a fingernail, so please be careful. And you are not allowed to bring anything back with you. Understand?"

Roan, Stuart, and Sun nodded and put on their respirators and headed up the path to the chamber.

The heat and humidity climbed to 136 degrees Fahrenheit and pressed on Roan like a wall of melting lead. He took slow, measured steps, pushing through the heavy air until he came to the opening of the cave and got his first look inside.

Crystal beams soared to the ceiling in majestic towers and fields of translucent selenite glistened along the path of his flashlight. Beds of crystals clustered like gardens with daggered edges.

Roan glided his hand along one of the beams. Even through the fabric of his glove, the crystal felt silky smooth and soft.

The cave was unlike anything he had experienced before. The grandeur and magnitude hit him like a wave. Energy radiated in the air with the concentration of life force, and he knew without a doubt that the answer to the ooparts was there.

"Magnificent." Sun came to stand beside him and they moved deeper into the cavern.

"Can you feel it?" Stuart whispered. He turned in a slow 360-degree circle, taking it all in. Then he brought out the ring, the key, and the compass.

When the ooparts met the air, they began to glow with an otherworldly light.

"My God," Stuart whispered. "Would you look at that?"

The ooparts came alive, shimmering in brilliance as they attuned themselves to their environment like three pitchforks being struck.

A harmonic resonance began to sound, like a far-off hum, and a colorful prism of garnet, emerald, sapphire, and ruby appeared inside the crystals, lit by a mysterious source, and illuminated the whole cavern.

Roan stood transfixed at the incredible symphony of light and sound unfolding before them.

The ooparts were keys, and they had just unlocked a door.

"You did it, Roan. This is it." Stuart had tears in his eyes. He placed Miguel's compass in his hand, setting the spoon on top of the heaven-plate. He held the plate out and watched the spoon spin on top of it and then stop. Like a divining rod used by the ancient magicians who'd held the compass before him, the spoon was guiding him to the center of the cave. The whole space was magnetized.

Roan stood still, unable to move. The crystal pillar next to him reminded him of the stone pillar at Gobekli Tepe—so easy to touch, and yet he hesitated, unable to push past his fear.

He took off both of his gloves and laid them aside. His bare palms could feel the energy permeating the space and his fingertips tingled. To prepare he brought his hands into an Abhaya Hridaya mudra, the Fearless Heart mudra he and Melicent had practiced together. But for the first time in his life the mudra fell short, because only her hand in his completed it. If he touched a crystal and an imprint overpowered him he might lose his life—and Melicent. The choice at this crossroads was clear.

He turned to Sun, his eyes shining with utter certainty.

"I can't," he told her.

For the first time he was choosing life over a memory.

Sun took his bare hand and squeezed it, just like her grandmother had done with her when she did something right.

"Good," she said. "Never be alone again." Her words moved him because she was right. He had walked through life alone, too caught up in the earth's pain and suffering to allow himself to live, or to love. He'd reached the heart of his own labyrinth. But he hadn't reached it alone. Sun, the strongest woman he'd ever met, stood beside him. She'd walked through the fires of this world and survived them, survived with a heart bigger than anyone he knew.

"I will try for both of us," she offered. But before she could, the ground beneath them began to rumble.

Roan turned to find Stuart had placed the Chinese compass on a crystal beam that was lying on its side like a table.

The spoon began to spin on the heaven-plate. Stuart was tapping directly into the energy of the cave with the ooparts. He let out a whoop. "It's working!"

"Stuart, don't!" Roan called out—but Stuart placed Hanus's key on the crystal too.

The ground began to quake and tremble, every crystal reacting. The ancient fault line was awakening.

Stuart placed Descartes's ring down last and knelt before the crystals. "Take me back. Take me back. Take me back," he whispered, looking like a desperate man praying at an altar.

The humming magnified and the compass spun faster, like a windmill signaling a storm.

"Move the ooparts!" Sun waved her arms, yelling at him.

Roan started toward Stuart. The walls of the cave shook harder, and the lights within the crystals turned blinding. The ground had become a tightrope. "The cavern's going to collapse!"

A violent tremor struck and Sun lost her balance, falling back onto a jagged bed of crystals. Her head landed on the rocks. Roan cried out and made his way to her.

"Everyone!" Oscar yelled from the entrance, a good fifty feet away. "You need to come back! We're having tremors."

"Someone's hurt!" Roan called back to him. "Get help!"

Oscar stepped inside the cave and saw the lights. He made the sign of the cross. "*Dios mío*." He swore and hurried back to the antechamber.

Roan yelled to Stuart over the deafening hum. "Stuart! We need to help Sun."

The ooparts were conjuring an electrical storm. A wild wind whipped around them. Stuart yelled back, "No! I can't leave! You go!"

Roan made his way over to him as carefully as he could, the ground threatening to give way. "Stuart, Nema's gone. The ooparts can't take you back."

Stuart turned to him in shock that he'd said Nema's name—that he understood. "How can you say that? This is a portal."

"We don't know what this is!" Roan tried to make him see reason.

But Stuart was beyond it. "I don't care! I have to try." The entire cave was vibrating like a rocket ready for liftoff, and a crystal beam nearby fell, heavier than a tree in a forest. The ground beneath the ooparts began to crack.

"Stuart, we have to go!" Roan tried to pull him away.

"No!" Stuart rose up and lunged at Roan's chest. Roan sidestepped, his body acting on instinct. Stuart charged at Roan again. Roan tried to wrestle him to the ground, but Stuart stumbled backward and the floor beneath him gave way like an avalanche.

Roan dropped to the ground and slid forward, using a deft

bouldering move to grab Stuart's hand and keep him from falling.

Stuart's body dangled over the ledge. The floor had suddenly become a cliff opening to a chasm.

When Roan held Stuart's hand, his breath hitched inside of him. Roan's father had always told him, *You never know a man until you shake his hand.* All these years Roan thought he had known Stuart. Now Stuart's hand was showing him the past and everything that he had done.

NORTHERN TERRITORY, AUSTRALIA

ONE MONTH AGO

MIGUEL WAS THE ONE WHO HAD SUGGESTED that he and Stuart visit Australia to see if the ooparts would respond. The Aborigines believed time flowed in a circle and every event left a record on the land. Miguel's theory was that the ooparts might react to the collective imprint embedded within one of their ancient sites.

They'd been traveling through the outback for two weeks and had journeyed to the Pinnacles, unearthly sculptures made of seashells from earlier epochs; the mysterious caves of the Blue Mountains; and Wilpena Pound, an amphitheater made of mountains that had formed a ring, creating the most magical stage on Earth.

"It's like tuning a radio," Miguel explained. "When you're in the middle of nowhere you get only static, but what if there is a certain place on Earth where these ooparts can get good reception and react?"

Stuart had been willing to buy into the idea, but so far it had yielded no results. Uluru was their final destination. The famous monolith had been a sacred site of the Aborigines for twenty-two thousand years. The collective imprint within the stone was immense. But the red rock didn't make the ooparts react either.

The trip was a clear disappointment. Before heading back to Alice Springs for their flight, they decided to venture deep into the Northern Territory, where Stuart had heard there were good climbs. Bouldering always helped him to refocus. Miguel could stay at camp and read his books while Stuart went climbing and tried to clear his head. Sometimes his best ideas came during that Zen-like window when he was gripping the rock with his bare hands.

Stuart scaled every rock face for two days without inspiration. No new thoughts or ideas were coming to him. He'd hit a dead end with the ooparts, and tomorrow they would be going home. Never had he felt so defeated. He had devoted the last three years to unraveling the ooparts' riddle. He'd used up all his savings, mortgaged his house to the limit to find the answers. He was almost out of funds and becoming desperate.

"There has to be a pattern that we're missing," Miguel said, laying out their sleeping bags at the campsite.

Usually Miguel and Stuart would go back and forth with theories at the campfire over dinner. But tonight, for once, Stuart didn't feel like talking. He brooded, watching the flames as he sipped his whiskey, and let Miguel ruminate on how there had to be some kind of order behind the locations where the ooparts had been discovered. He couldn't believe the phenomenon was random.

"We just need to figure it out." Miguel joined him at the fire and sat down. "Early next year we can pick another place and try again. I can take time off from the university. Maybe we should go back to Wiltshire for the next season of crop circles."

Stuart tried to swallow his frustration. For the past two years they'd visited sacred sites, walked crop circles with their ooparts in hand, and been around the world hoping to land on the answer. What his friend was suggesting didn't give him any hope.

"We need to know," Miguel said softly as he stared at the fire, "what the ooparts and crop circles are trying to tell us. They're like a compass leading us down a path, left by someone 'out there'"—Miguel pointed up at the stars—"or our ancient selves or our future selves. Maybe it's all one and the same." He went to get into his sleeping bag. "One day, Stuart, one day, my friend," he said with a smile, "we will travel far beyond this world. The earliest known maps are of the stars, not here. Don't give up."

Stuart didn't say a word. He really didn't give a damn about the stars or ancient maps. He was fed up with theoretical talk and whimsical ideas—what he wanted was to bend time.

If only Roan were with them, they'd have had a better chance. Roan could return heirlooms generations removed from their descendants. No one in their group was that good at unraveling imprints. Roan could read every imprint embedded within the ooparts and find the answers they were missing. The problem was that Roan was afraid to touch anything too old and trigger another heart attack. Somehow Stuart had to convince him the risk was worth it.

Miguel's scream jarred him from his thoughts. Stuart jumped to his feet, spilling his whiskey into the fire. The flames shot up like a spire. In the light he could see Miguel in his sleeping bag, kicking with his legs, trying to get it off.

Stuart ran over to him and dragged Miguel out by the armpits—an angry snake slithered away into the darkness.

Miguel had crawled into his sleeping bag without shaking it out first. The snake had been inside, making its bed for the night.

Terror gripped Stuart as Miguel writhed and clutched at his leg, his body suffering an anaphylactic reaction.

Stuart ran to his bag to get the shot of antivenom. His hands were shaking so hard he had trouble opening the emergency pouch. He didn't even know where to administer the shot—he'd never had to before.

"Hold on, Miguel! Hold on!"

Frantic, he rolled up Miguel's pants. The bite was small and barely noticeable, but Miguel was already gripped with paralysis from the neurotoxins in the venom.

He choked and grabbed at his neck as his airway closed.

One antivenom shot wasn't enough. Stuart ran to his bag and found the other two. He gave them both to Miguel within seconds, but it didn't matter.

Miguel's heart had stopped.

⌣

Time seemed to stand still. The stars looked down on Stuart like thousands of unblinking eyes. He sat numb in disbelief and stared at the dwindling flames of the fire. The unforgiving wilderness surrounded the firelight's edge, and its stark shadows echoed the violence of the night.

Stuart didn't know what to do. Deep shock had made his mind go blank. The thought of having to deal with the authorities and ship Miguel's body back to Lima was so overwhelming, the whole night began to feel like a dream.

Perhaps it was for this reason that a doorway in his mind opened and allowed a thought to slither in, just like the snake who had been waiting to strike. And by dawn's first light, Stuart had a plan and had convinced himself that Miguel's death would not be in vain.

Wrapping Miguel's body in his sleeping bag, Stuart dragged him from their campsite. Stuart had explored all the deep canyons and crevasses on the mountain for the past two days, and he knew the perfect burial place for his friend.

A three-foot crack in the rock face led to a hidden cavern below. He lowered Miguel's body through the opening and winced when it landed. He threw Miguel's gear into the crevasse too, keeping only Miguel's oopart.

Stuart crawled into the tight space and climbed down without a rope. It took three hours to shovel the dirt and bury Miguel's body and his things. Then Stuart slept beside the grave and rested his arms. He'd need all his strength to boulder back up.

It would be weeks until anyone realized Miguel was missing. Before that, Stuart would contact François in the guise of enlisting the psychometrist's help with their research. Earlier in the year François had shared that he'd been diagnosed with pancreatic cancer that was inoperable. Stuart's mind began working through all the scenarios of how he could speed the poor man's death without causing any pain. The key was to make the suicide look suspicious to the group. He'd be doing François a favor by ending his suffering early, a euthanasia of sorts. Then Stuart needed to disappear, stage his own kidnapping, and send an SOS to Roan. If Roan believed every psychometrist was at risk, including himself, then Roan would help him without question.

As the plan took shape a strong sense of purpose filled him. If finding the source of the ooparts' power gave him the ability to return to the past and save Nema from dying, he was willing to pay any price.

⁓

By the time Stuart arrived at François's house in Avignon, he had cycled through countless excuses for what he was about to do, but none of them gave him absolution: he would be killing a man. He'd done an anonymous internet search on a library computer to find the best poisons and had one of them in his pocket, ethylene glycol.

François spent a day going over Stuart's research. He held Hanus's key and Descartes's ring multiple times. Stuart also showed him Miguel's crop circles file.

"How is Miguel?" François asked.

The question was innocent, but Stuart felt the blood rush to his head. Stuart couldn't hear the words he was speaking as he said Miguel was fine and busy in Lima—Miguel wished he could have joined them and sent his best.

When François touched the key and the ring, Stuart held his breath, hoping François would summon the answer to the whole riddle and save Stuart from having to carry out his plan. But the poor man was in such pain, his shaking hands could barely discern an imprint. He was too weak from the cancer.

"I'm sorry, Stuart, I cannot be of more help," François said with regret, handing the ooparts back. "Has Sun looked at these? She's better than any of us."

"Not yet." Stuart gave a tight smile, knowing he would have to contact the Korean woman soon. He'd never been comfortable around Sun and was afraid she would see right through him. He'd have to tread carefully with her.

That evening Stuart snuck the powerful tincture into François's cognac. When Stuart went to hand him his drink, he hesitated. "If you could go back in time and save the love of your life from dying, would you risk everything to do it?"

The Frenchman smiled, a gleam of his younger self in his eyes. "Absolutely." Then he took his glass, raised it in the air, and drank.

38. THE CRYSTAL

STUART DANGLED FROM THE LEDGE, his hand in Roan's. He looked up at Roan, his eyes begging for forgiveness that wasn't Roan's to give.

"Only you could get us here," Stuart pleaded. "The others couldn't. I couldn't. I knew you wouldn't try unless the threat was real. It was the only way." He choked on the words.

Roan couldn't fathom what Stuart had done. Roan had witnessed the darkest imprints through history, left by those who were willing to sacrifice others to achieve their gain. Now he was holding the hand of such a man, a man who had been his friend.

There was no time to process the shock. Above them the electromagnetic storm was narrowing into a single point like a vacuum, forming a vortex of energy.

They had to get out. Whatever crimes Stuart may have committed, Roan wasn't willing to let him die.

"Hang on!" He tried to pull Stuart up, but he didn't have enough leverage.

The only thing Roan could grab on to was a crystal.

He made a split-second decision—he grabbed on to the crystal and used his strength to hoist Stuart up. How many times had they helped each other reach a summit?

Stuart crawled away from the ledge, gasping, and rolled onto his back. The crystal Roan was holding anchored him to it like a weight, its energy a magnet he couldn't let go of. Within the crystal an endless imprint stretched out before him, a strata of time hundreds of thousands of years old. It began pulling him like the powerful tide of an ocean.

"Can't . . . I can't," Roan whispered, trying to resist, but his body was frozen.

Stuart stood up, riveted by the vortex forming out of midair behind them. A pinwheel of energy was sparking like a Tesla coil. Stuart began to climb the nearest crystal pillar to reach it.

Roan struggled to stay conscious, knowing what Stuart was about to do. "Don't."

Stuart looked down at Roan and gave him a sad smile. "Sorry, mate. I've got to. Maybe you'll find where I've gone in an imprint someday." Then he jumped.

The vortex closed like a wink with a brilliant flash, and Stuart vanished. The cave plunged into darkness.

Roan couldn't hang on any longer. The imprint within the crystal was overtaking him as the cavern's heat pressed on his chest in a vise, making it harder and harder for him to breathe.

"Roan." Sun had regained consciousness. She called to him but her voice sounded muted to his ears.

Inside his brain ninety billion nerve cells with their trillion synaptic connections were all firing at once like a solar storm, and a light within his mind's eye opened. The last thing he felt before he stepped through its door was Sun's hand in his. She'd crawled over to him and taken it.

Sun had made the journey to the other side once before with her grandmother. Like Princess Bari, the first shaman who guided souls to the otherworld, she was coming with him. They were dying.

39. THE MOUNTAIN

MELICENT LOOKED OUT THE WINDOW of the passenger van, unable to see a thing. The Earth was swallowing them whole.

The ground beneath them began to shake. They'd been feeling the vibrations for most of the drive, but this tremor was the worst yet. Their driver and guide, Elias, swore and pulled over. The shaking lasted almost a minute.

Melicent and Parker were in the back of the van. Holly was up front with Elias, and Jocelyn was in the seat behind them. They had rushed through putting on their ice suits and were on the way to the Crystal Cave with less than five minutes to go.

"I thought there weren't earthquakes this far north," Holly said.

Elias shook his head. "There aren't."

"Then what is it? An explosion in the mine?"

Elias didn't know and seemed reluctant to put the car back into gear.

Jocelyn prompted him, "We need to keep going."

When another tremor didn't follow, he muttered "*Mierda*" and started driving again.

Parker leaned over to Melicent and whispered, "I don't want to die down here."

"We won't," Melicent tried to reassure him.

"I love you," Parker said. "In case we do die."

"We won't," she said again, her stress levels soaring when another tremor hit and they had to pull over. Rocks rained down, rattling the van. Parker shouldn't have come with her. What was she thinking bringing him along? Her mother would never forgive her if something happened to him.

When they started driving again the lights on their ice suits came to life. Parker held his arm out. "My suit is glowing like a superhero."

"Parker, can we be quiet until we get there?" Melicent was about to lose her mind with worry.

The radio crackled in the silence. A man was speaking in Spanish and sounded distraught. Melicent only understood a smattering of what he was saying from the classes she'd taken in high school Spanish: someone was hurt and needed help.

Her hands went to her mouth. *Roan.*

Elias radioed back telling him he was almost there.

"What's going on?" Holly demanded.

"We have a situation from the tremors," Elias said, tight-lipped. "Oscar said one person's hurt, possibly two."

"How many people are down there?" Holly asked sharply. "There's only supposed to be two."

"The man's brother joined them."

"Oh my God," Jocelyn said, sounding dazed. There was only one person Roan would call his brother.

Stuart was with them.

Melicent gripped her middle, on the verge of being sick. She didn't know if she could meet the person who had tried to kill her. It was more than a nightmare—now he was with Roan. Had Stuart hurt him?

Parker put his arm around her. No one said a word the final minute of the drive.

When they arrived, Oscar ran toward them in a panic, launching into an outburst in Spanish.

"What's he saying?" Holly jumped in. "What's happened?"

"There's some kind of geomagnetic activity in the cavern."

Melicent's and Parker's eyes met, both thinking the same thing. *The ooparts.*

"One of the men fell. The woman's badly hurt." Elias quickly ushered them out of the car. "They only have fifteen minutes before they run out of time."

Melicent tried to control her fear. "Which man fell?"

"Un momento." Oscar was gaping at the group. "Who are you people?"

"Holly Beauchêne." Holly stepped forward. "I'm in charge of the tour."

Oscar looked ready to lose it. "Are you from NASA too?"

"No." She ignored Oscar and turned to Elias. "Get us in there *now,* please."

Elias was already hurrying to the entrance. Melicent ran to catch up, with Parker right behind her. She folded her hands into a Ganesha mudra, hoping she was remembering the position right. The stance was meant to bring strength and courage, two things she desperately needed right now.

When she entered the cave, there was no evidence of any magnetic activity, no movement or light, only the feeling of a residual charge in the air. The magical, dreamlike chasm illuminated under her headlamp took her breath away and rendered her speechless, then her panic returned.

Elias had a portable floodlight and was shining a wide beam over the entire area. When it landed on a pair of bodies across the cavern, Melicent let out a cry. She made her way through the crystal beds, where she found them.

Roan was lying faceup, his face oddly peaceful. His right arm was wrapped around one of the crystals, his palm against it, like he'd used the massive rock to keep from falling. A bottomless crater was in the center of the cave where the floor had given way. Sun was unconscious on the other side of Roan, her hand clenched in his. From her body's position it was clear she'd crawled over to him.

What had happened? Where was Stuart?

Elias knelt down and felt Sun's pulse. "She's dead," he whispered in shock. He moved to Roan and placed his finger on his neck. "He's still alive but his pulse is faint."

Horror rendered Melicent immobile. Sun was dead and Roan was barely holding on. She knelt down beside him. "Roan? Roan?" She laid her hands on his chest. His energy, his vibrancy was gone. Yet she could sense the faintest trail of him. She looked to Holly and Jocelyn, who'd just arrived with Parker. "He can't get back. He needs our help."

Elias bent down. "I need to move him."

"Wait. Please wait," Melicent said, her voice quivering. If they moved Roan now he might never wake up. "It's like what happened to him before, in Turkey. The time span was too much." She looked to Holly and Jocelyn for support, willing them to understand. "I need to try and help him get back."

Jocelyn seemed paralyzed with fear and unable to speak.

It was Holly who stepped forward and ordered Elias. "You have to wait."

Elias shook his head. "He only has ten minutes in this heat."

"Then give us ten minutes." Holly stressed, "I'll take full responsibility."

Elias threw up his hands, muttering "*loca*" under his breath, and backed away.

Holly met Melicent's gaze, and for the first time there was clear trust between them. Holly nodded. "Whatever you're going to do, do it now."

Melicent lay down beside Roan and took several deep breaths to calm down. She had no idea if what she was going to do would work. Her and Roan's minds had met once, but he'd been conscious when they'd done it. What she was about to attempt was more like a search and rescue.

"Be careful," Parker said, scared.

Melicent held out her other hand to him. "Hold my hand." She knew in her gut she needed his hand in hers. Parker would be her anchor.

Melicent put her left hand over Roan's and the crystal he was holding. Her left hand had been her dominant hand as a child, the hand she'd been born to use, and she had to trust it was the correct one now. She wasn't trying to read an imprint today; she was going to try to find Roan.

40. THE EARTH

LEAVING THE WORLD IS EASY. It's returning that is hard.

Roan could hear Sun's thoughts. She was beside him, holding his hand. The imprint within the crystal had brought them to another place. They were in the center of a vast plane of vibrant consciousness, free of the Earth and the memories blanketing it.

The collective imprints of the billions of souls on Earth had become muted. Even the imprints of Roan's life were fading away from him, like the smoke of a firework whose light was nearly gone.

No longer bound by the constraints of his senses, Roan's mind expanded infinitely. Within the crystal's imprint was an ancient memory of the Earth being born, its crust, mantle, and core forged from a matrix of iron, oxygen, silicon, and magnesium. Like an astronaut, Roan watched the world circle around the sun and the sun spin around the galaxy. They were two perfect bodies, spiraling one within the other, in the universe's perfect dance.

A sense of peace he'd never known before filled him. And a fleeting thought crossed his mind. Was this death?

A brilliant star came to greet them, beautiful and beckoning.

Roan went to step toward the light, but Sun stopped him. She took his hand again and led him away gently.

You need to go back.

She raised her palms to his, communicating everything that needed to be said. He couldn't come with her.

Roan watched her step into the light and the star extinguish. His thoughts began to dim.

Sun was gone and he was alone.

The infinite landscape around him vanished and he felt the sensation of falling—falling backward—falling into a cloud of fear and doubt because he didn't know his way.

The world he was returning to was an ocean and its waters were too dark. His worst nightmare was coming true: that the memories of the world would drown him. He could feel the depth of the years pressing down on him.

No longer in the light, he was lost and alone in the mire beneath the ocean.

He could only hear the sound of his heart slowing down, like a clock about to stop.

41. THE LABYRINTH

MELICENT CLOSED HER EYES and began to breathe in long, deep measured breaths, following every instruction Roan had shown her as she tapped into the wellspring of her ability. She tried to keep the doubt, the panic, all the questions clamoring in her mind at bay. How could she find him? How could she bring him back?

She'd watched her mother die, watched the moment her spirit slipped softly from her body. Roan's life force was about to leave him too. She had to try.

She forced her mind to center on the crystal. An infinite landscape of endless moments was captured within the quartz—like snow globes—there were billions of them. Panic rose inside her again. These were memories. She could never find him there.

She was running out of time. She could feel the lingering warmth in Roan's hand ebbing. There had to be a way.

She found herself praying, praying to her mother. If Roan was trapped somewhere on the other side and unable to come back, she needed Sadie's help to find him.

Mom. The call resounded from her heart, traveling outward, and circled around her like a raging storm.

Its force brought her to another place and time.

She was standing in the middle of a hospital room. The smells of floor cleaner, flowers, and coffee down the hall greeted her, just as they had every morning during the final days of her mother's life.

Melicent reached out and touched the red roses on the bed stand and realized that what she was witnessing now wasn't a memory.

"Melicent."

Melicent turned to the bed and her breath caught inside her.

For a moment she was the lost little girl at Paddington station, hearing the sound of her mother's voice again. Sadie held out her arms and Melicent embraced her, her body infused with the powerful joy of coming home, and they gently rocked together in each other's arms.

"Tell Parker I'm never far away," Sadie said. "He's holding my hand now with you."

Melicent nodded, unable to speak.

"My Melicent." Sadie pulled back and framed Melicent's face with her hands. "Do you know why I named you that? Your name means brave strength. The bee and the honey. The one who can fly."

The door to the hospital room opened and radiant sunlight spilled inside.

Sadie's smile held every answer. "You have a fearless heart. All you have to do is follow it."

Melicent suddenly realized what to do.

She kissed her mother's lips and the room turned to stardust.

42. THE THREADS

ROAN COULDN'T BREAK through the mire of the past to return to the present. Every memory that had ever haunted him through the centuries circled his mind like barbed wire. The exquisite beauty he had witnessed with Sun was no longer there.

Here, in this chasm, he could not reconcile the geometry of life with the agony, destitution, and misery of those who had suffered in the world, were still suffering. There was no symmetry in suffering. No beauty in pain.

He'd lived his life as the boy who remembered, while everyone around him was blessed with amnesia. His ability had kept him apart and broken his heart time and time again. He'd grown up hating the world and yet he desperately loved it.

Now that he'd seen beyond the darkness and glimpsed the underlying fabric of life and its infinite beauty, he wanted to bring that fabric back with him and build a future. He wanted to live, to love, to endure. He wanted to grow old. He wanted to lay down his sword and relinquish his battle with time. But he didn't know how.

Then he heard a voice say in the darkness, "When you find yourself in a hole, quit digging."

The words sounded clear as day. Roy Rogers had said it. The memory was embedded in the guitar Roan's father had bought that had changed their lives forever. Roan remembered hearing Roy say those words when he was five. Suddenly Roan was back at the flea market, five years old and holding hands with his father.

The memory had become real.

More than real, the past was happening all over again. Time had just bent and bowed, bringing him back.

His father knelt down to embrace him. "Come here, son." Robert's arms came around him and hugged him to his chest. In that moment Roan was just a boy with so many years ahead, and yet they'd already come. He was standing in the center of time's circle.

Roan could feel every thought, every emotion emanating from his father. He wanted to tell his father so many things—that he was sorry he'd destroyed his parents' love for each other. That his ability had altered their lives. That his father had passed away in their old house in Mid-City alone. But now those words didn't seem to matter. Only their love was between them.

His father was still with him, never gone, because love was the strongest imprint in the universe. Roan felt all the moments of his life begin to weave back together like a tapestry. And his heart opened, for the first time, like a flower ready to be filled with life.

He heard Melicent calling to him.

Hold on to me.

Her voice was faint, traveling a vast distance.

Hold on to me.

Hold on to me.

He could feel her hand in his, wrapped in a Fearless Heart mudra.

Her voice grew stronger, nearer—until he could feel her all around him.

"Hold on to me." The words were clear and powerful. He could feel her presence beside him. Her hand was real, clasped in his, and their fingers were braided into a lovers' knot as she pulled him back to the world like gravity.

⌒

Roan opened his eyes. It wasn't a dream. Melicent was beside him in the cave with her hand holding his in the mudra.

Parker was holding Melicent's other hand. Holly was holding Parker's hand. Jocelyn was holding Holly's. They had formed a human chain to give Melicent all their strength.

Roan breathed in like a man who had been drowning and found air. Melicent let go of his hand with a cry of triumph and squeezed him tight.

"You found me." His arms wrapped around her. "You found me." Roan looked at the group in wonder. They had all helped to bring him back.

"I saw Dad," he told his mother. Jocelyn let out a laugh and a cry, hugging him to her. Roan's eyes fell to Holly, who was trying her hardest to keep her emotions in check.

She turned away to Elias and said, "Get him out of here, please."

43. THE GLOVES

THE HOSPITAL ROOM WAS STARK AND WHITE, filled with machines to monitor Roan's vital signs. His mind and body were tethered to the world once more.

Roan opened his eyes, waking up, and looked around the room. Two nurses right outside his door were speaking Spanish in the hallway. Melicent was in the chair beside him, dozing with her eyes closed. She had her arms crossed and a fierce frown on her face. She looked like a stern teacher waiting to reprimand him when he woke up.

He wondered how long he'd been asleep. The memories in the cave came flooding back . . . the ooparts, the portal, Stuart's insanity and jump into the abyss.

"You're awake," Melicent said, sitting up.

Roan turned to her. They gazed at each other for a long moment.

He reached out and took her hand, kissing it, and laid it on his chest. "I'm sorry. For leaving you." He wanted her to know how much he meant it.

She stared at him hard. "Don't ever leave me a note like that again."

"I won't. Ever."

"And Stuart . . ." His name on her lips was enough to convey everything she knew.

Roan squeezed her hand, pain lodging in his heart. "I'm sorry for what he did to you," he whispered. "He almost . . ." Roan couldn't get the words out. Stuart had set fire to her house and stood outside and watched.

"He threw rocks at my window until I woke up," she said sadly. "I thought it was a dream, but it was him."

Roan nodded, unable to speak. In the cave he'd witnessed everything Stuart had done: his descent into madness after Miguel's death and taking François's life. Roan's trip to L.A. to meet the budding psychometrist from YouTube had factored nicely into Stuart's plan to scare Roan into action. Stuart had set fire to Melicent's home and then Sun's. Stuart waited until Gyan's wife and daughter were out of town and then he contacted Gyan, asking Gyan to meet him at Savandurga outside of Bengaluru. Stuart concocted a story about the artifacts that the Ministry of Culture had recently found there, saying that they were tied to the ooparts, and he made Gyan swear to tell no one. He instructed him to leave Descartes's ring in his office before he departed. Stuart needed it left somewhere out in the open where it could be easily found. He told Gyan the ring needed direct light because ooparts became more reactive with the sun. Gyan did as Stuart instructed and showed up at the campsite to survey the artifacts. Stuart hired men to abduct Gyan in his sleep that night, drugging him in the twilight of a bad dream. He paid the men to hold Gyan captive while he finished his plan. As Stuart had surmised, the string of events had compelled Roan to act, and Roan's ability had gotten them to the heart of the answer.

Melicent broke the news gently. "The official word is that a series of earthquakes caused the accident and Sun's and Stuart's deaths. The mining company refunded the foundation with their deepest condolences."

Roan's vision blurred with tears and he blinked them away.

"What happened to Stuart in the cave?" she asked softly. "We found the ooparts." She nodded to her bag. "Did he fall, like the people at the mine are saying?"

Roan shook his head. Stuart's body hadn't been found and it never would be.

"The ooparts created a doorway and he jumped right into it."

Roan wondered if Stuart had achieved his desire. Was he in a parallel time with Nema, living a life where he had done no wrong? Or was he lost in a void, in a place of darkness? Or was he traveling beyond this world? They were questions that might never be answered.

The last time he'd seen Stuart before Mexico, they'd ascended the hardest climb of their lives, a towering rock face in Hatun Machay, Peru. At the summit, they were lying on the ground, catching their breaths and staring up at the vast sky swaddled with clouds.

"Do you believe one day we'll be able to time travel?" Stuart had asked him. "Not just see an imprint but go there? Relive it?"

Roan looked over at Stuart and caught the sadness in his eyes. Roan wasn't sure an imprint could ever be real again, but he did believe there was another aspect of time that had yet to be discovered. Souls left echoes of their lives on earth. Was there a way to follow the echoes back to the original voice?

It was a tantalizing thought, and if Stuart had asked Roan again for his help with the ooparts, in that moment, on that mountain, under that sky, Roan would have said yes and moved forward with him and Miguel with their research.

But Stuart didn't ask. Instead he kept his grief for Nema and his desperation to return to her close to his heart, where it continued to fester. After that trip to Hatun Machay, Roan returned to New Orleans. It was the last time he'd seen or talked to Stuart until his message about meeting in El Paso.

Now everything had changed. "He's gone and will never hurt you again. That's all we need to know." Roan held both of Melicent's hands in a promise.

A shadow passed over her face. "I'm sorry Sun didn't make it."

Roan nodded. He'd come back and Sun had not. He'd watched her step into a brilliant starlight and move on to whatever world waited next.

Now Roan would work to repair the damage Stuart had caused. He would put in a call to the authorities in Australia so Miguel's body could be unearthed and returned to his family. He would explain to François's children that their father's death had not been a suicide. Gyan was set to be released from his captors. He'd been kept in a motel room, unharmed. Roan would travel to meet with him and try to help him in whatever way he could. And Sun's young psychometrist in Korea who was about to join the group—Roan planned to visit her, too. The girl had never met them. She had been Sun's protégé, and Roan wanted to help her and present her with Sun's fan.

Maybe it was time to form a new network and continue the research that had begun. The riddle of the map may have been solved, but how the ooparts were jumping time and space and what intelligence was behind it—and crop circles—remained unknown. The Crystal Cave was the heart of the labyrinth and a portal, a true wonder of the world. Only a handful of people knew its secrets. For the time being it would remain that way.

Three psychometrists had died from Stuart's quest. Roan intended to honor their lives by sharing the knowledge he'd brought back from the journey he'd taken when he touched the crystal. Beyond life on Earth and the time we live in, there was an *elsewhere* and an *elsewhen* waiting. René Descartes had believed this knowledge existed in the hearts of all men and women, that it was forged from the stars and encoded within the geometry of life.

"What are you thinking about?" Melicent asked him, watching the expressions on his face.

"The future." He tugged her hand so she could crawl into the bed with him.

The nurses in the hallway watched them with a grin and discreetly closed the door.

Melicent laid her head on his chest, the sound of his heartbeat a perfect metronome. "I've been thinking about the future too. When we get back, I want to help you with the Heirloom Foundation," she said, raising her right hand. "I'm getting pretty good at reading imprints. I've been practicing on all your things."

Roan laughed. "I'm sure you have." He kissed her fingers. "I'd like nothing more." He brought their hands together in a Fearless Heart mudra, expressing the deep well of feeling that existed in his heart for her. Their lips came together in a kiss, its beauty becoming a part of the mudra itself.

He stared into her eyes. "Thank you for being the cavalry." Roan still marveled that she had been able to bring him back. Her ability was so much stronger than he'd imagined. Together with Jocelyn, Holly, and Parker, they had formed a powerful chain, holding hands. "How long have I been asleep? Where is everyone?" Roan knew his mother couldn't be far.

"Two days. They're downstairs eating lunch."

He looked over at the bedside table, where his gloves were waiting.

"Do you need to put them on?" Melicent asked, about to reach for them.

"No." He stayed her hand and tucked her fingers back into his. Sun had been right. After he'd pierced the veil of the world and come back, he didn't need gloves. He could touch anything.

Roan and Melicent lay together with their eyes closed,

holding hands, and followed each other's thoughts in perfect harmony.

Roan couldn't help but think it was like Mozart and Regina's sonata, and he found himself agreeing with Regina Strinasacchi. Miracles did exist.

ACKNOWLEDGMENTS

The past two years while I worked on this book went by both in a blink and a crawl. I'd like to give an enormous thank you to all my readers. I'm thrilled to finally share the book with you. This story was an adventure to research and to write.

Infinite gratitude goes to my agent, Brianne Johnson at Writers House, who is my sage. She was my first reader on the first draft so long ago and helped improve the story in countless ways. She is also the captain of the wonderful book ship I am sailing on. My deepest thanks to my publisher, Picador USA, beginning with Stephen Morrison and my editor, Elizabeth Bruce, for yet again giving my story a home. Elizabeth paired me with Emily Murdock Baker to edit the novel and it was such a pleasure to work together. Emily's story compass and in-depth insights were invaluable in bringing Roan and Melicent to life. Elizabeth also worked her magic as well in the process. A big thank you to my very thorough copy editor, Bethany Reis, designer Jonathan Bennett, and the whole production team: managing/production editorial group Kolt Beringer, Lauren Hougen, and Eric Meyer; marketing team Darin Keesler and Liat Kaplan; publicity with Sara Delozier; and Picador's associate publisher, James Meader.

The Time Collector's magical cover was designed by Tree Abraham with art direction by Na Kim. Thank you, Tree and Na!

During the research for this book I was inspired by many sources. A detailed bibliography is on my website, but I would like to include a few works in the acknowledgments. The book *Descartes's Secret Notebook* by Amir D. Aczel was a pivotal piece of reading, as was *It's About Time* by Liz Evers, *Mudras for Modern Life* by Swami Saradananda, and *Crop Circles: Signs, Wonders and Mysteries* by Steve and Karen Alexander. Maria Popova's *Brain Pickings* online essays on time were such gems, and *Ancient Origins* articles on ooparts led me to researching the phenomenon in further detail.

Before I started writing, I knew I wanted to set a major portion of the story in New Orleans. I cannot thank my dear friend Jacquelyn Castrogiovanni Migdal enough for her support and the three wonderful days we spent together going all over the city. The same thanks to John Migdal and the whole family. Much gratitude to my friends Julia, Indy, Charlotte, Asitha, and my sister Alex for their generous help, and a special thank-you to my fantastic web designer and manager, Jessica Foster, from Imagine Higher. I'd also like to give a warm thank-you to everyone in the book world who has been so supportive— and to authors Nancy Bilyeau, Kelli Estes, M. J. Rose, and B. A. Shapiro, who generously offered a quote for my previous novel, *The Fortune Teller,* thank you so much!

Thank you, Dad, for eternally cheering me on. Loving thanks to all my family and friends, especially my husband and son, Kurando and Kenzo, who encourage me daily. Sometimes I wish I could time travel and share right now all the stories I want to write, but that is for the future.